BLACK HAND GANG

Gazette was the first to get off a shot, firing a full clip at the great beast as it tore ravenously into Jessop's stomach, all in the time it took Atkins to bring up his rifle.

"Holy Mary Mother of God!" wailed Ginger.

"What the bleedin' hell is it?" shouted Mercy.

"Bloody ugly!" replied Gutsy, as the rest of the section brought their rifles to bear.

Atkins had never seen such a creature. None of them had. It was like some kind of monstrous hyena. Easily as high as a man, it had powerful shoulders, like that of an American bison; a mass of knotted, corded muscle rippling under its short, coarse fur. By comparison, its neck was short, its long snout filled with sharp teeth and it possessed powerful muscled legs ending in long claws.

"Don't just stand there," bellowed Hobson. "Five rounds rapid!"

The great predator roared as the bullets bit, but would not be denied its kill. It turned its blood-drenched snout towards them, snarling in pain and anger. Driven away from the body, it let out a howl of such fury that some of the men nearby dropped their guns and began running for the trenches.

WWW.ABADDONBOOKS.COM

An Abaddon Books™ Publication
www.abaddonbooks.com
abaddon@rebellion.co.uk

First published in 2010 by Abaddon Books™, Rebellion Intellectual
Property Limited, Riverside House, Osney Mead, Oxford, OX2 0ES, UK.

10 9 8 7 6 5 4 3 2 1

Editor-in-Chief: Jonathan Oliver
Cover art: Pye Parr
Junior Editor: Jenni Hill
Design: Simon Parr & Luke Preece
Creative Director and CEO: Jason Kingsley
Chief Technical Officer: Chris Kingsley
No Man's World™ created by Pat Kelleher

ISBN: 978-1-906735-84-5

Printed in the US

NO MAN'S WORLD

BLACK HAND GANG

PAT KELLEHER

Abaddon
Books

WWW.ABADDONBOOKS.COM

ACKNOWLEDGEMENTS

I would like to thank: Jean Spencer of the Broughtonthwaite Genealogical Society without whom I would never have stumbled across this story in the first place. I am also grateful to Bill Merchant of the Broughtonthwaite Real Ale Society for an insight into the history of Everson's Brewery and the Everson family in particular. I am extraordinarily indebted to Arthur Cooke, author of *The Harcourt Crater: Hoax or Horror?* for access to his own private collection of documents, letters and diaries pertaining to the incident and especially to surviving footage from the original Hepton film. I would also like to thank the Moore Family for their permission to view the letters and diary of Private Garside. I also owe a debt of gratitude to Stephen Maugham, secretary of the Broughtonthwaite Historical Society for his enthusiasm and tireless work in tracing original documentation. I should also thank Graham Bassett and the staff of The Pennine Fusiliers Regimental Museum for providing me with exhaustive details on the deployment and movements of the "Broughtonthwaite Mates" prior to November 1916 and whose otherwise polite refusals to supply further information only served to confirm and bolster my own research. I am also grateful to Sarah Purser of the Jodrell Bank Press Office and to Michael Wild for agreeing to discuss, over a pint of Everson's Old Fusilier, the speculations still surrounding the Harcourt event. Special thanks must also go to Jim Sherman of the War Museum of the North's Photographic Department and Mike McCulloch of the *Broughtonthwaite and District Mercury* in attempting to identify soldiers and individuals appearing in the Hepton footage. I would also like to thank my wife, Penny, for her continued support, encouragement and long hours transcribing interviews. Finally, I must also pay tribute to those descendants of the men of 13th Battalion of the Pennine Fusiliers who spoke to me privately for fear of ridicule and censure.

Any errors in this book are entirely the responsibility of the author.

13th BATTALION PENNINE FUSILIERS: COMPANY PERSONNEL

Company HQ.

C.O.:   Major Julian Wyndam Hartford-Croft
2C.O.: Captain Bernard Edward Grantham
        Company Sergeant Major Ernest Nelson
        Company Quartermaster Sergeant Archibald Slacke
        Pte. Jonah Cartwright (batman)
        Pte. Charlie Garside (batman)

        Royal Army Chaplain: Father Arthur Rand (CF4)
        ('Captain')

        War Office Kinematographer, Oliver Hepton
        2nd Lieutenant Henry Talbot, Battalion HQ,
        military conductor

'C' Company

No 1 Platoon
C.O.:   Lieutenant Morgan

No. 2 Platoon
C.O.:   2nd Lieutenant J. C. Everson
2C.O.: Platoon Sergeant Herbert Gerald Hobson

1 Section
I.C.:   Lance Sergeant William Jessop
2I.C.: Corporal Harry Ketch
        Pte. Thomas *'Only'* Atkins
        Pte. Harold *'Gutsy'* Blood
        Pte. Wilfred Joseph *'Mercy'*
        Evans Pte. George *'Porgy'* Hopkiss
        Pte. Leonard *'Pot Shot'* Jellicoe
        Pte. James *'Lucky'* Livesey
        Pte. *'Ginger'* Mottram

Pte. Henry *'Half Pint'* Nicholls
Pte. David Samuel *'Gazette'* Otterthwaite

No. 3 Platoon
C.O.:   Lieutenant Holmes

No. 4 Platoon
C.O.:   Lieutenant Gilbert W. Jeffries
2C.O.   Platoon Sergeant Fredrick Dixon

RAMC
Regimental Aid Post
RMO: Captain Grenville Lippett

Red Cross Nurses
Sister Betty Fenton
Sister Edith Bell

Driver Nellie Abbot (First Aid Nursing Yeomanry)

Machine Gun Corps (Heavy Section) 'I' Company
I-5 HMLS Ivanhoe
C.O.:   2nd Lieutenant Arthur Alexander Mathers
Pte. Wally Clegg (Driver)
Pte. Frank Nichols (Gearsman)
Pte. Alfred Perkins (Gearsman)
Pte. Norman Bainbridge (Gunner)
Pte. Reginald Lloyd (Gunner)
Pte. Cecil Nesbit (Gunner)
Pte. Jack Tanner (Gunner)

D Flight 70 Squadron: Sopwith 1½ Strutter
Lieutenant James Robert Tulliver (pilot)
Lieutenant Ivor Hodgeson (observer)

For Scott and Callum

PENNINE FUSILIERS

PREFACE

"There was a Front, but damned if we knew where..."

The Harcourt Crater is one of the greatest mysteries of World War One, along with the Angel of Mons, the Phantom Archers and the Crucified Canadian. At nearly half a mile wide, it was reputed to be the largest man-made crater on the Western Front. The official explanation was that German mines dug under the British positions in the Harcourt Sector of the Somme were filled with an experimental high explosive before being detonated on the morning of November 1st 1916, resulting in the loss of over nine hundred men of the 13th Battalion of the Pennine Fusiliers.

Indeed, this was the accepted explanation until nearly a decade after the event, when a French farmer ploughing fields which lay along the old front line dug up several mud-encrusted old film canisters and a package of documents. Inside the canisters were reels of film which, when developed, revealed silent, grainy footage of British Tommies seemingly on an alien world. The film itself was shown to great acclaim in Picture Houses around the world and it became a minor sensation. Although there were those who claimed they could identify faces in the footage, in the end most felt it to be it a hoax.

The success of the film nevertheless engendered an appetite for Space Fiction among the general public that persisted for decades; the film's grainy, iconic images inspiring thousands of lurid sci-fi magazine covers and pulp fiction stories.

My research further revealed rumours that the Government had approached the noted inventor Nikola Tesla, who had earlier claimed to have received extraterrestrial radio signals, to try to construct a device for contacting the lost men, but without any apparent success. The government of the day quietly closed the case. They officially declared the whole incident to be a "meticulously planned hoax" and it was consigned to the annals of British folklore, although documents believed to include letters and journals from the men of the 13th were discreetly returned to the families. Some eventually found their way into the hands of private collectors, where I had a chance to view them.

The original film stock from the canisters, I was disappointed to discover, did not fare as well as the letters. It was stored badly and the unstable silver nitrate composition of the film strips meant that in many cases the film decomposed, although some was salvaged and incomplete footage does still exist.

For a while, the Battalion War Diary, recovered with the film and allegedly detailing the Battalion's life and actions on another world, was relegated to the stacks in the Regimental Museum and was surreptitiously 'misplaced', having been considered an embarrassment and a stain upon the regiment's proud history.

But the myth refused to die. In subsequent years, men occasionally came forward claiming to be survivors of the battalion, returned with fantastic tales to sell, but none were believed. The story inspired the film *Space Tommies,* released in 1951 featuring Richard Attenborough and Richard Todd, and was the basis for a short-lived adventure strip in the boys' comic *Triumph.*

However, it has become apparent from my extensive research that the mystery of the Harcourt Crater and the *true* fate of the men of the lost 13th Battalion constitutes one of the biggest cover-ups in British military history. I hope that this, the first part of my account, will go some way towards setting the record straight. All of the major events have been drawn directly from primary sources where possible. Others, by necessity, are based on inference but nevertheless serve to hint at the trials, wonders and horrors they were to face, fighting on a Front far, far from home...

Pat Kelleher
Broughtonshaw
November 2009

CHAPTER ONE
"Waiting for Whizz-Bangs..."

The autumn sun ducked down below the Earth's parapet, staining the clouds crimson and, as the chill twilight wind began to bite, Broughton Street was busier than usual. Private Seeston fidgeted impatiently as an ambling ration party of Jocks on their way to collect food for the Front Line barged past, discussing rumours of the impending attack.

"Oi, newbie! Y'do know this is one way don'tcha, and it ain't yours?" one said as they shuffled awkwardly by.

"Sorry," said Seeston. "We've only just taken over this sector."

"Who you with?"

"Thirteenth Pennine Fusiliers."

"Thirteen, eh? Unlucky for some."

"Unlucky for *Hun*, we say, mate," said Seeston, bridling at the insult.

The Pennine Fusiliers was a regiment with a proud history that went back to Waterloo. They had served in the Boer and the Crimean wars, as well as during the Indian Rebellion. It was their proud boast that they were the backbone of the army in the same way their namesake mountains were considered the backbone of England. Their barracks were in Broughtonthwaite, a northern mill town nestling among the Pennine hills on the border of Lancashire and Yorkshire. The 13th Battalion of the Pennine Fusiliers was one of several local Pals Battalions raised in 1914 as part of Kitchener's New Army. With only a small standing army at the outset of the war, a million men were wanted to fight the Bosche. Towns vowed to raise as many of the new Battalions as they could muster. A patriotic fervour swept the nation as young men – driven by dull lives, poverty and the lure of adventure – signed up along with their friends, neighbours and workmates. They couldn't wait to get stuck into the Hun and were desperate to see some action before the war was over.

Their illusions didn't last. On the Western Front, along a strip of mud six hundred miles long, that stretched from the French Alps to the Belgian coast, they died in their tens of thousands, in the blasted, unhallowed ground called No Man's Land.

Seeston forged ahead. Shoulders stubbornly thudded against his as he pressed against the flow, but he was on urgent business, a runner for Battalion HQ. The air of importance that this status lent him bolstered his courage and he pushed on with the purpose of a man who knew his time was more valuable than that of those around him.

From somewhere up ahead, beyond the turn in the communication trench, a high scream punctuated the dull repetitive bass thuds of the German shells that had begun to fall.

"Make way there! Coming through."

Men backed against the walls as best they could. Seeston's advance was brought to a halt as a broad arm swept across his chest and thrust him against the revetment. He was going to say something, but as he glanced down at the khaki arm he noticed the three chevrons and thought better of it. "You an' all lad," said the Sergeant.

A couple of Linseed Lancers, red cross brassards on their upper arms, moved urgently past, carrying a stretcher. Seeston got a good look at the occupant. The man, his face swathed in dirty blood-soaked bandages, had stopped screaming and a pitiful whine surfaced though thick, wet gurgles. Inexpertly tied, the bandage had partially fallen away from his face. A couple of waiting men crossed themselves.

"Jesus. Poor bastard."

From the shattered visage a desperate, pleading eye looked up and briefly met Seeston's gaze. A small jewel of humanity set in a hellish clasp of splintered bone and bloody, chewed meat, the eye lost its lustre as its owner sank once more beneath a private sea of pain. There was a cough and sputter and the groan worked its way up into a scream again, a desperate arm clutching the air for something none of the soldiers could see. Seeston turned his head aside with a shudder. Jesus, that could be him lying there next time. There were countless ugly and obscene ways to die out here; sniper bullet, machine gun, shell fire, gas, grenade, shrapnel, bayonet, trench club. All for King and Country.

The stretcher-bearers disappeared round the traverse of the communications trench towards the Casualty Clearing Station. Seeston doubted their patient would make it. Once the stretcher-bearers were out of sight, Broughton Street came back to life, the incident consigned to a consensual silence and added to the list of things they'd seen but wouldn't tell those back home.

"That's why these things are one way, y'daft bastard," said the brawny sergeant, releasing him. "If yer going *up* you want High Street. Down, you take Broughton, got it? Now go back the way you came and turn left at Mash Lane."

Seeston had seen a map of Harcourt Sector back at Battalion but here, sunk into the ground between walls of wooden shoring and mud, he quickly lost his bearings. He came to a crossroads gouged into the earth. A crude hand-painted sign declared the place to be 'Idiot's Corner'. Below it, signposts pointed down different runs: Lavender Road, Parsonage Lane, Harcourt Trench, Gamble Alley. He stopped an approaching soldier.

"Excuse me mate, I'm looking for Moorside Support."

"Yeah well I wouldn't stand there and do it. It's not healthy. Idiot's Corner, that."

Seeston blinked.

The soldier rolled his eyes in exasperation. "These crossroads have been marked by Fritz 'aven't they? Every so often he drops one on it. Like I said, only an idiot would stand around here."

"I'm looking for C Company HQ."

"The Broughtonthwaite Mates? Down Mash Lane, turn left onto High Street and follow the smell of black puddin's."

"Ta, mate."

Seeston followed the direction indicated by the Tommy's outstretched hand and onto another narrow communications trench, this one linking the reserve trenches, several miles back at St. Germaine, to the front line. Having lost time, he started to jog up the trench.

He'd just turned the corner of another traverse when he collided with an officer. A few splatters of mud flew upwards from Seeston's hobnails as his foot missed the broken duckboard and sank into the open sump, splashing the officer's highly polished boots.

Crap.

It was Lieutenant Jeffries, Commanding Officer of 4 Platoon.

Crap, crap, crap.

Seeston snapped to attention.

There were some officers that you could get on with, but Jeffries wasn't one of them, with his airs and graces. In fact he seemed more concerned about his own appearance than anything else, to the point where they called him 'Gilbert the Filbert' behind his back; after that musical hall song by wassisname. And he could blow hot and cold. You never knew what you were going to get.

He was a dapper-looking cove with a thin, black, neatly trimmed moustache, not a brass button unpolished, not a crease out of place, cap set straight, everything just so. This man took care of himself, took care to remain different, *better*. Made a point of it. Not for him the new common purpose, all in it together for King and Country. Despite that, Jeffries had a reputation for taking suicidally dangerous risks on the battlefield.

The officer met Seeston's gaze and held it just a fraction too long to be comfortable, before his eyes flicked down to the mud on his boots. He had a way of looking at you, *into* you, as if he expected to find something and was profoundly disappointed when he didn't. A smile, like a shark's fin, briefly cut the surface of his face.

"Striking an officer, Private? That's a court martial offence."

"Sir, it was an accident, sir. I didn't see you. Sorry, sir."

"I'll be the judge of that. Handkerchief."

"Sir?"

"Get your handkerchief out, man, and wipe that slop off my boots and mind you don't scratch the leather."

"Sir?"

"You heard, Private."

Seeston pulled out his handkerchief and knelt down on the wet duckboard to wipe the splatters of grey chalky mud from the rich, tan, calf-length boots.

"Now why are you in such a hurry, hmm? Spit it out."

"Runner from Battalion, sir. Message for Captain Grantham, C Company, sir."

"Is that so? Short life, a runner. What's your name?"

"Seeston, sir."

"Well, Seeston, best be on your way."

"Thank you sir. Sorry, sir."

"Oh, and Seeston?"

"Sir?"

"I *never* forget a face."

Second Lieutenant James Charles Everson was making his way though the trenches towards Company HQ when, out of the corner of his eye, he thought he recognised the soldier skulking down a support trench.

"Evans?" he called in a hoarse whisper. The soldier stopped and turned sheepishly.

"Sir?"

Everson saw he was carrying a couple of hessian sandbags in his hands that, despite his care, clanked suspiciously. He shook his head in exasperation.

"Damn it, Evans. You're my best scrounger. I can't afford to lose you."

"Sorry sir, couldn't help myself. I got you a bottle of scotch though." His hand slipped into a sand bag and produced a small bottle of amber fluid. He handed it to Everson, who glanced about cautiously before slipping it inside his jacket.

"Merci, Evans," he said. "Just don't do it again."

"I won't, sir."

Everson arched an eyebrow. "Won't what, Evans?"

"Get caught, sir?"

"Good man."

Evans touched a finger to his temple in an informal salute and slipped away into the muddy shadows.

Everson, too, continued on his way. Heart pounding in his chest, his mouth dry and breath stale from too much coffee and fear, he took a moment to compose himself before pushing aside the heavy gas curtain. A warm fug of stale sweat, damp earth, the chatter of voices and soft oaths rose up the steps to meet him. Ducking his head, he started to descend into the Company HQ Dugout.

Private Seeston, coming up the steps, graciously backed down and stepped aside as Everson entered.

"Thank you, Seeston," said Everson.

"Sir."

Seeston had worked for Everson's father before the war and they often exchanged pleasantries in passing, but today Seeston's terse demeanour unsettled him. The men had been on edge for days. Supplies had been moving up from the support lines for more than a week now; ammunition, rations and medical supplies along with new troops, and still nobody had told them anything. The tension was palpable. Was this it?

Below, the Dugout was sparsely furnished but the furniture was of good quality, requisitioned from some bombed house, no doubt. Hurricane lamps lit the small room, casting large shadows on the crude wooden walls. Everson could hear the disciplined rattle-tattle-ting of the battered old Underwood typewriter as Private Garside typed out order sheets. Major Hartford-Croft, the Battalion Second-in-Command, stood over a makeshift table and looked up from the papers in front of him as Everson entered. Around him stood the Platoon Commanders of C Company. The Major had seen the men through the early summer of the Somme and had even been over the top with them. The men liked him all the more for that. He was a ruddy faced man who permanently looked as if he'd just done the hundred-yard dash and hadn't yet recovered, a raspy catch to his breath as he breathed out, his cheeks almost as red as the tabs on his lapels. His mood wasn't good.

Captain Grantham was there too, C Company's new commanding officer. This was his first time on the front line and he'd yet to prove himself to the men. Oh, he'd been round the trenches and tried to jolly them along with the odd joke in an accent you could cut glass on, but that had only served to confirm the men's original unfavourable impressions.

Also present were Everson's fellow subalterns, Morgan and Holmes. In the corner two men, neither of whom Everson knew, muttered together self consciously; a nervous-looking Second Lieutenant and another man, wearing small round spectacles and a British Army Warm.

Everson edged around to where Lieutenant Morgan was idly polishing his belt with a cuff.

"Is this it then?" he asked in a low voice.

"Looks like it. The old man's been huffing over those papers for the past ten minutes. It don't look good."

Everson ran his fingers under his collar and began to chew his lower lip.

"Sorry I'm late. Dashed sniper at it again, hmm?" Lieutenant Jeffries didn't wait to see if his apology had been accepted.

Everson glanced up at him with disapproval but found himself looking away as Jeffries caught his gaze. He was a queer fish that one, no doubt about it. He'd been with them a little over a month and didn't seem particularly keen on the company of the men, liked his privacy, of which there was precious little to be had on the front. Sometimes it seemed the sensible option he supposed. The life expectancy for an officer in the trenches was only months and eventually you got tired of making new friends only to have them blown to buggery.

"Gentlemen," began Major Hartford-Croft. "Orders have come down from Battalion HQ. We go over the top at 7.20 Ack Emma tomorrow morning. We are to take the German stronghold at Harcourt Wood at all costs. The general advance is being held back by the stalemate in this sector. This objective falls to us. We are to take the machine gun positions that have been holding back the line for the past four months. Bite and hold, gentlemen, bite and hold." Using his swagger stick, he pointed at the map spread out on the table. "The Germans have held the ground around the woods all summer. Unless we can break them before the winter sets in the whole advance will be held back until spring. I don't want that ignominy falling on the Pennines, is that clear? Tomorrow is the first day of November and we *will* take that ridge."

On taking over the trenches three days previously, Everson had studied the lie of the land well. Before the war, it had been gentle rolling farmland. Harcourt Wood sat on a low ridge about a half a mile beyond the front line, overlooking the British positions. After years of artillery bombardment, the long incline to the wood was a featureless shell-pocked quagmire. It wasn't going to be easy. He caught Jeffries smirking to himself and looking a tad more pleased than he had a right to, considering what they were being asked to do. As if he knew something the others didn't.

"Sir?" It was Holmes, Commander of No.3 Platoon. "The Black Country Rifles before us didn't manage it. The German machine gun emplacements will mow us down as they have every other assault. We can't get near them. We're well under strength. They can't seriously expect –"

Captain Grantham cleared his throat in a meaningful fashion.

"Thank you, Captain" said the Major. "GHQ have absolute faith in the Pennines to sort this little mess out. A bombardment will begin at 5.30 Ack Emma tomorrow to soften them up."

"Tomorrow, sir?" queried Morgan. "I thought a bombardment would start days before an attack."

"All very well in theory, Morgan, but that would only warn 'em of an impending attack. Blighters'll huddle in their deep dugouts until it's over and then come out like rats and cut us down. This way we have the element of surprise." The Major broke into a grin. "The Machine Gun Corp Heavy Section is putting a section of their new Hush Hush Boojums into the fray. They'll lead off the assault and clear a path through the wire. That ought to make Fritz windy enough."

There was a chorus of muttered approval. Tanks. None of them had ever seen one, although there were many wild rumours floating up and down the line. It was said they'd made a great show of themselves a couple of months back at Fleurs Courcelette. They had apparently scared the Hun witless– great roaring metal monsters crawling inexorably towards them through the smoke. By God, with a section of those it might just be possible. Despite his better judgement, Everson could feel himself getting excited at the prospect of an attack.

"The tanks will set off first and break through the wire. Here and here," continued the Major, pointing at the map. "They will also draw the machine gun fire, giving the Company a fighting chance. Your job will be to take the German positions and hold them until relieved, which may be a couple of days. The Jocks will be holding our flank, but I want this to be *our* victory. Understood? GHQ have such confidence in us they've even sent one of their flicker-wallahs to film the battle for the Kinemas back home." The Major turned to introduce the men in the corner. "This is Oliver Hepton and his conducting officer, Mr Talbot."

The bespectacled man in the greatcoat at least had the decency to give a weak apologetic smile. Everson wasn't impressed. This was going to be a difficult enough job as it was, but it looked as if GHQ wanted a circus, damn them. His men needed rest, but perhaps this might provide a momentary diversion in the lead up to the attack. Flickers were always popular among the men and the chance to appear in one might take their minds of things. Briefly.

"Don't mind me," said Hepton. "Just go about your duties as you would normally. I'm sure your chaps will put on a jolly fine show for the folks back home."

Everson shook his head; bread and bloody circuses.

There was a scuffle outside. Everson heard Seeston's deferential but firm voice. "You can't go in there just yet, Padre... *Padre!*"

They heard the heavy tread of boots upon the steps and the Padre half stumbled into the room. The only thing that marked him as an army chaplain was his dog collar and lack of a sidearm.

"Ah Chaplain Rand," said the Major. "Although a little late, I fear. Our prayers, it seems have been answered and without your intercession on this occasion," he said, chuckling. The subalterns laughed politely, but briefly.

"What can we do for you, Padre?" said Captain Grantham.

"I'm after a little Christian charity and a few of your men, if you can spare them. There's been an accident on the St. Germaine Road. An ambulance came off the road hit a shell hole. Thankfully the occupants weren't injured – they're shaken and a little bruised but generally fine."

"Well send 'em on their way again, Padre, they're no business of ours," said the Major.

"Well, it's just that they're VAD's – three of them."

"Women? Shouldn't they be in their hospitals instead of gadding about out here?"

"They say they were dropping off supplies for the Casualty Clearing Stations. Now they're stranded until they can get their ambulance on the road again. They've taken shelter in the cellar of the old Poulet Farmhouse. Do you think you can spare some men to get their motor out of the hole?"

The Major glanced at Captain Grantham, who eased his way round the table to the Chaplain.

"Sorry Padre, we can't spare the men. Big show on tomorrow."

"Well what about a couple of men to guard them?"

"Absolutely not," he said ushering the Chaplain towards the steps. "We can't afford to waste men to nursemaid silly gels."

"Who's going to look out for them until they can get back to their depot? You can't leave them alone out here."

"I can't think of a better man than yourself, Padre," said Grantham. "I'll send some men to help them out as soon as I can, but it probably won't be until late tomorrow. But feel free to stop by the kitchens and pick up some rations. Best tell 'em to keep their pretty heads down, eh? It'll be getting damn busy around here soon."

Everson watched the Padre's shoulders slump. He may have been God's representative to the Battalion, but even the Almighty cut no slack with Army bureaucracy. Resigned, the Padre left the dugout.

"Right, if there are no questions, that's it," said the Major. "Best get back to your platoons and inform the men. Oh, and I'd like some patrols out tonight, make sure the Bosche aren't up to anything that can put the kibosh on our little stunt. You'll also need to do the usual wire cutting. Same old, what!"

As the dismissed subalterns shuffled up the steps, Everson was approached by Private Cartwright. "Sir, Can you have a word with the Major? I'd really like to go over the top with my mates, tomorrow, sir."

"You were a member of the Broughton Harriers, weren't you?" asked Everson.

Cartwright nodded reluctantly.

"That's why you're needed as a runner to the Battalion. I need you to watch our backs. D'you understand? If the lines go down – and they will, your speed could save the company. I'm counting on you, Cartwright."

"Sir," said Cartwright heavily.

Everson mounted the steps up to the trench. Both he and Cartwright knew he hadn't being doing him a favour. Being a runner was a very hazardous occupation. He felt himself sinking into a distinctly black mood.

"At last. My first action old man. Bally good show. I've been waiting to give old Hun what for, eh?" Morgan was saying to others at the top of the steps.

"Oh yes, old thing. Give the Hun what for, hmm?" agreed Jeffries, but the twitch of a sneer at the corner of his lips betrayed his condescension.

"God help his men," said Everson, half to himself, as he watched him go.

"Oh I shouldn't think so, John. I shouldn't think so for one moment," said Jeffries. "In fact I should think that's the last we'll see of Morgan."

Everson looked at Jeffries in disbelief and shook his head.

They set off up High Street together, Everson slightly ahead as the way wasn't quite wide enough for two-abreast.

"I didn't see you at church parade this morning, Gilbert," said Everson. "All Hallows' Eve, you know."

"I don't require a third party to intercede with my god on my behalf, Everson."

"Ah, Presbyterian, eh? Say no more."

Jeffries just smiled.

Everson was about to say something when a familiar screech made him look up.

"Whizz-Bang!"

Everson shoved Jeffries down Garland Avenue, a foul- smelling latrine sap, to take cover against the wall. A second later there was an almighty explosion. They felt the concussion wave through their backs as they were showered with soil and mud.

There was a brief silence before the cries and wails began. Everson got up and brushed the dirt off his uniform. Smoke and dust rose over what was left of the sandbag parapet above his head. His hands were shaking. He took a deep breath, then he stepped round the corner into the chaos.

A soldier, blood streaming down his face, ran blindly past, screaming, almost knocking him over. Everson walked up the communications trench towards the sound of pitiful squeals and gruff shouts.

"Gilbert, there's men hurt down here," he called back. Jeffries sauntered out to join him. They rounded the corner of the traverse to a scene of devastation. The shell had burst in the trench, taking out a dugout, burying the men below. Severed limbs lay on the ground and slick red offal steamed in the mud.

Everson saw a soldier walking around unsteadily. He grabbed the fellow by the shoulder. "How many?" The man wheeled round and stared through him, eyes wild and rolling like a cow that had smelt the abattoir. Everson could see no blood, no injuries, but the vacant expression in the eyes told a different story if you cared enough to look. "How many? How many in the dugout?"

"Nine, ten. I only stepped out for a fag. Harris's talk was getting on me wick. I only stepped out for a fag," his gaze focused on Everson as if remembering where he was. "You got to help 'em, sir. You got to get 'em out."

"And we will do. Now get some entrenching tools and we'll need wood for levers and bracing. You there," he said, his eyes alighting on another Tommy. "Get back to the support trenches and muster up a rescue party. We won't have much time."

"Why bother?" said Jeffries. "They'll be dead before they can dig them out. Might as we'll just wait for the trench repair party. This whole section will have to be repaired overnight anyway. It'll be needed tomorrow."

"Damn it, Gilbert. There's still hope we'll find some alive."

"Sir!" Several men digging with their entrenching spades called him over. A hand protruded from the mud. Everson brushed the dirt from it and clasped it gently by the wrist. There was a pulse; weak and thready.

"He's alive. Quickly, but carefully."

The men nodded and resumed their task, excavating the body. He wished he could join them but that wasn't his role. They looked to him for leadership. It was his job to stand back, take in the chaos before him and shape it into order.

"Everson!" called Jeffries. He was holding up a wounded, insensate man whose face was covered with blood; a ragged wound in his side. "He can't wait for stretcher bearers. I'm going get him to the Regimental Aid Post. Can you carry on here?"

Everson nodded curtly and watched as Jeffries, staggering slightly under the weight of the semi-conscious soldier, started off down the trench.

* * *

Jeffries half walked, half dragged the man down the communications trench. The Tommy's hold on consciousness was tenuous. They came to a T-junction in the communications trench. A left turn would take them to the Regimental Aid post, where the Medical Officer could see to his charge and take him off his hands.

"Come on, not far now," Jeffries said. The strain was beginning to tell and his charge wasn't helping. He stumbled on past the junction and took the next right. This wasn't the sort of work he was used to, or usually deigned to do but needs must. His own dugout lay a few yards ahead.

The Tommy tried to mutter something, but with shattered teeth and bloodied lips, it was hard to make out. Not that anything he had to say would have mattered.

With a last effort, Jeffries reached his dugout and clumsily pushed aside the gas curtain. He glanced quickly up and down the trench and, seeing no-one, dragged the soldier inside.

Jeffries dropped the soldier to the floor, before striking a match to light a hurricane lantern hung from a joist. The dugout wasn't as well appointed as Company HQ but this one at least had a bed with a mattress of sorts. Over in one corner was a small writing desk and chair. The back wall had been panelled with the sides of tea-chests by a previous occupant. Several thick wooden joists ran the width of the dugout supporting a corrugated tin roof.

The Tommy on the floor groaned.

Jeffries looked down at the man and noticed, for the first time, the battalion brassard on his upper arm. A runner. "Seeston?"

A groan.

A grin opened on Jeffries' face like a knife wound.

"Well, well. This is fortuitous."

Jeffries went over to the back wall and, with a little difficulty, removed a section of tea-chest panelling exposing a sackcloth curtain behind. He lifted the curtain with all the solemnity of a priest unveiling a tabernacle, revealing a niche containing several objects; an ornamental dagger, several black candles, an incense burner, a small leather-bound volume and a carved totem of black stone.

He stepped over Seeston, cleared papers and ink pots from the writing desk before dumping them on the bed. Next he took out the dagger, the candles and a bag of salt from the niche and set them down on the table.

Seeston watched with mounting incomprehension.

Around the table and the prone soldier, Jeffries drew a circle on the floor of his dugout with salt. Seeston roused himself and began to cry, tears running down his cheeks and mixing with dirt and crusted blood. "Whatever you're thinking of doing, sir, please don't."

"Shh, don't worry. Your life's ebbing away anyway, but thanks to your sacrifice, mine is guaranteed to last much longer." Jeffries picked up the ornamental dagger and began intoning the words he knew by heart.

"By Raziel and Enrahagh, Hear me oh, Croatoan. Protect your servant. Take this life in his stead."

He stood over Seeston and cupped his chin, extending and exposing his neck. "I told you I never forget," he whispered. Then, with a single, practiced movement, he drew the blade across the man's throat.

CHAPTER TWO
"All the Wonders of No Man's Land..."

Once the NCOs turned up at the bombsite Everson found himself being thanked politely and gently sent on his way, dismissed like a hapless schoolboy. Feeling frustrated and vaguely empty he wandered along High Street towards the support trenches.

Back at his dugout, Everson found his Platoon Sergeant making a cup of tea. Hobson was a career soldier in his forties though his attachment to his waxed moustache made him look older than he was. His once imposing barrel chest had given way to an expanding waistline that he nevertheless insisted was "all muscle". Hobson was a godsend; an Old Contemptible and veteran of the Boer War, a man of infinite common sense. He had been assigned to Everson from the beginning and had stopped him making a fool of himself on more than one occasion.

"Well, sir?" said Hobson as he took a tin mug off a nail and poured another brew.

"Tomorrow. 7.20. Tell the men. They're getting restless."

"They've known summat were going on, sir. They're up for it. It's just the waiting that gets 'em."

"Yes, that does for us all. We've to send out a patrol, too, Sergeant. Dirty work to be done. Orders to cut wire for tomorrow's assault and spy out the German positions, check they've got no new surprises for us. Know of any likely volunteers for a hazardous mission like that?"

"For a Black Hand Gang, sir? Leave it to me. 1 Section are up tonight. Best lot I know. Some handy men there."

"Hmm." Everson knew it. Several of them had worked in his father's brewery – 'Everson's Ales: They're Everson Good!' He remembered them all signing up together at the outbreak of war, eager for adventure; after all it would be over by Christmas, where was the harm? The factories and mills seemed to empty that week as workers joined the raucous, ebullient crowds of men in flat caps and straw boaters jostling outside the town hall recruitment office. Then there were the months of drilling and training in the camp on the moors above the town. Months more before they got their uniforms and guns. But the pride they felt as the 13th Battalion of the Pennine Fusiliers, the 'Broughtonthwaite Mates', paraded in full kit through the town, down the cobbled streets lined with family, relatives and friends, to cheers and tears under hastily appropriated Wakes Week bunting and Union Jack flags was an almost tangible thing. Your heart swelled, your blood sang and you grinned with so much pride your cheeks ached. There was even a brass band to see them off at the railway station for the start of their Grand Adventure.

Not so grand as it turned out.

They'd come out to France in March 1916, spent some time at the training camps before being shunted up the line in Hom Forties for the Big Push. Since then they'd been up to their necks in mud and blood and bullshit, their sense of pride and patriotism long since tarnished by cynicism.

Hobson handed Everson a steaming mug of tea.

"Ah, just the job," said Everson wearily. "Whisky, Sergeant?" he added, pulling the small bottle from his tunic.

"Don't mind if I do, sir," said Hobson, offering his mug. "But just the one."

Everson poured a shot into Hobson's tea and one into his own. Hobson savoured the aroma and knocked the milkless tea back in one before slapping the enamel mug down on the table with a dull metallic clunk.

"Best go tell the men, then, sir," he said, before putting on his steel hat and venturing out into the night.

* * *

The men of 1 Section, No 2 Platoon, were passing the night as best they could in their dugout. It was a crude affair, with little to recommend it but six wooden frame and chicken wire bunks and several upturned tea-chests for tables.

Private Thomas 'Only' Atkins sat on his bunk reading a letter by the light of a candle stub. It was one he'd read a dozen times before. It was from Flora Mullins. The letter was full of the usual daily doings of a small terraced street but one sentence stuck out. One sentence that sent the bottom of his stomach plunging sickeningly.

"There is still no news of William. Every day your mam reads the casualty lists hoping not to see his name, then despairing when she doesn't. The not knowing is killing her, Tom..."

He read the words again and again, as if by doing so he'd wear them out, erase them somehow. Was it wrong to hope William didn't turn up?

He and his older brother had signed up together, even though, technically, Thomas was too young by eleven months, having only just turned seventeen.

"Go around the block until you've had another birthday, sonny," the Recruiting Sergeant had told him with a wink. So he did. But in those twelve minutes the queue had grown and it was another three hours before he was back before the Sergeant. Those hours had made the difference, not in years, but between serving in the 12th Battalion with his brother and the 13th.

His mother hadn't half torn a strip off William later that day when she found out he signed up. He'd never seen her so furious until ten minutes later when Thomas had told her he'd joined up, too. She was all for marching him down to the recruiting office and telling that sergeant there and then that her son was too young and what did he mean by signing up helpless little kiddies? Thomas had been mortified and begged and pleaded before appealing to his dad. Half an hour later, when she found out they weren't even in the same battalion and wouldn't be serving together so William couldn't keep an eye on him, it all blew up again.

And now William was missing. He'd been missing since the Big Push. Atkins had traipsed round all the field hospitals and questioned old mates, but there was no news and it was tearing him apart.

He watched 'Mercy' Evans stowing the contents of his latest 'trip to the canteen' into a haversack hanging from the ceiling, out of reach of the ever-present rats. Scrounging he called it, although looting would be the official charge. However, in a war where supplies were short, the Platoon Commander turned a blind eye, so long as he occasionally plied his skills on behalf of his comrades.

'Porgy' Hopkiss was shuffling though his pack of photographs, each a portrait. He had twenty-seven of them so far, every one presented by a sweetheart he'd met or so he claimed, although at least one was of Mary Pickford and several were of dubious taste and also in the possession of more than one man in the battalion. It was his avowed intent to collect enough to turn them into a deck of cards after the war.

'Gutsy' Blood, a butcher by trade before he took the shilling, was sharpening and polishing his best meat cleaver, because, quite frankly, it was his pride and joy and he didn't trust his wife or brother-in-law to look after it proper back home, so he'd brought it to France with him, When he charged towards the German lines brandishing it, it scared the crap out of Jerry, not to mention half of his own platoon.

'Lucky' Livesey had his trousers off and turned inside out across his bony white knees as he ran a lighted candle stub along the seams. "Nothing more satisfying than Chatting," he said, grinning gleefully at the small cracks as the ubiquitous lice popped under the heat.

"Maybe, but you'll still be hitchy-coo tomorrow, Lucky. Can't never get rid of the bloody things," said 'Half Pint' Nicholls, scratching his ribs fiercely. Half Pint was the greatest grouser in the regiment. You want to hear it true and unvarnished, then he was willing to give his opinion forth to all and sundry and, among a certain kind of man, he found a willing audience.

Lance Corporal Ketch, 1 Section's second in charge, entered, bringing in the post. He was a small man with a pock-marked face; just a shade too tall for the Bantams, worse luck, so they were stuck with him. His gimlet eyes glowered with resentment as he began handing out the brown paper and string packages and ivory envelopes. It seemed to be against his nature for anyone to have any measure of happiness.

Atkins leaned forwards eagerly, poised for his name. His heart began to pound in his chest, waiting for news, but dreading it at the same time.

"Porgy one for you, Package for Mercy. Half Pint. Gazette, *two*! Pot Shot, Lucky..."

The men snatched them up eagerly and were momentarily lost in their own private worlds as they proceeded to open them.

"Gazette and Pot Shot are on sentry duty, " said Gutsy, taking theirs.

"And lastly Juh Juh-Ginger," sneered Ketch, holding out a package towards a nervy, curly-haired blonde lad who was feeding a rat he'd tamed, taken for a pet and named Haig.

'Ginger' Mottram had made it through the entire summer without a scratch, but he was a wreck. Shell-shock, they called it. Malingering, Ketch said, but then he would. Ketch deliberately waved the package just out of his reach, taunting him. Ginger went bright red. The lad blushed so often they joked that one day his hair would turn red, hence his nickname.

"Guh-guh-give it here!" stammered Ginger.

"Leave it out, Ketch," warned Mercy. Ketch thrust the package into the lad's hand, his fun spoiled.

"Corp?" said Atkins leaning forward hopefully.

"Atkins," said Ketch gleefully. "Expecting something were you?"

"Yes."

Ketch made a show of patting himself down. "No, Sorry. Nothing."

"Ketch!" snapped Mercy, looking up from his own letter. "Only's brother is missing f'fuck's sake. He was hoping for news."

"Fuck you, Evans," muttered Ketch as he retired to his bunk.

Sergeant Hobson's ample frame filled the dugout door. "It's getting late, ladies. Time to get your beauty sleep. Waiting's over. Word has come down. We'll be up early and going over the top first wave tomorrow. Check your weapons. Where's Lance Sergeant Jessop?"

"NCO of the watch, Sarn't," said Mercy.

"Sarn't?"

"Yes, Hopkiss?"

"It's just that there's not much of a bombardment from our lot," he said jerking his chin in the direction of the Front. It was true. The night's artillery fire was sporadic at best.

"Don't you worry your pretty little head about it, Hopkiss. You just turn up in your Sunday Best for tomorrow's little promenade and we'll go for a nice stroll in No Man's Land. I'm sure wiser heads than yours have got it sorted," he said, turning to go.

"That's what we're worried about, Sarn't," said Mercy.

Hobson's eyes narrowed as he strode across the dugout.

"You think too much, Evans, do you hear me?" he said sternly, rapping Mercy sharply on the head. "And you do it out loud. If that ain't a bad habit I don't know what is. Don't let me hear you do it again!"

Evans winced and rubbed his scalp.

"Yes, Sarn't. Sorry, Sarn't."

"I'm watching you laddie," said Hobson as he left. "Ketch, I need a Black Hand Gang for a bit of business tonight. I want three volunteers to meet me in F8 at two Ack Emma. See to it."

"Right," said Ketch, gleefully. Hopkiss and Blood? You've just volunteered."

Ketch took his time, letting his eyes roam over the rest of the men, making sure to meet each of their eyes as if daring them to challenge him. His gaze settled on Atkins. Atkins, suddenly aware of the silence, glanced up. "Something better to do Atkins? Not now you haven't."

*　*　*

Atkins was woken by Gutsy shaking him. The last vestiges of warmth and wellbeing slipped away as realisation of where he was rushed in.

"Only? Come on lad, it's time. Let's get this over and done with."

Wearing leather jerkins, carrying their bayonets in sheaths, their faces blackened with burnt cork, the Black Hand Gang, Atkins, Gutsy and Porgy, made their way past scurrying rats up to the fire bay, where Hobson and Ketch were waiting for them.

There was a faint *fwoosh* as an enemy flare went up. It burnt a stark white, casting deep shadows on the wall of the trench that wobbled and tilted as the flare drifted down, until at last they ate up the last of the light and filled the trench again.

'Gazette' Otterthwaite and 'Pot Shot' Jellicoe were on sentry duty. Even in the dim light it was hard to miss Pot Shot. He was a large man, a shade over six foot, tallest man in the Battalion; the only man who had to crouch when stood on the firestep lest his head present a tempting target for German snipers.

Gazette was up on the firestep on sentry duty, Pot Shot sat on the step beside him, slumped against the side of the bay and snoring gently, his rifle clasped to his chest like a loved one. Gazette glanced down at them and kicked Pot Shot awake.

"All right, lads?" he yawned.

That helped ease the queasy feeling in Atkins' stomach. Gazette was the best sharp shooter in the platoon. If anyone was going to have your back on a Black Hand job you'd want it to be him.

There was a pile of equipment on the firestep by his feet.

"Right," said Hobson, "take these." He handed out pistols; Webley revolvers, usually reserved for officers but more practical in situations, such as this, that called for stealth. They each had their own bayonet and there were two sets of long-armed wirecutters. Atkins and Porgy got those. Hobson also gave them each a grey military issue blanket that he instructed them to wear across their backs in the manner of a cloak.

"It'll help disguise your outline against German flares. If a flare goes up, don't move. You'll want to throw yourself on the ground but don't, they'll spot the movement and you're a goner. If you freeze you could be tree stump, a shadow or a body on the wire," he told them. "We're goin'out to cut the German wire in preparation for tomorrow. So we make sure we do the job properly or it'll be us and our mates paying the price if we don't. We also want to take a shufti and make sure Fritz isn't planning any nasty surprises. Don't worry, I'll have you all back in time for the big show."

"Thanks, Sar'nt. You're a real pal," said Gutsy.

"Time for a fag, Sar'nt?" asked Hopkiss, trying to delay the inevitable.

"No. Follow me. Stick to me like glue. No one talks but me. Make sure you stay within an arm's length of the next fellow. If you get lost make your way back here. And make sure you dozy ha'porths don't forget the password: Hampstead."

Atkins checked his bayonet in its sheath. He checked the chambers of the Webley revolver. They were full. The pistol had a loop fastened to the handle, which he slipped round his wrist.

There being no sally port available, Hobson put a ladder up against the revetment and was about to step on the bottom rung when another flare went up. He stopped, waited for the flare to die out, before rolling over the sandbag parapet with practised ease. His arm appeared back over the bags signalling the next man up. Porgy was already on the ladder and climbing. Gutsy stepped on below him and began his climb. It was Atkins' turn next. As he stepped on the bottom rung, he felt a hand pat his thigh.

"Good luck, mate," said Gazette. Aktins smiled weakly. He could feel his heart lifting him fractionally from the ladder with every beat as he lay against the rungs. He hadn't felt a funk like this since that last night with Flora.

"Cheers. I'll be back for breakfast."

Another flare.

Above him, Gutsy froze, waiting for the light to die. Atkins looked up. All he could see was Gutsy's big khaki-covered arse eclipsing everything. Blood let one rip and looked down between his legs, grinning.

"Fuck's sakes, Gutsy!" hissed Gazette. "At least with the yellow cross we get a warning. Where's me bloody gas helmet?"

A hiss rasped from over the parapet. "Get a move on, you two!"

Puffing, Gutsy rolled over the sandbags with as much grace as a carcass in his old butcher's shop.

Atkins reached the top of the ladder. The nightscape before him never failed to chill him to the core. No Man's Land. It was a contradiction in terms. You were never alone in No Man's Land. During the day it was quiet, with generally nothing but the odd buzz of a sniper's bullet cutting low over the ground or the crump of a Minniewerfer to disturb it. At night, though, it became a hive of activity; parties out repairing wire, laying new wire, digging saps, running reconnaissance, conducting trench raids. Both sides knew it. It was the most dangerous of times to be out and never dark for long, as flares burst in the air, momentarily illuminating bleak Futurist landscapes that left hellish after-images in the mind's eye.

He saw Hobson and Porgy about four or five yards ahead, crawling along on their bellies. Gutsy was to his left. Atkins crawled forward using his elbows and knees. The mud was cold and slimy and within a minute his entire front, from chin to toes, was soaked. He and Gutsy made their way to where Sergeant Hobson and Porgy were waiting. About twenty yards ahead, they could make out the vague unearthly shapes of their own wire entanglements. Sergeant Hobson indicated a piece of soiled, white tape in the mud that led them to the gap in their own wire.

Now they truly were in No Man's Land.

They crawled on, their progress achingly slow. Every time a flare bloomed in the sky, they would press themselves into the mud. It took them nearly an hour to crawl through the blasted landscape – peppered as it was with shell holes – up the gently inclining slope towards Harcourt Wood. About them Atkins could hear the foraging corpse rats feasting on the bodies of the fallen. They reached the German wire, some thirty yards short of a low stone wall that bordered the wood. There was a muffled shout, some distance over to the left and a brief spatter of machine gun fire, then nothing.

More waiting.

Hobson gestured to the left and rolled with a barely perceptible splash into a shallow shell hole just short of the wire. The others followed. Atkins slithered over the shallow lip to join them and found himself in a pool of water. Hobson beckoned them closer with a finger. They gathered their heads together while Hobson spoke in a low, slow voice.

"Wirecutters get ahead. Blood and I will cover you. If it all goes off, get back here sharpish. Got it? Just don't take all night about it."

Atkins nodded. As they crawled out of the shell hole toward the wire, Hobson and Gutsy took up their positions on the lip of the crater, pistols cocked and ready.

Atkins looked at Porgy as they reached the entanglement. Porgy crawled forward with his cutters, slipped the blades around the wire and snipped. There was a sharp *tink* and a dull tinny twang recoiled along the wire. Atkins froze until long after the sound died away, expecting a burst of machine gun fire to cut them down at any moment. But nothing happened. Porgy cut again.

Atkins gripped the wire between his own cutter blades and snipped, and snipped again. It took nearly an hour to cut though the entanglement, working his way along on his back under the thicket of Jerry wire until his arms ached and his muscles burned, but eventually it was done. A section of wire five or six yards across had been freed from its mooring.

They made their way back to the shell hole.

"All present and correct?" whispered Hobson. "Good. Let's be off home shall we?"

As they began the slow crawl back towards their own lines, something gave way under Atkins' palm and his left arm sank up to his elbow in the thick mud. A bubble formed on the surface and popped, releasing a cloying, sickly stench. His hand had gone through a corpse's gas-distended stomach. Disturbed, several corpulent rats squeaked indignantly and darted off. He heaved, retching up several lumps of army stew and pulled his hand out of the mud. In an attempt to put some distance, *any* distance, between him and the corpse, he planted a knee down only to feel a crack of bones somewhere just below the surface of the slime. A red flare went up bathing everything in a hellish glow. Atkins looked down with horror to see the decomposing face of a French soldier lit by the lurid light, making shadows dance in the empty sockets of its eyes.

A burst of machine gun fire zipped over their heads. Hobson quickly indicated to a large Minnie crater with a flick of his hand. They headed for it, rolling down into the relative shelter of its shadow.

Unable to stop himself, Atkins slipped helplessly down the slick wet sides into the slurry-filled basin at the bottom, before coming up against wet muddy cloth. Fearing another corpse, he looked about wildly and met the gaze of a German soldier staring back with the same intensity of fear and surprise. They'd stumbled on a German patrol sheltering in the same shell-hole.

Atkins knew he had seconds to act. He clamped a muddy hand over the German's mouth. The Hun clawed desperately at his wrist. Atkins adjusted his position so he was astride the man's chest and was able to use his knee to pin the man's upper arm to the ground, leaving a hand free to unsheath his bayonet. The German tried to bite Atkins' hand, desperate to stop him. Out the corner of his eyes Atkins made out the other members of his Black Hand Gang engaged in similar private struggles. It was desperate fighting, no rules. This was war at its most raw, most visceral, most base. The only sound was the slap of mud or splash of water as boots sought for purchase on soft tissue; grunts of exertion as the struggle turned first one way then the next, each opponent knowing it was killed or be killed.

Gritted teeth. Little explosions of breath, spittle flecks bubbling up at the corners of the mouth, face red with effort, neck taut with strain as Atkins leant forward trying to use his bodyweight to press his bayonet home. The Hun kicked, trying to dislodge him. The point of his bayonet against the Hun's ribs. His eyes creasing, pleading, hands slick with mud losing their grip, the bayonet pushing into the thick serge of his uniform but not puncturing. It was all now dependant on who could last out the longest, but Atkins had gravity on his side.

The blade sank suddenly, plunging Atkins' face unexpectedly towards his enemy's, whose eyes widened in shock. He tried to focus on Atkins as his hand clawed weakly at his face. Atkins turned away and raised himself to avoid the filthy, clammy hand. Then, hardly able to see for the stinging tears welling up in his eyes he muttered, "sorry," and used his bodyweight to push the bayonet further in. Blood bubbled and frothed at the corners of the Hun's mouth. Atkins could feel the warm exhalation of breath on his face waning. The man's eyes lost focus and beneath him Atkins felt his chest fall for the last time. He collapsed with effort and relief onto the body feeling his heart beating fit to burst, a pulse suddenly pounding painfully at the base of his skull behind his right ear. He rolled over onto his back, his chest heaving with sobs he tried to stifle. To his left he saw Porgy sitting with his head in his hands. Hobson was wiping his bayonet on a German's tunic. Three Huns lay about the shell hole in unnatural positions. A fourth lay face down in the water. Gutsy grabbed Atkins and pulled him into a sitting position, holding his head between his knees as he dry-retched.

"Get it up, son, you'll feel better," Gutsy whispered. Atkins tried to make himself heave. It didn't take much before he vomited, spitting out the stringy mucus and half-digested bits that remained in his mouth. Gutsy pulled his bayonet from the dead Hun and handed it back to him. "You did well."

They made their way back to their line but when they came to their wire, they couldn't find the gap. Following Hobson, they inched their way along the wire, careful not to touch any of the makeshift alarms of tin cans containing pebbles that hung from them before finding one. They edged through and towards their lines until they could see the sandbag parapets of their own trenches. From the dark ahead of them came an aggressive hiss.

"Password."

"Hampstead" Hobson hissed back and began crawling forwards, beckoning the others to follow. There was sudden rapid fire, and the whole world went to hell. Porgy screamed. A flare went up from the trench. Hobson shouted: "You're shooting your own bloody men, hold your fire!" There were far away shouts from the German line, a German flare and then the whine of bullets splashing into the mud around them.

Shot at from behind, shot at from in front, Atkins scrambled for the sandbags and the trench. Hands reached up, grabbed him and pulled him over the parapet to safety. Hobson was already over and laying into the Jock sentry with a torrent of sergeantly abuse. Gutsy was sat on the firestep checking himself all over for wounds but there was no sign of Porgy. Atkins stood on the firestep and, against all his better instincts, he peered over the top. He saw something that could be Porgy some five or six yards away. Sporadic shots from the German line continued to bury themselves into the mud around him.

"Only! Only, I'm hit," whimpered Porgy.

Before he knew what he was doing, Atkins was scrambling over the parapet and wriggling forward on his elbows.

"Come back you bloody fool!"

Atkins slithered on, the odd bullet whining over his head. He reached Porgy who was lying on his side groaning. He gripped Porgy's hand and pulled, trying to drag him through the mud, but he was too heavy. There only one thing for it. As quickly as he could, Atkins picked him up under the armpits and hauled him backwards, step by muddy step, towards the trench amid the whine and splatter of German bullets. Reaching the sandbags, he tipped the barely conscious Porgy over the parapet and into the arms of his waiting mates, before leaping into the trench after him. Trembling, he sat down heavily on the firestep and watched as Gutsy looked Porgy over.

"Hell's bells, Porgy you're a lucky one."

Atkins could see a bloody groove on Porgy's left temple where a bullet had grazed him. "Head wound."

"Good job it didn't hit anything important, eh?" croaked Porgy.

"Barely a scratch, y'daft beggar. You'll live."

Porgy looked up as that sank in and seemed to rally, turning on the sentry loitering off to his side. "All the way to the Hun wire, an ambush by Jerry, and I get shot by my own bloody side!" he growled, attempting to get up, but Gutsy held him down.

"Och, sorry mate how wis ah tae know? This isnae your section o' the line. You could a been Kaiser Bill hisself fer all I knew!"

Atkins looked up as a grubby mud-slathered Hobson stood over him. "That," he spat, "was a bloody stupid thing to do."

"Couldn't leave him, Sar'nt."

"Quite, right lad," said Hobson, gently patting him on the shoulder.

As if that were all the permission he needed, Atkins felt great sobs well up within him and his shoulders started to shake.

"You'll be all right son. You did well tonight. Take Porgy to have his scratch seen to. Don't want him missing out on the fun later, do we? Then go and get yourself cleaned up and get some kip. Big day tomorrow."

"Sar'nt."

Atkins and Gutsy made their way along the fire trench, carrying a dazed and bloody Porgy between them, his head now roughly bandaged with a field dressing. They turned down a communications trench and weaved their way to the Regimental Aid Post. The MO wasn't very happy about being woken up, but soon cleaned and stitched the wound before packing them off.

Atkins went back to the water butts in the support trench to clean himself up.

Ketch caught up with him.

"I heard what you did, Atkins," he said.

"Any one of us would have done the same."

"But they didn't did they? It was you, weren't it? Bit of a glory hound are we? Your mates might think you're the bee's knees right now, but I know different. You're bad news, Atkins. I'm watching you."

Atkins was too weary to argue. He crept back into the dugout, crawled under his ration blanket and dozed fitfully as the rats scurried across the floor beneath him.

INTERLUDE 1

Letter from Private Thomas Atkins
to Flora Mullins

31ˢᵗ October 1916

My Dearest Flora,

*As I write to you tonight I have no further news of William.
Last week, out of the trenches, I tramped around the field
hospitals again. I showed his picture about and, though
I feared what I might find, I visited the army cemeteries
hereabout. I even buttonholed a relief column to ask if they'd
seen him. I can bring you no peace, I'm afraid. But do not
despair. He may still turn up. It might be that he is only lost
and taken up with another regiment, or else been wounded
and travelling between hospitals. It is too soon to give up. We
must both hope that he will come home.*

*Tomorrow we've a mind to go and bother the Kaiser for
some sport. We're taking a stroll up to the woods to see what
mischief we can make! My only fear is that I shall not see
you again, but do not fret for I am determined that I shall.
Tell my mam I'm well and will see her soon. I know she
worries so. Tell her I got the socks she sent. If she can send
some lice powder I would be very grateful.*

Ever yours,
Thomas.

CHAPTER THREE
"This World's Verge..."

He was safe. A million miles from the front line. He was home. Home on leave. In his uniform he waited anxiously outside the factory gates for her shift to end, afraid he'd miss her as the workers swept out. He saw her first, picked her out amongst the crowd of women surging towards the street, arms linked with her workmates, walking in step, laughing. He stood across the street, waving eagerly. "Flora! Flora!" She looked up and saw him. And smiled...

"Wakey, wakey, ladies!"

Atkins jerked awake and sat up in his bunk, cursing as he caught his hair in the wire of Ginger's bunk above him. Already the dream was slipping away. Sergeant Hobson, cleaned up and dressed for battle, his moustache as prim and proper as ever, stood in the dugout's doorway, his appearance sending the rats scurrying for cover.

"Oh God, what time is it?" groaned Mercy.

"Time you were in Jerry's face before I get into yours, Evans," hollered Hobson.

"It's not even dawn, Sarn't!" said Pot Shot. "What about me beauty sleep?"

"No amount of sleep is going to make you ugly bunch any better looking, and that's just the way I like it. I want Fritz to feel his balls shrivel when he sees you lot coming. Now get up and get yourselves sorted. Stand To in fifteen minutes."

Bleary eyed, Atkins rolled out of his bunk, his mouth dry and his empty stomach churning as he jostled over cold water and tarnished shaving mirrors, braces hanging limply from his waist.

They all clustered about Porgy with his new bandage, demanding all the details of the night's events, which Gutsy duly gave them, building up to Only's heroic dash and rescue.

"It was nothing," said Atkins awkwardly. "Besides, I couldn't let him stay out there. He promised me he'd introduce me to Marie down at the estaminet in Sans German." Never ones to learn the local language if they could get away with mangling it, it was one of the Tommies' jokes. St. Germaine was the nearest town to Harcourt Wood, well behind the British lines and so long as it remained behind British lines it would bloody well remain 'Sans German' - without Germans, too.

"Going to have quite a scar, the doc says," beamed Porgy. "The old 'war-wound', it'll have the girls flocking to me, it will."

"Luh-looks like a Buh-blighty wound to me," said Ginger quietly. "Why you still 'ere?"

"What, and desert me mates, today of all days? Bloody hell, Ginger, what's got into you?" said Porgy.

Atkins felt the knot in his stomach tighten. His teeth were furred up and his mouth tasted rank after vomiting last night. He pulled his braces up onto his shoulders, slipped into his tunic and fastened it before shrugging on his webbing. It was an attack so it was Battle Order equipment; rifle, helmet, backpack with iron rations, water flask, bayonet and 150 rounds small arms ammunition. Then they'd have to pick up spare sand bags, entrenching tools, grenades, spare grenades, flares and wire cutters, smoke candles and picks from the QM.

Atkins joined the queue with his dixie tin for his bit of bacon and fat. His mouth was so dry he could barely swallow. The tea was lukewarm and made with petrol-contaminated water, from using petrol cans as water carriers. It made him gag.

Then Lieutenant Everson and the Quarterbloke made their way down the fire trench, issuing rum from a stone SRD jar. Atkins gratefully accepted the slug of liquor that

Everson measured out into his greasy dixie tin and tipped the contents down his throat. He felt the rum burn all the way down.

Afterwards Gutsy kissed his little rabbit's foot on its leather thong and tucked it into his shirt. Porgy shuffled his pack of pictures, hoping that the one he drew as his Queen of Hearts for the day was one he actually fancied. Gazette listened for the crump of an artillery shell and tried to count to twenty before the next one landed. Ginger quietly confessed his sins to the pet rat hidden in his tunic. Atkins took out of his tunic pocket a much-read letter, the last letter he'd received from Flora, and eased it, like a sacred relic, from its envelope. He raised the letter to his lips and kissed it softly, almost reverently, then parted the folded corners, held the paper to his nose and gently inhaled as if smelling a delicate flower; if he could still smell her scent on it, even here amid the malodorous mud of the trenches, then he was convinced that he would survive the day. Finally, everybody touched or kissed Lucky's steel helmet with the two Jerry bullet holes in it.

They all had their little rituals.

Jeffries was going through his own ritual, quite literally. It had served him well in the past and garnered him a reputation as a fearless soldier on the battlefield, taking life-threatening risks as if he had no care for his own life, when in fact the opposite was very much the case.

He knelt in his dugout, within his salted circle, incense burning on the table next to him. He breathed deeply as, slowly, his mind centred on the Great Working at hand. Today, on the feast of Samhain, he would prove them all wrong. He had no need of fear. He had Seeston. Last night's ritual of protection should shield him from harm. And from this calm, centred place he offered up a prayer.

"I bless Enrahagh, fallen from the light, I bless Croatoan dwelling in the night, I bless the sword of Raziel that all the heathen dread. I bless the dirt beneath my feet, the earth on which they'll tread."

The clatter of rifles and shouts outside shattered the serenity of the moment as men scurried about the narrow culverts and alleys in readiness for the attack. Beyond the immediate shrill shouts, he heard the persistent dull bass thud of artillery shells. Dirt sifted down from the ceiling. He got up, put on his tunic and Sam Browne belt then searched for his hair brush and applied it in slow, considered strokes though his Brilliantined hair. Picking up his steel helmet, he placed it on his head and adjusted it just so before a shard of mirror. He admired his reflection for a moment and, irritated, turned to brush some slight dirt from his shoulder pips.

There were times when he really missed having a batman, but he needed privacy and they only got in the way. It had been a shame about Cooper. Good at laundry but a little too inquisitive for his own good. He'd proved useful in the end though, just like Seeston. Luckily the disposal of bodies at the front was less problematic than it had been back in England.

As he left, he turned and took one last look round his dugout for old times' sake.

This was it. All his preparation had brought him here, to this place, to this hour. After today nothing would be the same again.

Oliver Hepton chose his position and had set up his tripod in the cover trench by a loophole, the better to catch the costly advance of the Pennines as they went over the top. He began to crank the handle of his camera. He panned round the trench slowly, not an easy task when trying to maintain a steady camera speed.

Don't want to make the people at home feel motion sick.

He'd been filming for three days in the reserve lines, getting shots of soldiers coming up the line, waving their steel helmets, full of fun and bravado, posing for family back home. Plucky British Tommies waiting to give the Hun hell. But today was different. The men didn't care about the camera. They were tense, too preoccupied to give it anything more than a cursory glance and a weak smile. Hepton didn't mind. It was all good stuff and he began composing the accompanying caption cards in his head.

Atkins stood in the fire bay as dawn grazed the sky; Ginger and Porgy closest to him, Gutsy, Pot Shot, Mercy and Lieutenant Everson to their left, Lucky, Half Pint, Gazette, Ketch and Jessop to their right. C Company's other three platoons on either side of them. Behind them in the communication and cover trenches, A and B companies readied themselves for the second wave of the attack. In front of him on the firestep the scaling ladder stood up against the brushwood revetment and sandbagged parapet. Atkins stared at it with deep resentment. How could something so mundane hold such sway over his life? He hated it. Every rung left him more exposed, lessened his chances. It might as well have been a ladder to the gallows.

From along the trench Corporal Ketch glowered at them. Atkins knew he wanted them to funk it and he wasn't going to give him the satisfaction, but to Atkins' left Ginger was fidgeting uneasily, like a child on the verge of tears.

"I heard they got summat new lined up for Fritz today; them watchercallems, Boojums they used up Flers," said Pot Shot.

"What, here? Oh, what I wouldn't give to see one of them," said Gutsy.

"Boojums?" said Ginger.

"Like prehistoric monsters they is," said Porgy. "They knock down trees and eat houses. Bullets and bombs just bounce off 'em, I've heard,"

"Jerry up!" said Half Pint, pointing up into the sky. Glad of the diversion, Atkins looked up with the rest into the calm autumn dawn. Above, he saw a great long train of tall white clouds stretching almost from horizon to horizon moving in a slow stately procession across the sky. There, beneath their great white bellies but high above the scattered smudges of black air burst, were two small dots flying toward the British lines.

"Albatrosses, I'll be bound," said Porgy, shielding his eyes.

"There!" called Lucky. Atkins turned. Three small black dots were making for them slowly, almost casually, flying out across the British lines to meet them. The Royal Flying Corps. Atkins willed them on as if wishing could give them speed enough to smash into the enemy like jousting steeds of the air, dashing their foes from the sky and sending them plummeting to earth. Instead they drifted slowly toward each other, almost lackadaisically, then seemed to weave in and around each other, dancing like mayflies on a summer evening. Atkins watched the dumb show, spellbound. One of them left a dark soft streak across the sky as it began a slow balletic tumble towards the earth. Atkins held his breath.

"One of ours or one of theirs?" he asked nobody in particular as he craned his head.

"Dunno," said Jessop.

"Wait," said Mercy squinting his eyes. "It's one of theirs. I think."

Grasping for a sign, any sign, and fanning a small flame of hope for the day ahead, a ragged cheer went up along the line. They joined in.

Ketch growled and took a step towards them. "Quieten down. How can you listen out for the enemy, making a racket like that?"

"Well it's not like they're going to attack at the same time we are, is it?" said Mercy.

But the mood was successfully punctured and the cheer subsided. Satisfied, Ketch returned to his position with a smirk.

Indistinct barks came down the line.

"Fix bayonets!" bellowed Hobson.

Atkins slotted the handle of the seventeen inch blade onto the end of his rifle. He'd done it so often he could do it in his sleep.

Then they waited.

* * *

Everson looked at his wristwatch. The second hand swung its way inexorably round to zero hour. Ten minutes to go. He licked his lips to moisten them for the pea-whistle that waited in his hand. Everything that could be done had been done. He could feel the weight of the revolver in his hand but his world had shrunk to that small disc on his wrist, to that needle-fine finger rotating, as if winding up the thread of his life onto some celestial spool.

Once more he had to lead his men into battle. Except that this was never battle; no glorious charge, no smashing of shields or clash of swords. There was little honour or glory here; only death, despair, pain and guilt. You never saw the enemy. Death strode the field, no longer cutting men down with a scythe, but with a threshing machine, gathering in its harvest in commercial quantities. Death had been industrialised.

Everson had never wanted responsibility. When he joined up he'd just wanted to be one of the men, a small cog in a big machine, but when your father was twice mayor of Broughtonthwaite and owner of the largest brewery in town there were bigger wheels turning against yours. So he'd been given a commission. Men he'd known before the war, men whose families had been intertwined with his for generations, now depended on him for their lives and he didn't want the responsibility. But now that it was his he wasn't going to shirk it. He'd done his damnedest to keep them alive through the bloodshed of the preceding summer, and by God, he'd do the same today.

He ran a finger around the inside of his collar and unconsciously began chewing his lower lip.

The artillery bombardment began. It started in No-Man's Land and, every minute, crept forwards another hundred yards towards the German lines – a barrage designed to shield the advancing soldiers from enemy fire. They would then move behind the line of smoke and shells, with the huge armoured hulks of the ironclad landships crushing paths through the German wire. At least that was the theory.

The ground began to shake. A loud rumbling filled the air. Atkins felt himself flinch involuntarily, expecting a shell burst or trench mortar, but the sound went on and on, increasing in volume. Dirt started dancing off the sandbags on the parapet.

"What the hell is it?" said Porgy, looking round. Down in the trench it was difficult to tell where the sound was coming from.

Along with the deep bass roar came another noise now, a squeaking and whining, a repetitive metallic clank.

"Blood and sand!" said Atkins as, several bays down, a fearsome metal monster belching white smoke from its back rolled across the reinforced bridge over the trenches into No Man's Land.

It was an ironclad landship; armour-plated, its side-mounted sponsons seemingly bristling with guns. He'd never seen anything like it, not even in the adventure stories he read. On the side he could make out a painted identity number, I-5, and then underneath, painted in a scruffier hand, the legend, *HMLS Ivanhoe*.

"Boojums!" yelled Pot Shot ecstatically.

"Tanks! Read about 'em on leave," said Mercy. "The papers were full of 'em. Oh, we're going take that wood now. Fritz'll shit himself when he sees these coming at him, eh Ginger?"

Ginger managed to crack a weak smile but then, as soon as the huge great armoured rhomboid rolled over the firing trench, he began flinching and jerking.

Not now, thought Atkins. *Not now*.

If Ginger fled the Battle Police would get him. If they didn't, Ketch certainly would. This close to a show, he wouldn't get the courtesy of a court martial before they marched him out to a stake and his mates had to shoot him.

"Ginger, quiet!" But before he could say anything more to calm the boy there came the dull repetitive clang of a cracked warning bell and the cry of: "Gas! Gas! Gas!"

The Germans, now aware that something was going off and having the prevailing wind in their favour, had opened their gas canisters and, heavier than air, the sluggish green cloud had begun to slue down the incline toward the British trenches.

At once, Atkins put his rifle down, took off his helmet and began to fumble at the canvas bag on his chest, undoing the buckle to get at the P. H. gas helmet inside. Well, the Quarterblokes called it a helmet. The men called it "the goggle-eyed bugger with the tit". What he pulled out was a cloth hood. He flapped it to open it out and pulled it on over his head, tucking its neck down into his shirt collar to form a rudimentary seal. He bit on the rubber clamp inside and took a couple of breaths, in through the nose and out through the tube in his mouth with its distinctive red rubber valve. Peering out through the greenish eye-pieces, he picked up his battle bowler and placed it back on his head before feeling around for his rifle.

He felt himself jostled from the side. He had to turn his whole body round to see. Ginger was sobbing and sniffling, unwilling or unable to open his respirator bag. Atkins hurriedly did it for him then thrust the gas hood over Ginger's head. If the gas got to him while he was snivelling like that it would be the worse for him. Immediately Ginger started to panic and claw at the hood, trying to rip it from his head.

Atkins heard a muffled shout. Ketch, looking for trouble, had caught sight of the commotion and was coming towards him.

Atkins elbowed Porgy.

"Give us a hand with Ginger!"

Porgy stood one side of Ginger and grabbed his arm, Atkins stood the other side. They held him tight so he couldn't struggle.

Atkins felt a tap on his shoulder; he swivelled round as much as he could.

"Whaff gun eer?"

"Sorry, Corporal. Can't tell what you're sayin'," said Porgy.

He didn't have to. Ketch poked him in the shoulder in a manner that said 'I'm watching you.' "Pick up your gun!" he enunciated carefully though the chemically-impregnated flannel, before returning to his position.

"Thirty seconds!" called Lieutenant Everson.

Atkins picked up his rifle and held it at the ready. Ginger had been a useful diversion. There was nothing worse than waiting for the whistle. He stared again at the scaling ladder before him, noting its shabby construction. There was not even a basic joint. The rungs had been hastily nailed to two longer pieces. Whoever expected them to climb it obviously didn't expect them to have to climb it more than once. That about said it all.

"Ten seconds..."

Everson lifted his gas hood and blew his whistle before clumsily shoving the cloth back into his collar. Waving with his pistol, he watched his men scale the ladders. To his left, one fell back into the trench, immediately cut down. From beyond the parapet came cries and screams. He grabbed a rung and hauled himself up, cleared the sandbags, stepped out onto the mud and began to run, slogging through terrain the consistency of caramel, seeking to lead his men forward. He'd seen them all over the top with none left for the Battle Police to round up, which was no more than he'd expect of them. Another man fell in front of him. Everson stepped reluctantly over the body. It was not his job to stop and see if he were wounded or dead. The stretcher bearers would follow. Over to his left, he saw one of the tank machines as it nosed down into a shell hole and then reared up to clear it and rumble onwards along its terrible trajectory as spumes of earth exploded around it.

Atkins heard the whistle from far away, as if underwater, then another and another; some fainter, some louder. Up and down the line, dozens of subalterns blew their whistles or shouted their men forwards.

This was it. Under the tidal pull of fear he felt the swell of vomit and bile rise, and felt a growing urge to piss. He didn't want to go over the top. You'd be mad to.

Someone hit him on the shoulder. Twice.

Shitohshitohshitohsh –

Atkins screamed in rage and terror, which wasn't clever because it fogged up his eye pieces. He could barely see where he was going as it was. He scrambled up the ladder and over the parapet, and looked around. There to his left he saw sergeant's stripes. Hobson was walking resolutely forward. Somewhere amid the explosions he caught the rolling tinny snap of the marching snares and the harmonious wail of the bagpipes playing as the Jocks advanced over on their left flank.

Standing in the trench with his men was like standing by a pen of cattle waiting to be herded into the abattoir and meant just about as much to him. Jeffries felt no pity for them as he lifted his gas hood to blow his whistle. He caught sight of a man, his shoulders heaving as if with sobs, a dark wet patch spreading down his trouser legs. He wouldn't move. Others clambered over the top to meet their fate. This one wouldn't.

"I'm not going to have you ruin things, Bristow. Get over!" said Jeffries in cold measured tones. Bristow snivelled but didn't stir. Jeffries sniffed derisively then shot him. "A death is a death Bristow, out there or down here, it's all the same to me. You'll have done your part either way."

He climbed the ladder and stepped from the still security of the trenches into a maelstrom of noise and fury. Shots, cries, bullets and bombs raged about him but he felt no fear. Anticipation, excitement, even, but fear? No. What had he to fear, today of all days?

In front of him, Appleton fell. And Harlow. Burton just vanished in a plume of wet offal and dirt. Still Jeffries strode on, unencumbered by the pack, webbing and bandoliers that weighed down his men. Every step a step closer to his destiny. When the day's bloodletting accrued to a critical mass, charging the landscape with a talisman of binding, he would speak the words he had long practised. The air screamed as shrapnel burst overhead, tearing down through flesh and mud alike. But none of it touched Jeffries.

Tendrils of chlorine lapped at his feet. Beneath his gas hood he wore a contented smile as he waded into the choking cloud with a surety that took the place of heroism. To be a hero you needed to feel fear. Jeffries didn't feel fear. He didn't need to. The sigil that he had drawn on his chest with Seeston's blood, now beginning to crust and pull uncomfortably at the hairs there, saw to that.

Around Atkins, men were marching forward into the clouds of gas; a rising tide of asphyxiating death. The ground was soft and treacherous underfoot. Muffled by his gas hood, the crump and boom of shells assumed a continuous roar that made his ear drums crackle. He glanced to his left. Pot Shot and Mercy were striding forward. He could make out the weak sunlight glinting off the tin triangles on their backpacks.

It was nearly a quarter of a mile to the forward German lines. Running with full pack through this mud would tire you out before you got there and you'd have no puff left for the fight. Already he could feel the muscles of his legs begin to ache from pulling against the mud. It was better, so they said, to walk and conserve your strength. Fair enough. But that bollocks about carrying on and not seeking cover? Stuff that.

Following the tape he reached the British wire. He could hear the insistent stuttering of the British machine guns, while above them shells burst, leaving lazy black woolly clouds hanging in the air as shards of hot metal ripped down through bodies below. Ahead of him now, men began to drop, some hanging on the wire as if they were puppets whose strings had been cut. He walked on past the fallen, some dead, some wounded, crying and begging for help. Most still wore their gas hoods and Atkins was grateful that he could not see their faces. You weren't supposed to stop for them. You weren't allowed to. Carry on. Forward. Always forward. He walked on aware that every step could be his last. Was it this one? This one? This?

The great bank of greenish grey fog, a mixture of chlorine, cordite and smoke rolled over them, enveloping the soldiers like a shroud. Atkins lost sight of his Section. He stepped aside to avoid a shell hole that loomed up out of the ground before him and found his leg caught. He looked down; a hand had grabbed his mud-encrusted puttee. A man, maskless, green froth oozing slowly from his mouth, gagged and struggled, tearing at his own throat with a bloodied hand, drowning on dry land as the chlorine reacted in his lungs. Atkins tugged his ankle free and marched on. Shell holes were death traps now. The gas was sinking to the lowest point it could find, settling in pockets like ghostly green rock pools, where the weary and wounded had sought shelter.

As he walked on, he began to experience a light-headed feeling. Around him the gas cloud seemed to glow with a diffuse phosphorescence. The noise of battle, the rattle of machine guns and the constant *crumpcrumpcrump* of artillery, the zing of bullets seemed somehow muffled and distant. He stumbled as he missed his footing. He looked down. His body seemed to be longer than it should have been, stretching and undulating until a wave of vertigo overwhelmed him. Letting go of his rifle, he dropped to his hands and knees. The small area of ground before him seemed to swim and ripple gently and, no matter how hard he tried, he couldn't bring it into focus. Sweat began to prickle his face, he felt a pressure in his head, something trickled from his ear and he could taste the iron tang of blood running from his nose. The whole world seemed to tilt and from the periphery of his vision an oozing darkness spilled inwards until he could see no more than a few square inches of the Somme mud before his face. What remained of his vision filled with bursting spots of light as the world began to slip away...

Private Garside's feet skittered under him on the chalky mud as he ran through the communication trench. A German shell had brought down the telephone lines between Harcourt and Sans German. He'd been ordered to collect information from the Front. Battalion needed to know how the advance was progressing. He had to get to the Observation Post and run the latest reports back to Battalion HQ. That alone could take about an hour or two. If he survived. Already two others had failed to get through.

The first walking wounded were beginning to filter back in ones and twos down the trenches, helping each other where they could. Yells of "Stretcher bearer!" filled the air. A shell exploded nearby. Garside flinched, but ran on, pushing past a couple of RAMC sent up from the reserve trenches, carrying their as yet unused stretchers wrapped around their carrying poles as they headed towards the Aid Post.

"There's no hurry, mate. I'm sure Fritz'll 'ave a bullet or two left for you!" they called after him.

Garside ignored them. By the time he'd thought of a witty retort he was several traverses ahead of them. He turned into High Street. The OP wasn't far now. The trickle of wounded he'd noticed before was fast becoming a steady stream.

Two Battle Police were confronting a young soldier, tears running down his face. He's lost his steel helmet and had no gun.

"I can't," he was saying. "I can't..."

"Turn round the way you came, you fucking coward," the bigger, burly one said.

The soldier took a step forward, towards him.

"I *can't*!" he screamed, tendons straining in his neck, his face red with effort as he dashed the Military Policeman's face with spittle.

The smaller man casually put his pistol to the man's head and fired. His legs crumpled beneath him and he dropped heavily to the ground, his head lolling at a sickening angle.

"What the fuck are you looking at?" the burly one snarled as Garside tried to edge past. He lowered his eyes to avoid meeting their gaze, but as he did so his eyes fell upon the now lifeless body of the young private.

"Leave 'im, Charlie," the wiry one said. "He's going in the right direction, 'sides he's got a Battalion armband on."

Garside ran on. He rounded several traverses to put distance between himself and the casual brutality he'd just witnessed.

"Jesus, Mary and Joseph!"

He skidded desperately to a halt. Small pebbles skittered from under his boots – and off into empty space.

Before him, where the support and front line trenches should have been, where No Man's Land had stretched away toward the German lines, lay nothing now but a huge crater almost half a mile across and thirty or forty yards deep at its centre.

The entire front line of the Harcourt Sector had gone.

CHAPTER FOUR
"Though Your Lads Are Far Away..."

Blood pulsing in his ears, his breathing shallow and rapid within the claustrophobic gas hood, Atkins struggled to stand. About him, the featureless smog of war billowed sluggishly, draping itself around him, as if seeking a way through his respirator. Shapes swirled about him and he saw Flora's face, looking like she had that day outside the factory: threading her way across the street towards him between honking motor cars and horse and carts. Her joyous smile made his heart sing. He had to tell her. How would she react? He didn't know. He wasn't sure he could find the words at all. In the end he didn't have to. As she approached her face fell, but she caught herself and smiled again, although this time it seemed strained and polite.

"I – I thought you were William."

His stomach dropped away and his heart rose to his throat. "No, he said quietly, lowering his head and wringing his army cap in his hands as if in contrition. "I'm sorry."

She clasped his hands in hers gently. "No, I am."

"I've no news of William. He's been officially missing for weeks. Lots of lads have. But I'll keep trying for you. He'll turn up, I'm sure."

Unable to look her in the eye, he found himself looking at the small hands that embraced his, and the engagement ring his brother had bought her. He looked up, tears welling in his eyes to see the same in hers, united in grief.

"Hush, Tom. Walk me home."

As quickly as it materialised the shade dissipated. Unseen in the twilit gloom of poison gas, he could hear the gas hood-smothered cries of others.

"Porgy! Porgy! Where are you?"

He thought he heard an answer from somewhere over to his left but the lethal cloud around him left him completely disorientated. He could be stumbling straight towards the German wire for all he knew. And he wished his world would stop spinning. He leant on his rifle to steady himself but, unable to keep his balance, he keeled over again and the ground loomed up to meet him. He just wanted the great big world to stop turning. With a groan he moved into a sitting position and pushed himself to his feet with the help of his rifle butt.

A deep bass rumble filled the featureless miasma around him and his world lurched, lifted upwards and dropped with such a jarring force that it drove him into the mud up to his knees. An explosion? Not any kind of shell he was familiar with. It wasn't a Five Nine or Whizz-Bang or Jack Johnson, that was for sure. It seemed to come from below the very ground he was standing on. Perhaps a mine had been set off. That must be it. Hundreds of tons of high-explosive going off underground. That'd give Fritz something to worry about.

A bright, diffuse light illuminated the smog from above, penetrating its suffocating gloom and throwing strange, disturbing shadows onto the moving banks of mist. There were cries of alarm from all around, moans of pain; calls for help, for pals, for mothers.

An eddy of wind caught the gas cloud and, for a moment, it thinned. Atkins thought he could make out the shapes of others, before the gas closed in again. He lay back in the mud as far as he could, feeling the jumbled contents of his backpack pressing into his back, and slowly began to pull his right leg from the sucking mud. Men had died getting stuck in this mire.

His leg came free with a loud sucking noise. Scrabbling to gain a foothold with his free heel again he levered himself backwards, digging the shoulder butt of his rifle into the ground for extra purchase and slowly drawing his left leg free, almost losing his boot in the process.

Stopping to catch his breath, he noticed the silence. The wailing of the distant bagpipes had ceased. But even more disconcertingly, the guns had stopped. He had grown so used to their incessant roar that their absence now startled him. What the hell was going on?

"Only!"

He turned his body trying to gauge where the sound was coming from.

"Only! Where are you?"

"Over here!"

He could make out things moving in the mist. Three hunched shades with gaunt faces containing empty sockets resolved themselves into solid corporeal soldiers in gas hoods and Battle Order.

"Only!"

It was Porgy, Pot Shot and Lance Sergeant Jessop. Well, it was definitely Pot Shot. There was no mistaking the size of him, or Jessop's stripes.

"You okay, mate?" asked Pot Shot.

"What the hell was that, a mine going up?"

"Dunno, but they might have bloody warned us."

"What the hell's going on?" asked Gutsy joining them. "Why's the firing stopped? D'you think it's a truce?"

"It's bloody eerie, is what it is," said Atkins.

"Hey, maybe it's an armistice, maybe the war is finally over," said Jessop. "I can go home to Maud and little Bertie."

A gentle wind began to worry the edges of the gas cloud. The fog thinned and visibility gradually improved. They saw dazed soldiers picking themselves up off the ground. If that had been a mine and it was British, then they should be pressing home their advantage and taking the Hun trenches while the enemy were still dazed.

"Where's the rest of us?" Atkins asked, looking around.

"Over by that shell hole. Half Pint's trying to calm Ginger down. Lucky, Mercy and Gazette are still out there somewhere. Ketch? Who cares? Sergeant's probably taking the Jerry trenches by himself," said Porgy.

The battle fog was mostly gone, slinking shamefully along the surface of the mud, herded by playful draughts.

"Hoods off!" came a distant shout.

Thankfully, men began removing their steel helmets and pulling off their gas hoods.

"Uh, chaps?" said Pot Shot, staring off into the distance.

"Come on, give a man a hand here," said Atkins putting out an arm. Porgy and Jessop took it and pulled him to his feet.

"Chaps?" said Pot Shot again, more urgently.

Atkins wiped his muddy hands on his thighs. He felt a tap on his shoulder. Porgy was looking past him. "What?" he said in irritation as he rolled up his gas helmet and took a lungful of air. The acrid tang of cordite hit the back of his throat and the slight hint of chlorine hung in the air. He coughed and spat.

Porgy jerked his chin.

He turned and followed their gaze "Blood and sand!" The shell-ravaged vista of No Man's Land was as familiar as it ever was. Atkins turned round. He could see their trenches and the barbed wire. For around a quarter of a mile in every direction there was the pummelled and churned ground of the Somme. But beyond...

It was as if some pocket of Hades had been deposited in the vale of Elysium. Beyond the muddy battlefield of No Man's Land, lush green vegetation sprang up, a green so deep and bright after untold weeks of drab khaki and grey, chalky mud that it almost hurt the eyes to look upon it. Great curling fronds, taller than a man, waved in the breeze. Where there should have been only blasted hell-torn rolling farmland, now, on either side of them, deep green thickly wooded hills rose up as if cradling them, their peaks marked by glittering becks and scumbles of scree. Atkins was reminded of the hills and mountains of his Pennine home and felt a pang of homesickness. The air around them was no longer chill and damp, but warm and moist. In the distance, along the valley floor, was a forest of sorts and, above them all, arced an achingly blue summer sky.

But of Harcourt Wood and its splintered, shredded trees, there was no sign.

Men, stunned by the same sight, were taking off their gas hoods and shucking off their backpacks and webbing to stand dumbstruck. Some fell to their knees weeping openly with relief. In the distance, the sounds of a hymn, *Nearer My God to Thee,* rose up from the trenches. Soldiers slowly, cautiously clambered over the parapets, laying down their weapons to stand in the sunlight.

"Lay down your arms, brothers, for we are at peace in the fields of the Lord!"

Groups knelt in prayer amidst the mud, their hands clasped together, heads bowed. Others just sat, exhausted from the constant tension of the front lines or wandered dazed amid the trammelled corpse-ridden fields. Warmed by the sun, steam began to drift gently up, rising like the ghosts of the slain from the desolate earth.

"It's paradise!" said Ginger, his steel helmet held loosely in his hand, a beatific smile adorning his face. He wasn't shaking or jerking, he wasn't stuttering. It seemed as if a load had been lifted from him. Atkins had never known Ginger without his shell-shock.

"Paradise? You mean – "

"We're dead. Yes. Look. The guns have stopped. This isn't the Somme. This isn't France. It's heaven," Ginger sighed. "It's heaven..."

"Valhalla," said Pot Shot, nodding in agreement.

"You what?" said Jessop.

"Valhalla. Norse heaven of Viking warriors."

"Well, that's us, though, ain't it, warriors? That's us," said Lucky.

"Blimey you're a regular fount of knowledge, Pot Shot. I'm surprised you can get your head inside that battle bowler of yours," Gutsy said.

Atkins felt the great weariness that he had been holding at bay descend on him. It was as if the weight of his mortality was slowly crushing him, as if the mere thought of an end had robbed him of the tenacious will to cling on at all costs. Was this it then? If it was over, if it really *was* over, if he really could just stop and give in –

"There's just one thing bothers me," said Half Pint, scratching his head after a few seconds thought.

"Oh aye, what's that then?" said Jessop. "You found a problem with heaven, have you?"

"Well, there's no way they'd be lettin' Porgy through the pearly gates for a start."

Me, neither, thought Atkins.

It was all very well the chaplains preaching for victory and devoutly citing that the murder of a Hun was a good thing, but they were hollow words if your conscience was pricked by other matters.

Porgy inclined his head, pursing his lips as he nodded. "Man's got a point," he said.

"I'll say," said Gutsy, "All those saintly, virtuous young ladies and Porgy? Might be his idea of heaven, but it'd be their idea of hell."

"Don't blaspheme," said Ginger. "Look at it. How can it be anything else? Where did you ever see such beauty on earth?"

"Where's the Padre? He'd know," said Lucky.

"Well, if this is heaven he ain't going to be too happy about it," said Half Pint.

"Why?"

"He'll be out of a job, won't he?"

Seeing that the gas was now blowing away, Jeffries eagerly pulled the stifling hood from his head as he stood ready to receive his god with expectations of the glory and power due to him. So he was perplexed at his deity's absence and the idyllic sights surrounding them confused him. But beyond that that there was a growing anger. What had gone wrong? He had said the words *perfectly*, hadn't he? Yes, he must have. He was sure he had. He ran through his preparations in his head. He had been painstaking in their groundwork. It had taken months to put this plan together based on years of meticulous research. There was only one conclusion he could come to; he'd been cheated. At the moment of his greatest triumph, somehow he'd been cheated. He shook his head slowly, uncomprehensive as anger burned deeply within him until he was consumed in a wave of rage and vitriol.

"No!" he roared, throwing his helmet to the ground. "No!"

Sergeant Hobson stormed over to 1 Section. "You lot! Just what the hell do you think you're doing?"

"Nothing, Sar'nt. We're dead," called Porgy.

"You're not bloody well dead until I tell you you're dead!" snapped Hobson. "Now pick your kit up and follow me."

Atkins smirked at Porgy, who shrugged. "Well, it's something to do until Saint Peter shows up and demobs us," he said.

"Don't believe in heaven, anyway," said Pot Shot casually. "Opiate of the masses an' all that."

"Opiate of the masses, that you readin' again, is it?" retorted Gutsy.

"Opiate?" said Jessop thoughtfully. "No, wait lads, he could be onto something. That would explain it. What if ol' Fritzy-boy, is using some sort of experimental opium gas what got through our respirators? This, this could all be a giant illusination. You know like them Chinky opium dens they have in that fancy London?"

Everson felt disconsolate. Since the gas cloud cleared and the astounding change to the landscape had revealed itself he began to feel power dripping away from him. It was all he'd wished for, for months, yet now he was not yet ready to relinquish it so easily. Not until he was sure that it was over, that they were all safe.

"You men!" he called, brandishing his Webley in their direction. "Pick up your weapons!" They ignored him. "Pick up your weapons!"

It was as if, in the absence of an enemy, he'd lost all authority. Isn't that what he wanted all along? To shed the burden? It was the same along the entire front. Men had cast their rifles aside, sat down and were breaking out their iron rations and singing sentimental songs, sharing out the smokes, waiting... waiting for something. Nobody seemed sure what, but whatever it was, it wasn't a subaltern with a pistol.

"It's a higher authority we answer to now, mate," one brazen private told him, jerking his chin towards the distant hills. "If we're dead then the only route march I'm doing is through the pearly gates. Fag?"

Perplexed, Everson shook his head. Seemingly bereft of purpose, he wandered out along the wire entanglements that marked the British Line. Men lay where they had fallen, sobbing and crying in pain. Some were being tended to, some being ferried away on stretchers. If this was heaven, why were there still the wounded and suffering? Would heaven allow men to suffer with their guts hanging out? What kind of god was that?

He caught sight of 1 Section being herded towards him like wayward sheep by Sergeant Hobson, before he went to round up the rest of the scattered platoon. Everson addressed one of the men.

"Jellicoe?"

"Sir?"

"I don't know what the hell is going on here, but the last I heard we were attacking the German positions in Harcourt Wood."

"Wood seems to have gone now, sir," chimed in Hopkiss.

"Thank you, yes, I can see that, Hopkiss, but the point remains. Until we know what we're dealing with here I would prefer –"

An unearthly howl cut through the valley, echoing off the hillsides. As one, the Section raised their rifles, eyes surveying the landscape. Around them men started and turned to listen, uncertainty clouding their faces. Some began gathering their discarded equipment, looking expectantly towards the officer.

"What the bloody hell was that?" said Everson.

"It came from that forest, sir," said Jellicoe.

"Right. Yes," said Everson, feeling a resurgence of purpose and responsibility, "Jessop, stay here with your section, I'll tell Hobson to rally the Platoon and pass on any orders." He turned to address the other men. "The rest of you men get back to your platoon's trenches and stand to! Until we know what's going on I think we must remain on our guard."

As platoons of men slunk back to the trenches, overhead, Atkins heard a faint, familiar drone. High above he spotted two aeroplanes, each vying for an advantageous position from which to attack. One succeeded in manoeuvring above the other for a split second before it began descending in a slow smoky spiral. Atkins watched it drift down like a leaf until it was lost from sight behind the peaks of the newly risen hills. A high gust of wind had caught the untethered and slowly deflating German kite balloon, carrying it further and further away over the hills, buoyed aloft by swift currents of air.

A spatter of machine gun fire jerked him back to reality, if anything they were experiencing could be said to be reality. Another burst. And another. The field of fire swept across No Man's Land. Tommies fell. Men scurried for cover and dived into shell holes with shouts of alarm and dismay.

"There!" said Gazette, spotting the muzzle flash of the machine gun as it fired off another burst. "It's a Hun sap."

They barely had time to follow Gazette's stare towards a fortified shell-hole before the Maxim fire swept towards them. The Section scrambled for the cover of a shell hole, bullets spitting into the mud at their heels as they ran. As they threw themselves into the mud-filled pit a roar filled the air as the great ironclad bulk of *HMLS Ivanhoe* reared up out of a dip in front of them, like some great blind creature emerging from the primordial slime. It crashed down heavily, placing its metal carcass between them and the raking German machine gun. Atkins heard the bullets raining against the hide of the motorised beast.

Slowly its great six-pounder gun turned toward the emplacement. There was a brief pause before the gun fired. The machine gun emplacement erupted in a geyser of dirt and sandbags; smoke and screams filled the air as munitions went up in a series of secondary explosions. A ball of flame bloomed briefly within the remnants of the emplacement and mud and hot metal rained down, clinking dully against the armoured hulk.

Mercy banged on the side of the boojum. "Ere, conductor! Any room inside, it's ruddy raining out here!"

The Tank gave no indication of human occupancy although, in reply, its motorised growl rose in pitch as if in recognition. Gears ground as the left hand track remained still and the right hand track spun slowly, swinging the tank away from them as it continued it halting, lethargic advance.

"Christ that was close. Bloody boojums, though, eh, Only?" said Mercy cracking a grin and slapping Atkins on the back.

"Right, you lot!" bellowed Sergeant Hobson herding the rest of the scattered platoon towards them. "Take a dekko and see how far this mud pie of ours goes. We also need to make sure Fritz hasn't got anything else up his sleeve. One other thing. Nobody steps off this mud until further orders. Got it?"

"Yes Sergeant!"

"Right. Move out."

Atkins fell in with Mercy and Gazette with Jessop taking the lead. The initial eerie tranquillity had now been shattered, spurring the growing sense of unease he felt at their surroundings. Along the line several other platoons were being ordered to move forward through the shell holes towards where the German lines should have been.

They came across the remains of an aeroplane lying on its back, its wheels splayed in the air. It was one of theirs, the Royal Flying Corps roundel clearly visible on the fuselage. The front was covered with mud, the remains of the propeller splintered as though it had ploughed head first into the mud before flipping and coming to rest. Oil leaked onto the ground from the engine, turning the mud beneath it to a thick black viscous puddle.

"Only, check the pilot blokes," Jessop said, looking around warily.

Atkins passed his rifle to Porgy and got down on his hands and knees to crawl under the upturned machine. The observer was upside down in his cockpit, his head tilted back and his face planted in the mud. Atkins tried to push him up to relieve the pressure, but realised his efforts were futile. He was dead. Atkins moved towards the pilot. He crawled over the plane and let out a startled cry when his knee went through the doped cotton with a pop.

"Sorry, nothing! My fault," he called out to reassure his startled fellows. "Hang on chum, we'll get you out."

Once Atkins had wriggled through the snapped spars and wire he found that the pilot had fallen out of his cockpit and lay in the small crushed space between machine and the upper wing, his neck broken. Awkwardly, Atkins shuffled out from under the shattered plane. As he did so he spotted a line of bullet holes stitched across the fuselage.

Atkins shook his head at Jessop.

"Both dead. Pilot's got a broken neck. Looks like the other one was drowned in the mud."

"Nothing we can do here, then," said Jessop. "Ginger, Mercy, get those bodies out then salvage the guns and collect whatever ammunition you can from the plane. The rest of you spread out and move on."

Porgy had been looking at the rear of the aeroplane. "Look at this, lads. What do you make of that?"

The tail had vanished, not ripped off or shot through, but simply amputated by a clean cut. Atkins looked around but could see no sign of the missing section.

There was a dull snap as Ginger and Mercy tugged at the body of the observer and dragged him from the rear cockpit.

"Careful, you clumsy buggers," cried Jessop.

"It was the plane!" said Mercy defensively.

Jessop shook his head and moved on. The rest followed his lead.

In minutes they had reached the end of the mud. The German wire should have been twenty or thirty yards further on but, where once there had been fortifications, entrenchments, emplacements and entanglements there was now an abrupt drop of seven or eight feet. Beyond, they were surrounded by a thick green meadow, the grass maybe three or four feet high, the stalks flattened outwards as if by violent impact. Beyond the veldt, looking towards the head of the valley, was what could be termed a forest, perhaps a mile or so or away. Scattered across the meadow were what looked like trees, spaced singly or in small groves.

"Jessop?" said Pot Shot, standing at the very edge of what they knew as the Somme.

"What is it?" said the Lance Sergeant, striding over.

Pot Shot was stood over a body of a dead Hun. Or to be more precise, half a body. The torso was hanging on the wire. It was cut clean through and the legs were missing. Hobson pushed his tin hat back on his head, raised his eyebrows and let out a long, slow exhalation.

"Christ," he said.

"What do you reckon did that?"

"Nothing I know of," he said. There wasn't the usual mess they were accustomed to, just a clean, surgical cut.

All eyes turned to Gutsy.

"What? Just because I use to be a butcher? Bloody hell!" Gutsy, despite his protests, set about studying the body with an almost professional interest. There was no blood. It was as if the entire wound had been cauterised. "I don't know of any blade sharp enough or quick enough to leave such a clean cut."

Pot Shot had been examining a strand of the wire.

"Same here," he declared.

"How can you tell?" asked Gazette.

"You see here? Normally when you use wire cutters the wire is pinched thin before it breaks, resulting in a pointed 'v' cross section. This is flat."

Atkins stood at the edge of the lip and looked slowly left, then right along the fault line as it curved gently back away from him on either side. "Y' know," he said slowly. "It's almost as if something has severed cleanly through everything - ground and air. I'll bet if we follow this around we'll find the same."

"What are you saying, Only?" asked Jessop.

Atkins never got the chance to reply. Out of the corner of his eye he caught a flash of fangs as Jessop disappeared, propelled backwards by the weight of a large mound of greasy fur and muscle, leaving only a scream in his wake as foot long teeth ripped out his throat.

PENNINE FUSILIERS

CHAPTER FIVE
"Some Corner of a Foreign Field..."

Gazette was the first to get off a shot, firing a full clip at the great beast as it tore ravenously into Jessop's stomach, all in the time it took Atkins to bring up his rifle.

"Holy Mary Mother of God!" wailed Ginger.

"What the bleedin' hell is it?" shouted Mercy.

"Bloody ugly!" replied Gutsy, as the rest of the section brought their rifles to bear.

Atkins had never seen such a creature. None of them had. It was like some kind of monstrous hyena. Easily as high as a man, it had powerful shoulders, like that of an American bison; a mass of knotted, corded muscle rippling under its coarse fur. Its neck was short, its long snout was filled with sharp teeth and it possessed powerful muscled legs ending in long claws.

"Don't just stand there," bellowed Hobson. "Five rounds rapid!"

The great predator roared as the bullets bit, but would not be denied its kill. It turned its blood-drenched snout towards them, snarling in pain and anger. Driven away from the body, it let out a howl of such fury that some of the men nearby dropped their guns and began running for the trenches.

From out of the undergrowth, a pack of the same creatures answered, bounding towards the mud, howling and baying, the scent of fresh blood now on the wind, driving them into a frenzy.

Gazette and the others turned their rifles on the creatures and fired. The beasts staggered under the fusillade. Some yelped and fell, others skidded to a halt, uncertain. The volley hadn't entirely stopped their advance, but it had slowed it. Twenty, maybe thirty of the creatures were now bounding towards them, guttural snarls drawing back lips to reveal rows of sharp teeth. Others, more cautious, began edging round, trying to flank them, bellies low to the ground.

"Fall back!"

Atkins didn't need to be told twice. He began running with the others, which only served to excite the creatures more. He sprinted past the downed aeroplane, where Mercy was wrestling with the ammunition magazine on the Lewis gun.

"Run!" cried Atkins as he sprinted past. Gazette and Gutsy skidded to a halt by the wreck and, using it for cover, loosed off another clip each.

"Take Ginger!" yelled Mercy, stacking up the six circular ammo magazines by him and setting the Lewis gun on the wing. "I'll cover you!"

Gutsy and Lucky hauled Ginger to his feet and began herding him back towards the trenches.

Atkins dashed back towards the crashed biplane, firing off another clip as he ran before he slumped down by Mercy.

"You'll need a loader," he said. Mercy nodded grimly.

Mercy took aim and pulled the trigger, loosing the entire magazine in one burst. Atkins pulled it off, threw it aside and clipped on the second, but too slowly; the first wave of the creatures was nearly upon them. Mercy let off another quick stammer.

On their blind side, hidden by the fuselage of the aeroplane, they could hear the cries of other, less fortunate men as they fell to the pack.

Atkins loaded up the final magazine. A quick burst from the Lewis gun brought down a couple more of the creatures. Mercy was now getting the measure of the MG, alas with all too few rounds left. Another beast approached cautiously, its head down, a low growl emanating from its throat. It glared at them warily as it began tugging at the body of one of the dead aviators, seeking to drag it away. Mercy screamed and let fly another burst, bullets tearing into the beast, until the canister spun on empty. He shoved the gun aside, unshouldered his rifle, loaded another clip and waited.

Atkins heard a clatter above them. A creature had leapt onto the upturned belly of the machine. He could hear it sniffing. He lay still, not daring to move.

There was the rapid fire of five rounds and a roar of pain from the unseen creature, which seemed to stagger unsteadily on top of the machine and, in doing so, missed its footing, putting its full weight on the doped covering of the wing. Its claws tore through the flimsy cotton as the wing folded under it, the spars snapping under its weight and sending the wounded creature crashing towards Atkins.

Atkins rolled onto his back and braced the butt of his rifle against his shoulder. Unable to stop itself, the beast tumbled onto the blade of his bayonet. Atkins pulled the trigger, emptying his clip into the creature. It slumped heavily towards him. Inches from his face, its teeth snapped weakly; hot, thick saliva dripping onto him with the creature's last fetid exhalation.

Mercy dragged him out from beneath the carcass. "Come on, Only, we've got to get back to the trenches."

"No argument from me," said Atkins, kicking himself free.

Stooped over, they ran for the shell hole from where Gazette was providing covering fire and jumped over the lip to find the rest of the section sheltering within.

By now the machine gun emplacements back behind the firing trench were opening fire on the animals. Bullets zinged overhead, causing them to flinch back into the shell hole.

"We're on your side, you daft beggars!" called Porgy, clutching his steel helmet to his head.

Cautiously, Atkins peered above the rim. It appeared that competing packs of the creatures were now fighting among themselves and, now that he had a better view, he could see why.

It wasn't just the living that they were feeding off. Several beasts were tugging at the exposed limbs of corpses and attempting to draw the corrupt bodies from the mud's clammy embrace. They fought over rotting bodies, worrying the fragile cadavers until they fell apart, or else bursting gas-filled bellies and snuffling greedily at the contents. The scale of their predicament, the full horror of their situation, hit Atkins. They were sitting on a charnel field consisting of layer upon layer of decomposing dead, thousands of corpses of rotten Hun, French and British soldiers. They'd attract every predator, scavenger and carrion eater for miles around. This was just the start.

"It's now or never. Make for the trenches, lads, and don't spare the horses," said Hobson.

As one, they leapt from the shell holes and made for the lines. Distracted by the prospect of a live kill, some of the creatures turned from fighting over scraps to give chase. Ketch fell headlong into the mud, his rifle flung out beyond his reach. He cried out as he spotted the creatures bearing down on him, each trying to warn the other off their potential prize.

Sod him, thought Atkins, but he couldn't. "Damn!" He ran back.

"Get the hell away from me, Atkins. I'm not going to be party to your showboating heroics."

"Now ain't the time, Ketch. F'Pete's sake, take my hand."

Ketch's hand clasped his and Atkins hauled him up. The beasts, sensing that their prey was about to bolt, put on a burst of speed. They weren't going to make it.

The air filled with a high pitched drone, punctuated by the spatter of machine gun fire. Atkins dropped as a biplane swooped low over them, picking off the creatures as it came. He cheered as he caught sight of a gauntleted hand giving him a cheery wave from the cockpit before the plane began to climb steeply away again, waggling its wings briefly.

Atkins attempted to haul Ketch to his feet again but the Corporal swatted his hand away. "I don't want your damn help, Atkins," he snapped and, after a false start, slipping in the mud, he struggled to his feet and they raced for the trenches. As they ran Atkins could hear the machine circling round again, diving towards the packs of creatures and spitting lead.

As those on the firestep covered them, Atkins flung himself over the parapet into the safety of the trenches, almost knocking over Hepton who was feverishly cranking the handle of his camera, mesmerised by the scene before him. There, from the relative safety of the fire bay, Atkins saw the tank turning its Hotchkiss machine guns on knots of the feeding creatures. Some of the more cunning ones slunk in under the gun's field of fire and leapt onto the tank's back, growling and slashing impotently at its armoured hide. They started ripping at the anti-grenade gable on its roof, tearing at the chicken wire. Fore and aft of the gun sponsons, small round loopholes, no more than a couple of inches across, flicked open and the barrels of revolvers poked out and began to fire. Muzzle flashes buried themselves in the greasy hides of the beasts straddling the tank. They dropped to the ground with yelps and squeals, slinking into the undergrowth with howls of frustration to cheers of victory from the men.

Lieutenant James Tulliver peered back over the trailing edge of his wing down at the bewildering scene. Huge wolf-like creatures prowled over No Man's Land, which seemed to have shrunk to a circle barely half a mile across, surrounded by a halo of bright cinnamon earth. It sat in the wide green valley, looking as if it had been dropped there from a height by a careless giant. Well, to be quite frank, thought Tulliver, it looked like nothing so much as a freshly dropped cow pat in a field.

Normally he would return to the airfield, but from what he could see, there was no airfield left to which he could return. There were several hundred yards of No Man's Land but the persistent shelling meant that wasn't even an option. He could make out the fire and cover trenches and even a long section of support trench along with a bombed farmhouse near the edge of the grey-brown mud flat. Beyond that, some sort of long grass was flattened outwards as if by a shockwave. It wasn't ideal, but right now he didn't seem to have much choice. He selected his approach and cut the engine, gliding down towards the ground.

He felt the wheels of the Sopwith 1½ Strutter hit with a bump and the machine bounced along. He adjusted the flaps and the biplane came down heavily again, this time trundling along to a stop, the thing juddering and shaking so much Tulliver feared it would fall apart before it stopped, but stop it did. He pushed up his goggles revealing piercing blue eyes amid the oil-splattered face. He climbed out of his cockpit and checked Hodgeson his observer. He was dead, sat slumped forward in the rear cockpit, blood filling his goggles. Damn shame. He'd only been out two weeks. He clambered down to the ground, took off his fur-lined gloves and boots, then walked round to inspect his machine, noting the holes across the fuselage that the Hun had given him. They could be repaired. All in all she was still in admirable condition.

"Good show, old girl," he said gently. He looked round. About fifty yards away was the beginning of the mud patch. He strolled towards it with his usual insouciance, intending to report to the nearest officer, when he heard a scream. A female scream. It came from the bombed-out farmhouse teetering near the edge of the muddy escarpment. He ran towards it, pulling out his revolver, barely noticing the change of ground underfoot as he raced up the incline. The scream was suddenly drowned out by a frustrated growl.

Nearing the house, he slowed down and edged forward cautiously. He could hear some animal, probably one of those beasts he saw earlier, padding around inside.

From a boarded up window he heard the sound of sobbing, the murmur of prayer and an insistent, urgent whisper.

"Well, we can't just sit here. There must be something we can do."

"What on earth is it?"

"It must have escaped from a zoo!"

There was another roar from the beast, which could clearly hear and smell its prey but couldn't reach it.

Tulliver edged along the wall until he came to a faded wooden doorjamb, its paint peeling and the door long since carted off for firewood. Cocking his pistol, he peered round the door. The huge beast was stood in the passage sniffing at the closed door within. Its great claws had slashed through the plaster to the side to reveal the fragile wooden slats beneath. It wouldn't be long before it got through that way.

Tulliver withdrew. As quietly as possible he checked the chambers of his revolver. They were all full. He only hoped they'd be enough.

He took several deep breaths. He wished whoever was screaming would shut up. It was really getting on his nerves. Apart from which he wanted to make sure the animal could hear him. As the screamer stopped to take a breath, he stepped round the doorway and whistled. The beast looked up and growled before bounding at him, claws skittering over the debris on the floor. Tulliver got off two shots then stepped aside, back against the wall beside the door as the beast came through, bringing half the doorjamb with it. He got off another two shots before the beast realised where he was and could turn. Its back legs skidded out from under it.

It pounced. Tulliver let off the last two shots. One passed straight through its skull scattering its brains out through the exit wound. As he dropped and rolled aside, the beast crashed into the wall and collapsed to the ground, sending loose bricks tumbling down, prompting another round of screaming from inside.

"Edith! Do be quiet. I shan't have to slap you again, shall I?"

"Sister, please, no more violence!" said a man's voice.

"Well, if she don't, I will," came a third female voice.

"Hello?" called Tulliver as he walked slowly down the short passage and tried the door. It wouldn't budge. He tried knocking and was encouraged by the sound of scraping as if someone were moving large objects.

"Well for goodness sake, Edith, give the gel a hand."

"Thanks awfully," came the reply, dripping with sarcasm as the door scraped open and jammed halfway. Tulliver was just wondering whether he should do the gentlemanly thing and put his shoulder to it when a final wrench from a pair of grubby hands freed it. The door crashed open sending a woman dressed in a khaki jacket and long ankle length khaki skirt reeling back into the arms of a middle-aged chap in an army uniform, under which Tulliver could see the black cloth and white collar of a Devil Dodger. Two nurses looked on.

"Careful there, Padre, this is more my area of expertise than yours I think," said Tulliver, stepping into the room and setting the poor woman on her feet again.

"Gor blimey, a... pilot!" said the khaki-clad FANY. She blushed furiously against her better judgement but recovered admirably. "Nellie Abbott," she said with a little bob of a curtsey. "Where's your machine, then? Can I see it? What sort is it?"

"Driver Abbot! A little decorum, please!" said the Sister brusquely. "You *are* a pilot, then?"

"Lieutenant James Tulliver, RFC," he said, clicking his heels and giving a little mock bow of the head.

"Sister Fenton," said the nurse curtly, thrusting out a hand. "Red Cross. This is Nurse Bell," she said, nodding at a similarly dressed young woman.

"Yes," said Tulliver, shaking her hand. "The red crosses on your uniform did rather give it away."

"I don't think this is the time for flippancy, do you, Mr Tulliver?" interjected the Padre.

The young woman in the nurse's uniform, her once carefully pinned hair now a-tumble, let out a sigh and crumpled to the floor.

"Oh, for goodness' sake!" said Fenton, stamping her foot. "Edith!"

"I say, I don't usually have that kind of effect," said Tulliver. "Is she all right?"

"It's not you, you great oaf," snapped the other nurse. "We've just been though a lot, a motor crash, a freezing cold night in a cellar, the shelling and now to have that slavering great creature..."

"It's dead now," said Tulliver. "But this place isn't safe. There are more of them. We'll have to get you into the trenches."

"The trenches? Are you mad?" said the Padre. "There are hundreds of men there."

"Padre, believe me," said Sister Fenton, "The likes of that lot hold no fear for me."

"An' I've got four brothers so I've seen the worst of 'em!" said Abbott jovially.

"There, that's settled then," said Tulliver.

"It's totally out of the question. It's... improper," said the Padre. "We're waiting on a motor ambulance to take them back to the Hospital in St. Germaine."

"Ah," said Tulliver, awkwardly, rubbing the back of his neck and feeling the short bristles there.

"What do you mean, 'ah'?" said Sister Fenton.

"I mean, I don't think it's going to be possible, I'm afraid," he said. "At least for a while. Can she walk?" he asked, indicating Nurse Bell.

"Oh she'll be fine. Abbott, give me a hand," said Sister Fenton.

The khaki-clad girl hurried to put herself under the blonde nurse's arm in order to take her weight. The woman groaned softly.

"Come on, Edi," she said. "Time for a little promenade."

"Where to?" asked the dazed nurse weakly.

"Padre, I need to report to, well, to *somebody*. Can you take me to an officer? Whose Company Front is this?"

"13th Battalion Pennine Fusiliers. I can take you to C Company HQ. It's not far from here."

"It may be further than you think," Tulliver said cryptically. "Wait here." He slipped out of the door and peered outside. He held his revolver for appearance's sake. The nurses needn't know it was empty. He had some spare ammunition, but it was in the aeroplane.

"It's clear. Padre, you bring up the rear."

"Right you are."

They stepped over the rubble and out of the back of the ruined farmhouse facing the front line, to avoid the creature's corpse out the front. It took the women a moment or two to catch their breath at the sight of the lush green vista now surrounding them.

"Blimey!"

"Oh. My..."

"Hold fast, Abbott, Edith's going to faint again," said Sister Fenton. "Mr Tulliver, where exactly are we? These mountains weren't here yesterday. I should have been sure to spot them. How is this possible?"

"That," said Tulliver, "is the very question. Well, Padre, any answers?"

The Padre opened and closed his mouth several times before giving up and reluctantly shaking his head.

A strange cry startled them. Above, flocks of things that were not birds were beginning to swirl and wheel above the mud. Up ahead, they could hear the marshalling shouts and barks of NCOs giving orders.

"We'd best hurry. Watch your step, ladies," cautioned Tulliver as he led them across the mud and down into the nearest communication trench. He'd only ever once before had a trip up to the front lines, when visiting an artillery battery.

"That smell!" said Edith, faltering as she looked round for the source while Sister Fenton dragged her on like a tardy child.

"I know," said Tulliver, shaking his head. "Sweaty feet, unwashed men, cordite, army stew. If nothing else they should act as effective smelling salts, eh, Abbott?"

As they worked their way up the trench the party attracted cat calls and whistles from weary, mud-soaked and bewildered men. Tulliver turned back to check on his charges. Sister Fenton strode purposefully on, doing her best to ignore them, while Edith seemed to have recovered enough to smile coquettishly as she was pulled along in her wake. Abbott strode confidently behind. She looked longingly at a private drawing on a fag. "Aw, go on, duck, give us a Wood, I'm gasping!" she said as she passed.

The soldier leered at her. "Come 'ere, and I'll give you –" he began, before catching the eye of the Padre bringing up the rear. Flustered, he fished around in his tunic pocket producing two battered but serviceable Woodbines and offered them to her. "– I'll give you a couple," he stuttered apologetically, smiling awkwardly as his mates jeered and jostled him.

Abbott took them from his hand. "Ta, ever so, ducks," she called gaily as the Padre impatiently herded her away.

One man flung himself desperately at the Chaplain.

"Padre? What's happened. Where are we? We thought we was in heaven, like, but them devil dogs attacked so it can't be, can it? Is God punishing us? Tell us Padre, tell us!"

"I – I don't know, my son" answered the Padre as he pulled away from the distraught soldier.

Further along, the revetments leaned drunkenly, their sandbags askew. In places they threatened to topple over completely. In others they had collapsed and they had to scramble over the mounds of spoil. When they reached C Company HQ they found a captain sat in the remains of the trench with his head in his hands. There was a bustle of activity around him as men worked stoically shifting sandbags and timbers, using shovels, picks and buckets to excavate the dirt where the C Company HQ sign lay half buried.

"Captain Grantham!" said Padre Rand, kneeling down by him. "What happened? Is the Major all right?"

Grantham lifted his head from his hands. His face was streaked with dirt and tears.

The Padre took him aside. "For God's sake, compose yourself, Captain. Not in front of the ranks. Remember you're an officer! Pull yourself together."

Grantham made an effort to regain his composure as he stood. He brushed the drying mud and soil from his tunic, cleared his throat and straightened his collar and tie.

"Can we help?" asked Sister Fenton, stepping forward.

"Eh?" The Captain looked at the women nonplussed.

"The nurses I reported on last night, Grantham," said the Padre.

"Ah. Right. Yes, well there's nothing they can do here," said

Grantham waving away Sister Fenton's ministrations. "But I'm sure the MO can put them to work." He gestured to the pile. "The Major's dead, buried under that lot. I barely got out myself. There was a sudden jolt and the whole place just collapsed around us. There's the CSM, the orderlies and the signal chappie down there, too," he said earnestly. "And reports of other dugout collapses. I sent a runner to Battalion but he says it's gone. How can it not be there? And then there were those damn wolf things. I don't know what's happening."

"This man might be able to shed some light on it all," said the Padre, introducing the Flying Officer.

"Lieutenant Tulliver," said Tulliver, extending a hand.

Grantham took it. "Well I certainly hope you can. This is a right bloody shambles. The men are getting windy. It felt like a bloody earth tremor."

"A bit more than that."

"A mine explosion?"

"If it was it's blown us to God knows where," said Tulliver, looking up at the mountains on either side as he pulled his trench maps from inside his double-breasted tunic. He took a stub of pencil from his pocket and, after studying the map for a few moments, drew a rough circle on the paper around a section of trenches and No Man's Land. "As far as I can tell, sir, this area is all I could see from the air. It's as if someone had taken a giant pair of scissors, cut it out and dropped it down somewhere else entirely."

"Scissors? Talk sense man!" snapped Grantham.

"From what I could see from the air, sir," said Tulliver, "this circle of mud is all that is left of the Somme."

The tank rumbled and squealed its way implacably toward the trench and then stopped. Atkins could see where the beasts had clawed away at the trench paint – camouflage cover and the wire netting gable was torn and hanging off. By the time the engine had puttered and died Atkins and some of the others were out of the trenches and walking towards this new wonder machine. Its guns slowly lowered, as if bowing in obeisance or exhaustion. There were metallic clangs and bangs as a door, barely more than two feet tall, opened in the rear of the gun sponson and there clambered, from the pit of the armoured machine, one small man and then another. They were wearing oiled-stained khaki overalls covered with small burn holes and tight fitting leather helmets with leather masks across the upper halves of their faces, their eyeholes merely thin slits. From the bottom of the masks hung chain mail drapes that covered the rest of their face. They looked as if they'd stepped from the Devil's own chariot. Two more climbed out of a hatch on the top of the motorised mammoth and walked down the back of the now motionless track that encompassed the entire side of the tank.

"Bloody gas! Now I'm going to have to strip everything down and clean it to stop the damn corrosion."

"Jesus my head's banging!"

Atkins had never seen a more otherworldly group of men. They would have looked fierce and impressive, almost like some primitive tribal warriors, if two of them hadn't then fallen to their knees and started vomiting warm beige splatters into the mud, coughing and retching worse than a retired coal miner.

"Bloody hell!" said Porgy.

The little bantam bloke pulled off his helmet and mask to reveal a pale face covered with flaky, livid red patches. He took a swing with his foot, savagely kicking the body of a dead creature.

"That's for scratching *Ivanhoe*, you ugly mutt," he said, punctuating his invective with further kicks.

The lanky Tank Commander strode over and made a curt introduction. "Lieutenant Mathers. Who's in charge here?"

"That'll be Captain Grantham, sir," said Sergeant Hobson. "I'll get someone to take you to Company HQ."

Atkins turned his attention back to the others who were talking to the tank crew.

"Well if this ain't the Somme it's not my fault," the bantam tank driver was saying. "My map reading were bloody perfect!"

"Then where on earth are we?"

"Earth?" spat the bantam figure scathingly. "This ain't like no place on earth *I've* ever seen!"

CHAPTER SIX
"What's the Use of Worrying…"

"I'm going to need numbers, Sergeant; roll call and casualties," Everson said as he inspected the fire trench along his Platoon Front. After the attack by what they were calling hell hounds, the men were stood to on the fire step, rifles at the ready. Any questions the men might have were silenced by Hobson's stern glance, for which Everson was thankful. He had no idea what had happened. Right now he was as ignorant as his men, which was not a position he liked to be in and one he was even less likely to want to admit to. Latrine rumours were flying about. You couldn't stop them. Those that thought they'd suddenly materialised in Paradise and the Just Reward they so richly deserved were quickly disabused by the attack of the creatures. Now they were convinced they were in Purgatory. Others thought it Hell, although that argument was soon sunk by the virtue of them having been on the Somme which was itself the very definition of hell. Best to nip such gossip in the bud, if you could. Having stalled after the initial confusion over the strange surroundings and the attack of the beasts, the great military machine was beginning to reassert itself.

"I want you to keep the men busy," Everson told Hobson. "Don't want 'em getting windy. After they're stood down, set them to repairing the trenches. Work will keep them occupied until we can sort out what the hell is going on here."

Cries and moans from the wounded drifted over from No Man's Land, those wounded by Fritz in the initial attack and those poor souls left alive by the attacking hell hounds. That was the real morale sapper, he knew. In a Pals Battalion like the Broughtonthwaite Mates, those weren't just any soldiers, those cries came from people you'd known all your lives. That's what became unbearable; the knowledge that they weren't just going to die. With gut-shots or shrap wounds they could lie out there for days, begging for help, crying for their mothers, calling for *you* to help them, and you knowing that if you tried to help them, you'd be joining them on the old barbed wire. That's what broke men, that's what ground insidiously away at morale. Oh, the bombs and the shells and the sniping got to some after a while, but this was the clincher.

"Sergeant?"

"Sir?"

"Best, get a party together with stretcher bearers, too, and start bringing in some of those woundeds while we've still got daylight. Those damned beasts are still out there somewhere. See to it, will you?"

"Sir," he said. Everson left him to it, turned down the comm trench and began to work his way back to where the temporary HQ had been set up and a Company meeting arranged.

Hours later, with only the occasional reappearance of a wily hell hound or two, the men were stood down with only sentries left on guard against further attack. Those not on duty retired to the support trenches.

"Fuck, look lively here comes Hobson," said Porgy, sucking the last dregs of smoke from his Woodbine before dropping it in the mud to sizzle and die.

"Great. Ketch'll be in charge of the Section. Bet he couldn't wait," muttered Mercy as they noticed the Corporal skulking along behind the Sergeant, "and Jessop barely cold."

"Right, you lot, finished sitting around on our arses have we?" said Hobson. "Then there's work to do."

"Sarn't," said Porgy, putting a hand to his grubbily bandaged pate, "Me head's spinning. I think it's that crack I got last night."

Atkins could almost hear the rest of the Section groan and suppressed a smirk. Bloody Porgy. He had an aversion to manual labour. Had to keep his hands soft for his long-haired chums, or so he said.

"Right, Hopkiss," said Hobson, almost wearily. "Let's get you to the MO then and see what he has to say. If you're malingering, I'll have you. The rest of you fall in. Come on," he barked when they were slow to get up, "put some jildi into it!"

They got up and put themselves into lacklustre order.

"Jesus, Mary and Joseph, you're a sorry bunch. If your mothers could see you now they'd be ashamed!" he snapped. "You lot are on trench fatigue. I'll leave it to Corporal Ketch to sort the details out. They're all yours, Corporal." And he set off, escorting Porgy to the MO. Porgy turned and gave Atkins a quick wink before Hobson shoved him down the comm trench.

"Right," said Ketch slowly once Hobson had gone, the sneer on his lips smearing itself across his face. "We're going down Broughton Street for a bit of digging, so grab your entrenching tools."

There was a lot of muttering and sighing as they picked up the spades from their kits and began sloping off down the trench.

"Not you, Atkins," said Ketch. "I've got another job for you. Don't think saving me from them hell hounds has won you any favours, cos it hasn't. You suffer too much from cheerfulness you do. Well, I've got the cure. You're a cocky little shit, d'y'know that?"

"Here, steady on Corp!" said Mercy.

Ketch shot him a look and carried on.

"And shit should be in the latrine. Sanitation duty until I say so."

"Corp!" objected Atkins, but knowing it was an argument he was going to lose, Atkins bit his tongue. Mercy had no such reservations.

"Quit riding the lad, Ketch. You may be an NCO but *apres le guerre* I'll have you cold, mate," he said stepping between Ketch and Atkins and going to-to-toe with the Corporal.

"For that you can join him, Evans, you like getting yourself in the shit so much."

Once Ketch had dismissed them and they'd gone off to fetch their tools, Atkins turned to Mercy.

"What up with him? Why's he got it in for me?"

"Ketch? Regular four-letter man he is. He was foreman over at Everson's brewery before the war an' he didn't 'alf lord it over us. Thought he had it cushy 'til old man Everson decided to let the workers form a union, didn't he? Aggravated Ketch no end that did, but there were nowt he could do about it, was there? War broke out, we joined up to get away from the bastard only to find that, as a foreman, he'd been made an NCO. He's worse now than he ever was," Mercy said with sardonic grin. "He hates everyone and everything."

"Because?"

"Because they are and he's not."

"Not what?"

"Tall, handsome, rich, popular, sergeant, butcher, baker, candlestick maker. Take your pick. But don't worry about him, It's not worth it. Look on the bright side, Sanitation duty stinks but shouldn't take more than a couple of hours," said Mercy with a smile and a wink. "Gives us an easy ride while the others are breaking their backs, don't it?"

Padre Rand, having left Tulliver with Captain Grantham, escorted the VADs through the trenches drawing curious glances from some of the men as they passed.

"Where are we going?" asked Nellie Abbott.

"To see the Regimental Medical Officer. He's trying to set up a Dressing Station here until we can find a way back to your hospital."

"Looks like you're going to have to find the Somme first," said Nellie chirpily.

Edith bowed her head and smiled privately. She liked this young, tough woman.

"Driver Abbott, you may not be under my direct supervision, but I'll ask you to show some respect to your betters," said Sister Fenton.

Edith saw Nellie bite her lip and flick a dirty look to Sister Fenton and loved her all the more.

"But she's got a point, hasn't she Sister?" said Edith. "We don't know where we are and that... that creature...."

"It probably escaped from a zoo, or some such, Bell," said Sister Fenton. "Or it's a new kind of attack hound bred by the Hun. I'm sure they're not above doing that sort of thing. Remember poor Belgium?"

They followed a crudely painted sign and turned a corner to find a wide, bombed out shell hole appropriated as a sort of waiting room. Dozens and dozens of men sat about listlessly. Some bandaged, some staring vacantly ahead. Others lay on stretchers, still and lifeless. The group worked their way through the crowd of men, who parted quietly, politely, until the nurses came to a lean-to structure made from timber, corrugated iron and sandbags.

"Captain Lippett?" enquired Padre Rand.

A man, late thirties, with slickly oiled hair and a small pair of pince-nez sat on his nose, dressed in shirt sleeves and braces, wearing a blood-stained apron, looked up from a bare-chested, pale skinned man, whose arm wound he was cleaning. "Padre. If you've coming looking for work there's plenty. Many of these men will die today. I haven't the time or the facilities to deal with them here. I've got a large percentage bleeding from eyes, ears and nose. Never seen anything like it. Damned if I know what's caused it. Been tellin' 'em it was the gas. Seems to keep 'em quiet for a while. Tompkins," he called to a nearby orderly, "dress this man's wounds. Bloody lucky there, private."

"Light duties, Doc?" the man asked weakly.

"For you? Yes, I'd say so."

The man could barely disguise his smile as the orderly led him away.

"Actually, I've brought you some help," said the Padre.

Captain Lippett turned to look at the women over the top of his glasses. He obviously wasn't pleased with what he saw. He hurriedly took the Padre by the arm and dragged him away. There seemed to be a heated discussion going on between them. Edith made out the words "Women!" several times. It was clear that the MO didn't approve of their being there, but here they were and there was nothing to be done about it. In the end the officer threw up his hands in submission and returned to the nurses.

"Well, if you're so put out, Captain, I'd be obliged if you could just arrange transport back to the hospital," said Sister Fenton.

"Sister, I have absolutely no idea what's going on. And it would seem motor ambulances, or indeed transport back to anywhere, is beyond us at the moment. In the meantime, however, we have many injured men here and, while I believe that this is no place for a woman, frankly I could use your help."

Which was about as much apology as they were going to get. Nellie was set to sterilising equipment and finding bandages, while Sister Fenton assisted the MO with the more serious cases. Edith was assigned the duty of helping MO orderlies assessing and treating the crowd of walking wounded. She cast her eyes around the crater. There were so many of them waiting around stoically and the stretcher bearers were bringing more. There was a sudden rush as the more ambulatory felt they would rather be treated by a woman than the rough hands of Privates Tompkins and Stanton.

A soldier with a bandaged head caught Edith's attention, or rather, his grin did. She beckoned him over. He shuffled over humbly, steel helmet in hand, dirty bandages covering his head, and sat down on an ammunition crate.

"Ain't you a sight for sore eyes?" he said. "We don't ever get nurses this far up the line. I must have died and gone to heaven," he said.

"Any more talk like that and you'll wish you had," she said firmly as she began unwinding the bandage from around his head. She gently eased the dressing off his wound. He winced. Edith uncovered the now scabbing furrow on his temple. The wound, at least, seemed clean.

"My name's George. George Hopkiss, but my mates call me Porgy," he said. "Guess why?"

"I can't imagine," she said, keeping her business-like demeanour, working intently on his wound, feeling herself blush.

"Kiss the girls and make 'em cry, don't I?"

"Well that's not much of a recommendation, is it?"

"Do you fancy walking out with me down Broughton Street tonight?"

"Shhh. Or Sister will hear!"

"She can come too, if she likes," he grinned.

"Now, now I'll have none of that. I'll have you know I'm a respectable lady."

"Oh, I don't doubt it."

"I was a debutante. I was presented at Court before the war."

"You don't say! Cor, That's as good as Royalty to me. Fancy!" said Porgy amazed, trying to turn round, but she took his head in her hands and gently, but firmly turned him back to face front.

"Oh yes," she said as she carried on cleaning the burned and torn flesh. "So don't forget with whom you're dealing! I have friends in high places," She dabbed the iodine on and Porgy stiffened, sucking in a sharp breath.

"Let that be a lesson to you," she said. She wondered if it sounded too playful and improper.

"I knows me place," he said, touching his forelock, mockingly. Edith gently pushed him on his shoulder.

"*You*. Now you're teasing."

"Nurse Bell!" barked Sister Fenton. "When you've *quite* finished fraternising with that jackanapes there are other men waiting for your attention!"

Edith felt her face burn as she reached for a gauze pad. "Hold this," she told him as she placed it over his wound.

"Sorry, Miss," said Porgy. She began wrapping crepe bandage around his head. "Not too much," he said, "otherwise I won't be able to fit me battle bowler on."

"I've a feeling your head's way too big for it anyway," she said with a smile. "Away with you."

Everson reached the makeshift Headquarters. It was dug back into the side of a trench; all salvaged beams, corrugated iron and tarpaulins. News of the death of the Major hadn't taken long to filter down through the Company and the men had taken it quite hard, especially as the next in command was Captain Grantham. To be truthful he didn't have much faith in the new Skipper himself. Captain Grantham shouldn't even have been at the Front. He'd had some cushy job back at Battalion, but he'd probably whined and groused about a Front Line position, wanting to see a bit of action just so that he could say he'd been there before returning to his nice desk job in the rear. Now, for better or worse, they were stuck with him.

"Is this it?" Everson asked, stepping inside and looking around despondently. "Is this all of us?"

It was dispiriting how few officers were left. There was Slacke, the Company Quartermaster Sergeant, Padre Rand and Captain Lippett, the MO and Captain Palmer of D Company. Jeffries was sat on a wooden chair, slouching with his legs stretched out in front of him, his chin resting on steepled fingers, glowering blackly, lost in thought. His eyes flicked up as Everson entered, but seeing nothing to interest him, lost focus as he turned back to his own contemplations. Grantham looked up from talking to a Royal Flying Corp officer and an officer with Machine Gun Corp insignia on his uniform.

"Everson," said Captain Grantham. "I'm afraid so."

The Flying Officer looked young, even to Everson. He had blonde hair and there was something about the double breasted tunic and that RFC wing on the left breast that just looked so – dashing. Everson felt a pang of jealousy. Here he was caked in mud, dog-tired and aching to his very bones and here was a handsome young man seemingly unmarked by the terrors of war; an 'angel face' he believed they called it.

"James Tulliver, RFC," he said, turning, extending a hand and jerking his head in Jeffries' direction. "Who's that louche chap over there, I'm sure I know him. Hibbert, is it?"

"Jeffries, Platoon Commander, 4 Platoon, C Company."

"Jeffries?" said Tulliver, mulling the name over. "Oh. Are you sure? No, of course you are. Sorry, my fault. Thought he was someone else."

"I often wish he was," said Everson.

The other man turned too. Tall and lanky, he had dark circles under his eyes and a greasy pallid look to his skin. His uniform hung on him as if it were a size too big.

"Mathers, Machine Gun Corps, Heavy Section."

"Ah, the tank commander," said Everson. "Good show. You saved some of my men out there today," he added, gripping the proffered hand. He was disappointed to find the grip a little weak and clammy. "So what the devil's going on, d'y'think?"

"Hmm," said Mathers. He closed his eyes and rubbed his temples. "Sorry. Damned headache."

"Gentlemen?" said Grantham, bringing the meeting to order. The officers gathered round the rickety table covered with maps. "Casualty Reports?"

"We weren't up to full strength to begin with. Out of nine hundred and twelve officers and men, we had already lost twelve officers and two hundred and forty eight other ranks to German fire and gas, and we lost two officers and fifty-eight other ranks from shock of transport here. We have a further two officers and twenty seven other ranks killed by those creatures. There are three hundred and seventy wounded, some critically, most walking and nine suffering from severe shell-shock. In short, gentlemen, you're down to less than two hundred able-bodied men at the moment, barely a Company."

Seven. Seven officers left, thought Everson.

"We need to get the wounded to a Casualty Clearing Station," said Lippett, "I don't have the means to deal with them here."

"Well, Mr Tulliver here doesn't seem to think that's going be, ah, possible," said Grantham nervously.

Lippett peered at Tulliver from under his eyebrows in a way that reminded Everson of his old schoolmaster.

"That's right, sir," said Tulliver. "I'm afraid there *is* no Casualty Clearing Station to go to. I explained to Captain Grantham earlier, we're completely cut off. *This* is all that's left," he said, pointing to the pencilled circle on the map. The other officers leaned in to look. "The rest of the area outside the circle no longer seems to exist. You've all seen it. What's out there bears no resemblance to any maps or aerial photographs. It's as if we've been picked up and dropped elsewhere entirely."

"But the world can't just disappear!" muttered Grantham.

"Perhaps it didn't," said Everson. "Maybe *we* did."

"Preposterous!" agreed Lippett.

"You've seen it for yourself," said Jeffries sternly. "How can you doubt it?"

"Some of the men have suggested it's Paradise," said Padre Rand.

"Are you trying to say that we're all dead and this is some blasted afterlife?" said Grantham. Everson tried to ignore the tremor in his voice.

"Well, I certainly wouldn't say so after meeting those hell hounds earlier," said Mathers.

"Some think we're dead, yes," continued the Padre. "Some men have been saying it's Africa."

"Well, something, I have no idea what, has brought us here, wherever *here* is," said Everson. "There's no reason to think it might not snap us back to the Somme at any moment, like an Indian Rubber band."

"And if not?" asked Grantham. "What then? We have no line of communication, our supply line ends several hundred yards to our rear. If Tulliver is to be believed you can't ring up Battalion and ask for another truck load of Maconochies and Plum and Apple to be sent up. We can expect no replacements and no relief. What on earth do you suggest we do?"

"Survive," said Everson. "Survive until we return home."

"An admirable sentiment, Everson," said Jeffries. "but what if we don't return home?"

"We'll find a way. That's what hope is all about. 'If the mountain won't come to Mohammed, then Mohammed will go to the mountain.' Isn't that how the saying goes?"

"Very prosaic," said Jeffries. "But platitudes won't save us. What if there isn't a way? What if this," he said, gesturing at the foreign landscape beyond the tarpaulin, "is it?"

The discussion degenerated into a babble of voices and opinions, each seeking to be heard. Jeffries stood back and smiled to himself as if pleased with the discord he had sown.

"Gentlemen, please!" cried Grantham, but he was unable to bring any kind of order to the debate.

Jeffries leaned forward and began whispering quietly into his ear. Grantham pinched the bridge of his nose between thumb and forefinger. For a moment Everson thought the man had found an ounce of gumption.

"Mr. Jeffries, what is your opinion?"

Jeffries drew himself up and glanced at the men one by one. They fell silent. He took a moment before he spoke, to make sure he held their attention. "It is my belief that we are no longer on Earth at all."

Over in the corner CQS Slacke barely stifled a snort of derision. Jeffries ignored it and pressed on. "One, the sun is slightly larger than we know our sun to be. Also, we attacked Harcourt Wood at dawn mere hours ago. The sun is now sinking towards the horizon. Two; the temperature here owes more to the tropics than to winter in France. Thirdly, those creatures that attacked us exist in no bestiary I'm aware of. And fourthly, my compass." He shoved his brass compass onto the table. The needle swung round and round indecisively. "North seems to be everywhere."

"Then where the deuce are we?" said Lippett.

"I have no more idea than you, Captain," said Jeffries, "but Everson is right in one respect..."

Startled by his name, Everson looked up and found Jeffries regarding him curiously.

"Something, it seems, has snatched us up and delivered us here. As to how and why, well, I wonder if we'll ever know," mused Jeffries. "However you may be sure that there are things in this universe, gentlemen, of which you have no conception, no conception at all."

"So what do we do now?" asked Grantham.

"I suggest an inventory of all rations, supplies and equipment," said Slacke.

"For the moment we should keep to Standing Orders, sir," said Palmer. "Confine the men to the trenches just in case, as Everson says, we should be returned as abruptly as we arrived."

"So that's your answer? We stay on this charnel pit on the off-chance we should be catapulted back to France?" Lippett said.

"Which is fine in the short term," said Everson. "But if supplies start running low we shall have to find water and food. We need to find out about this world if we are to survive it. We should think about sending out scouting parties."

"And what happens should we get snapped back to the Somme while they're out? What will happened to the those left behind?" said Padre Rand.

The men around the table fell silent as they ruminated on the possibility of their being marooned under such circumstances. It was a fate nobody wanted to contemplate.

"Padre," said Grantham. "I think it would be a good idea to arrange a church parade for tomorrow. I think the men could use your moral guidance and faith right now."

The Chaplain looked startled. "Er, certainly Captain."

"Captain," Jeffries urged Grantham. "*You* should address the men. They need to be told *something*. We must keep up morale and quell any thought of desertion or mutiny. A few words from you, sir, would help."

Grantham slumped into a chair, completely overwhelmed by the situation. His eyes searched the floor of the dugout as if they might find the answer there. "I don't know. What the hell can I say?"

Everson swore under his breath. Grantham was funking it. And what was Jeffries' game? He seemed to have made a good job of undermining Grantham while appearing to support him. After Grantham, as the next senior officer left in line, command would fall to Jeffries himself. If something wasn't done this whole situation would turn into a bigger disaster than it already was. The men needed leadership. Now.

"Sir!" said Everson, rather more sharply than he had intended. Grantham started. "Whatever you're going to tell the men, tell them quickly. The sun is setting and we'll need them to Stand To. God alone knows what else is out there."

Grantham looked up and nodded wearily. "Of course," he said. "Order the men on parade."

"Men!" began Captain Grantham. He was stood on an old ammo box, Everson Jeffries, Lippett and the Padre standing in the mud behind him as a show of unity. "As you know from our current troubles we face a predicament the like of which the Pennines have never faced before. There is a rumour that this is some kind of hallucination or afterlife and that your fighting days are over. I am here to tell you that they are not. You took the King's shilling, made the oath and signed up for the duration, the *duration*, gentlemen, and as such you are still soldiers in the King's Army. We are still at war. Any insubordination under the present circumstances will be dealt with severely. Standing Orders are still in effect and all men are confined to the trenches. If we are to get through this we must all pull together. I am informed that the world around us may not even be Earth, but we have faced adversity in foreign climes before and triumphed and we shall do so again. We do anticipate an eventual return to Blighty but, as the Pennines, we know that there's always a long hard climb before we reach the top. But reach it we will, so we must bear our current troubles with fortitude. Onward and Upwards, the Pennines!"

The men cheered and waved their helmets in the air. It was half-hearted, but, nevertheless, Grantham seemed pleased with the response. It wasn't the most rousing speech Everson had heard, but nobody expected much of Grantham. It would be left to the subalterns and NCOs to pick up the pieces. Oblivious, Grantham smiled magnanimously. Enjoying the brief moment, he spoke out of the corner of his mouth to his poker-faced staff. "Come on, smile boys, *that's* the style."

CHAPTER SEVEN
"The Evening Hate"

The sun began to set. The fact that perhaps it wasn't *their* sun was only just beginning to dawn on the soldiers. 2 Platoon were stood to on the fire-steps of their trench as they had stood dozens of times before; rifles, bayonets fixed, resting on the parapets, one in the spout, ready to repel any attack. Though from what, they had no idea. If the hell hounds earlier were a taste of what this place had to offer, it was going to be a long night.

Atkins stood in his bay with Gazette and Ginger. Porgy, Gutsy and Mercy manned the bay to their left. Beyond them were Captain Grantham, 1 Platoon and a flanking Vickers machine gun post. To their right was a second machine gun emplacement and the remains of 3 and 4 Platoons, under Lieutenant Jeffries. Atkins didn't envy Pot Shot, Lucky and Half Pint. They'd drawn the short straw and were twenty yards further out in the forward observation post in No Man's Land.

"Psst!" It was Ginger. Atkins tried to ignore him. "Psst!"

"What?" Atkins flicked his eyes from his rifle barrel. Ginger grinned at him and lowered his eyes towards his own tunic. Atkins followed the glance. There, peeking out the top of Ginger's shirt, was Haig, his pet rat. Ginger looked absurdly pleased with himself and started making *chtching* noises into his chest.

"Bloody hell, Ginger," Atkins rolled his eyes, a smile flickering at the edge of his lips as he returned to his vigil. Hunkered in the distance the nearby forest seemed as impenetrable as the old Hun line. The noises emanating from it changed as the sun sank, becoming wilder and more guttural as if the night signalled the onset of some feral reverie. He shivered involuntarily. The howls and chatterings played on his nerves more keenly than the never-ending drum roll of artillery barrages ever had. By comparison the abrupt ferocity of Whizz-Bangs, Jack Johnsons and Woolly Bears were as comforting as a home-fire.

More unsettling though was the evening breeze. He was so used to the smell of gangrene and feet, of shell hole mud and corpse liquor, of cordite and overflowing latrines, that the eddies of warm, damp wind caught him by surprise, bringing with them, as they did, brief intoxicating respites to his deadened senses. Tied as he was to his post, fleeting siren zephyrs of air laden with captivating scents danced lightly around him, allowing him snatches of exotic perfumes or heady animal musks; the ephemeral aromas tempting and teasing, offering a world beyond imagination.

There, that note. He closed his eyes and inhaled gently, afraid the scent would evaporate before he could savour it, it was like... like Lily of the Valley – Flora, that last night. They'd been to see the latest Charlie Chaplin at the Broughtonthwaite Alhambra. She was laughing. The cobbles – the cobbles were slick with rain, the faint smell of hops from Everson's Brewery hung in the night air. Her foot slipped on the greasy sets as they crossed the road and she'd linked her arm through his to steady herself. She chattered on about Old Mother Murphy, young Jessie in the end terrace and Mr Wethering at Mafeking Street School but he didn't hear her.

He'd known Flora forever. They'd sparked clogs and scabbed knees together as nippers in the same back alleys. They'd lived two streets apart their whole lives but she'd never really looked at him that way until he'd got the khaki on.

"You look ever so handsome in your uniform, Thomas."

"Get away!" he said, dismissively, then: "Really? Well, it's a bit on the large side and these trousers don't half itch, but if you ask the Company Quart –"

"Sssh." She put a finger to his lips.

She was so close he could smell her hair, the scent of her perfume – Lily of the Valley – the brief scent vanished and the familiar fug of war and corruption closed about him once more.

Raucous cries rang overhead as furred creatures with long necks, leathery wings and hooked beaks flocked into the sky from somewhere in the hills, congregating over the muddy sea of the battlefield. They dived and banked with rasping calls, like gulls in the wake of a fishing trawler, tempted by the human harvest of No Man's Land.

From somewhere down the line a couple of shots went off into the flock followed by the sharp, scolding bark of an NCO. The shooting ceased.

Atkins shifted his body uneasily against the wooden planking of the revetment and wiped his sweat-slick hands on his thighs before repositioning the stock of his rifle more snugly against his shoulder. He looked out again across the landscape of mud and wire towards the forest. He hated this time of day; as the light failed, shifting shadows played tricks on the eyes. It seemed to him that whatever gloom slunk sullenly in the forest was now flowing sinuously from it.

"What else is out there, d'y reckon?" he wondered. "I'm hoping for wild women myself."

"Don't know, but a target's a target," replied Gazette, his eye never leaving his rifle's sight. It was clear he had his 'business' head on. "It's either alive or dead."

"Yeah, either way, Porgy'd probably make a pass at it, eh?"

Gazette didn't reply.

"Never thought I'd miss Fritz," said Atkins. "At least with 'im you knew what to expect; the odd Minniewerfer or Five Nine. You knew where you were."

"Reckon you'll have cause to be even more nostalgic by the time the night's out," said Gazette. That was Gazette – a real barrel of laughs, but you didn't have him round for his sparkling repartee. He was the sharpest shooter in the platoon, so you forgave him the odd lapse in manners.

Ginger was no company at all, either. He whimpered and patted absent-mindedly at his tunic. The squeaking from inside it grew more frantic and agitated. As Ginger fumbled to catch his wretched rat his rifle slipped from his grasp. It landed heavily, butt first, on the duckboards. Atkins flinched but it didn't go off.

"Fuck's sake, pick your gun up y'daft sod. If Ketch catches you, that's 'casting away your arms in the presence of the enemy'," Gazette hissed, his eyes never leaving the darkening landscape.

Ginger ignored them and carried on wittering and cooing to Haig.

"Shhh. Ginger. Button it!" Atkins' brow creased, he cocked his head. "Gazette, you hear that?"

From out in the mud came a desperate scrabbling sound, like a drowning soldier trying to claw his way out of a slurry-filled shell hole.

"Just some poor injured sod out in No Man's Land. Usually is. That or one of them hell hounds from this afternoon caught on the wire. Either way, be dead by morning."

A scream went up from the forward observation post but it was stifled, drowned out by thousands of shrieking squeaks and the splatter of countless feet. In the fading light the mud itself seemed to ripple like a mirage. But it was no illusion.

From further up the line, the sound of surprised yelps, the discharge of rifles, spattered bursts of machine gun fire leapt from bay to bay towards them.

Alert, Gazette altered his stance almost imperceptibly, shifting his centre of gravity, bracing to absorb the anticipated kick of his Enfield.

"What is it?" Atkins asked.

Gazette just shrugged. He either didn't know, or didn't care.

Ginger shuffled about on the firestep as Haig skittered around inside his clothes, squealing, while his arms flailed and contorted trying to reach his ersatz pet. He pirouetted clumsily. Atkins tried to grab his webbing but Ginger tumbled from the firestep, falling awkwardly and cracking his head on the sodden duckboards, writhing and screaming as the rat seemed to bite and claw at him inside his clothing.

"Jesus! Shut him up!" snapped Gazette.

Atkins jumped down and clamped his hand over Ginger's mouth.

"Keep quiet, you silly sod. You'll end up getting us all killed if not up on a bloody charge!" Atkins was astride his chest now, a hand clamped over his mouth, trying to keep eye contact with the thrashing soldier, to calm him somehow, all the while trying to undo his tunic and shirt buttons one handed in order to free the damned rat.

"Ginger, calm down, mate. Stop it! It's me, Only."

Ginger's eyes bulged and he tried to scream, but it was muffled by Atkins' hand. Ginger sank his teeth into the skin between the thumb and forefinger.

"Agh, y'bastard!" Atkins snatched his hand away. Ginger bucked under him.

There was a sudden volley of unintelligible oaths from Gutsy's bay next door.

"Only!" said Gazette. "Only! Get up here!"

As Atkins looked up Ginger arched his back, turned his head awkwardly to see down the traverse and screamed. Racing round the corner and tumbling pell-mell towards them, over the parapets and channelled by the trenches, came a stampede of thousands of panic-stricken corpse rats scrabbling and scrambling over each other, driven headlong in a frenzy through the fire bays by something out in No Man's Land, something that had alarmed them enough to flee their cosy cadavers in droves. Not even the artillery shells had ever moved them like this before.

"Jesus!"

Atkins instinctively gulped a mouthful of air and drew his arms up over his head in a desperate attempt to protect himself as the routed rats swarmed over him. Their urgent piping squeals filled his ears as they covered him in a heaving wave of mud, blood and viscera-matted fur. Myriad cold paws scratched and scuffled exposed flesh; clumsy legs and feet finding his mouth, ears or nose while the acrid tang of voided rats' piss left him spluttering and nauseous.

And then they were gone, the verminous tide receding, washing over 3 and 4 Platoon's positions to yells of consternation.

Gasping and spitting filth from his mouth Atkins cautiously lifted his head. Ginger was still on the duckboards, curled into a foetal position, sniffling and whimpering, a damp warm patch darkening his khaki trousers.

"Gilbert the Filbert'll feel right at home among that lot," said Gazette. He was impassively inspecting three of the buggers he'd managed to impale on his bayonet. "Three with one blow. That's a dugout record, is that."

"He's gone," Ginger said with a snivel, patting his torso. "Haig's gone."

"Yeah, well good riddance," said Gazette scraping the rats off his bayonet on the edge of the step. "Here, Only, give us a hand." He stood his rifle against the revetment, stepped down, grabbed Ginger by his webbing straps and hauled him to his feet. Atkins picked up Ginger's rifle and put it back in his hands.

"Look, I know your rat's gone. Looks like they've all gone, frankly and good bloody riddance. But if you don't get back on the step, Ketch'll do for you, got it?"

Ginger sniffed, wiped his nose with the cuff of his tunic and nodded sullenly.

"Sorry. Sorry, Only."

Atkins straightened his battle bowler for him and helped him up onto the step.

"Good lad."

The sun was almost gone now. The dark velvet blue of night advanced relentlessly, overwhelming the last crimson smears of retreating dusk; a salvo of stars pock-marking its wake in the night sky.

Atkins had always found some measure of comfort in the constancy of the stars, but not tonight. Tonight, he couldn't find a single constellation that he recognised. And no moon either, nothing but a faint trace of reddish gas trailing across the firmament. Disconcerted, Atkins shifted his gaze back down to Earth, or what there was left of it.

"What was that all about? Never seen 'em act like that before."

"They're rats. Who knows?" said Gazette.

"Something scared 'em."

"You do surprise me."

"Something out there. The bodies in No Man's Land are going to attract every scavenger and predator for miles around."

"You may have a point," said Gazette. "But I've got this," he added patting his rifle. "And I'll put my faith in this any day over anything you think may or may not be out there."

They'd been here less than twenty-four hours. From what Atkins had seen of this place whatever was out there was probably far worse than anything he could imagine or, more worryingly, something he *couldn't* imagine.

"Everything all right here, men?"

Lieutenant Everson came round the traverse into the bay, Webley revolver in his hand.

"You mean apart from the rats, sir?" said Atkins.

"Yes, apart from the rats, Atkins."

"Yes, sir," Atkins managed a perfunctory smile. "Leaving the sinking ship, d'y'think, sir?"

"Sorry?"

"The rats, sir. Leaving the sinking ship?"

"Well I wouldn't put it quite like that, Atkins, but I'm certainly not going to miss the buggers if they really have gone."

Ginger stifled a sob in the crook of his elbow.

"Is he – is he all right?" said Everson with a jerk of his head in Ginger's direction, his voice tinged with concern.

"Mottram, sir?" said Gazette. "Yes sir, just got the wind up, sir, that's all. He'll be fine."

Aktins wasn't so sure but Everson didn't seem to want to press the point.

"Very well. Any idea who Hobson put in the OP?"

"Jellicoe, Livesey and Nicholls, sir," said Atkins.

"Right. Better check in with them. No doubt Nicholls will have something to complain about. Keep your wits about you." Everson slipped round the next traverse and was gone.

Somewhere out in the dark, where the Somme mud met alien soil, the fading pitiful squeals of the rats were met by the snarls and growls of unseen predators.

Atkins' tried not to listen, humming a few bars of 'I Want To Go Home' under his breath. He stopped as he felt, rather than heard, the noise; a deep bass note that thrummed against his chest and vibrated the soles of his feet through his hobnailed boots.

Dull alarms began jangling in No Man's Land; tin cans containing pebbles that hung from the wire rattled out their beggar-like warnings, the cries from the injured and dying stranded in shell holes rising to a crescendo.

From either flank of the line, bursts of machine gun fire opened up in reply. Each machine gun post was positioned so that it could lay enfilading fire *along* the lengths of wire entanglement. They had been laid in an extremely shallow 'V' out in front of the fire trenches so, even at night, once the wire alarms had been set off they had every expectation of hitting whatever it was that had set them off.

From Captain Grantham's position over in the centre of the line came the *phut* of a Very pistol as a flare arced up into the night sky. Atkins, Ginger and Gazette bobbed instinctively below the lines of the sandbags as it burst with a *whuuff* high over the battlefield, illuminating the scene with the stark white brilliance of a photographer's flash powder.

Atkins wished it hadn't.

About fifty yards out half a dozen great, glistening wet worm-like creatures, thicker than a man was tall and some thirty yards long, had broken the surface of the grey-churned mud, like land whales. Atkins could see no eyes, but long probing tentacles quested the air around facial sphincters that contracted and relaxed to reveal barbed gullets. No sound issued from their gaping, clenching maws as they set about scooping the dead and decomposing into their pouting orifices, grazing like elephants, lifting food into their mouths, or else dragging the corpses down into the vermiculate earth. From the terrified yells and sobs it was clear that it wasn't just the dead they were taking.

All along the fire trenches soldiers champed at the bit, wanting to shoot but constrained by orders.

The Very light went out. Another shot up into the sky from the observation post, burning whitely.

"C'mon, give the order," muttered Atkins, a finger playing restlessly on his SMLE's magazine cut-off.

Sergeant Hobson's voice rang out. "Five rounds rapid. Fire!"

"About bloody time," muttered Atkins as he flicked open the cut-off, took aim and fired before cycling the bolt and putting another cartridge into the receiver. He took aim, fired again, cycled once more.

Along the trench tattered bursts of rifle fire raked across the alien worms.

Trench mortars popped and flew into the air, arcing out into No Man's Land.

Beside Atkins, Gazette was in his element now. Calmly, surely, he fired off his shots, taking his time, making each bullet count. Ginger on the other hand had completely lost it and was huddled on the firestep, by Atkins' legs, his arms cradling his knees to his chest, sobbing and shaking uncontrollably.

The Very light went out again but the ungodly wet suction noises and weakening screams continued unabated. Another Very light went up from the observation post.

The worms were closer now. One reared up over the observation post itself. An officer, it must have been Lieutenant Everson, fired the Very pistol almost at point blank range. The flare shot up leaving a brief white trail before embedding itself in the hide of the creature where it continued to burn with a white-hot fury, causing it to thrash about in voiceless agony, its tentacles flailing helplessly. Some agent in its mucus coating, or subcutaneous fatty layer, must have been flammable for, under the intense heat of the flare, the great worm began to burn like a wick. Its bulk crashed down into the mud – right on top of the observation post.

"Everson's bought it," said Gazette, matter of factly.

"Are you kidding?" said Atkins. "Lucky's out there. He'll see 'em all right."

"Thruppence says they're landowners now."

"Thruppence says they ain't," said Atkins, spitting on his palm. Gazette shook his hand, barely taking his eye from his rifle sight.

With the landscape now dimly illuminated by the burning carcass Atkins could make out the other worm creatures. One rippled over to the burning body, reaching out its tentacles, but was driven back by the heat of the flames. It raised its head up as if giving a great call, arched its body and dived into the ground. The others followed.

A ragged cheer rose from the trenches.

"They're going!"

The elation didn't last long. Thirty feet from the line one of the great worms broke out of the mud, ploughing toward the fire trench with a fluid peristaltic motion, through the troughs of shell holes and the crests of their craters, heedless of the twenty yard length of barbed wire entanglement it had ripped from the ground in its sinuous advance, and which was now hanging from its body.

Men who had seen comrades blown to so much meat, who had stoically suffered days of continuous bombardment, who had risked death every day, found it hard not to flee in the face of such a monstrous vision.

The command came again. "Fire!"

As Gazette took aim, carefully squeezing the trigger and firing off five more rounds at the monstrous creature before them, Atkins felt the ground beneath him tremble and the revetment against his chest begin to creak and strain. Sandbags tumbled into the trench from the parados behind them. He and Gazette glanced at each other.

"You don't think –"

"Thinking's for officers. Run!"

They slung their rifles over their shoulders and jumped back off the fire step as the revetment begin to splinter under a great wave of pressure building up from below. Ginger remained sobbing on the step, oblivious or incapable of reacting as plank after plank behind him burst free of its frame.

"Shit!"

A hand under each armpit Atkins and Gazette dragged him off the firestep and round the corner into the traverse. Barely had they vacated the fire bay before it erupted behind them in a shower of dirt, dust and splinters as another worm burst up through the trench.

Probing tentacles appeared around the corner of the traverse. One caught hold of Ginger's ankle and pulled, tugging Atkins and Gazette off balance as the screaming man was dragged back towards the shattered fire bay. Atkins unslung his rifle and thrust his bayonet into the tentacle, pinning it to the ground, and fired, point blank range, severing the member. The other feelers let go of Ginger and retracted back round the corner, the lopped pseudopod trailing a dark viscous slime behind it.

Gazette grabbed Ginger by the scruff of the neck as he and Atkins half-scrambled, half-stumbled with him into the next fire bay where Gutsy, Porgy and Mercy were laying down covering fire as the wounded worm reared up. They kept it up as Atkins and Gazette retreated round the far corner to the adjacent traverse and the next fire bay, held by Sergeant Hobson and Corporal Ketch.

There they dropped Ginger to the duckboards and took aim at the mindless monster as it blindly sought for its attackers. Gutsy, Porgy and Mercy, abandoning their own position, fell back and joined them, as Gazette and Atkins in return gave them covering fire. Gazette had fired his five rounds and was reloading from a pouch on his webbing, while Atkins was still chambering and firing his third as the great worm, flinching under the hail of bullets, sought a way forward. It fell back from sight, retreating into the ground from which it had come.

Atkins spied a bandolier of grenades on the firestep. "Gazette, cover me!" he yelled, snatching up the bandolier. He dashed forward to their ruined fire bay where he saw the tentacles of the beast vanish as it retreated back into the dark earth. He looked briefly into the darkness of the hole in the side of the trench as he opened the pouches on the bandoleer. He took out the string from his pocket and threaded through the ring pulls of about half a dozen grenades. Holding one end of the string in his hand he tossed the bandoleer into the hole. Left holding nothing but the piece of string and its collection of grenade pins he threw himself to one side. Seconds later the grenades went off with a muted roar. The ground heaved and the hole erupted with smoke and fire as torn and shredded flesh shot out of it.

Atkins picked himself up from the mud, his ears ringing with the high pitch buzzing of the concussion. Helping hands pulled him to his feet as Porgy and Mercy dragged him clear. Smoke drifted from the collapsed tunnel. The ringing in his ears distanced him from the scene around him. He was thankful for the brief respite as he could no longer hear the screams of pain and the cries of terror. Only faintly, as if from a great depth, could he hear the tattoo of the guns as the Tommies drove the worms back into the ground.

Jeffries was barely aware of the explosion. The sight of the creatures held him spellbound. He had read of such things in texts older than the regiment itself, but never expected to see them. "Shaitan," he murmured under his breath as he watched them harvest the dead and dying out in No Man's Land. "Messenger of Croatoan. It's a sign." He climbed the ladder and stood, exposed, on the sandbag parapet, arms flung wide in supplication.

"Sir!" hissed Dixon, his Platoon Sergeant. "Sir, get down!"

One of the giant worms burst up through the sodden ground half a dozen yards from the trench. It opened its maw, pseudopods flailing. Jeffries stood his ground and stared down the barbed throat.

He was vaguely aware of Everson stumbling down the sap from the observation post, his arms around one man's shoulder as they helped each other along the narrow ginnel. Two others followed on behind, all four of them covered in mud and slime.

"Jeffries, for God's sake, man! Are you mad?" he called, reaching for the Very pistol in his belt. There was a dull click and a *whoof* as something rushed past Jefferies' head. A Very flare ricocheted off a failing tentacle and skittered down the creature's length before whirling across the mud and into a shell hole. The great worm veered away from it and plunged back into the earth. However the encounter was enough to convince Jeffries. He turned jubilantly and jumped down onto the firestep.

"Everson," he said, "you might have been right."

"Right?" said Everson quizzically. "About what? What did I say? Jeffries!"

But Jeffries was already strolling down the fire trench, elated.

The great worms, it seemed, had retreated, beaten back by the firepower of the Battalion. The relief along the line was almost tangible. There were exultant, if weary, cheers as the last of the creatures retreated into the earth under the burning glare of another flare.

Slowly the concussive ringing in Atkins' ears faded to be overwhelmed by the rising tide of groans and screams from those in No Man's Land.

He plugged his ears with his fingers as if trying to restore the blissful distance granted to him by the explosion, wishing the cries would cease and hating himself for it. The screams continued all night, though none would venture from the trenches to lend aid or succour, the cries gnawing relentlessly at each man's conscience. Those that could survive out there until morning might have a chance.

Atkins' guilt threatened to rise up and choke him. Had William died like that, slowly, alone in agony and fear with no one willing to help? If he was truthful even that wasn't what bothered him. What bothered Atkins was the unspoken thought that somewhere, deep down, he hoped his brother was dead.

CHAPTER EIGHT
"In Different Skies…"

Over the next few days a broken telegraph pole was erected to serve as a makeshift flagpole. Hanging from it, not proudly and defiantly, but limply, fluttered a dirty and ragged Union Jack. It seemed to reflect the worn, exhausted mood of the men who wandered aimlessly about beneath it, devoid of any great purpose now the battlefield in which they toiled had ceased to exist. However, the veneer of normality was maintained, as it always was, in the most damning and ignominious of circumstances. Or perhaps because of it, because of the sheer scale of it.

The battalion fell back on a comfortably familiar routine despite their unfamiliar surroundings. The physical labour and variety of the fatigues reassured the men, keeping them occupied and busy. In Kitchener's Army there was never any shortage of tasks.

Captain Grantham had forbidden anyone to leave the sodden circle of Somme. It was all that now remained for them of the world they knew as home, blighting the fresh green landscape around them like a canker, an unutterably dark stain on their souls, made visible. For Jeffries that wasn't too far from the truth. Jeffries, who was technically now next in command being a full lieutenant, feeling constrained for the moment by orders he had no compunction to obey, began seeking more signs and portents. The molten rage he felt at the ritual's failure was, thanks to the sight of the giant worms, even now being forged into cold, hard intent. And he was given to wandering to the far edge of the mud pack and peering out into the unknown land.

It was something many of the other ranks did when not working. Egged on by pals a few daring or stupid ones had tried scrambling down the mud banks onto the verdant foreign plain, wading out into the green tubular fronds and turning to wave at their friends, only to be snatched away with a scream by the hell hounds that still loped about perilously near. That put a stop to such expeditions. Those that didn't get eaten alive were just as quickly chewed up and spat out by equally voracious NCOs.

Not that many wanted to leave the confines of their claustrophobic muddy trenches, for there, at least, was a sense of familiarity and belonging. There, among the avenues, streets and homes they'd carved and burrowed for themselves they shared a commonality of purpose, of experience, of comradeship that no one back home could, would or should understand. The fear that it might suddenly vanish in an instant, returning to France without them, leaving them stranded, was more than incentive enough to keep most in line. Battle Police and Field Punishments did for the rest.

With the aid of several privates Lieutenant Tulliver wheeled his aeroplane onto the drying mud flat in order to protect it from the indigenous life that seemed to be gaining in courage by the day.

Swamped in his Aid Post, Captain Lippett, with the help of the nurses, began to set up a Casualty Clearing Station on the open ground above, behind the support trenches, using what they could to erect makeshift bivouacs. There they found themselves having to deal with a new kind of shell-shock victim, ones who could not deal with the new reality they now faced.

The tank crew didn't really fraternise with the other soldiers, preferring to keep themselves to themselves, the secrecy of their training had been drilled into them and was not easily relinquished. They slept in bivvies alongside their machine, politely declining to mix with the others, happy in their own company and in allowing their commander, Mathers, to speak for them. This is not to say they were unfriendly, merely guarded. The landship created a great deal of interest among the infantry men and, when brief moments between work arose, whole platoons would gather round examining the great armoured war beast, circling it and expressing their approval with low whistles and amazed shakes of the head. While pleased with the attention lavished on it, the tank's crew guarded its secrets enviously, like priests at a shrine, and requests for a ride or a look inside were politely, if firmly, declined.

The length of the day was timed. It came to twenty-two hours. The night sky offered up no clue to their whereabouts, other than it was no sky they recognised. Whatever myths might have drawn its constellations, they were none they knew, so some men began sketching their own; 'The Pickelhaub', 'Charlie Chaplin', 'Big Bertha', 'Little Willie.' The brightest star in the night sky was soon named 'Blighty.'

By day the warm sun began to dry the Somme mud out until it developed a light dry crust that contracted in the heat until it cracked. The decomposing bodies beneath began to rot faster. Foul smelling steams and vapours rose from the flooded shell holes as the fetid liquor within evaporated.

The hell hounds, still drawn by the smell of carcasses, unable to help themselves, slunk forward in ones and twos only to be driven back by sentries' rifle fire.

2 Platoon were on trench fatigues again, working on the stretch of support trench behind the front line. Meant to house off-duty and support troops it needed to be turned around to work as a front line in order to protect their rear. It was a job they were familiar with. Captured German trenches needed such work doing to them in order to make them defensible; changing parados to parapet, cutting new fire steps and laying new wire. The idea here though was to turn the entrenchment into a circular defensible stronghold. It was still an unnatural feeling to stand in the open on the lip of the trench in the full glare of the sun

with nothing to fear but sunburn, but the bright warm sunlight eased their brittle nerves a little.

"Bloody rotten job!" said Mercy, sucking fiercely on the end of a fag as he shoved his entrenching spade into the dirt with his foot, seeking to prise loose another spit-worth of claggy mud.

"I'm sure you'd rather be on burial duty," said Ketch, walking towards them as they slung the spoil over the top. "It can be arranged."

Pot Shot put a warning hand on Mercy's shoulder. Mercy grunted and stubbed the butt of his woodbine out on the damp wall of the trench, grinding it purposefully into the grit, his eyes never leaving Ketch.

"Now put your backs into it! This section of trench is to be finished before dark" he said, before wandering off.

"One of these days," said Porgy, spitting on his palms and gripping his shovel before starting to fill another sandbag. "Burial party? I know it's a bad lot but –"

"It's worse than you think," said Atkins. "Don't tell me you can't smell it?"

"Thought that were Gutsy's feet," said Lucky.

"Oi!" warned Gutsy from where he was leaning against the side of the trench taking a slug from his water canteen.

Ginger, who was on watch, sat on an old ammo box, his eyes nervously darting around the unfamiliar landscape.

"I hope you're keeping your eyes peeled, Ginger. I don't want to become a devil dog's dinner," griped Half Pint.

"Uh huh!" he said, nodding his head.

"He seems to have calmed down a bit in the last few days," said Atkins to Gazette.

But Gazette wasn't listening. At least, not to him.

"Shh!" he said, holding up a hand.

"I wish you'd stop doing that!" said Atkins.

Gazette silenced him with a scowl.

There came a low soft roar like the roll of distant thunder.

"Take cover!" yelled Ginger, leaping down into the trench. The roar continued building. It wasn't a shell or thunder, it was an earth tremor.

The walls of the trenches began to vibrate, sandbags jittering over the edge.

"Get out, get out!" Atkins yelled as Porgy thrust his hand down from the lip. Atkins shoved Ginger towards him. Porgy grabbed his hand and yanked him up. Atkins scrambled up using an old scaling ladder. The wall collapsed, sliding down into the trench and undoing several hours of hard work before the tremors subsided. Muted yells arose from all around as men scrambled out of the trenches onto the open ground above. A more plaintive and urgent, if unintelligible cry issued from nearby.

"Someone's trapped," said Pot Shot. They slipped back down into the trench and worked their way along until they came to the junction that led to the latrines.

Ketch had been doing his business, sat over the hole in the plank across the pit. When the tremors hit, the plank must have juddered loose because there was Ketch, khaki pants round his ankles, in the slurry pit of excrement below. Buckets of urine had also fallen over, drenching him in their pungent contents.

"Get me out!" he screamed through the filth.

The section looked at each other, smirks breaking out on their faces as their corporal struggled to right himself. No one was willing to go near the collapsed latrines and risk a similar ducking themselves.

Atkins looked around the collapsed trench. Seeing Ketch's rifle, he picked it up and, checking that the lock was on, held the butt as he thrust the barrel towards Ketch.

"Grab hold!

But the corporal's hands were slick with sewage and, as he pulled himself out, he slipped back with a splash causing the section to double up in raucous laughter.

Atkins persisted though and Ketch was able to loop his arm through the rifle's shoulder strap as he pulled him out, almost losing his own footing in the process.

Ketch lay panting on the floor of the trench coughing and spluttering, his sodden trousers round his ankles. Atkins slit open a sandbag with his bayonet and passed it to Ketch who snatched it from his hand ungratefully and began to wipe the excreta off his face.

"You!" he spat. "You did this!"

"Corporal?"

"You were told to put this latrine right. You and Evans. Did you think it would be a big joke? A big laugh? Well you'll be laughing on the other side of your face one day, Atkins. You mark my words. You'll get what's coming to you." He got to his feet and advanced towards them. They backed off, unwilling to be smeared by the malodorous mud.

"It was the earth tremor!" said Atkins. "You must have felt it, we all did."

Ketch opened his mouth to say something, stopped, gagged and wretched. The section's delight turned to disgust. They backed away from him out of the trench, hearing another heave as vomit splattered wetly on the trench floor.

Still snorting and guffawing over Ketch's misfortune they got back to the section of trench they had been rebuilding and found Ginger billing and cooing. In his arms he held his tunic inside out and crumpled like a nest. They could hear something snuffling about inside it.

"Look, Only!" said Ginger thrusting his hands out towards Atkins, inviting him to examine the jacket's contents.

"Oh god, don't say Haig's back!" muttered Gazette.

Atkins peered over cautiously, not knowing what to expect, half anticipating something to leap out of the bundled cloth and bite him. He caught a flash of yellow fur and saw a long nose sniffling about in the makeshift khaki nest.

"What the hell is that? Ginger, what on earth have you found this time?"

"His name's Gordon," he replied beaming. He moved his hand under the tunic to open it out, revealing a small rat-sized creature with short yellowish fur, small black beady eyes and a long tubular snout. It didn't seem to have jaws or teeth. It snuffled eagerly around in the jacket, completely uninterested in the soldiers now gathering around it. "I found it," said Ginger. "He was just sort of wondering around, like he was lost... like us."

"Fuck's sake, Ginger, everything we've come across so far has tried to kill us or eat us or both. You've got no idea what this thing is!" said Gutsy.

Mercy did. He knew what it was straight away. It was an opportunity.

"No, no," he said. "Steady on, lads. I think Ginger is onto something. Look."

They looked. Then they looked puzzled.

"All I see is some blonde rodent with a furry trunk," said Porgy.

"At what it's doin', smart-arse!"

Atkins looked again. It seemed to be excitedly running its snout along the seams of the jacket. A small long red tongue flickered out. "It's chatting," he said. "Bloody 'ell. It's eating the lice!"

As they watched, the otherworldly rodent pushed its snout into and along the seams, sucking up eggs and lice alike with great relish.

"We could clean up with this, fellas. This is the proverbial golden goose. No more feeling hitchy-koo. They'll pay through the nose to have their regulations cleaned of chatts. Gawd love us, any of us would! Gordon, here, is what you might call a Hitchy-kootioner."

There was a chorus of nods.

"Me next!" said Porgy hopping to pull off his boot before carefully pulling off his woollen sock and dangling it in front of Gordon. "Here, boy. Here," Gordon lifted its head and sniffed tentatively at the warm, damp, writhing sock. Porgy dropped the stinking sock into the coat. Immediately Gordon thrust its snout into it.

"And what good is all that money going to do out here?" said Pot Shot. "Where can you spend it?"

"Jeez, steady on, Pot Shot, can't a man have a dream? I'll save it and spend it when I get back."

Gordon was now totally enclosed by the sock, although from the snuffling and snorts that were issuing from it, it didn't seem to mind.

Already Atkins and the others were thinking of the booming business ahead; five hundred lice ridden, lousy men at thruppence a head? Gordon was going to make a killing for them.

Grantham had taken to pacing about his new HQ, trying to avoid the vista outside, as if by ignoring it it would go away. He couldn't cope with it. There was no section about this in the Field Manual or the Standing Orders. Without them he didn't know what to do.

The man was fast becoming a liability. He commissioned innumerable reports, seeking to bury the stark horror of their situation under a mountain of minutiae, so Everson found himself mired in endless company meetings.

"Trench repairs are well under way," Everson reported. "The backfilling, blocking and fortification of the open trench ends will be complete soon. Nothing should be able to enfilade or flank us then. Second Lieutenant Baxter of the Machine Gun section is constructing new emplacements for his guns. We've also set up a trench mortar in the old farmhouse. However if we want to repair the trenches properly then we're going to need more wood. At the moment we're down to cannibalising duckboards for revetments."

Grantham's face was drawn, his eyes red-rimmed.

"This is a nightmare," he muttered.

"At some point we're going to have to send out working parties to cut down trees from that forest over there."

Slacke nodded emphatically.

"Sir," he said. "We have potable water for three more days. We have food rations enough for perhaps twice that. Rum ration won't last. If we're here much longer we'll have to start looking for supplies locally."

"No," said Grantham, hoarsely.

"But, sir..."

"I said no. We will return home."

"Begging your pardon, sir, but we can't just sit here and wait for that to happen." He paused. "It may *never* happen."

Grantham exploded. "That is defeatist talk, man, and I won't have it, d'you hear?"

Everson took this as a further sign of Grantham's growing instability. The man needed to believe they would be returned home. If it became apparent that their fate was otherwise he feared that Grantham would really funk it.

"Sir?" It was Jeffries. "With all due respect we may have to face the possibility that we are here for an indefinite period. While I am sure you are correct in your assumption that we shall be returned I feel it prudent that we should prepare for the worst. At the very least it will keep the men occupied. An army with nothing to do will soon become a mutinous rabble."

Everson was surprised by what he heard. "I have to say I agree with Jeffries, sir. It should be understood by all that we shall be returned home in order to keep up morale. However we should consider sending out scout patrols. We need to know what we might face in the short term and if we can find water."

"I could make a short reconnaissance flight, Lieutenant," offered Tulliver. "That would at least give your men some possible directions in which to explore. I should have enough fuel, but with my observer dead, I'd need someone to spot and map-make for me."

"Jeffries can go," said Grantham. A smile bloomed briefly on Jeffries' lips before fading.

"Very well," said Tulliver. "I suggest we go straight away. There's enough light left for a short flight."

"You need to look for rivers, streams, lakes; sources of water. Look for cultivated fields or others signs of civilisation," suggested Lippett.

Civilisation. It wasn't a thought that had even entered Everson's head until now. He had been too preoccupied with simple, brutal survival and thoughts of home. But yes, civilisation. The existence of a civilisation that might have achieved dominion over this wild and untamed country had never really occurred to him. What cities might they have constructed, what wonders might they have achieved? What marvels might they work? Surely they would recognise a fellow creature of equal intellect and extend a hand in aid? Unless they were responsible for their sudden journey and arrival here. In which case one would have to try and divine the motives for such an act.

There was a confused chatter as everyone suddenly attempted to talk over each other, each speculating on what it was they expected to find; certainly nothing to which the British Empire was not an equal.

"Gentlemen, please," said Jeffries. "This is all idle speculation. There is no point in raising false hopes at the moment though, as Captain Lippett so rightly states, it is something we should keep an eye out for. And when I'm up in Lieutenant Tulliver's machine I shall certainly endeavour to seek such signs as will assuage your doubts."

Under the covering watch of a Lewis machine gun section, 1 Section had pulled the Sopwith out onto the plain and had spent an hour trying to beat some kind of take-off strip from the tubular undergrowth there. They'd managed to clear about a hundred yards or so and hoped it would be enough. Tulliver walked the strip wincing and sucking in breath through his teeth. The ground was bumpier than he'd wished. Ideally he'd have the AM's fill the pot holes, but here that wasn't going to be possible, at least not this time. Maybe he'd have a word with the infantry captain.

Tulliver and Jeffries climbed aboard the Sopwith. Tulliver had checked it out earlier. There was about half a tank of fuel left. Quite what he'd do then, he didn't know.

"We won't be going too high today," said Tulliver. "But you'll have to be prepared to use the machine gun. We don't know what kind of flying creatures are up there."

"Oh don't worry about me," said Jeffries. "I'm sure I can handle myself."

"Well, bear in mind you're going to have to stand to fire and there's no safety harness. Contact!"

A private swung the propeller around. It juddered to a halt. He seized the blade in his hands and swung down again. The engine caught. "Chocks!" Two more soldiers pulled the makeshift blocks away from the wheels and the aeroplane began to inch forward as if impatient to get into the air and be free of the heavy, lumpen earth. It began to bounce clumsily across the uneven plain. The jarring stopped as the wheels left the ground. Tulliver pulled back on the stick and angled the nose up as the ground dropped away. He peeled to the right and flew over the pat of Somme mud as he climbed. He was excited to be in the air again. Only here did he feel he could be himself. Over on the horizon he could make out a line of thick black clouds as he reached a thousand feet and the world below began to take on a familiar map-like feel. Far from feeling alienated by this wondrous new landscape, up here he felt as if he were in the company of an old friend. He began looking for conspicuous landmarks; the flashes of sunlight off water caught his eyes. He looked down and saw a ribbon of silver a mile or so from the brown stain of the Somme. He turned to Jeffries behind him and pointed down. "A river!" he bawled over the sound of the wind and the engine.

Jeffries formed his finger and forefinger into an 'O'. Tulliver thought that a little odd. He'd only met a couple of other people that had used that specific gesture. Most just used thumbs up. One was an American flying with the Escadrille Lafayette, the other, more recently, was that Artillery officer, what was his name?

"Are you sure we haven't met?" he yelled over the engine's roar. "You seem familiar! Do you know a chap named Hibbert?"

Jeffries shook his head and Tulliver shrugged, but couldn't dismiss entirely the feeling he knew the man from somewhere. He turned the machine and from their vantage point, the circle of Somme was sat near the head of a wide valley, enclosed by hills on three sides. On one side of the valley stretched a large forest. Beyond it lay a large plain bounded by a range of hills. The silver ribbon of water ran down from the hills and threaded itself through the forest before reappearing on the plain. If it was coming down from the hills maybe it led to some sort of –

There was a tap on his shoulder. He wiped away the oil spray that was beginning to mist his goggles and glanced back over his shoulder, Jeffries pointed down. Tulliver tilted the wings so he could see a herd of tall, three-legged creatures moving across the plain. That's when he noticed the shadow ripple over the ground and pass over his machine. He immediately pulled up and banked so he could look around. He pointed up, indicating that Jeffries, who was sat behind the wings and had a better view, should look around. Then he saw it. A great shape above them like a flying manta ray, but it had hind legs with large talons and a long neck that ended in a small head with a wide mouth, displaying sharp teeth. It was easily bigger than the Sopwith and with claws and teeth like those could rip the aeroplane to shreds if it got close. It had obviously been following the herd of whatever-they-were and saw the Sopwith as a territorial intruder. It came at them from the side. Tulliver hoped Jeffries was on the ball. He was. Standing up in his seat he swung the Hotchkiss machine gun round and opened fire. The creature closed its wings momentarily and dropped out of sight below them.

Damn. He couldn't afford to let it get beneath them.

"Hang on!" he yelled to Jeffries. Tulliver banked sharply and spun down in a wide spiral looking for the creature. It reared up almost immediately in front of them.

"Hellfire!"

He pressed the fire buttons on his machine gun, spitting lead and tracer bullets at the beast. It let out a long, pained cry and vanished over the top of the machine as Tulliver pushed the stick forwards sending the aeroplane into a shallow dive. As the creature passed overhead Jeffries fired, raking its body with a line of bullets that left it spurting a bluish viscous liquid.

"Go round!" yelled Jeffries. Tulliver banked, keeping the wounded creature within the circle of his turn. Jeffries kept it in his sights and let off another couple of bursts, one ripping through the membranous wings, another shot hitting it in its head, exploding the skull. The lifeless beast plummeted from the air, the drag from its wings sending it careening into a drunken tumble.

"Calloo Callay!" Jeffries yelled triumphantly as he leaned over the lip of the cockpit to watch the dead beast crash into the plain with an explosion of blood and offal.

Tulliver, wary of any more of the creatures, was eager to get down.

"Have you got enough?" he shouted.

"Yes, it's dead!"

"No, have you got enough information for the map?"

Jeffries turned, sat back down in his seat and pulled out the clipboard. He marked the stream and the forest. He'd seen no sign of cultivation or farming, no patchwork of fields, no smoke, which was vaguely disappointing. He nodded emphatically and gave his ringed okay sign to Tulliver, who turned the aeroplane about and headed back up the valley towards the muddy charnel field they had to call home for the present.

As he did so, Jeffries caught a glimpse of something gleaming in the far distance across the plain, as if it had caught the light from this world's sun. He struggled to turn around and see. He could have sworn he saw some sort of huge spire far off, almost smeared into obscurity by the intervening aerial perspective of the atmosphere. The machine bucked on a pocket of air as it descended and dropped heavily, leaving Jeffries' stomach briefly somewhere above his head. When he looked again the fortuitous angle was lost and the spire had vanished. But it had nevertheless ignited a gleam of hope in his heart. He smiled to himself. This was one thing he wouldn't mark on his crude, despairingly blank map. He well knew the value of information as currency. This would only strengthen his position in the long-term and, until he knew its true value, he would sit on it and let his investment accrue.

Tulliver circled the field of mud as he came down and brought the machine about so that the hastily cleared green strip was ahead of him. He pulled back on the stick, opened the flaps, slowing the aeroplane down to just above stall speed, and cut the engine before they hit the ground. He saw the waiting soldiers run towards them as the Sopwith bounced and trundled to a halt.

He tore off his flying helmet and goggles before clambering out of the cockpit. The Tommies gathered round the machine like excited schoolboys, barking questions at him and Tulliver took the opportunity to bask in the moment.

Jeffries was left abandoned by the machine as Tulliver and the adulating scrum around him moved off. The airman had almost recognised him. Of all the damned luck to get stuck with the same pilot that took him up when he was using Hibbert as an alias. He didn't need anyone putting the pieces together yet, he needed more time. He would have to do something. He was reaching over to put the helmet goggles and gloves back in the cockpit when he noticed the tool box in the bottom of the craft. His usual methods might attract too much attention now, but an accident? He looked back toward the mud flat. No one was about. He leant over and dragged the box towards him. Something to make sure that Tulliver didn't come back from his next flight? Flicking the little hooked catch he opened the wooden box to reveal a jumble of tools; spanners, wrenches, screwdrivers, wire cutters. He smiled...

INTERLUDE 2
Letter from Private Thomas Atkins to Flora Mullins

4ᵗʰ November 1916

My Dearest Flora,

Things haven't gone quite the way the top brass expected here so I don't know when I'll get a chance to post this.

I know you must be sitting at home thinking me among the missing, too. Although we're not so much missing, as lost. It's the rest of the world that's missing. What will my mother do? Both her sons among the missing. She must be heartbroken. I wish I could tell her I'm alive and well, although I'm not sure I like it here. The wildlife seems none too friendly. I thought rats and lice were bad, but they've got things here that put them to shame.

I've been picked as part of a foraging patrol, going out into the countryside to pick fruit and berries and the like. Mercy says it sounds like a bit if a lark. It'll make a pleasant change from digging trenches though and no mistake. With no Hun to fight, that's all they've had us doing the past few days, and on rations too. I tell you, we're all getting fed up of Maconochie and Plum and Apple here. Half Pint says we'll end up looking like jam tins at this rate. So here's hoping we find something edible.

Ever yours,
Thomas

CHAPTER NINE

"Death, Where is Thy Sting-a-Ling-a-Ling…"

"God damn it!" said Captain Lippett. It had been a bad couple of days for the surgeon. Apart from the usual round of battlefield wounds and infections there was a new rash of cases as the perils of the world about them began to make themselves known. The carcass of one of the worms was hacked up and roasted on the open ground between the supervision and support trenches, by some men who hadn't had fresh meat in weeks. Those who ate the meat died agonising deaths in the night. It seemed from what Lippett was able to determine that the flesh was poisonous, containing some kind of toxin to which man had no immunity.

A Lewis gun team broke out in bloody pustules after eating a variety of knobbly yellow fruit that hung full and ripe, weighing down the rust-coloured boughs in the small grove of trees near the mud perimeter. The boils proceeded to swell at an alarming rate and to a grotesque size, disfiguring the face and body until the skin became taut like a drum, causing immense pain, before bursting so that those infected were left with terrible open wounds and died of blood loss or septicaemia.

After that the order was not to taste anything but to bring it back for the Medical Officer to conduct tests on to determine whether it was fit to eat or not.

* * *

2 Platoon had been ordered to scout out the wood that lay maybe a mile away. It was the farthest any party had yet been. Although they didn't say it Everson could tell the men were nervous. A platoon had gone out on a search for water the previous day, following the directions garnered from Tulliver and Jeffries' reconnaissance flight. They had lost four men to animal attacks.

After Stand To, breakfast and parade the forty-two strong 2 Platoon headed out across the plain in Indian file. Every man had one in the spout. They all remembered the attack of the hell hounds and knew they were out here somewhere. Behind Atkins came Hepton, carrying his camera and tripod and several canisters of film in haversacks. He had asked for permission to join them, eager to record the wonders of this new world, if not the horrors, for he knew such vivid sights would sell seats. Then came Ginger, cooing happily into his gas helmet haversack in which he had stowed his new pet. Gordon's flaccid whiskery snout poked out of the flap. Pot Shot, Gazette, Gutsy, Porgy, Half Pint and Lucky brought up the rear of the section, carrying a couple of rolled up stretchers to help carry whatever they managed to harvest. Sergeant Hobson and the other three sections of 2 Platoon followed on behind.

Atkins felt his stomach tighten. If the entrenchments disappeared back to Blighty while they were away they would be stranded. He, and every other man in the platoon, kept glancing back anxiously until the small escarpment of the mud field was lost from sight amid the thick tube-like grass. After that, their only comfort was the distant bark of NCOs heard through the man-high fronds that now surrounded them.

"At least if they stop we can tell that they've disappeared back to Blighty," said Pot Shot.

"Yeah, I never thought I'd be grateful for an NCO," said Mercy, throwing a glance behind him at a sullen Corporal Ketch.

Atkins watched as the edge of the forest grew closer. The fronds began to thin out and become shorter until the platoon found themselves merely wading though them, hip deep, as they approached the edge of the woods. The trees, if that was what they were, seemed to be similar to those in the odd copses they had observed growing in the vale about the entrenchment; great thick trunks that split into boughs protruding radially from the trunks and ending in large, flatish leaves. Those facing the sun were open. Those that faced away had closed, like inverted gentleman's umbrellas. Some were already beginning to open in anticipation of the sun's movement. A number of the trees vied for supremacy, some growing taller than their fellows in order to best deploy their umbrella leaves and absorb the maximum amount of sunshine.

At the edge of the wood Everson called a halt. "We're here to find food. Don't try anything yourselves. You saw what happened to 1 Platoon. We're just here to bring back samples of anything we find that might be edible. Captain Lippett has ways and means of testing them, so let's leave it to him, shall we? We need to be careful in there. We don't know what kind of wildlife we'll find. The damned beasts we've found so far have been none too friendly so watch your back. Don't take any chances. We've got two hours, and frankly that's longer than I want to spend away from the trenches under the present conditions and I'm sure you all have similar concerns."

There were noises of agreement among the platoon.

"Right. 4 Section will hold this position in reserve with the Lewis gun. We'll meet back here in two hours. If you get into any danger, your NCOs have whistles. I'll go in with 1 Section. Good hunting!"

As they moved deeper into the wood, the trees they saw on the perimeter, unable to obtain enough sunlight, soon gave way to stranger vegetation. Some of this had great green tubers running down its sides, embedded in its huge thick trunks, like great veins. The trunks rose straight up, without interruption from bough or branch, into the canopy where they seemed to explode with foliage, each competing with its neighbours for the nourishing rays of the sun.

Further in, they came across a tree, an entanglement of thorny weed wrapped around its base. Here and there the mass supported large dark red blooms. Strands of the weed climbed up the trunk, wrapping itself so tightly about it that its barbed thorns drove deep into the bark, a clear thick liquid oozing from the puncture wounds.

"It's like living barbed wire," said Lucky, scuttling sideward to avoid a tendril as it moved weakly towards him.

"What kind of hell world is this?" said Porgy, shaking his head.

Even as they watched it Atkins could see this wire weed grow, spreading out feelers across the ground under some vegetable imperative he couldn't fathom. The men skirted the slowly spreading carpet and pressed on.

The clatter of their weapons and gear was smothered by the surrounding vegetation and, every now and again, sharp cries and calls from the canopy or rustles and snaps from the undergrowth startled them, but they saw nothing.

As they advanced cautiously through the wood Everson heard something ahead. He put his hand up to hush the rest of the section. They stopped and cocked their heads, listening intently, fingers poised on the magazine cut-off catch on their rifles. The Lieutenant beckoned them forward, a warning finger on his lip. They pushed slowly through the undergrowth until it parted to reveal a large sunlit glade.

There, hopping about, feeding on close cropped grass, were a pack of Gordons. They squeaked as their furry snouts probed the ground, no doubt looking for some sort of insect or ground dwelling creature upon which they depended. In the middle of the clearing, towering over them all like some beneficent totem was a tall plant. It consisted of several stems, each as thick as an average man, entwined about each other and rising to a height of around eighteen feet. At its tip was a large bulbous yellow head and around the underside, hanging from the nodule, were small pods of varying sizes, like ripening fruits. A sweet smell hung around the glade. Atkins' mouth began to water.

"Fascinating," said Hepton, as he fixed his camera box to the tripod and began cranking away.

"Sir," said Pot Shot, addressing the Lieutenant. "Do you think we should try picking one of those fruits for the MO, sir?"

"My thoughts exactly, Jellicoe," said Everson, "once we make sure those damn creatures aren't harmful."

As if in answer, Ginger's haversack began to writhe impatiently. Closer to its own kind again, Gordon became excited and sought a way out of the bag.

"Fuck's sake, here we go again!" said Gazette as he saw Ginger struggle to control his haversack.

"No, Gordon!" cried Ginger as the creature wriggled its way out from the under the flap and jumped down to the ground, scampering across the glade to be with its fellows, squeaking gleefully. The others stopped and stood on their hind legs, squeaking in answer.

"What the deuce!" Everson exclaimed.

"Gordon, come back!" hissed Ginger, striding into the glade. Startled, the creatures scattered and Ginger clumsily switched this way and that, raising sniggers from his mates as he tried to catch his pet, or the one he thought was his pet, for they all looked the same. The creatures panicked and squealed and ran around bolting into holes in the ground. Others poked their noses shyly out of their holes all except, presumably, Gordon, who sat calmly by the plant in the middle of the glade, preening itself.

"This is better than Charlie Chaplin," said Hepton, as he followed the slapstick antics in the glade.

"Mottram, get back here!" hissed Everson.

Ginger, a look of grim determination on his face, advanced on his pet. There was a soft *pfffft* and a giant red thorn exploded from the ground where he stood, ripping up through his groin, the tip exiting through his shoulder. The force of the thrust hefted him off his feet and he hung suspended on the thorn. He screamed, struggling to free himself, but barbs protruding from the spine held him fast. At the bottom of the thorn, large leaf like structures fell open, forming a cup at the base.

Hepton stopped cranking in horror.

"Ginger!" cried Atkins as he Porgy, Mercy and Lucky dashed into the grove.

Atkins saw now, as he ran across the ground, that it seemed soft and springy, yielding under his weight, like boggy earth. It undulated with shallow tussocks. Lucky's foot came down on one and another thorn sprang up from the earth. He squealed as the point tore up though his gut, ripping out through his back, jerking him off his feet. Lucky's helmet rolled across the glade and came to a halt near Atkins.

Porgy, Mercy and Atkins stopped dead still.

"It's burning me! Burning!" screamed Ginger. His pleas degenerated into a meaningless, agonised wailing. He twisted his head and fixed his bloodshot, watery gaze on Atkins. "Help me!"

"God help us," croaked Gutsy hoarsely. "That thing in the middle – it's some kind of carnivorous plant. This must be how it feeds."

"Don't move," said Everson. "You may trigger off more of those things."

Lucky was screaming too, thrashing about in a frenzy as he tried to work himself free, but only succeeding in driving himself further down the thorn. As he slipped down he revealed little sacs that pulsed at the base of small barbs, pumping out some vile secretion. Atkins realised that similar sacs, caught within Ginger and Lucky's bodies, were even now pumping this stuff into them; some sort of poison or digestive juice. The whole glade was a honey trap. Gordon and its little friends had been safe, being too light to trigger the plant's mechanism.

Pot Shot had his hands over his ears in a vain attempt to blot out the anguished screaming. "Somebody do something!"

Everson cocked his pistol and aimed at Ginger's head. It was the only thing to do to save him from a slow, agonising death by internal liquefaction. He pulled the trigger and the back of Ginger's head exploded across the glade. He turned and re-cocked his pistol, this time aiming at Lucky who looked straight back at him.

"Thank –"

Everson met his gaze as he fired again and Lucky slumped lifelessly down on the thorn. Everson sagged visibly as he holstered his pistol. Atkins didn't envy him. But they were still stuck. One wrong move and their fate could be that of their companions.

"Right," said Everson eventually. "These things are obviously set off by weight. Otterthwaite, can you shoot the tussock things and trigger the remaining thorns?"

"Begging your pardon, sir," said Hobson. "But there's a quicker way. Jellicoe, give me your Mills bombs."

Atkins, Mercy and Porgy exchanged glances. Atkins watched as the Sergeant got down on his hands and knees to sight along the floor of the glade, looking for the tell-tale tussocks of untriggered thorns.

"Right-o, watch yourself, lads, sir," said Hobson, pulling the pin from a Mills bomb. Hobson counted to three and tossed it towards the edge of the clearing, away from the trapped men, who crouched down where they were. The grenade exploded and Atkins felt himself showered with dirt as one, two, three huge thorns, triggered by the concussion wave, sprang up around him. The engorged sacs on the barbs pulsing and ejaculating their venom impotently.

Hobson threw a second grenade and it landed in the cup of the furthest thorn before it exploded, shredding the plant. "There's your way out," said Hobson, indicating the path of triggered thorns. "Watch where you step."

Mercy and Porgy edged their way carefully past the thorns, now oozing with digestive acids.

"We can't leave them here, sir," said Atkins, looking back at the impaled bodies.

"I'm sorry, Atkins, it's too dangerous."

"Then just their pay books, sir?" he pleaded, William foremost in his mind. If someone had taken his brother's disc and pay book they might now have known his fate.

"Very well, but be careful."

Atkins stepped as gingerly as he could in his hobnails towards Ginger's slack body. Standing on his tiptoes and leaning over the shiny red collecting cup at the thorn's base, he tentatively opened up what was left of Ginger's tunic and pulled the cloth-covered pay book from his inside pocket. God, this was never a pleasant job at the best of times. A wet splash made him jump as half-liquified organs and viscera slipped out of Ginger's torso and fell into the waiting plant cup. The stench drove Atkins back a step. Used to the charnel stench of the trenches as he was, this was a foul odour that turned his stomach. A squeak startled him. He whirled round almost losing his balance, his foot coming down inches from another tuft. It was Gordon. He'd almost trodden on the creature. It looked up at him, squeaking. He felt a hot flush of anger burst across his face.

"Piss off. This is your fault, you little shit!" he took a swing at it with his boot but it hopped back. It looked up at him from the safety of a tussock.

"Atkins, come on!" called Everson from the edge of the glade.

As he moved round to Lucky's body Atkins blatantly ignored the creature even though he was aware of it turning to watch him. He tottered precariously on his toes as he stretched to reach Lucky's torso. Carefully retrieving his now bloodstained pay book, he made his way back across the glade slowly, step by step.

Atkins leapt thankfully to the edge of the glade only to hear a wistful squeak behind him. Gordon had followed him. He tried shooing the creature away as Everson ordered them away from the glade one by one, but it hopped mournfully after him. With a huff of exasperation, Atkins picked up the creature and put him into his gas helmet haversack as Hepton packed up his camera and tripod.

They moved off sombrely through the undergrowth, knowing now to avoid the large airy sunlit glades, which they saw were dotted everywhere.

"Watch it, more of them damn Sting-a-lings," said Mercy. The name seemed morbidly appropriate and, for want of anything better, it stuck, adding a new level of poignancy to the old soldier's song.

Hobson took the lead followed by Ketch, with Everson bringing up the rear. As they progressed through the wood, each man glanced nervously about; every rustle, every breeze that stirred fronds or leaves or tendrils, every crack, every snap was now potentially something lethal. From elsewhere came the sound of muted rifle fire, screams and a whistle. One of the other sections was in trouble. There was nothing they could do about it but it didn't help the tension any.

Out of the corner of his eye Atkins caught a flash of something. Before he could shout a warning, something man-sized and mottled green detached itself from a trunk and sprang at Lieutenant Everson. Large, saw-toothed mandibles clicked lustfully on empty air as the Lieutenant dived out the way.

Even as the men ran to their commander's aid there was a husky cry and a figure hurled itself out of the undergrowth onto their assailant, deftly working a blade between the chitinous plates on the creature's neck and, with a twist of his arm, severing the head.

There were three bayonetted rifles aimed at him as the man looked up, while the soldiers lifted the partially decapitated body of the man-beetle from their struggling, spluttering commander. Everson, red faced, kicked it away angrily and sat up, struggling to contain the wracking sobs of relief. With their rifles and a jerk of the head, Gazette, Mercy and Gutsy herded the wild man against a trunk and disarmed him. Sergeant Hobson examined the curved blade he carried.

"Bloody hell, he looks human," said Gutsy, peering at the wild man.

The Lieutenant's saviour was a wiry, well-muscled middle-aged man with wild greying hair and a scrubby grey beard. His face and arms were tanned and weathered. He was dressed in clothing that looked as if it had been assembled from various animal hides and vegetable barks. Across his chest and tied to his upper arms were chitinous plates, worn like armour, that looked as if they'd been acquired from creatures similar to the one in front of them.

"Here, Kameraden, you speak English?" asked Mercy.

"Don't be so bloody silly!" said Gutsy. "Does he look like he can?"

The man's eyes flicked from one to the other as they talked.

"I am Urman," said the man, standing erect and thrusting out his chest proudly.

Gutsy's mouth dropped open. When it came down to it, though, the Tommies were not too shocked that the man spoke English. As soldiers of the great and glorious British Empire, they were used to the idea that Johnny Foreigner would speak at least some English, even if it was in an odd accent. It was only right and proper, after all.

Everson was too shaken up by his near miss to question it.

"Where'd you come from, eh? Eh?" challenged Gazette, jabbing the air with his bayonet, causing the man to flinch.

"Leave him, Otterthwaite," said Everson, who had just about recovered his composure. "He's not a Bosche prisoner. He saved my life. He might just be the first friendly face we've seen here." He stepped between his men and held out his hand towards the man.

The man looked at it blankly then tilted his head to examine the back of the Lieutenant's hand as if there might be some concealed offering or weapon. Everson grasped the man's hand gently and shook it.

"Well, I never!" said Pot Shot.

"Hands across the sea!" declared Gutsy, dumbstruck.

"Hands across my bloody arse!" muttered Ketch.

"We," said Everson, "are Human. My name is Lieutenant James Everson, 2 Platoon, C Company, 13th Battalion Pennine Fusiliers of His Britannic Majesty's Army. And yours..." he looked expectantly at the man, "is...?"

"Naparandwe," he said, pointing at himself, then, eyes narrowing, "to what colony do you belong?"

"Colony?" said Everson frowning. "None."

"You are Free Urmen?"

"Free? Well, yes."

The man grinned again as if this was the right answer. "Yrredetti almost had you. Killed two of my clan," he said, pointing at the lifeless bulk of the humanoid beetle creature.

It seemed as if it had evolved to walk upright, and it was evidently able to blend in with its surroundings to almost devastating effect. He spat. Mercy spat, too and the man clapped his hands and grinned. "You are lucky they are solitary hunters."

"Yes, thank you for that," said Everson, running a finger underneath his collar, relieved that his neck was still there.

"Free Urman!" he said offering his hand to Mercy as Everson had done to him. As he repeated this with every man in the section his stomach gurgled obscenely.

"Are you hungry?" asked Atkins, rubbing his own stomach with pantomime gestures. The man nodded eagerly. Atkins opened his pack and took out his iron rations.

The action caught Ketch's wary eye. "You touch that without permission, that's a punishable offence," he snapped. "Emergencies only."

Atkins knew all too well. Two men in his last platoon were court-martialled for eating their iron rations while trapped in a shell hole in No Man's Land for four days. Apparently that wasn't emergency enough.

"He has my permission," said Everson. "Go on, Atkins."

Ketch grunted but backed off.

Atkins opened the tin of bully beef, prised a piece out with his fingers and ate it. He proffered the tin to the man who sniffed it cautiously before devouring the contents within moments, never taking his eyes off Atkins. The act of gouging and prising out the meat was something he seemed to be accustomed with, though probably not from tins, thought Atkins with a quick glance at the green mottled body of the dead Yrredetti. Pot Shot and Porgy offered him their tins and that all went the same way, followed by a large and satisfied belch. He looked hopefully around for his next offering.

"No mate," said Gutsy shaking his head. "Napoo left. Sorry. All gone."

"Napoo?" the man repeated with a grin, his white teeth showing in his berry brown face.

"Yeah. Napoo. I guess that's what we'll call you, too. Napoo," said Gutsy, raising his eyebrows and nodding at the others for agreement. Uncomfortable with a culture not their own and unwilling to show their ignorance, this was easier than trying to pronounce the native's own name.

"Can't say he hasn't earned it," said Porgy with a sigh, looking at the empty tins. He reached up idly and plucked a ripe-looking fruit from a low hanging bough, absent-mindedly shining it on his trousers before lifting it to his mouth to take a bite.

"No!" The man suddenly leapt up and hit him squarely on the back between the shoulder blades. The fruit flew from his hand and was sent rolling across the ground.

Porgy turned round angrily and started to rise.

"What the hell did you do that for you, you little –"

"Hopkiss, sit down," barked Hobson. "The man was doing you a favour."

He pointed to where the fruit had fallen. It had cracked open and juice oozed out from fresh ripe flesh onto the grass, burning it away with acidic sizzles and pops.

"That's the second time he's saved our lives," said Everson. "He seems to know what's what around here. Frankly we could use his kind of help." He turned to Napoo. "Can you help us? We need to find food. And water."

"Food and water," repeated Napoo, nodding.

"You help us?" Everson asked.

"In exchange."

Everson, surprised, glanced up at Hobson who shrugged. Napoo was obviously shrewder than he looked. "Yes, if we can," replied Everson.

Napoo took his weapon back off Hobson and began to walk away through the forest. The men watched. When he realised they weren't following he stopped and turned around. "Follow." The men looked at Everson. He nodded slightly and readjusted his helmet. Hobson took the lead and the rest fell into line. Eventually they came to the edge of a small clearing in front of a cave. Outside the cave a fire burned, tended by a woman of similar age to the man, her hair tied back. A younger girl was scraping out the inside of a large beetle shell, the way one might scrape the fat and meat off a hide.

"Wait here," said Napoo. He went ahead into the clearing where Atkins watched him talk to the woman with big, expressive gestures, pointing back at the woods where they waited. The woman called out. Several other adults appeared from the surroundings or from out of the cave entrance.

Napoo turned and beckoned the Tommies into the clearing where several men stood holding crude spears and bows, eyeing the newcomers suspiciously.

The soldiers walked slowly into the encampment, Sergeant Hobson surveying the area warily. The two parties studied each other. The woman seemed interested in their clothes, plucking at Atkins' sleeves. She felt the rough texture of the khaki cloth between her fingers and tested the strength of its seams with apparent approval.

A lean-to had been built over the entrance to the cave using thick branches and leaves. Theirs seemed to be a miserable existence, at least as miserable as living in the trenches, thought Atkins.

"Let the men rest, Sergeant. Post a sentry. I don't want to be surprised again. I'll go and see what this Napoo needs. Atkins, you're with me."

Atkins groaned. He just wanted to sit down. Instead, he followed the Lieutenant and Napoo into the cave. As they did so the ground rumbled and shook. Small pebbles and rocks bounced down the side of the rock face, showers of dirt loosed from the roots of trees clinging to lips on the cliff drummed down,

"It's another earth tremor!" said Atkins. They staggered hard against side of the cave to stop themselves from falling over. Napoo had stopped and crouched for balance.

Almost as suddenly as it began, it stopped.

"It always happened this time of year," said Napoo, unconcerned. "The world shakes." He led them to the back of a cave where a young man lay on a litter of vegetation and fur, his skin slick with a fever sweat, his eyes rolling in delirium. A wound on his thigh had been smeared with some sort of poultice.

"You help him," Napoo said.

Atkins pulled out his field dressing pack and tore open the paper packing. He placed it over the wound and fixed it with a length of bandage. "It's infected. The MO needs to take a look at him, sir," Atkins said. "I can't help him here."

Everson was silent for a moment. He appeared to come to a decision.

"Very well, we'll take him back to the trenches."

CHAPTER TEN
"If You Were the Only Girl in the World…"

Coming across Napoo had been fortuitous. It was obvious they hadn't succeeded in finding much to eat on their own and Napoo had information that could greatly aid their chances of survival. So it was that Napoo accompanied them as they carried the injured Urman from the forest.

They met up with what was left of the rest of the platoon at the rendezvous point. 2 Section only had two surviving men. Sting-a-lings had killed several, wire-weed had caught another man and one soldier had been lost to a cave-dwelling creature that had snatched him down into darkness before anyone could get a shot off. 3 Section didn't return at the appointed time. The rest of them waited for a quarter of an hour. Everson would have waited longer, but the men were anxious to return to the trenches, if indeed they were still there. All in all the losses were slightly better than if they had attacked Fritz head on, but that seemed of little consolation.

Atkins' arms began to burn with the effort of carrying the wounded Urman on a stretcher as they headed back. He and Porgy had to stop every hundred yards or so. It wasn't easy, carrying battle order kit and lugging a loaded stretcher over a mile or so of uneven ground, especially when he was weary from lack of sleep and weak from lack of food and had Gordon mewling and wriggling about in his bag.

He felt a great wave of relief when they first heard the sound of work parties and the reassuring refrains of songs drifting over the plain. They passed several groups of men digging mass graves some hundred yards out onto the plain and seeding it with sacks of Chlorate of Lime. They were preparing to bury the rotting corpses from No Man's Land that had been attracting predators. Another working party was hacking up the fire-crisped carcass of one of the giant worms.

Sporadic cheers and looks of amazement greeted their arrival back at the trenches. Napoo strode through with Everson and Hobson, wide-eyed at the muddy encampment and holding his nose as the stench hit him. It prompted Pot Shot behind him to start singing: "To live with any luck inside a trench / Your nose must get accustomed to the stench / Of the rotten Bosche that lie/ On the parapet and die / 'cos they make a smell that Hell itself can't quench..."

Off-duty soldiers gathered to watch 1 Section pass. Word got round fast and the discovery of native people living on this world made quite a stir. On seeing Napoo, a number of old soldiers, having served in India, expressed the opinion that it was only right and natural to find someone to whom they were superior. If they were to be stranded on some other world now, at least, it was a place where they could be masters. Britannia's Colonial spirit was, in some quarters it seemed, still alive and well.

Everson and Napoo accompanied Atkins and Porgy as they carried the injured Urman to the newly established Casualty Clearing Station. Bell tents and crude tarpaulin marquees served as wards for the bedridden. The walking wounded lay about outside chatting and smoking. The shell-shocked had been fenced in for their own protection, under guard like POWs; their minds broken by the horrors of war and this strange new world that had suddenly appeared around them. Most of them sat quietly and wept, rocking themselves, or else shook and jerked in spastic fits and screamed. Some sought shelter and cover for themselves, desperately scraping sap holes with their bare hands. Every now and then one would completely funk it and run at the wire only to be brutally sedated by the butt of a guard's rifle. Many men hadn't time for the malingerings of cowards such as these. Atkins watched them mull about as he passed, his thoughts turning to Ginger. Poor bloody Ginger. He'd rather the lad had funked it proper and ended up in that compound than die the way he did.

The MO's hospital bell tent had a big red cross daubed on it and they made for that. The walking wounded seemed to give this tent a wider birth than the other and Atkins soon found out why. The sound of fast rhythmic sawing came from within and set his teeth on edge. In a place like that, there was only one thing you could be sawing. Atkins and Porgy put the stretcher down. The young Urman groaned feverishly. Everson collared an orderly. "Fetch the MO immediately." He turned to Atkins and Porgy. "Go and get yourself some grub," he said.

"Sir," they said, saluting. Atkins turned to leave when Porgy caught him by the arm.

"'Alf a mo, eh, Only?" he said.

Nurse Bell was ambling their way, exchanging pleasantries with cheeky wounded soldiers who fancied their chances. Flirting made them feel alive, made them feel wanted, valued. Human. She was talking and laughing with a soldier leaning on crutch, Lance Corporal Sandford from 3 Platoon. Porgy's eyes narrowed. This meant war. He ran a comb as best he could through his hair over his bandage and splashed his face with water from his canteen.

"Bloody hell, Porgy, you're going all out today," said Atkins. "Give the poor girl a chance!"

"Oh, I intend to, at the very least," he said with a grin. "I'm still looking for my Queen of Hearts."

"You again," Edith said as she approached.

"Yeah, I know," said Porgy. "Can you take a look at me noggin again? I'm feeling a bit light headed. Especially around you."

"You are incorrigible, Private," she said, smiling.

Atkins coughed discreetly.

"Oh, this is my mate, Only," said Porgy shuffling awkwardly.

"Only what?" she asked.

"Go on, tell her," said Porgy, digging him in the ribs.

Atkins rolled his eyes wearily. "My name's Thomas Atkins," he sighed. Tommy Atkins, the nickname for the common soldier, and didn't he half get ragged about it?

"Tommy Atkins? Really? That's your real name?"

"Certainly is, nobody would make that up. This," announced Porgy, enjoying his friend's discomfort just a little too much, "is the One, the Only Tommy Atkins!"

"It sounds like a music hall act," she said, putting her hand over her mouth politely as she laughed.

"I know," said Porgy, slapping Atkins on the back, "so we just call him Only."

It was what passed for a Tommy's humour. No sense making jokes you had to think about. You could be dead before you got it. To Tommy though, 'Only' also served as a constant reminder of his missing brother. He might well be the only Atkins brother left, the sting of conscience he experienced at its every mention was a penance he accepted for his uncharitable thoughts regarding William.

Leaving them to talk, he made great sport of Gordon, charging the waiting casualties thruppence an item to have their clothes chatted by the creature. Porgy caught up with him as Nurse Bell went on about her ministrations.

"She's a fine lass, isn't she, Only?"

"Oh no doubt," said Atkins, "But I do doubt she'll put up with you."

"She's a debutante," he said, plainly enamoured.

"And clearly out of your league. A Northern lad from a brewery stepping out with someone who's been in the same room as Royalty? I'd say you need your head examining."

"I have," he sighed. "By Edith."

"What? And she found nothing wrong with it? Can't be much of a nurse then."

*   *   *

Lippett operated on the young Urman with an orderly and Sister Fenton assisting. Napoo was reluctant to leave him alone, partly because Gutsy had explained to him in a slow, loud voice – which was the best way, in his opinion, to communicate with natives – that they were working their juju magic on him, which seemed to alarm Napoo. He hung around the surgical tent, his face etched with worry as he and Everson waited. To Everson's relief, the operation was a success. Lippett came out of the tent wiping his hands on his apron.

"It was some sort of poisonous thorn, embedded deep in his muscle," he said. "We've cut it out. He's young and strong. He should pull through. Remarkably, that poultice muck they'd spread on it seems to have some medicinal properties, slowed the spread of the poison. We might be able to use something like that if we're here much longer."

They moved the Urman to a tent, where Sister Fenton and Nurse Bell checked on him hourly. Owing to his chiselled, unshaven appearance, reminding them of the Gallic soldiers they'd treated, and not knowing the unconscious man's name, they nicknamed him Poilus. It seemed to suit him, or at least their romanticised notions of him.

Napoo was nervous and edgy, never leaving his bedside until the man eventually came round and opened his eyes. The wound on his thigh had been bandaged and he was still suffering from a slight fever, but Sister Fenton explained that they expected it to come down after a couple of days' rest.

Poilus looked around nervously, panic building behind his eyes. However, Napoo stepped into his eye line and laid his hand on his forearm, tears welling up in his eyes. He looked up at Everson across the bed.

"Yes," he said, his voice choked with emotion, "we will help you."

*   *   *

Napoo was at first suspicious when Oliver Hepton, delighting in him as some sort of indigenous novelty, wanted to film him. He persuaded Napoo to pose, which he did grinning nervously, surrounded by the men of 1 Section.

"Wave for the folks back home," Hepton directed them. "Valiant Tommies meeting the local natives of the Wonder Planet."

"Who's he kidding?" said Half Pint sourly as they performed for the camera. "Everything on this bloody planet is poisonous or dangerous. This place is going to kill us before we get a square meal out of it."

"Give it a rest Half Pint. Tell us something we don't know," said Gutsy.

"Whuuugh!" yelled Half Pint ducking down as something buzzed over his head; a fat bloated thing about the size of a pigeon with feathery antennae and large compound eyes. He started flapping his arms around. "Get it off, get it off!"

Napoo grinned, snatched it out of the air and bit its head off, spitting it onto the ground before tipping back his head and squeezing the carcass. A slop of dark viscera fell into his mouth. He chewed and swallowed.

"Gawd, that's disgusting!" said Porgy.

"It's good!" said Napoo, wiping his mouth on the back of his hand, offering it to Atkins.

Another flew by Pot Shot. He reached up a long gangly arm, and caught it. He was about to use his bayonet to cut the head off when Napoo stopped him, laughing.

"No, not that one,"

"Why not? I did what you did," Pot Shot protested.

Napoo shook his head and rapped his knuckles on Pot Shot's head.

"No, look. This one is thin. It hasn't fed yet. You wait until it has fed and fat. You eat that now you taste only bile. Make you sick." He picked it up and threw it away.

"Excellent!" yelled Hepton. Pleased with the unexpected footage he capped his camera.

*   *   *

Everson was right in his estimation of Napoo's knowledge. Over the next few days, he taught them many things. He showed them safe food to eat and where to find more. He told them what firewood to use without it spitting hot poisonous sap at them. He showed them edible fruits to gather, how to dig up the roots of the Tergo plant where they could find large, wriggling grubs the size of a man's forearm nestling in swollen tubers. They brought down one of the tall three-legged herbivore 'tripodgiraffes' as it fed. They also shot one of the hell hounds from a pack that was trying to stalk it. After several days of hunting and gathering, they had managed to build up quite a store of food.

"I think it would be a good idea," suggested Everson to Captain Grantham, "that is, I think it would boost the men's morale if we could celebrate our first meal with indigenous ingredients,"

The Captain nodded and waved his hand dismissively. "Whatever you want, Everson. Whatever you want."

However, Everson knew their survival would depend on more than food and water and morale. It would depend on information and there was more that Napoo might tell them about this planet. Therefore, he, Jeffries and Padre Rand sought to question him further. Padre Rand's bright flame of faith had guttered alarmingly in the face of the Somme and seemed extinguished by the wind of circumstance that had blown them to this world. Now it seemed Napoo's arrival fanned the embers of his dying belief. He had been a missionary in Africa and knew a heathen when he saw one. He wanted to know if Napoo believed in god, whether he had been baptised. He believed it to be his sacred duty to save the man's soul. If indeed he should have one. For if this place was not Earth, then he could not be a son of Adam, a creature of God.

"We believe in GarSuleth the sky god, weaver of the world, and in his brother, Skarra," said Napoo, reciting in the manner of a credo.

Everson could see the Padre's eyes narrow in the face of this new heresy but of Jeffries' countenance, he could make nothing.

"You do not know of them?" said Napoo uncertainly. "But all Urmen worship them, the Ones decreed it..."

Everson shook his head and shrugged.

"The Ones. The Children of GarSuleth," said Napoo impatiently. "Whose land this is? How can you not know? This place borders Khungarrii territory. They killed many of my clan, so we stay away. You should too."

"Khungarrii?" queried Jeffries.

"The Khungarrii of the Ones, aye."

"When we first met you spoke of Free Urmen. I take it there are those who are not free?" asked Everson.

"They serve the Ones."

As Napoo continued to talk it seemed to Everson that, here on this world, Man had never risen to his full potential. Here, the majority were indentured servants to a race greater than they. Those Urmen that chose freedom rather than serve the Ones grubbed a meagre subsistence, living among the unforgiving fields and beasts of this god-forsaken world. That Man should be so humbled was an anathema to him and, for a moment, he felt the same hot fury that he had once felt toward the Bosche.

That evening, cooks prepared the foods as best they could. The men built and lit fires and gathered round them, some digging out such treasures as harmonicas or penny whistles. Mercy even managed to find a battered wind-up gramophone and a surviving record. The strains of old songs and laughter rose with the smoke from the myriad campfires towards the unknown stars above.

Edith Bell, Nellie Abbott and Sister Fenton sat apart on empty grenade boxes nibbling tentatively at skewered alien meat.

"So why did you become a VAD, Edith?" asked Nellie Abbott.

Edith was silent for a moment as if considering something before deciding to speak. "I was running away, I suppose."

"From what?"

"The past."

"Well they say it always catches up with you."

"That's why I thought the Front would be the best place to confront it."

"The Front? You deliberately came to the Front?"

"To face it head on, to punish myself for surviving," said Edith, shaking her head. "Oh, I don't know anymore. I don't care. Seeing all this suffering – at least here, this time I can do something. I can make a difference, can't I? You see I know we're all going to die, it's just that on the Front you have a better idea of when."

"What could be so awful that you think you're punishing yourself by serving here?" asked Fenton.

"It was two years ago," she said in a hushed voice, half hoping that they wouldn't hear her and she could pretend she hadn't said anything and not have to go through with it.

"What was two years ago, the start of the War?"

"No, it was before that."

Fenton and Abbott exchanged questioning glances, each shrugging. They waited. Nelly took Edith's hands in hers and gave them a small, warm squeeze then held them lightly.

"The Lamb –" she could barely get the words out. She stopped, smiled apologetically and cleared her throat. "The Lambton Grange Murders."

There was a sharp intake of breath from Nellie. "Oh you poor thing. Were – were you there? That was an evil thing what happened there. Our Bertie read it to us from the papers, he missed out the worst bits to spare us, silly sod. But I read the paper myself, later. Horrid, simply horrid."

"No, that's the thing, you see," said Edith. "I was supposed to be there."

"What do you mean?" asked Fenton.

"I knew the girls that were murdered, Elspeth Cholmondley and Cissy Pentworth. We were a bit of gang. We met him, at a party a month earlier."

"Dwyer the Debutante Killer? Strewth!"

"Yes. I believe that's what some of the more sensationalist newspapers called him. He seemed so charming. Of course, we knew he had a bit of a reputation. That was what poor Cissy found so alluring. He invited us out to his place for the weekend. Only I couldn't go at the last minute. Great Aunt Lil decided to come up from Brighton."

"That was some luck."

"But I let them go alone, don't you see? I should have been with them," she said, sobs welling up. "It should have been me, too."

Edith saw Lance Corporal Sandford approach them tentatively, hobbling along inexpertly on a crutch, a pal by his side, and hastily wiped her eyes, cursing herself for weakening and sharing her private burden. She pasted a smile on her face for Nellie's sake. "I'm all right," she said. "Really."

While the Corporal and his mate stood talking to them, Edith could sense Nellie's awkwardness. Spotting the tank mechanic in his overalls, Nellie made her excuses, got up and slipped away, trying to catch his eye.

Sat round their own campfire, Atkins noticed Porgy stealing glances towards the nurses as the corporal sat down next to Edith, his injured leg out straight as he put an arm around her shoulder. Next to her, Sister Fenton wriggled away from his pal, rebuffing the NCO's advances. He tried again to put his arm around her shoulders, but she stood up. He couldn't hear what she was saying but he was obviously getting a bollocking. Fenton wrapped her cape around herself and stalked off in the direction of the casualty tents. Porgy had just decided to go and cut in when he saw Edith rise and help her suitor to his feet.

"Bad luck old chap," said Atkins sympathetically. "Perhaps if you'd got yourself more of a Blighty one."

"Fat lot of good a Blighty One does here!" he spat, glancing pointedly up towards the brightest star in the sky.

They watched as Edith helped Sandford walk along with his crutch. The pair passed beyond the light of one fire only to be silhouetted against another and met by encouraging whoops and catcalls as they passed the men gathered round it.

"Come on, Porgy. Face it. You lost out. Best man and all that, eh? Come and sit down," said Atkins.

"If he hurts her...," he muttered, tearing viciously with his teeth at the chunk of meat in his hands.

"My god," said Atkins, the truth dawning on him. "This isn't just about your deck of cards is it? You're actually serious about this one, aren't you?" The helpless look in Porgy's eyes said it all. "Look, he's crippled. What's he going to do, stand on her foot with his crutch? Come back to the campfire."

Atkins guided a reluctant Porgy back to where the rest of their section sat. After a while Half Pint turned the conversation to the thing that was on all their minds.

"What if we never get back? We're marooned here, I tell you. This," he said with a sweep of his arm, "is it and we'd better make the most of it."

"No, I don't believe that, I can't believe that," said Porgy. "Whatever brought us here might send us back just as quickly; the officers must think so too, why else do you think they've kept us on this stinking pile of mud?"

"Hope?" said Gazette. "But I don't think we can depend on miracles. If there's a way back I reckon we're going to have to find it ourselves."

"And what if there isn't a way back?" challenged Half Pint.

"We got here didn't we?" said Mercy angrily.

"Someone must be responsible. I say we find them and make them send us back," said Ketch.

"If there is someone, why did they bring us, what are we here for?" asked Gutsy.

"Do you really want to go back to the Somme?" said Half Pint.

"No," said Pot Shot. "I want to go back to my family."

A woman's horrified scream cut off the murmurs of assent.

Porgy was the first to jump and grab his rifle from the tee-pee of arms, causing the others to clatter to the ground.

"That bloody bastard. I knew it. If he's harmed her –" he said as he dashed off into the dark past other men, now standing up from the campfires and looking out into the night.

Atkins grabbed a rifle and ran after him, weaving between the fires and the muttering troops. Reaching the edge of the mud flat Atkins jumped the three or four feet to the plain and, without breaking step, ran on after Porgy toward the small copse of trees not twenty yards from the mud.

The screaming continued hysterically.

Atkins made it to the trees to find Porgy standing silhouetted against the light from a hurricane lantern hanging on a low bough. He rounded Porgy, accidentally standing on a discarded crutch as he did so. Then he saw Edith kneeling on the ground, her apron and nurse's uniform drenched in blood. The headless body of Corporal Sandford lay sprawled across her lap, blood now only gently pulsing from the open neck and pooling in the trough of her apron. There was no sign of his head.

A crack and a rustle from the foliage above alerted them and Edith screamed again, attempting to straighten her legs out in front of her and push her way back from under the trees. Porgy went down on one knee and clamped a hand across her mouth. Her eyes darted wildly to the canopy. Atkins put the rifle butt to his shoulder and scanned the foliage.

With his boot, Porgy clumsily struggled to push the headless body of the dead soldier off Edith's legs. "Shhh," he whispered in her ear before dragging her to safety.

Several other soldiers came running. Atkins beckoned them to stop and dropped down on one knee, eyes still fixed above him. He heard the sound of magazine cut-offs opened and loading bolts ratcheted back as one or two of the men circled round warily. He was aware of the sobbing nurse somewhere behind him, the noise growing fainter as Porgy took her back to the safety of the entrenchment.

His awareness immediately refocused as he caught movement on a bough above him. He gave rapid fire, five rounds as per. There was a sudden crack and crash as it fell through the canopy. The men backed off as something hit the ground. It was the soldier's head. The rustle continued high up in the tree as something jumped from one branch to the next in an effort to escape. Atkins and two other men followed the sound, firing blindly up into the foliage. Several others moved round outside the copse to cut it off. Whatever it was, they had it trapped now.

There was a scream as something snatched a soldier up into the foliage. His rifle clattered to the ground. There was a wet crunch accompanied by a strangulated sound before a head dropped down, bounced on the ground, and ended up staring, horrified, at Atkins.

Men blazed away into the trees, lost in fear and anger.

"Stand back," said a voice.

It was Porgy. From somewhere he had acquired a Lewis gun, slung from his right shoulder by a canvas strap and carried on his hip, a fresh circular magazine fixed to the top and several others in their canvas webbing slung over his other shoulder.

"Where?" he growled.

Atkins jerked his head upwards.

Somebody, an NCO, fired a Very flare into the trees. It burst with an angry hissing white light, setting the leaves ablaze and casting its stark glare over the area. There came a hoarse throaty screech and a rapid chattering as something thrashed about in the tree.

"There!" shouted someone as the dying glow of the Very light caught something shiny and brown. Porgy opened fire. The magazine rotated and the rapid rattle of the Lewis gun ripped through the foliage. There was an ear-splitting screech, like nails on a blackboard, and a large body crashed down followed by another.

Atkins stepped forward to examine the large, insect-like creature. Nearby, there was the decapitated body of the second soldier. "Yrredetti," he said, recognising the creature and its mottled markings from their mission in the forest, before putting his rifle against the creature's head and firing.

Rather than dying, as he had every right to expect it would, the now headless insectoid body began trashing about and only stopped when Porgy unloaded another entire magazine into it.

As the flames from the flare spread above them and the trees in the copse began to blaze, stretcher-bearers arrived to carry away the two dead soldiers. They left the body of the Yrredetti to burn.

INTERLUDE 3
Letter from Private Thomas Atkins
to Flora Mullins

9th November 1916

Dearest Flora,

I should be writing this from Sans German, by rights. We should have been relieved and back in the reserve line by now, but all that's gone to pot. We're sans Germans all right, but we're sans everything else too. Although things are looking up. We had a picnic this evening, al fresco, as they say, to celebrate our first harvest. Like all picnics we got pestered by insects, well only the one, but you should have seen the size of it.

Porgy is sweet on a nurse. He's quite serious about her, I think. It's sad and funny to see. But all the boys love our 'Roses of No Man's Land' and she has a fearsome Sister over her who forbids fraternisation, so I don't hold out much hope for him, though he seems proper determined and pines like a lost puppy.

Mercy is up to his scrounging ways again. He's found something special for Lt Everson that he won't tell us about. Loves a secret, does Mercy. Hasn't stopped Gutsy starting a book on what it might be though. I put a tanner on a bath tub, because well, we haven't washed for nearly two weeks now, so God knows we could use one. Well, I say a tanner, but we haven't had any pay for the last few weeks and it don't look as if the payroll will come any time soon, either.

Ever yours,
Thomas

PENNINE FUSILIERS

CHAPTER ELEVEN
"If the Sergeant Steals Your Rum…"

After the Yrredetti incident, fires were set on the plain in a controlled slash and burn policy, forming a *cordon sanitaire* around No Man's Land to deny further cover to any predators. Atkins watched as the smudgy black smoke drifted into the sky. It felt as if they were finally making their mark, conquering the land that had seemed so hostile to them when they first arrived.

As the days passed, hope began to fade that they would be transported home as quickly as they had arrived and the new survival practices became an established part of the daily military routine. With the most suitable trees nearby having been cut down for firewood, shoring or building materials, the Foraging Parties had to move further and further afield. Poilus continued to improve and Napoo, in high spirits, continued to educate the soldiers in hunter-gathering.

He had pointed out a fruit tree, the large purple fruits of which were the size of mangoes and wincingly sweet. This gave Mercy an idea. To be fair it was obviously an idea he'd had for quite a while because it didn't take him long to put it into action. In an abandoned dugout, Mercy constructed a crude still from water drums and Ticklers' jam tins, and even managed to scrounge some copper piping for a condenser. He also acquired some yeast from the cooks' supplies.

One night Mercy slunk into the Section's dugout carrying an old stone rum jar, almost tripping over Gordon as the creature chatted the seams of Pot Shot's shirt. "Here, he said. "Try this. I've already sold half to some lads from 4 Platoon."

"You haven't been nicking the rum rations, have you? Hobson'll have your guts for garters," said Porgy.

"Relax, this is my own mixture, isn't it?"

"You mean –"

"He's been brewing this stuff in secret for days," said Gutsy, shaking his head. "I tried telling him it wasn't a good idea. If he gets caught he'll be for the high jump."

"So what's this gut-rot called then?"

"Flammenwerfer," said Mercy with a grin. "Who's first?"

Porgy and Half Pint pushed Atkins to the fore. "Go on, Only! Put hairs on your chest, will that."

Mercy, laughing, poured a large tot into a dixie can and thrust it towards Atkins.

"Down! Down! Down! Down!" the others chanted.

Egged on by the rest, Atkins, wanting to be a good sport, grudgingly emptied his dixie in one draught. He immediately regretted it, stumbling back, half-blinded by stinging tears as the liquor burned down his throat. Flammen-bloody-werffer indeed. Although, as he fought for breath, he thought 'Gas Attack' would have been a more appropriate epithet. He could feel a pounding begin at the base of his skull until the beat of it filled his head. The burning liquid etched a path down his insides to his stomach where it seemed to reach flashpoint and ignite, expanding to fill his entire body. His limbs began to tingle and throb to the beat of his pulse. As he wiped the tears from his cheeks, he began to feel dizzy and light-headed. Blinking, he tried to speak, but it seemed that his vocal chords had melted.

The faces of the men before him began to contort, twisting and turning like a Futurist canvas, their features malleable, fading and shifting. The khakis and mud greys around him began radiating kaleidoscopes of geometric patterns that burst against his retinas. He squeezed his eyes shut and shook his head in an attempt to rid himself of the vision, opening them again only to find the scene around him stubbornly ablaze with guttering colours. He tried to speak again, but his voice sounded so far away and foreign he could barely hear himself let alone distinguish what he was saying or whether it made sense. He was finding it hard to breathe. He thrust a finger down the collar of his shirt and pulled at it. He looked down at his feet impossibly far below him and a wave of vertigo washed over him. Arms reached for him but he batted them away and struggled to put one foot in front of the other as he broke away from the garish India rubber limbs that tried to claw him back.

He clambered out of the blue-tinged trenches that expanded and contracted in waves before him, threatening to swallow him, and ran over sky blue mud with teal vapours rising in convection eddies. Above him, the sky boiled gently off into magenta hues. Time seemed to contract and expand in waves, too. One moment he was stumbling across crusting mud then next he found himself oozing slowly across the deep red stubble of the burnt open ground beyond as the orange fronds loomed towards him.

Two lidless eyes stared back; multicoloured whorls like oil on water dancing on their dark surface, watching him from the foaming purple undergrowth before shadows crept in from the periphery of his vision, occluding all...

Noises intruded on the blackness. Atkins felt himself surface from dark depths as diffuse light seeped into his consciousness. The noise grew until he thought his eardrums would burst. He sat bolt upright, gasping for air like a drowning man breaking the water's surface.

"Eyes!" he cried. "There's something watching us!"

Gentle hands urged him back down. Everything seemed raw and tinged with garish colours, like a hand-tinted photograph. The after effects of the Flammenwerfer, he expected. Things still wavered slightly, washing gently to and fro. He went with it and sank back into the pillow.

"There, there, you're safe. You've been hallucinating," said a soft warm voice. It was Sister Fenton. She soaked a cloth in a bowl of water by his stretcher and gently wiped his face. "That was a stupid thing you did. It could have killed you. How many of you drank that filthy stuff? Three are over there. One is blinded, another two have lost their minds. One poor wretch stumbled into a flooded shell hole and drowned. You were lucky." She held his head and gave him a sip of water. His dried, cracked lips stung as the water moistened them.

"Where..."

"You're safe. You're in the Casualty Clearing Station. Your friends brought you in. They found you wandering about – out there."

"Mercy," asked Atkins.

"Pardon?"

"My mate, Mercy."

"Is he the one who brewed the liquor?"

"Yes," he rasped.

"Hmm," said Fenton with a note of disapproval. "Well he'll get what's coming to him. He's in custody on a charge. There's to be a Court Martial."

Captain Grantham, Second Lieutenant Everson and Lieutenant Jeffries sat behind the table. Everson hated this part of the job. Already that morning they had heard several cases. The penalties for even minor infractions were often excessive and out of proportion for the supposed crime. And as the accused this time was one of his own he felt a little ashamed too. Evans had always been one to run close to the wire. He looked along the table. Captain Grantham was playing nervously with his fountain pen, clearing his throat every minute or so. The only person who seemed relaxed with the situation was Jeffries. Since most of the men who tried the liquor were in 4 Platoon, Lieutenant Jeffries had a personal stake in the case. One of his men had died, another had been temporarily blinded and another had been relegated to the stockade with the shell-shocked. Everson heard Hobson's bark outside. He shifted position, sitting upright.

"Prisoner and escort, halt! Right turn!"

Evans entered the dugout flanked by two soldiers.

"Prisoner and escort, halt! 'tenshun!"

Evans stood to attention, his thumbs extending down along his trouser seams, looking straight ahead at the wall over the officers' heads, his face emotionless but for his eyes betraying a flicker of fear.

"What's this one?" asked Grantham.

Everson read from the charge sheet regretfully, "The accused, 98765 Private Wilfred Joseph Evans, 13th Pennine Fusiliers, a soldier of the regular forces, is charged with, when on active service, wilfully destroying Army property without orders from a superior officer and with brewing and distributing alcohol."

"Which frankly doesn't cover the half of it," said Jeffries. "Several of my men are in hospital and one is dead because of this man's actions. Brewing and distributing alcohol in the trenches. In fact, worse than alcohol. The report from the MO says here that the liquor, while being extremely alcoholic, also contained some form of noxious opiate, causing hallucinations. This man's expertise with the still equipment suggests to me that this isn't the first time he's done this."

"With respect, Lieutenant," said Everson. "There is no evidence he knew the ingredients to be harmful."

"Nevertheless," pressed Jeffries in clipped and measured tones. "I would ask for the maximum sentence."

"Has the accused anything to say in his defence?"

Even if he had, thought Everson, it wouldn't do him any good.

"With respect –" began Evans.

"Respect?" barked Jeffries, shouting him down. "You know nothing of respect, Private!" He turned and whispered to Grantham.

The Captain had a glazed look in his eyes, almost as if he had given up. He nodded, and then spoke up. "The unauthorised use of Army property will not be tolerated. I will be issuing a general order expressly banning the fermenting of alcohol for consumption forthwith. Sergeant, make sure his equipment is put beyond use. As for you, Private, penal servitude not being practical at this point, I hereby sentence you to Field Punishment Number One. I trust you will learn from this. Dismissed."

"Sah!" barked Hobson. "Prisoner and Escort left turn. Quick march."

Hobson marched Evans and his men away.

Grantham sighed, pushed his chair back and began shuffling his papers together in preparation to leave when Lieutenant Tulliver and Lieutenant Mathers entered.

"Excuse me, sir," said Mathers. "Tulliver and I have a request. If I might?"

"Eh?"

Jeffries leaned forward and looked past Grantham at Everson, his eyes narrowing. Everson shrugged.

"It's about the still your private constructed, sir. I understand you've given orders for it to be dismantled."

"Yes, dashed bad show. Showed the fella what for, though, eh, Jeffries?"

"Sir," said Jeffries darkly.

"Damned right."

"Well as you know, my tank and Mr Tulliver's plane only have limited supplies of petrol. Without it, our machines will be useless. Although unfit for human consumption we might be able to use this liquor as a petrol substitute."

"Of course!" said Everson, "that's a capital idea!"

"You agree with this, do you, Mr Everson?" asked Grantham.

"Resources are scarce, sir, and petrol supply is very limited," said Everson. "I believe Quartermaster Slacke only managed to find forty gallons. With Napoo's help, we've managed to find food and water and started to build up our stores. If we can solve the fuel problem as well, then that will increase our chances of survival. Without petrol those machines are just, well, so much junk, if you'll excuse me gentlemen."

Mathers shrugged indifferently.

Tulliver nodded in agreement. "No, you're right. If we can gather more of these fruits that your man found then we can distill as much fuel as we need. You know what they look like, where to find them?"

"Napoo does," answered Everson.

"Ah, yes, Napoo," said Jeffries quietly. "And just what exactly are this Napoo's motives?" He had been sat quietly listening, thinking. Jeffries seemed to do a lot of thinking, to Everson's mind. Which wasn't a bad thing in general. Too many officers didn't think at all. Jeffries, though, seemed to think altogether too much. Now, he uncoiled from his nest like a snake. "Who is he? What do we know of him?"

"He offered us help and knowledge when we needed it in exchange for aid with his kinsman," said Everson.

"Oh, and he has been helpful," admitted Jeffries. "To a point. He has warned about these... Khungarrii, yes. But the question is what else does he know? Is there anything he isn't telling us? You know virtually nothing about this world including, I might add, how we got here."

"I'm sure he'd tell us if he knew," said Everson.

"Your faith in human nature is heart-warming," said Jeffries, condescendingly. "But *is* he human? If this is a different world how can he be?"

"He seems to be an honest soul," said Everson.

"And again," said Jeffries. "Does he even have a soul at all? I'm sure Padre Rand could dispute your claim."

"What's your point Mr Jeffries?" asked Grantham.

"My point, sir, is that we know nothing about this native, his loyalties, his people. How do we know they aren't hiding anything from us?"

"They have no reason to lie," said Everson.

"Speak plainly, Mister Jeffries," pleaded Grantham, rubbing his temples as if the very concepts Jeffries iterated pained him.

"Aren't we rather getting off the point here?" said Mathers. Jeffries shot him a glance as he continued. "Captain, have we your permission to commence distilling fuel for our machines?"

Grantham sat down heavily in his chair with a sigh and waved them away with his hand. "Yes, yes, of course. Take whatever you need. We must keep them going, I suppose."

Tulliver grinned and patted Mathers on the shoulder as they left, eagerly talking about plans to construct a bigger still.

Jeffries watched them go, like a cat watching another, warily, as it skirted its territory.

"Captain, if I may?" said Everson, rising.

Grantham, looking tired and worn, glanced up at him and nodded mutely.

"Sir," said Everson, putting his cap upon his head and adjusting it. "Mr Jeffries."

"So you have no objection then, sir?" asked Jeffries, in Everson's hearing.

Grantham looked up. "To what?"

"To my questioning this Napoo character, of course?"

"No, none at all."

"Good," said Jeffries under his breath, "good."

Everson realised that Jeffries was playing a dangerous game over this Evans incident. Since the repeal of flogging, the British Army had to resort to other imaginative forms of corporal punishment. Field Punishment Number One consisted of the convicted man being lashed to a fixed post or gun wheel for two to three hours a day without food or water, often deliberately in range of enemy fire. Asserting authority and discipline was one thing, but there was no telling how the men might respond to the brutal and public punishment out here. Separated from their home, their loved ones and now their planet, the trenches were a powder keg right now. The men were discontented, fractious. The last thing they needed was a reason to riot.

Everson entered the small dugout that was being used as a guardroom. "That was a damn foolish thing you did, Evans, bloody irresponsible!" he said, sitting down on the bunk bedside him. He pulled a hip flask from inside his tunic.

"A drop of the real stuff?" asked Mercy, meekly.

"You should know," said Everson as he unscrewed the cap and passed the flask to Evans. Evans took a slug.

"Aaah." He wiped his lips on his sleeve and passed it back. "Gilbert the Filbert's really got in for me hasn't he, sir?"

"Oh, believe you me; he's like that with everyone. No quarter given, but you bloody well asked for it. I warned you. What the hell did you think you were doing?"

"I didn't know the damn stuff made you see things and worse, sir, I swear! I didn't mean any harm. Those poor lads. It was only meant to warm the cockles and raise morale a bit."

"Damn it, Evans, There's a whole world out that that's trying to kill us. I don't need to worry about my own men doing it as well!"

Mercy lowered his eyes.

"This has got to be done, Evans. Discipline is important. Sometimes I think it's all that's keeping us together at the moment. If things go too far, I fear the men might mutiny and there are precious few officers to maintain order. If the men took it into their heads there's nothing we could do to stop them."

"Won't come to that, sir."

"How can you be so sure? No officer has the answers. I don't know where we are, or how. But I have to believe we'll get back. I have to. Because without that, without hope, then it all falls apart."

"The men know that too sir. Right now, they can grouse about the officers all they want but they know that if they usurp them, they'll have to fend for themselves. To put it bluntly sir, they don't want the responsibility. That and the fact, with the exception of Captain Grantham, you're all front line officers. If you weren't it might be a different story. But the men know you sir. They trust you."

"Well that's something I suppose," sighed Everson. "Can you take it, Evans?"

"Sir?"

"The punishment?"

"Had worse, sir," Evans said stoically.

Everson let a smile play briefly on his lips as he stood up, before scowling. "I can believe it. But I've already lost half my best men. I can't afford to lose any more. Straight and narrow after this Evans, or you'll answer to me."

"I don't suppose you'd care to leave that with me, sir?" he asked, nodding at the flask.

Everson looked down at the engraved silver hip flask and, after a moment's thought, tossed it over to Mercy. "It won't be enough, you know."

"Every little helps sir," Evans caught it cleanly. "Every little helps."

The next morning Grantham summoned all able-bodied men to witness Mercy's punishment. Discharged by the MO, Atkins still felt a little delicate when he joined the rest of his Section on parade. Ketch gave him a self-satisfied smirk as their eyes met.

"Bloody 'ell, Only, you look pale, you sure you're all right?" whispered Pot Shot.

"A little light-headed," Atkins replied. Spots still burst in his vision like Very lights and he had to keep moving his head to prevent Pot Shot being lost in drifting after-images. "What the hell happened?"

"We thought you were just foolin' around at first," muttered Gutsy, "but after you went doolally Ketch happened, that's what. The moment them blokes from 4 Platoon began screaming and blundering about in a blind panic, it didn't take him long to follow the trail back to Mercy. Hobson confiscated the booze and the still, but it were Gilbert the Filbert that pressed for a Court Martial."

"Parade! Parade 'shun!" bellowed Sergeant Hobson.

The guards brought Mercy out, stripped to the waist. He looked in a bad way; he'd been beaten black and blue. Jeffries' men had obviously given him a seeing to during the night, revenge for the men they lost. Jeffries stepped forward from the rest of the officers and addressed the men.

"98765 Private Evans, 2 Platoon 13th Pennine Fusiliers has been found guilty of wilfully destroying property without orders from a superior officer and endangering the lives of fellow soldiers while on duty. The penalty: 14 days Field Punishment Number One."

Mercy was led out into No Man's Land, beyond the barbed wire entanglement, to where a T-shaped post had been set into the ground. He was tied to the post in a crucifixion position, facing the trenches, so the men could see him, abandoned to the torment and torture of the alien sun, and whatever creeping, flying pests and predators might happen by.

A restless mutter arose from the watching troops.

"Silence!" bellowed Sergeant Hobson. "Parade! Parade fall out into working parties. Dismiss!" cried Sergeant Hobson.

Section NCOs began barking their orders and groups fell out, smartly marching off to their work details while Tulliver and Mathers' crew set off in the tank in search of more of the 'petrol fruit' for their newly acquired fuel still.

2 Platoon was due out on another Forage Patrol. They set off over No Man's Land, past Mercy who, despite bruised ribs, black eye and split lip, gave them an encouraging smile and a thumbs up. With uneasy glances back towards their pal they set out across the burnt clearing and across the veldt toward the forest.

Everson was uneasy that Napoo wasn't coming with them. Jeffries wanted to question him and Grantham had given him permission. Jeffries seemed to have Grantham eating out of his hand recently. He had been taking advantage of Grantham's weakened state; the man was obviously susceptible to whatever suggestions Jeffries was making. Of course, it was perfectly possible that Jeffries was just trying to bolster the old man's nerve...

As the Urman entered the dugout, escorted by Sergeant Dixon, Jeffries studied him with some disdain. He didn't see the Noble Savage Everson claimed he saw but a wily indigent. From his occult researches he knew primitive peoples had caches of sacred knowledge forbidden to outsiders.

"Thank you, Dixon, that will be all."

Dixon saluted and left.

"So, you're the barbarian, the one they call Napoo?" said Jeffries as he watched the Urman pick up objects and study them briefly before putting them down and moving onto the next thing that caught his eye. He was like a child. Simple things delighted him greatly. Britannia was a Mother to many such peoples and Jeffries held none of them in any great regard. This man, though, was different. This man was wiry, but it all seemed to be muscle and he had survived to live to an age where his hair had greyed. Obviously he had a survivor's instinct that shouldn't be underestimated. Jeffries reached down to the holster on his Sam Browne belt and slowly undid the revolver cover. He grinned at Napoo as the man looked up at the sound of his new nickname, smiled, and went back to gazing with wonder at the things he saw.

"Everson has not such things," he said. "You are mightier than he is?"

Jeffries allowed himself a smile. The man amused him.

"Oh yes. Mightier than he knows, old chap."

"You are king here, then?"

"No, but I do like the sound of it. Are you not king of your own people?"

"No, only the Ones have kings," said Napoo as he picked up a pen from the small wooden crate that served as a writing desk. He sniffed the instrument then put it down.

"You're not one of the Ones, then?"

"No. Urman."

"The Ones," said Jeffries, "I wanted to ask you about them."

"This is Khungarrii territory. You should not be here. Not safe."

"Yes. So you said. And where are these Kungry –"

"Khungarrii," corrected Napoo, now sniffing, now licking a sealed tin of Tickler's Plum and Apple jam.

Jeffries took it off him and, using a tin opener, scythed it open before handing it back. He couldn't stand the stuff himself. It was just his luck that one of the foods they had did have in large supply was damned Plum and Apple jam.

Napoo stuck his fingers into the tin, scooped out the runny jelly and shoved his fingers into his mouth with great delight. "Mmm hmm," He smacked his lips.

"I saw a gleam over against those hills in a forest out beyond the veldt. A high spire. Is that them? Is that where these Khungarrii of yours live?"

"Aye, that's the Khungarrii Edifice," said Napoo. "Croatoan curse them!"

Jeffries froze.

"What?" he said. That the name of his chosen god should be uttered by one such as this who should not know of him at all stunned Jeffries. This was more than mere coincidence. Within the Great Working there *was* no coincidence. It was another sign. Of that he was sure. He rounded on the savage. "What did you say?"

Napoo was startled. He offered the half eaten tin of jam back to Jeffries. "Forgive me, I didn't not mean to –"

"What did you say?" he asked again, urgency in his voice.

"I – I said Croatoan curse them! Forgive me."

"What do you know of Croatoan?" said Jeffries, advancing on Napoo. "Tell me!"

"Nothing," he answered, puzzled at his host's sudden change in bearing. "It is an old curse that once had meaning to my forebears."

"You don't... worship him?"

"No, it is forbidden."

"By whom?"

"The Ones. There is only one god, GarSuleth, Weaver of the World," said Napoo reverently bowing his head.

Jeffries picked up his journal and leafed impatiently through the pages until he reached one on which was scrawled a symbol. He thrust the page under Napoo's nose. "This symbol. This sign. Do you recognise it, the Sigil of Croatoan?"

"No," said Napoo, shaking his head.

"Are you sure?"

"I have never seen its like."

"Never?"

"No, Only the Ones make such marks."

"What marks?"

"Like these," said Napoo gesturing at the open book. "Like the ones outside, the telling marks."

"The trench signs? Writing? Urmen don't write?"

"We do not know how to make the telling marks."

Jeffries slammed the book down. The rickety table juddered under the impact. These savages were so simple they had no written language. If Napoo was speaking the truth then they were of no immediate use to him. But, clearly, the Khungarrii were. After days of confusion, his path was now clear. These Khungarrii were the key.

"Are you telling me everything?"

"Yes. We do not mark-make."

"What are you not telling me, Napoo?"

"I don't understand."

"This is your world, are you seriously telling me you know nothing more than how to pick fruit and hunt animals?"

"What else is there to know?"

"Don't play games with me, Napoo," said Jeffries, picking up his ceremonial dagger, allowing the blade to glint in the dim light. "Either you tell me what I want to know or I will divine the truth from your entrails."

"All they would tell you are what fruit is good to eat and what animals good to hunt," said Napoo calmly.

There was a commotion outside. Jeffries did not want to be disturbed now. Whoever it was would pay for it. "Stay here," he told Napoo. "I haven't finished with you yet." He heard shouts and rifle fire. He lifted aside his gas curtain and stepped out into the trench. A private almost knocked him over.

"What's going on?" he snapped.

"We're being attacked! They came at us from the rear near the unfinished trenches!"

"Napoo, come with me," Jeffries called back into the dugout. If something was mounting an attack, this savage's knowledge could prove vital. Napoo appeared and he pushed him along the trench, the revolver in the small of his back urging him forwards.

A petrified solider ran down the trench toward them, screaming. "They're not human!" he cried as he tried to barge past Napoo and Jeffries.

"Private! Halt. This is desertion. Turn back or I'll shoot." However, the panic-stricken soldier was no longer listening. Reason had fled. Jeffries pointed his pistol and fired. The man fell back and slithered down the trench wall. Jeffries urged Napoo on. He could see smoke rising now from the newly fortified trench and the noises of battle filled the air. Blue flashes crackled over the lips of the communications trench followed by brief screams. Approaching the rear fire trenches Jeffries saw men retreating towards them along the bays, fighting a defensive action.

"Khungarrii," said Napoo calmly, gazing towards the blue flashes that lit the trenches. "I warned you."

Jeffries glared at Napoo furiously. There was nothing he could do here now. If he were to face these Khungarrii, he would do it on his terms, not theirs. He turned to slip back down the communications trench. Round the traverse, he caught a glimpse of something manlike. A bright blue flash filled his vision. His body went numb and the duckboards swung up to meet him.

CHAPTER TWELVE
"The Sacred Call of 'Friend'…"

"One of these days I'm going to have that buggering bastard Jeffries, officer or no," said Gutsy as they moved swiftly and quietly along now well-trodden paths through the forest, thankful to be out of the heat of the alien sun. They were all painfully aware that, back at the entrenchment, Mercy had to endure its unforgiving glare, tied to the post as part of his punishment. To a man, the Section resented the example Jeffries had made of their pal and Ketch's part in it. Army justice could often be swift and cruel and discipline unavoidable, but there was a point beyond which it ceased to be effective. Given the conditions the men were living and fighting under, morale was brittle and they would only bear so much.

"Keep your voice down," hissed Atkins, nodding forwards to where Ketch ambled along, his ears no doubt burning, "or you'll be up on charges, too."

The routine of food collecting had now become a practised one for 1 Section. They knew now where to find the fruits that would not poison them. They had set traps and nets to catch animals. Fruits they slung into sandbags suspended from a pole carried between Porgy and Gutsy. The rest of the men had emptied their packs and were now carrying them in what they called Forage Order. The constant bombardment of Hun shells seemed a distant memory; many of the men had taken to wearing their regulation soft caps instead of their steel helmets, which proved uncomfortable in the heat.

Ketch had shuffled forward and was talking to Sergeant Hobson.

"Yeah, but Field Punishment?" said Gutsy. "He didn't have to go that far."

"Quiet back there," said Hobson, walking back along the line.

Atkins saw Ketch, up ahead, turn back and watch, scornfully. He pointed at his own eyes, then at Atkins – *I'm watching you.*

"If I hear any more 'mutinous mutterings' I'll make the lot of you sorry you were born," snarled Hobson in a low, dangerous voice. "And you, Atkins. You should appreciate just how stupid your mate Evans was. You nearly died. He knew the consequences when he started that racket. And he took 'em like a man. Scroungers and chancers like him may do you a favour every now and again, but they'll all get caught out somewhere down the line, you mark my words."

"But couldn't the Lieutenant do anything, Sarn't?" asked Porgy.

The Sergeant's face softened. "He did what he could, lad."

"Shh!" hissed Pot Shot. The column froze.

"I don't hear –"

Muffled by the forest canopy and the undergrowth they heard the faint sound of a whistle blown three times.

"The entrenchment!" Ketch blurted.

Blood and sand, thought Atkins, *please God don't say the entrenchment is vanishing without us.*

From the fleeting looks of panic on the others' faces, he could tell they were thinking the same thing.

"Make for the rendezvous point" said Lieutenant Everson. Immediately they dropped the carrying pole and sandbags of fruit and pelted back along their trail, hobnail boots pounding out an urgent tattoo.

It took them ten long agonising minutes of occasional stumbling, shouted encouragement and blasphemous urgings to reach the edge of the forest and Lieutenant Baxter's covering Lewis gun section. They had blown the whistle. Between deep wracking breaths, Atkins peered out across the plain; down the trail they'd made though the tube grass. Nothing seemed amiss.

"Baxter?" queried Everson.

"Shooting, sporadic gunfire from the direction of the entrenchment."

"Flare?"

"No."

"Oh, thank god!" muttered Everson.

"Is it vanishing, sir?" asked Pot Shot, through a hacking smoker's cough.

"No. Signal for that's a red flare. From the gunfire, sounds like they're being attacked. Right. Back to the entrenchment at the double. Set up covering positions and OP at the edge of the razed clearing. Stay under cover of the grass. I want to know what we're getting into before we go charging in blindly."

"Christ," said Atkins. "Now what?" he checked his rifle's magazine and flicked the cut-off open. He didn't like surprises. And this planet was just bloody full of them.

For the last hundred yards or so, 1 Section dropped into a crouch and edged their way forward through the bush, fanning out from the path. Everson peered across the charred earth that lay before the tilted muddy escarpment ahead of them. Smoke rose from beyond the lip and the cries of wounded reached them, carried on the wind.

"Hobson, take three men and proceed to the lip of the entrenchments. Hold that position," said Everson quietly. "We'll cover you. If it's all clear, we'll leapfrog you."

Hobson looked around. "Atkins, Hopkiss, Blood, you're with me."

Gazette, Half Pint, Pot Shot and Ketch took up covering positions in the tube grass. The Lewis gun section set up their gun. To their left Atkins spotted another couple of foraging parties that had returned in answer to the shots and now held back on the edge of the tube grass awaiting further orders. Everson indicated they should wait for his order before advancing.

Keeping low, Atkins followed Hobson as they ran across the scorched earth before throwing himself down against the chalky embankment of Somme mud.

"Atkins," hissed Hobson, with a jerk of his head.

Feeling vulnerable without his battle bowler Atkins cautiously peered over the lip of the mud across the remains of No Man's Land and towards the trenches a couple of hundred yards away. He could make out the tents of the Casualty Clearing Station beyond the Front Line. The remains of several tents were smoking. Figures wandered about dazed. Atkins looked back over his shoulder. "Looks like the aftermath of an attack, Sarn't. I can't see any enemy troops."

"Hopkiss, Blood, get up there with Atkins. Cover the Lieutenant's advance."

They scrambled to the top of the lip alongside Atkins, their rifles aimed, unnaturally, towards their own Front Line as the Lieutenant, Gazette, Pot Shot, Half Pint and Ketch scurried past them before dropping down into the cover of a large shell hole. Further to their right, they saw several other sections moving towards the trenches. There was a brief wait before Everson waved Atkins and the others forwards. Atkins leapt up and ran low across the drying mud, kicking up dust as he did. He slid down into the shell hole, Porgy, Gutsy and Sergeant Hobson almost coming down on top of him.

"I can't see any sign of occupation," said Everson. "Hobson, stay here. I'm going to take a butcher's. Atkins you're with me. Straight for the firing trench."

Atkins took several deep breaths and launched himself out of the shell hole. It felt distinctly odd to be charging your own trenches. This is what the Huns must have seen as they attacked. There was a buzz and crack as a bullet crunched into the crust of mud at his feet. He threw himself aside, into a crater.

"Ally Pally!" called Everson. "Ally Pally!"

A head appeared above the parapet. "Sorry, sir. Thought you were another of them Chatt bastards!"

Everson glanced at Atkins. Chatts? Atkins shrugged and shook his head. Everson stood up and walked towards the fire trench, Atkins following. Behind them, the rest of the section made their way in, along with other forage patrols, alert and nervous. Atkins grabbed a dazed private with haunted eyes.

"What happened?"

"They came out of nowhere."

Atkins shook him out of frustration. "Who? Who did?"

"Them!" said the soldier pointing at a body on the ground nearby, half obscured by the bend of the traverse. "Dozens of 'em."

Atkins took a step towards it. "Blood and sand! Lieutenant, I think you should see this."

"Good God," Everson gasped as he looked down at the corpse before them. Was it some sort of insect? It would take a more scientific mind than his to determine, although it certainly seemed to elicit that level of primal revulsion.

Porgy and Gutsy came up beside them and stared down at the sight.

The body that lay on its back at their feet wasn't human, although its proportions were. It would have stood between five and six feet tall. Its large black eyes were set in a wide flat armoured head and Atkins realised with a shock that he'd seen ones like them before, staring back at him from his hallucinatory episode. Below the eyes, at the bottom of the fused chitinous plates that covered its head was something he scarcely recognised as a mouth. Two shiny black mandibles, closed over a mucus-slick muscular maw. Four smaller articulated palps lay slack and lifeless about it. At the top of its head protruded two antennae, segmented and each about a foot long. One had snapped and lay at an odd angle. Two wiry looking arms, each covered with a series of barbed chitinous plates, extended from shoulder joints in the thorax. Each arm ended in what may have been a hand with two fingers and a prehensile thumb-like appendage.

Where, on a man, one might expect to find the ribcage, this creature had a hardened plate that shimmered with an iridescent gleam. There was a gaping hole in the plate from which a bluish liquid oozed. Atkins poked it with his bayonet. The edges of the hole gave way with a brittle crack. He drove the bayonet home, just to make sure. The thing didn't move.

He thought of the beetles that used to scuttle about his mam's kitchen. He and William used to crush them under their clogs with just such a frail, moist crunch.

Below this was an unarmoured mid-section from where two smaller, less well-formed limbs projected, each ending with a single curved claw of the same iridescent black as its carapace.

"Yrredetti?" asked Atkins.

Everson shook his head. "Wrong colouring. Besides, Napoo said they hunt alone. This must be Khungarrii."

"They're just big fat bloomin' lice!" exclaimed Gutsy. "Nothing more than vermin!" He kicked the creature's thorax. "'Chatts' is bloody right."

"Atkins, Hopkiss, see what you can find out," said Everson, still staring thoughtfully at the alien body before them. "Jellicoe, Otterthwaite and Nicholls, pull together as many able bodied men as possible. I want this entrenchment secure. Hobson, order the men to stand to."

Atkins and Porgy weaved their way through the fire and communications trenches. They came across several Khungarrii dead, lying among the bodies of their own. They stopped for a line of men, their faces roughly bandaged, one hand on the shoulder of the one in front, led, blind and stumbling, to the Casualty Clearing Station.

"Bastards spit acid," said the Lance Corporal leading them.

From a shelled section of trench, they ascended onto the open ground. Between the lines, they passed Hepton who was excitedly filming a group of grinning Tommies posing with a dead Khungarrii, like Big Game hunters. Amid the chaos and aftermath of the attack, Atkins could see the punishment post beyond the wire. Mercy was still there, crucified. His torso was now one great purple and black bruise.

"Mercy!" He ran towards him, stopping only to find a breach in the wire entanglement.

"Huu –"

"Mercy, you okay?"

"'S it look like?"

"Hang in there, mate."

"Oh, ha ha, very funny," said Mercy through dry, cracked, lips. "You should be in the musical hall, Only." Atkins held him up as Porgy used his bayonet to cut the rope binding his wrists.

"You two, what do think you're doing? I'll have your names for this!" It was Ketch. "Atkins, I might have known it were you!"

"Back off, Ketch," snarled Porgy. "Lieutenant Everson asked us to find witnesses. No thanks to you and Gilbert the Filbert, Mercy here was front and centre for the whole attack."

Mercy managed a weak grin. "Nice to see you, too, Corp," he rasped before insolently hawking a gob of mucus in Ketch's direction.

Mercy sat on an ammo box, Everson and 1 Section gathered round him. He gulped down the proffered water as Everson and the others waited impatiently.

"What happened?" asked Porgy, indicating the confusion around them. "Where's Edith?"

"I don't know. Couldn't see much from where I was," he said hoarsely. "They moved fast, rounded up prisoners. I think they must have come in through one of the unfinished OP saps. They must have taken out the sentries. Nobody saw them until they were in the trenches. I heard some shooting, then they swarmed across the top, some leaping ten, twenty feet at a go. Ugly buggers, like great big fleas."

"Yeah, we seen 'em," said Half Pint.

"They were well organised. Some of them spit, like, an acid. Others had lances and backpacks. Looked like a flammenwerfer, but it shot blue crackling fire stuff. Like electricity. But mostly they had swords and spears. They seemed to take a lot of loot as well, trench equipment, weapons and the like."

Among the missing were Captain Grantham, Padre Rand, Lieutenant Jeffries, Napoo, the three nurses and about twenty-five other ranks.

"Seems to have been a well-planned raid," Sergeant Hobson said bitterly.

"We've got to go after them, sir," said Porgy.

"We will, Hopkiss, we will," said Everson. "But first things first. We have to secure the entrenchments. We have to wait for the other Forage Parties to come back. And we have to find out exactly what we're up against. Then we have to put together a plan of attack and get a party together to go after them. Rushing into this won't do us any favours."

It seemed though, from Ration Dump rumour, that wasn't good enough for a section of Jeffries' Platoon, who had grabbed their guns and just gone after them; it was twenty minutes before anyone noticed that they were missing.

"Idiots!" said Everson. He was now the ranking infantry officer in the entrenchment. "Hobson, order the NCOs to take roll calls. Find out if anyone else is missing."

Tulliver and the tank crew returned in *Ivanhoe* from their petrol fruit forage trip, unaware of the raid until they were met with the organised chaos of mobilising infantry.

"Tulliver, how quickly can you get your machine in the air?" asked Everson.

"Give me ten minutes," said Tulliver.

"They've got about three hours on us by now. Can you track them, see which way they're headed?"

"Yes, I can do that but the state of the strip isn't perfect. I don't want to do too many take off and landings there without flattening the ground more."

"Right, I understand, but for now?"

"I'll chance it."

Everson watched anxiously as Tulliver and a couple of soldiers pulled the aeroplane out of its makeshift tarpaulin and brushwood hangar. The pilot waved at him as he stood by his machine. Everson raised his hand in reply and watched the young lad climb into his cockpit and strap himself in. A soldier pulled the propeller. Contact. Tulliver ran up his engine, testing it. Finally, the Sopwith began to run forwards eagerly. Tulliver gave it its head, the tail left the ground before the end of the take-off strip, and it lifted up across the fronds of tube grass. The aeroplane wheeled around the entrenchment before climbing and veering off, following the path Everson told him the arthropod raiders had taken. Everson turned from the aeroplane and headed back towards the trenches and the Casualty tents.

In the dank-smelling tent, Everson sat down next to Poilus. The young savage sat up in his cot, drinking a dixie of water. He looked disconcertingly out of place wearing striped pyjama bottoms. God knows where they'd come from. "Tell me about the Khungarrii," he said.

"They are of the Ones," said Poilus, as if that explained all.

"They've taken my men. Napoo, too. We intend to get them back but we need to know what they're going to do with them."

Poilus sighed. "Khungarrii always take Urmen. They make them work for them in Khungarr; building, mending, growing, cleaning..."

"But not you. They didn't take you."

"The sick and frail are no use to them," said Poilus with a hint of disgust at his own weakened state.

"Because they can't work them as slaves?"

"I don't know this word."

Everson didn't feel like explaining. He pressed on with his questions. "How many Khungarrii in Khungarr?"

"I do not know. Many. A great number."

"And Urmen?"

"Many."

"Damn," muttered Everson. For someone who resented the weight of responsibility, it looked like his load had just become a lot heavier.

Tulliver banked his machine with a little left rudder and turned to follow the trail that was plainly visible from this height, cutting a swath through the tube grasses of the valley, but of the raiders and their prisoners there was no sign. The valley side's fell away diminishing into foothills before a vast veldt opened up below him. He followed the trail across it for some twenty miles until he saw it vanish into a huge forest that seemed to extend for hundreds of square miles. Amid the forest, something glinted in the sun. A large tower-like structure rising above the tree canopy, twinkling as if –

The engine started to cough and splutter fearfully. That wasn't good. Best head for home. He throttled up, pulled the stick back to gain more height, and turned the machine towards the khaki coloured smudge of drying mud in the distance.

"Just another ten minutes, old girl," he urged. But he wasn't going to get it. He grimaced, throttled back and put the nose down before shutting the engine off. Better not to risk the engine, not in this place; there was no machine-shop to repair it if it went. The choking cough of the engine silenced, the only sound now was the wind whistling through the struts and interplane wires as he glided in, making for the burnt strip ahead. He circled to make his landing, skimmed over the top of the tube grass and came down a little inelegantly for his tastes, but without any further mishap. He jumped out to examine the machine. The fault didn't take too long to find. The petrol feed pipe had been crudely punctured. Since there was no corresponding hole in the fuselage, it could only indicate that someone had tampered with it from inside. Luckily, it shouldn't be too hard to fix. The control lines were another matter. Someone had tried to file through those as well. If they had failed while he was in the air he would have lost complete control. Thankfully, whoever it was hadn't done their job too well. Nevertheless, there was only one word for it. Sabotage.

It had been Porgy's idea, but nobody was against it, if it took his mind off Edith for a while.

"Gilbert the Filbert's had it coming," said Porgy as they crept down the comm trench.

"We can do his dugout over and blame it on them Chatts. No one'll ever be the wiser. I'll bet there'll be some good loot in there. Whisky. God, what I wouldn't give for some good whisky."

Mercy had insisted on coming with them, hissing, sucking and cursing with pain from his beating all the way.

It wasn't long before they reached the switch where Jeffries' dugout was located.

"We'll be up for it an' no mistake if we get caught, fellas," said Pot Shot hesitantly.

"We're here now. We're only looking for a little payback, Pot Shot, that's all," said Mercy, wincing. "The least that bastard can give me is a decent malt." He pushed back the gas curtain and stepped down into the dugout.

Atkins looked apologetically at Pot Shot and shrugged, "Look, stay here and keep watch. We won't be long, I'll stop him from doing anything too stupid." He knew this was a bad idea, but then so was going over the top and that had never stopped them before. He dealt with it the same way: one step in front of another. It was dark in there and smelt of stale sweat, hair oil and damp earth, and there was another peculiar odour, like sour potpourri. It began getting crowded as Gutsy and Gazette entered behind him, their bulks blocking out what little light filtered down from the entrance.

Porgy went over to the small crate that served as a writing desk. On it were a pack of worn cards and a leather-bound journal surrounded by a circle of salt. "Diary of an officer," he said, holding it up with a leer and a wink. He riffled through the pages. His face screwed up in frustration and disappointment.

"'Ere, these entries are all in code. Look, there are symbols and things... I can't make head nor tail of it."

"Let me have a look," said Gutsy, picking up the volume and licking the tip of his index finger before turning a page.

"I'm telling you. It's in code," said Porgy. "You don't reckon he's in military intelligence, do you? We're in deep if he is."

"Bloody 'ell, you're right," said Gutsy, throwing the book down as if it had stung him. "You think he's a Jerry spy? He seems the sort. Hates his own men worse than Fritz."

Mercy casually glanced around the place, looking for anything of value. Seeing nothing of immediate or obvious interest, he bent over with a grunt and began feeling about under the thin straw mattress on the wire frame bed. "I wouldn't be at all surprised. I always thought there was something a little 'off' about him. He was always a bit too full of himself. Only, give us a hand will you?"

Atkins dropped down on his knees by his friend, who, finding nothing under the mattress, put his hand under the bed. Mercy pulled a suitcase into the light, the oxblood red leather case scuffing along the dirt-covered floor as they did so. Half-heartedly, Atkins tried opening it and was relieved to find it locked. But Mercy wasn't going to be beaten. He pulled his bayonet from its sheath, jimmied the lock and opened the suitcase.

"Bloody hell."

"Hey, you chaps ought to see this," said Gutsy, pulling at a loose-fitting piece of tea-chest panelling. It came away exposing a sackcloth curtain which he pulled back to reveal a hidden niche. "What do you make of this little lot?"

They peered into the niche. There were ornate silver candleholders and a ceremonial dagger of some exotic foreign design, along with a black stone with a symbol carved in it.

"Loot?"

"Looks expensive, like he's robbed a church or museum or summat."

"Yeah, but why keep 'em there? Not exactly hidden is it?"

Atkins turned his attention back to the contents of the suitcase. There, he found a private's uniform with patches indicating it to be from the Black Foresters – the Midland Light Infantry, and an Artillery officer's uniform, neither had any links with the Pennines. There were five pay books, one of a Private and the others of several officers and an assortment of identity discs, cap badges and regimental patches. Stuffed under the uniforms were maps and papers; maps of Harcourt Sector showing British artillery positions and barrage targets, Battalion papers with dates of leaves and transfers; some old, some yet blank and undated.

"Something bloody odd's going on here," said Atkins.

"Who'd have stuff like this but a bloody spy!" said Mercy. "Gawd almighty!"

"Do you think the Lieutenant knows?" asked Porgy.

"Do *you* want to ask him?" Half Pint said. "Sir, we were just looting the Lieutenant's dugout when we came across these?"

"We have to tell him," said Atkins. "It's the right thing to do. If we don't it's *failing to inform*. Look, I trust Lieutenant Everson. I don't trust Jeffries. And certainly not now. There's something rum going on here and frankly I'd feel a lot more comfortable if we had the Lieutenant on our side."

Unfortunately, Atkins couldn't go straight to Everson. This was the army. You didn't just barge up to an officer. It wasn't done. You had to go through an NCO. He had to go through Hobson. He was more worried about the Sergeant's reaction than the Lieutenant's. Nevertheless, with the 'evidence' bundled up in an Army blanket, Atkins sought him out.

The Platoon Sergeant looked at him sternly and not without a little suspicion, glancing through the items, singling out the coded journal and the exotic knife as Atkins explained his finds.

"I think you'd better come with me, lad," he said.

They found Everson with Tulliver in the Company HQ. He was having a heated exchange of words with the Flying Officer.

"Sir," said Sergeant Hobson. "Atkins here has something to say. I think you'll want to hear it."

"This'll have to wait, Tulliver," said Everson. Exasperated, Tulliver turned to leave the tent. "What is it Atkins, I've got a lot on my plate right now."

"It's about Gilb– Lieutenant Jeffries, sir."

Tulliver turned from the tent flap when he heard the name. "Wait, did you say Jeffries?"

"We were combing the entrenchments, sir, and thought we heard something in one of the dugouts," said Atkins. "It was Lieutenant Jeffries' one, sir. We- we found this stuff scattered about the floor." Atkins emptied the blanket's contents; clothing, papers, maps, pay books, discs and museum loot onto the table. "We didn't pay much heed at first, sir, until we noticed the pay books. They aren't for men in his platoon, sir. They aren't even for men in this battalion. Blood thought he might be a Jerry spy, sir, and that we ought to report it."

"Stop right there, Atkins," said Everson. "Those are very serious charges. You can't just bandy about such accusations like that."

"But, sir..."

"Leave this with me. Thank you Atkins. That will be all. Dismissed."

"Sir."

Atkins saluted and left, feeling disappointed and dismayed by Everson's noncommittal reaction. However, he told himself, he'd done the right thing this time, or at least he hoped he had.

Although his dismissal of Atkins might have been brusque, it was only because the evidence in front of him troubled Everson. He been sorting out the logistics of a raid on Khungarr and frankly the odds weren't in their favour. "Do you believe him, Hobson?"

"I believe they found this stuff in Jeffries' dugout, yes, sir."

"And what about these? Any of these names mean anything to you?"

The Sergeant flicked through the pay books and shook his head. "No, sir."

Tulliver began leafing through the books himself, opening and discarding one after another. "Wait. This one. Hibbert. I know this name."

"From where?" asked Everson.

"Artillery officer. I took him up for a look-see three or four weeks ago. It's not something I've done often, so it stuck in my mind. Fella had this queer way of signalling 'okay', with his thumb and forefinger, which I thought was odd. Most people use a thumbs up. Then when I met that chap, Jeffries, I thought he looked damned familiar, you remember? He half convinced me we hadn't met at all, then, when I took him up the other day, he used the self-same signal. I'd swear it's the same man, although he didn't have a moustache then. And this," he said, picking up the officer's jacket with the artillery patches and badges. "This was Hibbert's mob. How do you explain this? It could have been he who sabotaged my machine, because it *was* sabotage. The petrol feed was punctured after he thought I recognised him. And he couldn't have failed to notice that spire I saw in the distance, reflecting the sun the way it did. You didn't believe me ten minutes ago, but surely you can't ignore this? The man's up to something, though God knows what his bloody game is."

"Hmm." Everson studied the papers for a while and then looked at the artillery barrage maps which showed a pattern of bombardment marked over the Harcourt Sector "There's something peculiar about these maps, too."

He turned to the Flying Officer and came to a decision. "All right, maybe there are allegations to answer here, Tulliver, but Jeffries will have to wait. Our main objective is to rescue our people and our secondary objective is to free these subjugated Urmen from the... Khungarrii." He turned to Sergeant Hobson, who was leafing through a sheaf of Jeffries' blank battalion orders. "Sergeant, get the men on parade."

*　　*　　*

Twenty minutes later Everson stood under the ragged Union Jack, before a parade of weary, discontented men as NCOs barked and cajoled them into order. It had long been a point of contention among the Red Tabs that, at the Front, the men's aggression should be channelled into attacks and trench raids to prevent them becoming an idle, disaffected rabble. While he was sure they would be glad of the opportunity of action, he may well have to convince them of it. However, as much as they needed an objective and motivation, above all they needed hope.

"Men!" he began. "You know by now that these Khungarrii have captured some of our own. We will get them back, but this cannot be our sole objective. For, whatever reason we find ourselves here, we are still British. We are a long way from home, on a foreign world where Man has been subjugated by an inhuman race who may very well know how we came to be here. They may even know how we can return home. But we also know our duty. It is clear. It is the reason you took the oath and the King's shilling in the first place. It is the reason you volunteered."

"We didn't volunteer for this!" came an anonymous cry. There were mutterings of agreement among the ranks.

Everson ignored them. "Did we turn our backs in '14 when Belgium pleaded for our aid? No! We answered their call. Honour bade us do no less. Can we do any less now, when our fellow Man suffers here under the oppression of a cockroach Kaiser?

"Or will we let the fate of these Urmen be our fate too? I say to these Khungarrii that whatever you do to the least of my brethren you do unto me. We will show them that 'no gallant son of Britain to a tyrant's yoke shall bend.' We may no longer be on the Western Front, but we have found ourselves a new Front. Here is where we draw the line, here in this Somme mud, where we always have. This corner of a foreign field is all we have left of England and we shall defend it – and all it stands for.

"I want volunteers to mount an expedition to free our companions and perhaps rouse these subjugated Urmen into rebellion. We do not know the number of the enemy or their disposition, but we put the kibosh on the Kaiser. We can put the kibosh on these Khungarrii! What do you say, Pennines?"

A raucous cheer rent the air. Everson's chest heaved as much with pride as with relief. These were the men he knew, men with a purpose, with a challenge. These were the 'Broughtonthwaite Mates.'

"I think you got 'em, sir," said Hobson.

CHAPTER THIRTEEN
"Hasty Orisons"

Small ripples of consciousness lapped at the shores of Jeffries' oblivion, washing up a flotsam of sensations. A flare of light. Flashes of russet and damson.

Darkness.

A feeling of warmth. An aroma of mint and sweat.

Silence.

A cacophony of noises; cracks, crunches, sobs, howls, whistles and clicks, sloshed over into the silence surrounding him.

Jeffries came round to find himself lying on narrow wooden planking that moved under him with a disconcerting rocking motion. Looking up, walls woven from branches arose either side of him, framing a view of violet and magenta foliage that drifted past above. It took several minutes before full use returned to his arms and legs and he was able to sit up. Pins-and-needles lingered in his limbs and spots cluttered his vision like drifting Very lights.

He found himself in a long narrow cradle-like structure with Napoo and several despondent privates. He peered over the edge. He could see that the cradle was slung from the side of a great grub-like creature easily twice the height of an elephant and some twenty to thirty yards long. Along its length, it wore a great harness of ropes and straps from which hung similar cradles containing further captives. Presumably, they also hung from the far side in a similar arrangement. Along the back of the mammoth caterpillar-like crawler, their captors – insects the size of men – patrolled its length, looking down on their captives, their antennae, twitching.

As the path curved gently he was able to look over the edge of the basket and see another caterpillar beast ahead of them. It crawled along on stumpy legs with an elegance and agility that belied its bulk. A rider sat behind its head on a howdah, guiding the thing with a series of reins. It cleared the trail before them, crushing undergrowth and boughs in it way or eating its way through overgrown vegetation. Another larval beast of burden brought up the column to the rear; this one slightly shorter and covered in sharp spines. It was purple-black in colour with fearsome looking yellow markings on its face. Whether this was just defensive colouring or not, Jeffries couldn't tell, but it definitely looked more warlike than did its pale, plodding cousin.

Around him, the small cheerless khaki-clad band of warriors sat hunched in groups under the ever-watchful eyes of their captors. Some Tommies glanced back with glowering, baleful and resentful stares, others with fear and anxiety, some muttered amongst themselves about 'the Chatts'. Jeffries could only assume they meant their captors and not the lice that infected their clothes. A snort of derision escaped his nostrils. It was a suitably derogatory term. However, where they felt beaten and defeated, he experienced a curious sense of self-confidence he had not felt since he arrived here on this world. He sat with the rest of the prisoners, although he never for one moment considered himself one of their number. He felt buoyed. He had wanted to talk to the Khungarrii and here they were. Of course, those great insects, walking upright in a dark chitinous mockery of man, didn't talk to him, but then he deduced they were merely soldiers. Soldier ants.

Peculiarly, with every peristaltic ripple that took him further and further from the entrenchment and the possibility of it returning to the Somme without him, Jeffries began to feel increasingly free.

Ahead, in another cradle, he could see Captain Grantham slumped, head bowed, defeated. The man was a joke. A weak insipid leader whose mind could barely take the brunt of war, let alone this magnificent world. He had long ago exceeded the limits of his comprehension. The nurses sobbed, cried and comforted one another; the apparent repugnance of their captors reducing them to the emotional imbecilic wrecks their gender inevitably devolved to under stress.

The soldiers weren't tied or chained and several decided to leap over the side of their cradle and made a break for freedom into the surrounding jungle to the encouraging cheers of their less opportunistic fellows. The vicarious victory didn't last long, brutally quashed as it was by the subsequent roars and screams from the undergrowth that, to Jeffries amusement, muted his fellows enthusiasm; there was no need for shackles when their captors knew the environment would seek to kill them at every turn.

There were about eighty of the Khungarrii, some riding in cradles, some stood on the backs of the caterpillar beasts, others walking alongside them. If they fell behind, they would use their powerful legs, bounding ten or twenty feet at a time until they caught up. Jeffries made sure to keep Napoo close to him. He was his best source of information right now and, for the moment at least, that made him valuable. He asked low whispered questions out of the side of his mouth.

"Where are the Khungarrii taking us?"

"To Khungarr," replied Napoo. There was no doubt the Urman might escape and indeed survive, but he obviously had mixed feelings and felt some loyalty to the soldiers.

"Are all Khungarrii like these?"

"No, these are Scentirrii. Soldier caste. You can tell by their armour. It is thicker and heavier than those of the Worker or Anointed castes. They spit a burning spray."

From behind came the irritating mumbles of that sham priest, muttering his feeble invocations and prayers. A sneer curled Jeffries' lip as he listened and he shook his head in disbelief.

Some of their captors held hollow lances attached to clay packs on their backs. Some sort of gun? Occasionally they would threaten the captives with them, chattering unintelligibly through gnashing mandibles in their harsh, guttural language.

"There!" hissed Napoo, grabbing Jeffries' arm and pointing. Through brief gaps in the canopy, Jeffries caught sight of a huge mound-like edifice. It must have been hundreds of feet high. Its colour was the same dark cinnamon upon which the caterpillar beasts walked, flecks of mica bound into its walls reflecting the sunlight in a myriad places and directions. Jeffries realised that this must have been what had seen from the aeroplane.

Jeffries' heart sank. He had been hoping for something more... *civilised*, that would belittle everything the British Empire had to offer. Nevertheless, the brief glimpse afforded him by the aeroplane couldn't do justice to the enormous scale of the structure. This was a feat of engineering on a par with that of the ancient pyramids of Egypt. Its sheer height and bulk dwarfed many of the great and noble British Institutions, although it could not match them for grandeur.

As they neared the edifice, the trees grew thinner and the path along which they travelled grew wider. They left the forest and entered a huge, well-managed clearing that spread for hundreds of yards around the earthen edifice. The sight drew gasps and groans of despair from the others in marked contrast to the seemingly excited clicks and chittering from the Chatts alongside them. Huge asymmetrical buttresses rose up the sides of the tower to varying heights as if shoring up the earthen mound. Small balconies could be seen dotted about the shell of the edifice, each occupied by an insect.

As the great caterpillar beasts undulated across the clearing, Jeffries noticed lines of other arthropods filing from various forest paths towards apertures in the base of the mound. They were of a different genus to their captors, less well armoured with smaller heads and shorter antennae. As they approached, Jeffries saw that men – Urmen – were among their number, carrying baskets or dragging litters, transporting food and materials to the edifice under the watchful eyes of the accompanying Khungarrii.

In the cradle ahead of him, Jeffries could hear those damn women wailing at the sight. And from behind came the throttled voice of the Padre, "Oh Lord, we are delivered into bondage."

As they passed into the shadow of the edifice, a large archway gaped before them and they entered into a great cathedral–like space. There the larval beasts were drawn to a halt against raised jetties, berthed there like boats so that the passengers, guards and captives alike might make an efficacious exit from the cradles. They were then led up sloping passages, before coming to a circular portal.

The door seemed to be made of tough, fibrous plant material, covered with sharp, close-set thorns. One of the Chatts hissed at the door, expelling a spray from its mouth. The portal recoiled from the chemical mist, dilating open. Once the last man was ushered through, the door sealed behind him. Twenty-five soldiers, Napoo and three nurses found themselves incarcerated in a circular cell.

Jeffries looked around their gaol. He noted that this side of the door was also bristling with close set thorns. Dim light filtered down from small windows high in the wall of the chamber. Also high up in the wall was a hole, from which could be heard a profusion of clicks and pops and from which proceeded a draught of air. A ventilation system, Jeffries thought. There was another source of light coming from a small hole in the floor at the far side of the room. Jeffries, suspecting what it was, peered over it gingerly. Through the hole, he could see the side of the tower plunging vertiginously away. The hole was a *garderobe* of sorts, a primitive toilet. Well, that was something, he supposed. He looked around the rest of the chamber. In places, the rough cinnamon-coloured walls were shiny, having been worn smooth over time by previous occupants, presumably. Captain Grantham sat against the wall, all pretence gone now, his authority all but evaporated. "I'm sorry. I'm sorry," he kept muttering. Jeffries, on the other hand, felt entirely calm and was quite content to wait.

*   *   *

He waited some hours and amused himself watching a group of Tommies commandeer one of the nurse's white aprons and push it down out of the garderobe, to hang like a signal flag for any potential rescuers to see.

It was several hours before the membranous plant-like door dilated open again. A few of the Tommies, who had been muttering together, suddenly rushed the aperture; no doubt in the hope of escape.

"No!" cried Napoo, but it was too late. Crackling blue bolts of electrical energy met them as two Khungarrii Scentirrii discharged their lances. The soldiers jerked spasmodically for a moment before the light died and they crumpled to the floor. One of the nurses let out a scream, though the involuntary twitching of the fallen bodies showed that they were still alive. The two guards then stood to either side of the doorway, holding their lances.

Three more arthropod creatures entered the chamber. One was tall and slender and wore a light cloak with a cowl over its head, covering its antenna. Its chitin was smooth and off-white, like bone china. Other than its eyes, maw and antennae, the dermal bone of its head was a featureless ovoid. Beneath the cloak, the creature wore a long length of tasselled white cloth wrapped over its right shoulder and down across its thorax, through which stunted, vestigial middle limbs tipped with single claws protruded.

Hunched with subservience, the second Chatt was of a similar build. It wore no cloak but it did wear the same manner of cloth, though it had fewer tassels. Was that a rank thing? Jeffries realised its antennae were broken off, leaving little more than stumps.

The third Chatt was more thickly built and heavily armoured than its companions, its faceplate flatter and broader with a suggestion of horns or antler nubs. It was similar in build and stature to the Khungarrii warriors behind it but for the surcoat of scarlet cloth it wore over its heavily armoured form, which did little to hide the bony protuberances rising from its armour.

The cloth they wore seemed to be some form of silk, though whether it was spun by the creatures themselves or farmed from another species Jeffries could not fathom; the garments served no practical purpose that he could see, they were probably more ceremonial, like ecclesiastical vestments, he surmised.

"Who among you speaks for your herd?" the tall, cowled one rasped, the clicking of its mandibles punctuating its dialogue. It spoke with a breathless, hissing vocalisation as if, like a cancer patient struggling to communicate via oesophageal speech, it was forcing itself to use organs for purposes other than for which they had evolved. All eyes turned warily towards Captain Grantham. He looked up with red-rimmed eyes, hardly seeming to comprehend what was happening. Jeffries watched the man struggle briefly with his conscience before remaining seated, stifling sobs. He felt no pity for the broken man. He was half-tempted to stand himself, but he had no idea of the Chatts' intentions. They could merely want to kill the leader. He would wait and see.

After a moment Padre Rand stood and, faltering, cleared his throat.

"I am. These people are under my protection," said the chaplain, his voice cracking as he held aloft his battered leather Bible, "and that of our Lord God, who watches over us."

Jeffries gave the man kudos for that. That was one thing you could say about the Catholic chaplains. They had guts, going up to the Front Line with only a copy of the Bible and their faith for protection. That was what endeared them to the men generally, that and the fact that many of them came from the lower classes and weren't all well-to-do la-de-da-types, like the C of E chaplains.

There was a brief discussion among the Chatts, with some animated waving of antennae, before they turned back to address the Padre.

However, Jeffries did not want this man, this mewling milksop of a shepherd, to speak for him, to assume authority over him.

Whatever secrets and confidences these creatures had to share, they were his. He would not give up now. Seeing that it was safe, at least for now, Jeffries rose to his feet and coughed politely. "Thank you, there's no need, Padre," he said. He turned to the Chatts. "I'm next in command."

Padre Rand, unsure, looked at him then down at his Bible. Jeffries put a reassuring hand on his shoulder. "Sit down, Padre. This is my responsibility."

Padre Rand nodded and sank thankfully to the floor.

Jeffries stepped forward, his arms wide.

"I am Lieutenant Gilbert Jeffries, Number 4 Platoon, C Company, 13th Battalion of the Pennine Fusiliers."

The tall, regal Chatt regarded him, its antennae waving gently in his direction.

"This One is Sirigar, liya-dhuyumirri, high anointed one of the Khungarrii Shura," it said, its mandibles clicking and rubbing together like knitting needles. "That One is Chandar, this one's gon-dhuyumirri olfactotum," it indicated the smaller, submissive Chatt, and then the larger creature. "And that One is Rhengar, Scenturion, njurru-scentirri of Khungarr."

Introductions complete, the creature turned back to the huddled captives. "This One offers you a blessing in the name of GarSuleth," it said. It opened its arms, pulling wide the robe it wore, revealing more clearly the smaller vestigial limbs at its abdomen, also splayed, and then raised its head. From somewhere within its mouthparts it sprayed mist into the air. Jeffries breathed in and, within seconds, recognised the feeling of mild drug-induced euphoria. Keeping eye contact with the round, glassy unblinking eyes before him he inhaled again, slowly, deeply, deliberately.

Edith hugged Nelly and Sister Fenton for reassurance. Some of the men closed ranks in front of them. The horrors of the last few days had begun to numb her, but the sound of the Officer's voice picked at the thick scab of denial that had grown over her recent experiences to the raw emotional wound beneath. There was something about his tone, supercilious and defiant. The insect spoke back. In English. Edith could feel the hairs on the back of her neck bristle with fear. There was a hiss of spray as the creature dosed the air with a vapour from its mouth. Almost immediately, the world seemed to slow down. The fears and terrors of the recent past lifted from her, like dandelion clocks drifting away on her outward breath. A languid sigh escaped her lips as she sank down to the floor with her companions. Senses baffled, a great lethargy overcame her. She looked up. The officer was still standing as the others sank to the floor around him. She was sure she knew his voice but her thoughts had become as thick and slow as treacle and then they ceased to bother her altogether. These creatures would not harm them. She forced her eyes slowly upward and looked at them, feeling content.

Jeffries smiled. Rather helpfully, his own personal drug use had rendered him less susceptible than his fellows.

"Last man standing," he said with a wry smile.

The antennae stumps on the smaller creature were moving feebly. It reminded Jeffries of the hospitals back in 'Bertie with their beds full of raw amputees, their fresh tender stumps waggling clumsily, as if manipulating phantom limbs.

"Interesting defensive technique," he said, "dosing potential threats with a mild euphoric."

Rhengar spoke, preceded by a curious expansion of its chest, as if the creature was unfamiliar with filling its lungs with enough air for the effort of speech. Jeffries found the process quite engrossing.

"You will come with us," it said.

Rhengar turned to address the accompanying scentirrii in the harsh guttural smattering and clicks of its own tongue. They went over and picked up the Padre, who looked at them happily.

"Both of you."

*   *   *

They were taken out though the membranous aperture of the gaol chamber and led along passageways that sloped gently upwards and spiralled round. Set in niches along the way, luminescent lichen glowed, giving off a gentle blue-white light.

Sirigar walked on ahead, its silken vestments billowing out behind it. Before it now walked a smaller Chatt, some sort of juvenile nymph, perhaps, Jeffries thought. Its armour was translucent and not yet fully hardened and it swung some sort of censer before it, the heady incense masking all other smells. The accompanying Khungarr scentirrii escorted Jeffries and the Padre, while Rhengar brought up the rear.

Chandar was limping badly on one leg and attempting to keep up with Sirigar. Jeffries watched it trying to engage the creature in its own language. Its chattering grew excited before being abruptly cut off by a harsh plosive exclamation from Sirigar. Chandar dropped back, almost sheepishly, to walk beside Jeffries. The creature looked up at him, its antenna stumps twitching. "Your clothing is unusual," it said, picking at the cloth of his jacket.

"If you mean clean, then yes. I pride myself on my appearance," Jeffries brushed the Chatt's questing fingers away from his jacket before straightening his tie. "I find people respond favourably to a good first impression. It's always worked for me."

Chandar looked at him. Jeffries was used to reading people, prided himself on it in fact, but it was frustratingly impossible to read the expressionless facial plates of his captors. The tone of voice they used offered few clues either, speaking in what was, to them, a foreign language.

"The Khungarrii have been watching you for some time," it chittered. "The presence of your herd has provoked much debate."

"So I saw," said Jeffries, nodding towards Sirigar.

"Are you an anointed one? Dhuyumirri of your herd, like Sirigar? That One is high anointed one of the Khungarrii Shura."

"Oh, if it's faith you want, ask him," said Jeffries, jerking his head at the chaplain. "He's full of it."

More scentirrii marched past. Approaching Chatts obediently stopped to let the party pass. Urmen, on the other hand, vanished out of sight down side passages at their approach; heads bowed, eyes averted. Jeffries caught sight of them cowering in openings or cloister-like passages. Sirigar swept on past them all. The creature led them to a spacious and well-lit passage, whose dominating feature was an imposing ornate opening, decorated around its edge with some sort of hieroglyphs. Jeffries very much wanted to examine them, but he wasn't given the opportunity.

"We are come," Chandar chittered. "The chambers of the Anointed Ones, the goro dhuyumirrii."

A strong smell of incense greeted Jeffries from the darkened void beyond the door, an infusion of aromas that overwhelmed his senses and began to sting the inside of his nostrils, making his eyes water. Sirigar entered and the scentirrii ushered Jeffries and Rand into the chamber after, Chandar and Rhengar following.

The walls of a great domed chamber rose up, disappearing into the gloom above. Around the walls were curved man-sized alcoves that extended up from the ground, most were in shadow and the few he could see were occupied by more Chatts, who stood in them, facing the wall, their heads bowed. A low soft susurration filled the space, echoing in the dark space above. There was a noise like the soft clatter of cutlery in a canteen that, Jeffries realised, was the constant ticking and scissoring of mandibles in prayer. This was obviously some sort of sacred space, a temple of some sort, he mused.

Overhead, in the gloom, was what appeared to be a giant web. Sirigar paused to perform a gesture of deference and worship as they passed beneath it, clicking in what Jeffries assumed were reverent tones. The web, or what it represented, must have some great significance for them and he recalled what Napoo had said about this GarSuleth weaving the world. He noticed that some points on the web had been picked out with pieces of the bioluminescent lichen, but the meaning of their arrangement was lost on him.

"Pay homage to GarSuleth, the creator of all. Very few Urmen have the privilege of entering these chambers," said Chandar, bowing its head, touching its hands to the base of its antennae and then to its thorax and waiting for Jeffries and Rand to do the same.

Even through his euphoria, Rand frowned slowly. "I will not bow to a heathen god," he slurred drunkenly.

A hiss escaped from Rhengar's mouthparts. The scentirrii stepped closer, their lances poised, ready to punish any perceived blasphemy.

Jeffries, unwilling to lose whatever trust he might have gained, grabbed Rand firmly by the upper arm and brought his mouth close to the chaplain's ear. "Just do it, Padre. We're in the midst of a nest of insect savages. If you know anything of entomology, there are probably a hundred ways they might kill us and I, for one, do not intend to be a martyr. Now bow!"

Reluctantly the Padre repeated the movement Chandar had shown them, and Jeffries did likewise. The scentirrii relaxed their stance and, as they continued their way across the chamber, Jeffries glanced up at the web. Was it home to some primitive creature that they kept and worshipped as a god? He briefly envisioned being cocooned and left as a sacrifice to some great bloated thing and then, more pleasantly, imagined the Padre there instead.

They were ushered through an arch at the far side of the room and along a series of passages and interconnecting chambers where members of Sirigar and Chandar's caste were engaged in various alchemical tasks. Finally, they were led into a smaller room, the main feature of which was several large piles of plundered trench equipment. At a glance Jeffries saw thigh boots, scaling ladders, waterproof capes, cooking utensils, fleabags, rifles, an old grenade catapult, trench mortar shells, a primus stove, Mills bombs, periscopes, a pickelhaube, latrine buckets, a gas gong, a sniper's loophole plate, several steel helmets, cases of small arms ammunition and, he noticed – partially hidden by tarpaulin – what looked to be several rusted old pressurised canisters of chlorine gas. Where the hell had they found those?

"These things are unknown to the Ones," said Rhengar. "They stink of decay and corruption as do you. The Ones would know their uses and your intentions."

"Intentions?" said Jeffries.

He was being judged and everything hung on how well he passed the test. He assumed that if they found out the true nature of some of the things around them, then whatever dialogue they might have would be cut very short indeed. A degree of diplomacy was called for.

"Most nomadic Urmen know better than to resist the Ones," continued Rhengar, "yet your herd is large and aggressive and you have made your clumsy delvings in Khungarrii territory. Our scentirrii were alerted to your presence spinnings ago. Your odours were carried before you on the breath of GarSuleth. The Khungarrii could not fail to notice it, it overpowered everything, almost obscuring the sacred scents themselves."

"And the Unguents of Huyurarr have long heralded the coming of a great corruption. There are those amongst the Ones who, upon sensing your putrescence, fear for their very existence," said Sirigar. "Are those Ones wrong?"

To Jeffries it sounded very much like the case was already stacking up against them. He had to think fast.

"If GarSuleth wills it," he said.

Chandar had been rummaging through the pile of looted trench items with a degree of curiosity, making smacking and clicking noises with every item he examined. "And this," it said, picking up a piece of field kit. "What is it?"

"An entrenching tool. For digging. These other things are harmless, I assure you."

"And these?"

"Boots, gum, soldiers, for the use of," Jeffries answered, mocking the Chatts with a parody of quartermaster's speech.

Rhengar picked up a rifle. "And this? What is this? Khungarrii fell before these without being touched."

"Skarra take them," intoned Chandar, head bowed.

"As we did before your electric lances. You know this is a weapon and I assure you we are quite adept at using them"

Rhengar snapped its mandibles together rapidly, rising up on its legs until it towered over Jeffries. The effect was unsettling, which was probably the entire point.

"Do not presume to threaten the Ones," the Scenturion chittered, its mandibles slicing furiously. "If you are a harm to the Ones, then the Ones will cull you the way it has been done with Urmanii in the past, otherwise you shall be absorbed into Khungarrii worker caste to toil for the good of Khungarr."

"Rhengar, you forget yourself ," said Sirigar. "This Urman can not harm us. Is it not still under my benediction?"

Rhengar backed off.

"I do see your dilemma," said Jeffries tactfully. "Believe me, I do."

"Your dilemma too, Urman," reminded Rhengar.

"You do not worship GarSuleth," said Sirigar. It was a statement rather than a question.

"No," said Jeffries, turning from Rhengar. "I worship... another." He wanted to pursue the subject but Napoo had told him Croatoan was heresy here and now probably wasn't the right moment. He would have to bide his time. He just hoped he had enough. At best, he had a day to get the information he required. Bloody Everson would see to that. The man was transparent. He'd come charging to the rescue like he was the BEF.

"Take your despicable claws off that, heathen!" said the Padre drunkenly. Chandar had attempted to take the Bible from the Padre's hands.

"Chandar!" Sirigar scolded. "You are not here to indulge your inconsequential and heretical studies. You are only here under sufferance, do not test this One."

Jeffries' ears pricked up at the word 'heretical'. This Chandar, despite its broken appearance, might be more interesting than it at first appeared.

Chandar responded to Sirigar in a rapid rattle of mandibles. Sirigar retorted. They sounded like a pair of angry crows. There was obviously a great difference of opinion being expressed and it was being expressed physically, in a series of stylised movements. Actions seemed to define and punctuate argument and proposition, counter-argument and denial. Like dancing bees, thought Jeffries.

The attention of the other Chatts was momentarily drawn to the sparring pair and, seeing his chance, Jeffries deftly palmed the pistol he had been eyeing on the nearby pile of equipment, thrusting it under his jacket and down the waistband of his trousers.

Chandar sank lower and backed away, obviously losing the exchange to Sirigar, who hissed triumphantly, its mandibles and arms splayed.

Jeffries, however, had come to a decision. There must have been a reason the rest of the battalion had been spared the blood sacrifice that brought him here. Until now, he hadn't been able to see it.

He turned smartly and addressed his captors. "Gentlemen!" he said brightly, with a clap, as if about to suggest a bracing snifter down the club. "You say we have a choice between annihilation and subjugation?"

Rhengar and Sirigar exchanged glances, their antennae twitching.

"It'll be difficult, but, yes, I believe I can deliver my people," said Jeffries. "For a price."

INTERLUDE 4

Letter from Private Thomas Atkins
to Flora Mullins

16th November 1916

Dear Flora,

I am well and have acquired a pet now. Gordon is a blessed nuisance, but he ain't half good at chatting shirts. I thought once the Lt. found out about him I'd have to get rid, but he says Gordon's fancy for the verminous louse has sent cases of trench fever down, so I guess I'm stuck with him.

Thanks to a local native we met, called Napoo, our diet has improved. After days of bully beef and hard tack we now have fresh fruit, although my hands are raw and my back is aching from picking the stuff. I don't think I'm cut out for country life. Living in holes and grubbing a living from the land isn't easy. We need more than this if we are to survive. An estaminet wouldn't go amiss, for a start, although after an unfortunate incident I've sworn off drink for the duration.

We were out picking more fruit when there was a raid on our trenches by some bug-eyed Bosche and some of our chaps were snatched. Lt. Everson gave a speech and whipped the lads' dander up good and proper. We're setting out to get them back. The Lt. says they've enslaved the local natives, too. It's disheartening to find that there are tyrants everywhere, but I suppose this is why I volunteered.

These Chatts, as the lads call them, make you feel squeamish just looking at 'em and, after what we had to put up with on the Somme, that's saying something. Anyway, the Lt says these things may know how we can get home too. That is my dearest wish, next to William returning safe and sound.

Ever yours,
Thomas

PENNINE FUSILIERS

CHAPTER FOURTEEN
"There's a Long, Long Trail..."

The rescue party set off several hours after the attack, the patriotic cheers of those left guarding the entrenchment ringing in their ears, the pride singing in their blood as the tank led the column off. Everson had made his point and without having to order them, in all, sixty men had volunteered for the dangerous raid, including 1 Section. Porgy said it was the biggest Black Hand Gang he'd ever seen. Poilus reluctantly agreed to accompany them, despite his fear of the tank, which he believed to be some sort of demon. Even Hepton volunteered, the chance of obtaining more heroic and fantastical footage proving too great to resist. Among those who stayed behind was Tulliver. Until he could repair his machine, he was grounded.

Morale had been high as they set off. Everson knew there was a long hard march ahead of them and estimated the action, with the return trip, might take three days to four days to accomplish. He charged Lieutenant Palmer with fortifying the entrenchments against the possibility of a repeat raid or retaliation.

The Chatts' trail wasn't hard to follow. Their passage had crushed and flattened a wide path of tube grass, fronds ripped and chewed in places as if by some great beast. And, despite a constant vigilance against hell hounds or anything else that might skulk out here, the march out of the valley and across the veldt, although steady and relentless, was relatively uneventful, thanks in part to the measured mechanical pace of the ironclad, whose dark, menacing shape and perpetual growl seemed to ward most things away.

Everson remembered the long marches along the Front whenever the battalion moved sectors. Forty miles in a day sometimes wasn't uncommon with your boots rubbing your feet raw. Now, with the heat and the load they were carrying many of the men were already becoming weary, even as NCOs worried at their heels like agitated terriers chasing motor cars. Everson was aware of it, which was why he had to push them now, so that they could camp for the night and be fresh for the assault the next day.

That afternoon, Everson stood on the roof of the tank and, through his binoculars, surveyed the dark line of forest ahead. Under him the tank growled impatiently, snorting smoke, as if the trees were a personal challenge and it was preparing to rip them up by the roots, each running up of the engine like the pawing of a bull's hoof. Everson called down into the square hatch in front of him.

"It looks as though they've gone into the forest," he bellowed above the din of the engine. There was no answer. He stamped loudly on the armoured plating. A sweaty, oily face peered up from below. Everson could only tell who it was by the fact that he was wearing an officer's cap. A hot damp waft of muggy air, sweat, oil and engine fumes hit him as he squatted down to yell into the vehicle. "All right, Mathers. Take us in."

The Tank Commander nodded and disappeared again. Everson walked back along the line of the tank and jumped down the back of the ironclad landship. The tank moved off with a jerk, rumbling and clanking, belching out black plumes of smoke from its rooftop exhaust as it followed the trail into the treeline.

The platoon followed behind the tank as it grumbled its way through the forest, following the clear trail, every now and again making minor course corrections so that it appeared to be sniffing out a scent, like a bloodhound. The canopy above was so thick that the exhaust fumes billowed back down towards them, creating a gritty grey smog that had the men coughing in fits.

They passed through a grove of pallid trees, whose gnarled and twisted trunks were interspersed with boles and fistulas and down which dripped thick, viscous slime that had the sweet sickly smell of gangrene about it. Small creatures drawn to its scent found themselves trapped in the substance. The whole effect of the grove conspired to produce an atmosphere that sought to absorb sound so that it fell dead almost the moment it was created.

Gordon started whimpering from inside Atkins' gas mask bag. Damn thing. He didn't even know why Lieutenant Everson told him to bring it. "Shut up," he grumbled at the bag. Gordon didn't. If anything the intensity of the mewling increased.

4 Section were bringing up the rear. They'd been singing half heartedly to keep their spirits up, however, travelling though the grove the singing grew harder to hear. "Sing up, Carter, I can barely hear you," called Atkins, the sound of his own voice sounding leaden and curiously clipped. Hearing no answer, he glanced round. 4 Section had vanished.

"Carter?"

Atkins heard something above him. He looked up. A thick, gelatinous string was dropping towards him. Before he could move or scream the warm, wet mucus landed heavily on him and it slithered down over his head and torso, enveloping him. The world about him vanished behind a grey-green film. It was thick and heavy and his struggling bore no fruit. He tried to breathe but the slime was smothering him. He began to panic as he felt the ground disappear from beneath him. Something began drawing him up into the canopy. He thrashed about and kicked his legs but the thick glutinous mass held him firm. His struggle only succeeding in using up what oxygen he had left and his lungs started to burn. He began to lose consciousness. His last thought was of Flora kissing him on the cheek – Blushing, Flora pushed away from him and, smiling fondly, busied herself brushing lint from his lapels before holding him at arm's length for inspection. She nodded approvingly. "Come on, walk me back. Mam will be wondering where I've got to." As he walked her home from the Picture House, her arm through his, he felt as if his very heart would burst. He blushed furiously, feeling as if every step he took would thrust him skywards. She didn't look at him; she kept her eyes straight ahead and kept the small talk polite and parochial. If only she were his. He envied his brother's good fortune. William. His momentarily buoyant heart sank, weighed down by thoughts of his brother. His cheeks still burned, but with shame at the conflicting feelings that now tugged at his heart –

He felt another tug. Something began pulling at his feet, against the suction of the mucus shroud. Another tug threatened to pull his head off as he was drawn down, inch by inch. The mucus wall in front of him thinned and began to tear. More light. A face drifted into focus against the grey green wall of snot. He felt the suction against him weaken. Muffled voices began to reach his ears. He felt as though he was being ripped in two, the webbing and pack resisting the downward pull. He felt strong arms grab his thighs and hold him tight. The mucus began to slide up over his face until he fell heavily, landing on top of Pot Shot and Gutsy and heaving down great lungfuls of air. He looked up to see the long stringy mucus tendril begin to recede back up into the canopy.

"Oh no you bloody don't!" He leapt up and grabbed it, wrapping his left arm around it.

"Jesus, Only what the hell are you doing? That streak of snot just tried to kill you," said Gutsy.

Atkins' right hand fumbled around in the pouch on his chest as he drew out a Mills bomb. Pulling the pin out with his teeth he thrust his arm shoulder-deep up into the ball of mucus.

"Oh god, you're not!"

"He bloody is. Run."

"You're a bloody lunatic, Only!"

With a satisfied smile he opened his fist, releasing the trigger, pulled his arm out with a *schlorp* and rolled behind a tree trunk. A snort from somewhere in the canopy above drew the mucus back up into whatever orifice it had oozed from. There was a brief pause followed by an explosion as the hand grenade detonated. A huge shapeless, invertebrate carcass fell down through the branches. It crashed to the floor of the grove with a large, sodden thump, followed by an accompanying rain of wet spatters.

Sergeant Hobson and Lieutenant Everson came running down the line as the platoon took up defensive positions.

"Just what the bloody hell is going on!" demanded Hobson as he found 1 Section crawling from out of their places of shelter, laughing with exhilaration.

"There was something up in the trees, Sarn't," said Porgy. "Some kind of snot monster. It had Only, I mean Atkins, sir."

Everson gently poked the steaming remains of the huge, many tentacled slug-like creature with his foot.

"From above, you said?"

"That's right sir. Seems to drop a huge string of snot on something then suck it back up, sir," said Gutsy. "Looks like it got 4 Section an' all."

"Hobson, better take a roll call. See who's missing," said Everson. He turned to Atkins, seated on the ground as the slime began to dry out and crust his uniform. "You all right, Atkins?"

Atkins cleared his throat and looked up. "Sir."

"Right, get cleaned up. Hobson, I guess you'd better tell the men to keep their eyes peeled for... what was it?"

"Snot, sir. Great thick sticky strings of snot," said Gutsy.

"Yes. Well," he said, as he walked back up the line. "Handkerchiefs at the ready then."

Jeffries waited. The three Chatts jabbered amongst themselves, their antenna waving and their arms gesticulating. Jeffries found it incredibly frustrating being unable to read their faces. It made them so hard to play.

"What do you mean you can deliver them, man?" asked the Padre.

"Exactly what I said," replied Jeffries, not taking his eyes from the trio.

"You don't mean sell them into slavery?"

"You're not going to get all Moses on me, are you, Padre?"

Chandar came over to them. "Do you mean what you say?"

"I always do," said Jeffries.

"We do not know the meaning of 'price'."

Backward savages. No concept of a monetary economy. Jeffries thought for a moment. "I want something in exchange."

"What?"

"Knowledge. I want Chandar to teach me the Khungarrii ways."

Chandar relayed the request to the others. There was a brief agitated discussion before Chandar returned. "Those Ones do not trust you. Those Ones want a portent, a sign."

This was becoming too much. He didn't have the time to play games here, but he could see no way forward other than to acquiesce.

"What kind of sign?"

"An ordeal."

"Ordeal?"

"Jesus, Mary and Joseph!" muttered the Padre.

"Those Ones require a ritual of purification," said Chandar. "It is a spiritual cleansing expected of Urmen when they reach adulthood. A symbolic pupation, a casting off of the old ways, the old life. We need this from you to show that you accept the Khungarrii and the will of GarSuleth."

"Is that all?"

The Padre, on the other hand, seemed to be having some problems with the idea.

"No!" he said, rousing himself from his induced ennui. "I will not renounce my faith. I will not renounce my humanity and bow down before false idols!"

"Excuse me," said Jeffries, smiling briefly and nodding politely to Chandar before wheeling round on the Padre, grabbing his elbow and steering him away from the Khungarrii. "Padre, I won't tell you again. Negotiations are at a very delicate stage here. This Chatt has... intelligence I need and I'm willing to play along and do whatever they want if it means I get what I want, do you understand?"

"I don't know what your game is, Lieutenant."

"And I can't tell you, Padre. Need to know. Hush-hush and all that." Jeffries tapped the side of his nose.

"Ah," said the Padre. "I had heard rumours. Military Intelligence, eh?"

"So let's go along with it, hmm? Think of it as a – a test of faith."

"Well –"

"Look at me, Padre," said Jeffries. The Padre cast his eyes down. "Rand, look at me. Do you mean to tell me that anything these heathen, soulless creatures could do would shake your faith?"

"Well –"

"Good man," said Jeffries, before turning back to Chandar. "Very well. We shall undertake your ritual. Lay on, McDuff."

"Chandar will explain to you the ritual," said Sirigar, before sweeping from the chamber. Turning to chatter something at Chandar, Rhengar left too.

Chandar and the ever-present scentirrii guards escorted them to another part of the temple area. The chamber in which they now found themselves was smaller than any they had so far seen and could have accommodated perhaps only six or seven people. It was bare apart from some sort of small brazier in the centre, like a large clay oil burner, fashioned from the same cinnamon-coloured earth as the rest of the edifice, almost as if it had been moulded from the floor. From above hung a shallow dish that contained the same luminous lichen that provided the light to the rest of the interior. It reminded Jeffries of a Native American sweat lodge.

"Sit," said Chandar.

Jeffries eased himself to the floor, his back against the wall, and made himself as comfortable as he could. The Padre sat down across from him, looking apprehensive.

"So what happens now?" Jeffries asked.

"You will begin the Kirijjandat, the cleansing," explained Chandar. "The ordeal will divest you of the past, help you relinquish old ways and atone for them so you may embrace the will of GarSuleth."

An acolyte, wearing a thin calico-coloured, tassel-less garment draped over its shoulder and wrapped around its segmented abdomen, entered carrying an earthen jar. Chandar scuttled backward as the acolyte proceeded to pour a thick, oily liquid from the jar into the bowl. Jeffries caught a whiff of a heady musk mixed with a light, almost fruity, scent. The acolyte then introduced a lit taper to the oil and it began to burn. It pulled on a cord and the shallow dish, holding the lichen light, was drawn up against the curve of the roof above until it clamped tight to the top of the chamber, extinguishing all light, apart from the burning oil.

"GarSuleth guide you," Chandar said, before withdrawing from the chamber with the acolyte, the door dilating shut behind them.

Fumes began to fill the chamber. Jeffries just smiled, relaxed and began to breathe slowly and deeply. If this thing was going to happen, there seemed no point in fighting it and it wasn't as if he hadn't done anything like this before. He was quite familiar with hallucinogenic rituals. Prior to the War he had participated in a good many. This was merely a drug he hadn't tried yet and he positively welcomed the experience. That old bastard, Crowley, always claimed he could take more than anyone else could and, while Jeffries had never actually called him on it before they fell out, he always suspected it was quality more than quantity that affected the experience. He'd read of rituals like this among primitive tribes and he would be lying to himself he if didn't feel a little apprehensive, but also excited as well. An otherworldly drug. He couldn't wait.

In the dull red glow of the burning oil he could make out the Padre muttering the Lord's Prayer under his breath, his fingers moving feverishly over the rosary in his hands.

Jeffries, beginning to feel uncommonly hot, pulled at his collar and found his fingers numbed. He struggled to control them as he fumbled clumsily at his shirt buttons, the simplicity of their mechanism outwitting him. His skin began to prickle unpleasantly and it was with a vague sense of detachment that he watched the Padre gazing ahead, slack-jawed, before slumping over. Jeffries, in a gargantuan effort of will, focused on the little rivulet of saliva that dribbled slowly from the chaplain's mouth, soaking into the earthen floor. He felt sweat trickle down his face and collect uncomfortably in his moustache. As the very air around him seemed to bleed shapeless colours into the world, spreading and blotting out the scene in front of him, he relaxed, giving himself over entirely to the alien fumes.

The gas cloud enveloped him. Sick and green and heavy it shifted sinuously around his body. His breathing was hard and laboured. He clawed at his gas helmet only to find the mask had become one with his face, his eyepieces become round dark eyes, the breathing tube a proboscis, his tunic a shiny carapace. His insistent buzz was lost amid the continual thunderous rumbling drum of the artillery barrage that modulated to become the slow sonorous chant of unseen male voices gradually becoming more urgent, more abandoned.

The gas drew back like an outrushing tide leaving him beached at the door of the London Presbytery. The heavy ornate oak door stood ajar. The sound of a rich, sardonic laugh drew him inside. He knew that laugh, knew the supercilious grin and the piercing eyes. He made his way across the tiled floor of the entrance hall toward the door to the inner sanctum. There he was, 'The Great Beast' himself, Crowley, fornicating with his mistress within his ritual circle. His mundane angelic transcriptions served him no purpose. Magickally impotent he could not take the leap that was needed to broach the spheres. Sex was not the answer. And now Jeffries knew it. Red Magick was the answer, the way...

"You were wrong!" he cried. "Wrong, you horny old bastard!" his voice shattering the vision in front of him He found himself in a woodland and saw a great beast, slavering, its phallus

protruding lasciviously from its sheath. He watched as a large snake writhed through the grass beneath the soft underbelly of the beast, where it struck, sinking its fangs into the flesh. The beast howled in pain and fear and bolted, unaware that the venom would nevertheless do its work. First blood to the Great Snake. The snake began to shed it skin and a naked man crawled out wet with viscera, clutching an onyx stone carved with a sigil. The sigil began to glow red and expand.

Jeffries stepped through it onto the cool moonlit lawns of Lambton Grange that rang with thrill-seeking drunken giggles. He looked up at the once familiar stars that augured such a propitious moment, felt again the adrenaline surge, the confluence of fear and excitement. He recognised the ritually inscribed circle, the fug of incense, the lost Enochian codex in his hands, the drug-addled groans of the two barely conscious sacrificial virgins - no chance of an Abrahamic reprieve for them here. He stepped inside the moment to relive it again.

The words, the words he had spent months learning tumbling now out of his lips. Their blood, their life force, charging the cone of energy, powering the evocation. Once again, he felt the penumbra of Croatoan's shadow creep towards him before the very little power he had harnessed waned. He howled, both in frustration and triumph. He felt the power, proof that his Grand Working was sound.

Betrayal. The sound of barking pushed him on as he found himself running, a wanted man. Shedding skin after skin, the Great Snake changed and grew. The outbreak of the Great War galvanised his purpose. What greater cauldron of blood sacrifice could there be? Wholesale slaughter, the extinguished lives going to waste. If only one could channel it. And so his great working took shape. On the field of battle, charged by the blood of thousands, he would evoke the Old One once more. He looked up to see the shells and Very lights and saw, instead, the eyes of the arachnid being he intuited to be GarSuleth, at the centre of a star-bejewelled web. He began to relax and feel calm, then content as he accepted the being above him, welcoming it.

A mine went up, blasting thousands of tons of dirt and soil into the air, ripping apart the web and banishing its occupant to the cold dark shadows of space. The giant earthen plume took the form of a huge, terrible being, squatting on its haunches, skin like onyx, the surface of which cracked and split to reveal a burning core from which rivulets of blood flowed, hissing and steaming like lava as it oozed out across the foreign world on which he now stood.

"Croatoan," he gasped.

Jeffries came round to the sound of retching across the chamber as the Padre vomited. Feeling light-headed and nauseous, Jeffries levered himself upright. His eyes met those of the Padre. They were wide with fear and doubt. Jeffries watched him snivel. Whatever he had seen had shaken him. Wiping the snot from his nose and the drool from his mouth he grinned at the broken Padre, whose chest was now heaving spasmodically, wracked with sobs.

The burner had been extinguished and Chandar stood over them, studying their faces expectantly. "The Kirijjandat is complete," the creature said. "How do you feel?"

Jeffries felt a calmness and certainty. Whatever doubts he might have had had been assuaged. He looked up at Chandar and smiled contentedly. He eased himself to his feet and stretched his cramped limbs. If they thought, after this rite of passage, that he would be more compliant to the will of GarSuleth they were wrong. He had passed through and not only was his conscience unaffected by the visions that had assailed him, but his convictions remained steadfast and his faith in his own actions had been reaffirmed. Most importantly, he felt vindicated by his final vision of Croatoan and, unfortunately for the Khungarrii, gloriously unrepentant.

"How do I feel? Never better, old chap. Never better."

* * *

The party had been marching for several hours now. The air was thick with cloying forest scents and the acrid smell of exhaust fumes from the grumbling tank ahead. Atkins was sweating in the oppressive heat. His uniform was beginning to chafe and his boots rub so he was thankful when, at last, the trees thinned and opened out into a stretch of heath land. The forest, they found, was not continuous but here and there were changes in terrain. A large outcrop of rounded boulders, yellow-grey in colour, worn and pitted by the weather and stained with a peculiar indigo-coloured moss dominated the heath to the left of the trail. Either side was a mass of tangled tendrils some several feet high, looking like overgrown brambles.

They walked slowly along the trail. If this world had taught them anything, it was caution. Frequent use of the track had kept the indigo-hued vegetation cropped close but anything could be hidden within the rest. They reached the centre of the heath without incident, the outcrop of boulders to their left.

Atkins thought he caught a movement out of the corner of his eye. But it was only the vibrations caused by the tank setting small pebbles skittering down the outcrop.

Or then again, maybe not. One of the large boulders shifted then began to unfold. Six legs extended from underneath and two great curved horns revealed themselves. The huge bulk of the boulder revealed itself as a giant beetle.

Moving quickly, it struck out at the line of men, mandibles scything the air snatching two up and severing them in half. Shouts went up and the Tommies scattered, some racing back the way they had come, others seeking cover among the brambles. Thinking it would afford them protection, some raced toward the tank. The rock beetle snapped angrily at them, catching up with a third man, his screams briefly echoing around the heath until it crushed him.

Gazette squeezed off several shots. He hit the beast squarely, but to no effect.

" Rapid fire!" the order came. A number of men, Atkins among them, opened fire, which only served to aggravate the creature.

However, it did buy time for the tank to slowly, haltingly turn round to face the attacker.

Atkins heard the tank's engine rev above the shouts and screams as the boulder beetle snapped at the fleeing soldiers. Hearing the grating roar it turned its attention to the tank.

"It thinks the tank is some sort of rival!" said Pot Shot.

With a loud, venomous hiss, it ran towards the landship. The mechanised behemoth gunned its engine and lurched forward, two titanic beasts charging each other. They crashed together with the tortured squeal of stone on metal, the tank pushing inexorably forward, forcing the huge rock beetle back. Stunned, it retreated briefly as if considering its next move. It lowered its head and shoved forward trying to lodge its great horns under the vehicle and turn it.

The tank reversed away from the beetle which raised itself up on its legs and hissed, spitting a stream of fluid at the ironclad. It sizzled and smoked as it hit the tank between its front tracks. The tank reversed and the beetle scuttled forward, clearly thinking its challenger was retreating.

"Come on!" Atkins muttered under his breath. A movement on the trail distracted him. Hepton was running clumsily, carrying his camera on its folded tripod before finding himself a vantage point for the battle. Planting the tripod down and splaying its legs out, his eye to the box, he began cranking at a measured pace.

"What the hell's he doing?" said Gutsy. "Hasn't he seen what that thing has just done to the *Ivanhoe*?"

"Give me strength," sighed Atkins. As much as he wanted to leave Hepton to his fate, the weight of his brother's fate lay heavily on him. He'd like to think that nobody had left William behind. He hoped somebody might have done what he was about to do. "Gazette, cover me."

"What?"

He started running toward Hepton as the tank roared its defiance and lumbered forward, snorting smoke. The beetle lowered its head and charged, meeting the tank head-on with a clash of armours. Atkins shouted at the kinematographer, who continued to crank his camera as the titanic battle played out before him. "What the hell do you think you're doing you idiot! Get out of there!"

"Are you mad?" cried Hepton, shrugging Atkins off. "This is money in the bank. People will pay through the nose to see this!"

Hepton had a point, Atkins thought. Gears grinding, engine screaming, the tank was holding its ground and edging forwards, pushing the boulder beetle back foot by foot. The beetle struggled to gain a purchase on the ground. It spat its acidic venom at the tank again. It splattered thickly against the plate armour, etching and pitting the metal.

The beetle braced itself against the tank's relentless advance and the landship's great tracks began slipping in the churned earth. Seizing the advantage the beetle's great mandibles sliced through the anti-grenade mesh roof before it turned its attentions to the upturned snout of a track horn, where the caterpillar tracks protruded forward from the body of the tank. The metal groaned in protest under the pressure. One tank track stopped and the other carried on running, rotating the tank clockwise before that track stopped and the other ground back into action, swinging the tank back the other way. Atkins realised that the tank was trying to shake off the giant beetle. The rear end of the creature slued round, its rear legs nearly taking out Hepton and his camera.

Atkins grabbed the cameraman by the collar and hauled him back. "God damn it, you've got your moving pictures, now let's go!"

The near loss of his equipment shocked Hepton into action. He gathered in the legs of his tripod, hoisted it onto his shoulder and ran.

By now, the rest of the company had made it across the heath, covered by a rapidly deployed Lewis gun on the far side.

The tank backed away from the creature, throwing it off balance so that it released its grip. Engines roaring, gears grinding, the valiant *Ivanhoe* threw itself forward once more, clashing with the giant beetle.

The tank stopped for a moment before pitching forward, catching the beetle off guard for a second before it began to push it back. The front of the tank rose up off the ground, forcing the beetle to rise with it. They looked like two primal beasts grappling chest to chest, locked in a titanic struggle.

Pushing the stumbling Hepton across the clearing towards the waiting company, Atkins glanced back over his shoulder and saw the *Ivanhoe's* right-hand sponson six-pounder swivel forward. It fired a shell point blank at the unprotected underbelly of the beetle. The force of the explosion threw it over onto its back, a huge gaping wound in its side. The front of the tank crashed down again and the machine lurched unsteadily forwards.

The beetle was struggling to right itself, its legs flailing in the air and squealing just within the threshold of human hearing. The tank drove purposefully up onto the fallen beast and came to a halt on its upturned belly. Then it shifted gears so that one of the tracks fed backward and the other forwards; it began to rotate, the metal tracks grinding the beast beneath it, disembowelling it. The squealing and the frantic leg waving ceased. The tank stopped, re-engaged its gears and rolled out of the pit it had gouged in the beast, its tracks leaving a trail of blue-green blood as it drove across the clearing. The company were cheering and whooping at its triumphant approach. As one, they rushed forward to mob it and slap its flanks as if it were a cup-winning thoroughbred.

"I missed it!" cried Hepton in disappointment as he turned to see the pulverised beetle lying slain.

"Well you got away with your life, and whatever film you did shoot, so count yourself lucky," said Atkins, delivering the kinematographer into the hands of Sergeant Hobson. Atkins nudged Hepton in the ribs and whispered confidentially, "If you ask him nicely he might do his Charlie Chaplin routine for you."

The company, jubilant and in high spirits after the *Ivanhoe's* victory, continued marching on through the forest. As the sun began to set the track widened into a tree-lined avenue.

"Holy mother of god!" gasped Porgy as, through breaks in the canopy, they caught their first glimpse of the edifice.

"They seal the edifice at night," Poilus told them. "Any Khungarrii or Urman outside will have to fend for themselves until dawn."

"Fine Christian attitude that is," said Porgy.

"I think we can say they're probably not Christians," said Pot Shot.

"I wouldn't be so sure. They've had the Padre for a while now. He'll be on a mission," said Mercy. "If he can convert 'em before we kill 'em at least he'll have saved their souls. That'll get him to the front of the queue at the pearly gates.

"That's if these Chatts have souls," said Atkins. "Which I doubt. I mean, not exactly made in His image are they?"

"Load off my mind then," said Gazette. "If they've got no souls, killing them will be just like reading my shirt."

By now darkness was rising in the depths of the forest. They halted for the night. Unwilling to light fires for fear of giving away their presence, they ate cold meals of bully beef, hard biscuit and pozzy before bivvying down as best they could.

Atkins found himself on watch with Ketch, whether by accident or design, he wasn't sure. The Corporal glanced sullenly about the undergrowth. Ketch had been riding him for weeks and he didn't have a clue why. He'd always tried to do the right thing. Why had Ketch taken against him? He started to ask the question several times, but hesitated. Finally, he worked himself up enough to get it out. "Look, Ketch, what the hell is your beef with me, anyway?"

"You, Atkins?" he growled.

"You've had it in for me since I joined the platoon."

Ketch sat hunched like a gargoyle, ready to pour forth venom like a waterspout. Atkins could smell the man's rank breath as he spoke.

"Always want to be seen to be the good man, the hero, don't you, Atkins. Why is that?"

"I don't know what you mean."

"This desperate desire to be accepted. What is it you're afraid people will see? Your true colours, the kind of man you *really* are?"

"What do you mean?"

"You know. You carry it with you, in here," Ketch said, tapping his chest. "It eats away at you. Gnaws at you like a corpse rat; feeds on you," he said, with relish. "And I'm glad."

"You... you know?"

"About Flora Mullins? Yes. I was on leave, too, remember? I know Flora. I was sweet on her myself, but she spurned me. Spiteful bint. Didn't give a shit about Old Ketch. But then I saw you both. At the Picture House. Outside."

"You spied on us?"

"Didn't have to. You weren't exactly discreet."

"It was a kiss... one kiss and... and... it wasn't like that. It didn't mean anything."

"Affianced to your brother. Your *own* brother!" he said in mock outrage, then softly. "How many weeks had he been missing?"

"You bastard, you've no right. No right at all."

"Nor did you."

"We vowed it would never happen again; that we would never speak of it again."

"Oh well," said Ketch nodding, as if in sympathy, "that's all right, then."

"It's true. If William were to find out..."

"Ah. William. Your beloved brother. The Atkins boys. Always together, never apart. A bit different now, isn't it? You haven't got William to stand up for you now."

"You know he's bloody missing in action."

"Yes, and more to the point, so did you," hissed Ketch. Atkins felt warm spittle spray his cheek. "Always want to be seen to be a good man, the hero, don't you, Atkins?"

"What is this, blackmail? Just what the hell is it you want, Ketch?"

"Me, Atkins? I want you to suffer."

CHAPTER FIFTEEN
"When John Bull Starts to Hit..."

Before dawn they prepared themselves for the attack. Atkins was still smarting from his confrontation with Ketch; he could barely bring himself to look at the man. The seedy little corporal revolted him almost as much as the damn Chatts did. The fact that he had intentions towards Flora just riled him even more. Ketch looked over and grinned at him, obviously enjoying his discomfort. Atkins responded with a sullen stare. The rest of the Section didn't notice his change of mood; men acted differently before going over the top, they sank into themselves and resorted to prayer or their little rituals to marshal their own fears. Atkins took out his last letter from Flora, held it close to his face and inhaled, gently. He could still smell her perfume, although it was not as strong as it once was. If he closed his eyes, he could still feel her lips on his cheek. No. No, he would not die today.

Everson went to set up a forward OP to spy out the lie of the land, Mathers and Baxter accompanying him, Poilus scouting the way. They crawled on their bellies through the undergrowth towards the edge of the clearing. As the rising sun seeped over the trees it illuminated the top most towers of the Khungarrii edifice, bathing it in a rich crimson light that made its mineral deposits sparkle. Everson raised his field glasses and scanned the mound. The earthen structure rose hundreds of yards into the sky, towering over the cultivated area around it.

It looked as if the Khungarrii had built the edifice over generations, each generation repairing and maintaining as well as expanding the towering colony, buttressing the main thrust of the spire with additional towers of various height and thicknesses. The excavated earth used in its construction had bonded and toughened over the years to a sedimentary rock-like hardness. Everson could see no sign of structural defences although he did notice small holes at varying heights, but whether these were window or vents he could not be sure. Maybe a combination of both. A movement about two thirds of the way up – about fifty or sixty feet above the tree canopy – caught his eye. He watched for a second. Hanging from one of the vents was a piece of white cloth. As it fluttered in an updraft he could made out a small red cross. It was a nurse's apron. "Good girl!" he muttered. That was one question answered. They were in there. However, fighting their way up inside two thirds of that thing wasn't going to be easy. "Hobson," he called softly.

The Sergeant crawled up through the undergrowth with a grace that Everson never thought possible for a man his size. "Sir?"

"Prepare the men and tell Evans that we'll need my little acquisition, will you?"

"Sir."

Everson returned the field glasses to his eyes and refocused his view on the base of the edifice. A series of large midden piles lay slumped against the sides and, clinging precariously to their slopes, was a jumble of crude dwellings. These, Poilus told them, were Urman dwellings. Not part of the colony, they nevertheless sought whatever protection their proximity to it could afford them. The Khungarrii themselves did not concern themselves with these casteless Urmen unless they became too numerous or they affected the running of the colony. They lived on whatever detritus and chaff they could scavenge from the colony, scouring the midden heaps that accumulated like scree round certain portions of the edifice. Even at this early hour,

Everson could see figures moving about, searching for food or other items they considered to be of value.

Over to one side of the vast clearing stood what looked like several small pyramids fifteen feet high or so, each composed of clay spheres, about four or five feet in diameter. Some of the pyramids appeared to be incomplete. "What are they?" he asked Poilus.

"Khungarrii dead. Each ball is a Khungarrii body encased in clay. They are left there for Skarra, the dung beetle, god of the underworld to roll down into his domain, where they undergo a final change into their spirit stage to join GarSuleth in the Sky World. I remember when I awoke in your camp, with the stench of the dead all around me and your great metal beast squatting there in the mud, at first I feared I'd been taken by Skarra, too."

There was a tap on his shoulder and an urgent whisper: "Everson, there." Baxter made him refocus his field glasses on the base of the edifice, on one of several huge bark-like doors. Boughs and trunks were embedded in the wall around the doorway, branches interwoven so they formed a jamb, roots thrusting into the ground. Out of the great openings began to spill Chatts, some bearing the electric lances and clay backpacks he'd heard about. They spread out across the clearing, behind them followed a mixture of Chatts and Urmen. Great elephantine larva-like beasts brought up the rear, bearing large panniers along their lengths.

Everson and the others crawled back to the camp and the waiting platoons, where they quickly mapped out the plan of attack. Everson noticed the Chatts avoided the dung ball pyramids of the dead and so, too, did the Urmen. If that was the case then they could use them as cover to get them in close to the Edifice. From there they could head for the midden heaps which would provide cover for their break-in.

"I suspect we have a window of opportunity now before the workers start returning to the edifice. I'll lead the assault with 1 Section," he said. "I doubt that we'd win an all out pitched assault. Stealth is the only option. We'll have to bypass those entrances; they'll be too heavily guarded. We'll make our own way in. Dixon, see that the rest of the party take up defensive positions on the outskirt of the clearing. Baxter, your Vickers and Lewis MGs I want set up to provide a field of fire to cover our escape from the edifice. Mathers, hold your tank in reserve. We may need it. And if Hepton gives you any trouble, you have my permission to stick his camera so far up him he'll be able to use himself as a darkroom. If we're not out in six hours don't waste time attacking. Get back to the entrenchment. You'll have a better chance of survival there. It's easier to defend."

"If it's still there," muttered Ketch.

Blood glanced at him blackly.

"Hobson, Ketch. You and your men are with me. Poilus, you're coming too." Everson had no doubts. He knew the men could do this. He had every faith in them. After all, hadn't Hobson himself told him they were the best Black Hand Gang he knew? He raised a hand and the entire section melted into the undergrowth.

"Bloody hell," said Atkins when he got his first full view of the edifice. "It's not quite what I was expecting." The scale of it tied a knot in his stomach. How many Chatts lived in there? Thousands? Tens of thousands?

"What were you expecting?" asked Half Pint.

"I don't know; exotic palaces, gleaming towers, metal roads, automatons, flying machines. Not this. Not earth. Not dirt. We can do that. We have done that. Look at the way we're living, we're still bloody doing it."

"Well, then you should feel right at bloody home, then shouldn't you, Atkins," sneered Ketch as he crawled up beside him.

Atkins' mouth was dry. He took a swig from his canteen. The thought of attacking the Khungarrii edifice made his balls shrivel. He'd done trench clearance and even been down the mines dug under No Man's Land as a guard, neither of which could prepare him for invading a giant insect nest.

He and William had poked twigs into wood ant nests as boys.

He remembered Flora squealing, equal parts delight and horror, urging them on. Emboldened by her, they squatted down on their haunches and thrust their sticks further in with more and more savagery, taking glee in watching the ants pour out frantically – just before the biting began as they swarmed over their clogs. William threw away his stick and danced around yelping and howling, much to Flora's delight.

There were probably thousands of the revolting Chatts in there – and they'd do a damn sight more than just nip.

Poilus tapped Everson on the shoulder.

"We must move to keep down wind of the scentirrii."

"Scentirrii?"

"Soldier Khungarrii, may Croatoan curse them!"

He hadn't factored in the wind. He was getting slack. Even in the trenches, it was one of the main factors of a daily report. Gas attacks were dependant on wind strength and direction. Here, apparently, these considerations were just as important.

"You," said Poilus to Atkins, thrusting a grey army blanket into his hands. "We will need to capture a Khungarrii to help us get into the edifice. As soon as I grab it you must throw the blanket over its head and wrap it tight, do you understand?"

No, he didn't, but he knew when to follow an order. Atkins nodded.

They watched and waited as the parties of workers and Urmen disbanded across the clearing, each appointed their daily tasks. Chatt soldiers accompanied the groups who walked off into the forest. As the Chatts drew near they heard the harsh, clicking language for the first time.

"Bloody hell," hissed Mercy. "They're only talking flamin' iddy-umpty. We should've brought a Signaller."

Atkins noticed that the Urmen each had a mark on their foreheads, a blue rune of some description.

"Why don't they make a break for it?" said Porgy.

"You've seen what's out there. Where the hell would they go?" said Atkins.

"Better that than serving some chatting tyrant race of insects. Makes my blood boil, does that," said Gutsy.

"Well maybe it just takes someone to show 'em eh? That's why we're here. Get our men back and just maybe teach these Urmen a thing or two about standing up to them bloody bug-eyed Bosche," said Pot Shot.

One Chatt wandered too close, its curiosity piqued by some sign or spore. Poilus gave an almost imperceptible nod to Atkins, who gripped the edges of the blanket firmly and tensed his legs. The Chatt's segmented antennae started twitching moments before Poilus leapt up from the undergrowth. He grabbed the creature from behind and Atkins tossed the blanket over its head, wrapping it round as Poilus sliced through its neck with a bayonet. The creature dropped with Poilus still on top of it. Atkins tensed, expecting a cry of alarm at the Chatt's absence, but none came.

"They can raise the alarm by scent," explained Poilus in a hushed tone as the men gathered around the kill. "It looks like we caught it in time though." He carefully unwrapped the blanket from the creature's head and handed it to Atkins. "Take it and bury it, carefully. We don't want the scent getting caught on wind."

Poilus then sliced his bayonet into the segmented abdomen of the dead Chatt, ripped down, pulled the wound open and exposed dark, swollen organs, sheathed in a slick wet cawl. This he tore from the body before easing his hand inside.

"Poilus, what the hell are you doing?" asked Everson.

"Looking for scent organ," Poilus pulled his hand out, holding a soft translucent greenish-red bag that sagged over the end of his palm. "We need to smear ourselves with its contents. We need to smell like Khungarrii."

"Oh Jesus!" groaned Porgy.

"He's right," said Pot Shot. "Many insects use scent as a primary sense. Those that don't smell like them are attacked as enemies."

"That'll be you and the Worker's Institute Library again, will it?" said Half Pint.

"What, you mean we cover ourselves with this stuff and we can just walk right in?" said Mercy.

"That seems about the size of it, Evans," said Everson. "This may fool them but we don't know for how long."

Poilus tore a small hole in the organ, pushed his fingers in and brought them out, covered with a greenish grey slime that he proceeded to smear around his face and exposed skin. He passed the organ round. Everson took it, cleared his throat and dipped his fingers into the wet sac, smearing himself with the warm goo.

Once the men had anointed themselves with Khungarrii scent they set off around the edge of the clearing. Leaving the rest of the party in the capable hands of Sergeant Dixon, Everson, Poilus and 1 Section edged toward the pyramids of dead, each man hauling extra weapons and ammunition with which to arm the hostages while Mercy lugged a mysterious tarpaulin-covered object. From the cover of the shunned pyramids they then made their way, cautiously, to the midden piles and the Urman dwellings.

It seemed the dwellings slumped up against the side of the edifice were empty. There was no sign of any Urmen. Atkins knew if you scratched a living on this world, or any world for that matter, there was no time for idleness. It was obvious that the Chatts themselves never came here unless they had to, so it was an ideal place to make a discreet entrance. In the shadow of a huge midden: an accretion of dirt and gnawed animal bones, pottery shards, composting vegetation, dung, and rotting food, Gutsy and Pot Shot started work with a couple of pickaxes. Their points hammered into the hardened earth at the base of the edifice with very little initial effect, while the rest of the section kept watch nervously.

"Put your backs into it," growled Hobson. Gutsy and Pot Shot swore and swung their picks, grunting vigorously with each impact in a practiced alternating rhythm. After a few minutes, the surface began to pit and flake. Then it began to crumble. Blood stopped, panting, to wipe his brow.

"Good work. Change over," said Everson.

The men changed over. It was no use doing all the fatigue work only to end up too knackered to fight once you'd actually breached the wall.

Atkins heard a clatter of refuse skittering down the far slope of the midden pile to their left and signalled the men to stop digging. Slowly, eight loaded Enfields converged toward the sound as something clambered towards them.

Everson licked his lips and cupped his pistol hand in his free palm to try to disguise the fact that it was shaking. He couldn't let the men see. The clattering grew closer. He flexed his trigger finger and caught Hobson's eye. The Sergeant gave him a barely perceptible shake of the head and patted his trench club, 'Little Bertha'. The cruelly customised truncheon, its end studded with hobnails, had seen good service in many a trench raid. Everson felt a surge of disgust at the sight but thankfully lowered his revolver, realising that its report would give them away. He watched as the burly NCO tensed himself, his face compressed into a twisted snarl of hatred ready for whatever came over the brow of the slope. A small hand appeared over the lip and, a second later, there emerged a small boy, no more than six or seven years old. The Section let out a collective sigh. All except Gazette, who kept the boy in his sights.

For Atkins it was like looking at his own past. He'd been a boy such as this one, running round the streets of Broughtonthwaite, so far away now, in soot and grime and clogs. The boy was thin and covered with dirt and sores. He wore a tunic of animal skins and breathed heavily though his mouth, his nostrils plugged with dried green mucus. He continued to stare at the soldiers with a surly pout.

Poilus started to approach the boy, but Hobson raised his arms and stepped towards the child, snarling in the manner of an ogre. The boy took fright and ran off down the slope. "There, that's got 'im."

"You're losing your touch, Sarn't," said Mercy, nodding his head downhill. The boy had stopped someway down and again stood staring at them resentfully before disappearing round a bluff.

After five minutes, Gazette and Atkins were up on pick-axe duty, taking over from Mercy and Half Pint.

"Just imagine it's Ketch's head," said Mercy.

Atkins was glad of something to do. The nervous expectation of being caught by a swarm of gigantic insects was almost interminable. It was much better to keep yourself occupied. As they continued to swing, the picks bit deeper and deeper into the wall. It was some twenty minutes and four feet before Porgy's pick broke through to the other side. Hobson crouched by the opening and beckoned the men closer.

"Right," he said in a low voice, "just like Trench Clearance. You know the routine."

Except this was worse than trench clearance and Atkins knew it. He still had nightmares about the mines. Nevertheless, he swallowed hard and tried to put it to the back of his mind as, one by one, the Black Hand Gang entered the short tunnel. Blood took the lead as ordered, slithering through the hole and disappearing into the darkness. There was a brief, tense moment of silence before he hissed back the all clear. They passed through the extra rifles and grenades, boxes of ammunition and a couple of Lewis guns, before following.

Atkins looked back at the silent urchin, now watching them again, sitting atop a pile of bones. "See you," he said with a wink and joined his pals in the Chatt-ridden gloom beyond.

High above, in the labyrinth of tunnels and chambers, Jeffries, having successfully passed the ritual, had spent the last few hours recovering from the ordeal. Thankfully, they had hauled the snivelling Padre back off to the gaol chamber. He had no idea what the chaplain had experienced but he did hope it wasn't pleasant. As for himself, he only felt mildly disconcerted by his vision. He had no idea how long he had been under the influence of the oil; it could have been a couple of hours or a couple of days.

The Khungarrii saw the Rite as one of submission, of acceptance to the colony, but, on a more personal level, for him it had been one of control, of discipline. His will against theirs. And he had won.

His Great Working had taken months to prepare and years to perfect. Only a handful of people would have understood the significance of what he had done on the Somme, of what he had achieved or, more gallingly, attempted to achieve. Everything he had read, everything he had learned had led him to believe that the Old One would be summoned within the great pentacle laboriously calculated and etched on the battlefield; that the blood of thousands would have summoned him and confined him in a crucible warded by a circle of geographic proportions. When their transportation to this world had occurred in its stead, he'd felt confused and angry. Loath though he was to admit it, there had been several small flaws in his calculations. There was the fact that vital commentaries to the Ritual had been long since lost, and that the ritual itself was an Enochian translation of manuscripts that Voynich, the old antiquarian book dealer, had discovered and got rid of, not knowing what they were but rather *fearing* he knew what they were.

Had this whole experience been a salutary case of 'be careful what you wish for'? Had his invocation inverted, torn them from Earth only to deposit them in Croatoan's own domain? A case of 'if the mountain won't come to Mohammed, then Mohammed must go to the mountain,' as Everson had so innocently suggested? A lesson in humility? If so, then he was suitably humbled, but not by these insects. These Chatts were a step on the road to his personal mountain, so to speak, and he had no compunction about treading on ants to get there.

Napoo's mention of Croatoan, his recent ritual vision, his Great Working; there had to be a connection. Was he brought here as an unforeseen consequence of his working? Were these insects just a means to an end?

"When you are ready, Sirigar has instructed this One to share knowledge about Khungarr society as you asked," said Chandar, watching intently as Jeffries tore hungrily into the loaf of fungus bread. "Then you will deliver your herd."

Jeffries looked up and regarded the old Chatt. That something had passed between Chandar and Sirigar, Jeffries was now quite sure. Now he knew there was a crack in their relationship, all he had to do was apply pressure.

"This One has made its work to study wild Urmen," said Chandar, "and you are unlike any others this one has come across. You have a keen intelligence almost matching the One's own. Your garments are complex and of a quality this One has never smelt, yet the scouts report that you live in your filth, among your own dead. It was these odours that the breath of GarSuleth carried to us spinnings ago, alerting the scentirrii and dhuyumirrii to your presence on Khungarr territory. Sirigar and Rhengar are of conflicting opinions, although each has their views rooted in holy scentures. Even now the Khungarrii Shura debate your presence. Some hold that you should be culled without consideration for your initial resistance but it seems to some that your earth workings and burrows imitate, in a primitive fashion of course, the great tunnels and chambers of the Ones' own colonies. It marks your herd as different. This, and your bargain, is what has what saved you," Chandar said.

"And those Urmen you keep here, are they so different from us?"

"They are Khungarrii."

"Not Urmen then?"

"Khungarrii Urmen. They smell Khungarrii, they belong to Khungarr."

"They are kept here by force?"

"They submit to the will of GarSuleth daily in their decision to wear the mark of Khungarr. It is reapplied, willingly, every day. By doing this they show their obedience and gratitude."

"But surely if these Urmen of yours are as much a part of the colony as you say, what culture do they have left for you to study?"

"It is true their culture is now that of Khungarr. They, too, worship GarSuleth but their ancestors and the wild Urmen, the remnants of their culture, fascinate me. I have been studying them for many spinnings."

"And Sirigar allows your studies?" said Jeffries, probing to see where the cracks between them lay.

"That One tolerates them," Chandar replied. "There are those of us among the dhuyumirrii that have long believed Urmen have a place in our Osmology. Other Ones, Sirigar among them, dispute this, believing that Urmen can have no other purpose but to serve the Ones."

A theological schism, thought Jeffries. That would certainly account for the animosity between Sirigar and Chandar and was certainly something he could exploit. "But you believe differently?"

"Come, let me show you something," said Chandar.

Intrigued, Jeffries followed Chandar back to the temple. He noted again the niches all round the walls. Hieroglyphic script of some form covered each niche. Chatts had their faces to the walls of the niches, their feelers moving dextrously over the surfaces.

"Here dhuyumirrii read and study sacred texts and debate on points of interpretation," explained Chandar.

Jeffries could see now that what he took to be contemplation, praying and bowing, was in fact the action of their antennae over the glyphs. Now he understood. Not only was there information contained within the hieroglyphs themselves, but there were other olfactory layers of meaning contained within chemical scents *attached* to the text. Layers of nuance, subtlety and context lay impregnated within the glyphs. Chandar led him on through the archway through which Jeffries had been taken previously. It led to the chamber of trench equipment. Along the way they passed through the alchemical chambers he had seen only briefly before. Now Jeffries was able to study it in more detail. Its walls were filled with small niches and recesses. Galleries led off the large room, each one containing bays crowded with stone bottles, pots, urns, beakers and amphora; ceramic vessels of all shapes, sizes and ages.

"This is the receptory of Khungarr, the repository of all our knowledge. The sacred odours stored here are the thoughts of our prophets and gon dhuyumirrii."

"A library," said Jeffries, nodding in appreciation at the vast accumulation of containers and the knowledge they must represent. Each bottle, each jar, contained what must have been an essence of scripture or holy aromas; bouquets of bibles, prophetic perfumes, olfactory encyclopaedias. There was so much he might learn, but it was like giving a blind man the key to a library.

He was not allowed to dwell on it for long as Chandar ushered him into the next series of interconnecting chambers. They passed through what looked like an apothecary's storehouse, hundreds of niches filled with earthenware bottles, jars, tubes filled with oils, essences, liquids, tinctures, extracts, secretions, resins, saps, powders, pastes, samples of plants, leaves, flowers, barks, bones, skins, fur, shells, all arranged, classified and organised. The smell was overpowering and made Jeffries' nostrils sting and his eyes water. Beyond them, blinking though teary eyes, he could see further chambers where more of the Khungarrii priest caste, the dhuyumirrii, were engaged in their great alchemical endeavours.

"For many generations the dhuyumirrii have been attempting, amongst other things, to distill the true quintessence of our creators' odour of sanctity, the scent of GarSuleth. Some believe certain notes of the Urmen musk may yet be relevant to our studies, but teasing out the lone indivisible base notes is a long and arduous task."

"Why?" asked Jeffries. "Why Urmen? They're not Chatts, I mean; they are not of the Ones. Why should they be relevant?"

"GarSuleth dwells in the Sky World, his web spanning the firmament above us. Ancient incenses tell us in his wisdom he once descended from his web to spin this world, this orb, where his eggs were laid and his children, the Ones, hatched. The Ones, the children of GarSuleth, then spread out across the world and begat the colonies," Chandar picked one of the knotted tassels on the cloth draped over its shoulder and lifted it up, almost nostalgically, its antennae stumps waving feebly. "Although this one can no longer read this odour, this one has committed its scents to memory. It tells how, many generations ago, a sickness infected the line of Queens who now ruled each colony. Eggs laid to be djamirrii -workers- hatched malformed and continue to do so to this spinning. Djamirrii populations were decimated and the Ones struggled to survive. The Ones knew of the Urmen's existence, but treated them as competition for scarce and hard won resources, until some came to believe they were created by GarSuleth for the Ones' own use."

"You used them to replace your own shortage of workers."

"Not without price. There came a dark time. The Urmen then worshipped a different god, the forbidden one."

Jeffries saw his opportunity. "This is all very interesting, but what I require is specific knowledge. Tell me about Croatoan."

Chandar rounded on Jeffries, its mandibles chattering, the vestigial limbs at its abdomen fidgeting.

"That's right," Jeffries said, deliberately relishing the opportunity to say the name again and forming each syllable clearly: "Croatoan."

Chandar glanced around at the alchemist dhuyumirrii. None of them seemed to have heard. "That name is forbidden!"

"Nevertheless, that is my price. You want my cooperation then tell me what you know," said Jeffries firmly. "Or should I shout the name out loud, here, now?"

"No! You must not," said Chandar, rising up on its legs in the threatening manner Jeffries had seen Sirigar use before.

"But your own studies? If you could tell me about your... forbidden one, how much might I be able reciprocate, to advance your own Urman studies with information I have? What is it that Sirigar and its acolytes don't want you to know? You have hinted yourself that passages in your scriptures concerning Urmen are ambiguous at best, maybe excised at worst. What if my information could shed light on them?"

Jeffries held the Chatt's gaze, looking deep into its dark orbs. He had the old fool's measure now. Give this old louse enough rope and it'll hang itself. It was like leaving a trail of sugar for an ant.

"Very well," said Chandar. It shrugged its shoulders and waved its antennae stubs in a way that seemed to indicate agitation. "But not here, I have somewhere we can talk. Come with me."

Chandar led him out through the chamber where they had stored their collection of items pilfered from the entrenchment. The jumble of trench stores and arms were still there, no doubt waiting to have their odours investigated, distilled and broken down. From there the passage became narrower and showed signs of disrepair. It seemed to be a little used part of the colony.

"Where are we?" asked Jeffries, a hint of suspicion in his voice, the reassuring pressure of the pistol barrel pressing against his abdomen.

"Somewhere we will not be overheard," said Chandar as they stopped before a chamber sealed by a fibrous membrane.

"Here are stored many Urman artefacts that I have found, lost in undergrowth or left in caves over many spinnings," said Chandar. "Indications of how Urmen lived before the Ones subsumed them. Maybe in return you can enlighten me as to the nature of some of them."

"Yes, yes," muttered Jeffries dismissively. He had no interest in the old Chatt's collection of archaeology, almost certainly a fusty amateur assortment of broken pottery, arrowheads, flints and bone jewellery with no context and less meaning. No, Croatoan was his only concern now. The need overwhelmed him. He fought the desire to take the Chatt by the shoulders and shake the information out of it there and then, and watched impatiently as it exhaled a mist from its mouthparts, in response to which, the door shrivelled open. Chandar stepped through and beckoned Jeffries to do likewise. Preoccupied, Jeffries stepped into the chamber totally unprepared for what lay inside.

PENNINE FUSILIERS

CHAPTER SIXTEEN
"The Last High Place"

Atkins knelt in the short stretch of tunnel. Before him the stack of equipment he was passing through to the others barred his way. Eager to be inside himself, he gave the last of it, Mercy's mysterious tarpaulin covered thing, a last shove with his heel, and it fell down into the passage with a dull metallic *clang.*

"For Christ's sake, Only, watch it!" hissed Mercy as Atkins dropped down into the passage after it.

The passage itself was about six feet high, four feet wide and rounded, almost as if it had been burrowed rather than built. A faint draft of air was blowing towards them down its length.

Everson nodded and Sergeant Hobson walked cautiously into the breeze until he disappeared around a gentle curve ahead.

Along the length of the curving passage small recesses were stuffed with some sort of glowing lichen that imparted a dull but diffuse blue-white light.

Mercy crouched down to inspect the damage to his bundle.

"How are we doing, Evans?" asked Everson.

Mercy glanced up at Everson and nodded.

"So what the hell is this mysterious thing we've lugged all the way, sir?" asked Porgy.

With a broad grin and the flair of a showman, Mercy flung back the tarpaulin.

"The Lieutenant thought we'd need a bit of an edge. An' I found one, didn't I, in the remains of that Jerry sap. Isn't it a beauty? Am I good or am I good?"

"Bugger me!" said Gutsy. "It's a flammin' Hun Flammenwerfer."

Mercy grinned and nodded slowly. "Oh yes. After what I saw them Chatts do when they raided our trenches I think a little payback is due, don't you?"

"What is it?" asked Poilus.

"A liquid fire thrower," said Atkins, in awe.

"Bloody hell," said Gazette, in a low voice.

"Them Chatts'll get what's coming to 'em now," Mercy said with a sneer.

"If it works," said Half Pint.

"Tell you what," hissed Mercy, "you look down the barrel and tell me if you see a spark."

"I was just sayin'," said Half Pint.

"Yeah, well don't come looking to me next time you want a light for your Woodie, is all I'm sayin'."

"Quiet!" hissed Everson as Sergeant Hobson returned.

"Tunnel leads to a broader one up ahead. I can hear voices beyond," he reported.

"Right," said Everson. "Poilus, you're sure this scent trick will work?"

"For a while," said the Urman.

"Let's hope so." He nodded to Hobson. "Carry on, Sergeant."

"We're not anticipating trouble going in, so long as this insect stink continues to do its work. Chances are we're going to have to fight our way out though, so save your puff and your ammo. Atkins, you're bayonet man with me. Hopkiss and Blood, bombs. Evans and Nicholls, you take the damned flammenwerfer."

"But Sarn't," Half Pint began.

"It takes two to operate," explained Mercy. "I can't reach the fire lever. You have to do it for me."

"Ketch and Jellicoe, you're on mop-up. Poilus, you stick with them," said Hobson. "Otterthwaite, you take the rear with the Lieutenant. Move out."

As they set off, all encumbered not only by their own equipment but also by the sacks of rifles, grenades, Lewis MGs and ammunition they were carrying for the others, Atkins began to feel the old familiar dread he'd felt in the mines as a guard.

The miners dug tunnels deep underground, far out under the German positions in order to plant high explosives. It was hot, cramped and dirty work, even more so if you didn't like confined spaces with little air. And God forbid you should think of the thousands of tons of earth above, constantly being shelled. Then there were the Germans who would be doing the same. It was a game of cat and mouse hundreds of feet below the peppered surface of No Man's Land. Sat breathless in a listening alcove trying to determine where the Hun was. Too close and you could hear them digging and they could hear you. Occasionally you'd accidentally break through into a German shaft and then, oh God then, the close fighting, the fear of grenades and being buried or cut off from escape by a tunnel collapse.

"You all right, Atkins?"

"What?"

"I said you all right?" asked Hobson as they advanced.

"Yes sir, just remembering something."

"Once we start killing these Chatts, the Urmen will rise up against their insect masters, against their Oppressors, that's right isn't it, Sarn't?" Pot Shot asked.

"If we're lucky," said Hobson.

"Just think what we could do with an army of Urmen. We could conquer this world," Mercy pondered.

"You're forgetting mate, we're going home," said Gutsy. "I ain't staying to conquer nothing. I've had a belly full o' conquering and a fat lot a good it's done me."

The passage began to slope up gently before forking. Atkins hesitated. "Which way?"

Hobson glanced down the smaller tunnel and dismissed it. It was a cul-de-sac. "Carry on. We want to go up."

Atkins advanced cautiously on up the tunnel. He began to hear sounds now carried on the draught; scuttlings and scufflings, poppings and clickings. He shuddered to think of the tunnels ahead teeming with giant insects. It had been bad enough in the trenches with the rats, but these things; they just filled him with horror. He couldn't help himself. A little way ahead, the passage opened out onto what seemed to be a main thoroughfare. Behind him, the Section flattened themselves against the walls as, in the lichen-lit twilight, Chatts scurried about mere feet from them. Urmen, too, went about their chores, unaware of their presence. Atkins tensed himself, ready to make the bayonet thrust they had been trained to make without thinking.

Several heavy chitinous plated scentirrii, one or two carrying Electric Lances that reminded Atkins of Mercy's Flammenwerfer, marched past. He glanced back down the passage to see Mercy's eyes narrow. As a group of Urmen came along, they slipped in behind them and then off down the first rising passage to which they came.

It led them up to a great hall, the roof of which arced high overhead. Shafts of light punctuated its domed ceiling on one side, sunlight penetrating deep into the structure. Many passages led off the cavernous hall. A wide sloping path spiralled round the walls at a shallow gradient to a gallery about twenty or thirty feet up. From here, more passages led away into the edifice. Chatt soldiers were standing there, armed with lances, overseeing the workers below. Hundred if not thousands of Urmen toiled at the raised beds that covered the floor of the chamber, each filled with some sort of mould or fungus. They seemed to be cultivating the substance. A damp, earthy smell filled the hall.

Urmen were not the only creatures tending the fungus beds, there were Chatts, too, although they were outnumbered by the Urmen about them. They seemed to be smaller than the Chatt soldiers above and there were fewer segments to their antennae. Their chitinous armour was smoother, lighter. These, Atkins assumed must be the worker Chatts.

The fungus from the beds was loaded onto large sled-like litters before being transported elsewhere, presumably for storage or distribution.

From the shadows of the tunnel, Atkins watched the Urmen, fascinated. They seemed like ordinary humans. They were dressed in roughly woven tunics and each wore some sort of blue mark upon their foreheads. Looking into the hall he was reminded of his first job in Houlton Mill, the men and women intent on their task as the foremen looked on. Fourteen he'd been when he left school. Those foremen hadn't been armed, though. Atkins counted twenty soldier Chatts, five in the gallery, the rest patrolling the floor.

"Bloody slave labour, that's what it is," muttered Pot Shot, appalled.

"Up there" whispered Everson. Atkins and Hobson followed his finger to the gallery. They watched Urmen enter it with their laden sleds.

After an urging shove from Hobson, Atkins stepped warily out into the hubbub of the fungus farming chamber, his bayoneted Enfield at the ready. The noise about him didn't suddenly subside and deteriorate into an ugly, tense silence as he half expected. In fact, the world carried on around him, the Urmen continuing with their tasks and pulling harvested litters of fungus along using shoulder harnesses woven from what looked like plant fibre.

Cautiously the rest of the section stepped out to join him. They kept to the edge of the chamber and headed in an anticlockwise direction for the gallery ramp. Poilus broke away from the group to acquire an apparently abandoned sled-like litter. He loaded the sacks and sandbags of extra weapons onto it, then heaped it with fungus to the cover the weapons. An Urman woman approached him to protest and Atkins felt himself tense for a fight, but Poilus, gesticulating, seemed to be making some sort of argument. Angrily, she gesticulated back. Poilus trumped her by pointing to the soldier Chatts on the gallery above and she threw her arms in the air, shook her head and wandered off sullenly.

They were making headway toward the spiral ramp when several soldier Chatts appeared out of a passage and advanced purposefully towards them. Urmen scuttled out of the way as, behind the squat, heavy-set soldiers, a taller, more regal-looking Chatt followed them; its head and antennae covered with a rich carmine hood that masked its features. It wore a length of silk thrown over its shoulder and tied around its abdomen from which hung a great number of tassels. The soldiers knew a member of the ruling classes when they saw one. Atkins and Hobson froze, unsure how to react.

A flat-faced soldier Chatt stopped in front of them, its lance sparking faintly. Its black, featureless eyes scrutinized them. Its antennae waved petulantly as it sought confirmation of the expected chemical mark of Khungarrii scent. Atkins became very aware of the sweat on his hands and his forehead as it continued its inspection and hoped his human smell wouldn't wash away his scent mask. Finally satisfied, its antennae stopped waving and it began scissoring its mandibles belligerently. "Move, dhuyumirrii comes."

Poilus, helped by Pot Shot, dragged the litter to the side of the chamber before dropping his harness and making a curious gesture, touching his hands to his forehead and then to his chest, while bowing to the imperious Chatt approaching them.

"Move." he hissed urgently at Atkins and Hobson, who moved clumsily back against the wall under the watchful gaze of the soldier Chatt. With a nod from Everson, the others followed suit. Atkins caught a waft of cloying perfume from the head covering of the stately Chatt. It was so strong that he had to suppress a cough as it swept passed without acknowledging their presence.

Pot Shot glared after the haughty arthropod. "Same the bloody world over," he muttered. "There's always them on top. Now I find out it's the same on different worlds an' all. I can't say I'm particularly encouraged. Still, all will be different when we get the Urmen to stand up for their rights and take these folk down a peg or two."

"Yeah, well don't forget our first priority is our own," hissed Gutsy. "Save your Labour rhetoric for later, eh?"

"Move on," ordered Everson, once the regal Chatt party had passed.

Pot Shot ducked into the shoulder harness, braced himself and stepped forward, taking the weight of his sled. Ketch, obviously unhappy with his own sacks of ammunition, sought to do what Poilus had done and requisition a litter the better to carry his load. However, a restraining hand on his wrist stopped him. A tall Urman glared down at him.

"Where is your mark?" he asked. "I see no mark."

"Mark? But I have the scent, you saw," he said, indicating the receding Chatt with its guards.

"Urmen Khungarrii don't smell it. You are required to wear the Mark. You know that. Where is it?" he hissed, staring hard at the Corporal's forehead and pointing to his own blue glyph.

Ketch raised a questing fingertip and wiped it across his own greasy brow. "It must have come off? I sweat. A lot."

"Then reapply it before someone else notices and takes you for Casteless and godless and calls the scentirrii. GarSuleth wills it," he snapped, before shoving Ketch away and returning about his business. The Corporal snarled and brought up his bayoneted rifle ready to thrust the point home, but Atkins grabbed him by shoulder.

"No, Corp," he said. "Not here. Not now."

Ketch glared after the Urman, growling under his breath before relaxing his stance. He turned and shrugged Atkins' hand off his shoulder. "Fuck off, Atkins." He grabbed the vacant sled-like litter, loaded it up and began dragging it along sullenly.

The social injustice of his surroundings continued to gnaw at Pot Shot, like a dog with a bone. He grabbed the arm of a passing Urman woman. "Why do you submit to their rule?"

"We are all Khungarrii. GarSuleth provides. GarSuleth wills it," said the woman.

Everson stepped up and gripped Pot Shot's arm. "Jellicoe, that's enough. Now isn't the time to organize a general bloody strike."

"But, sir –"

"I don't want to hear it, Jellicoe. We're here to do a job."

Reluctantly, Pot Shot returned his attention to pulling the sled, shaking his head and muttering while the Urman woman stared wonderingly after them for a moment, before turning back to her task.

The Tommies approached the ramp and began to make their way up its incline.

"What's the matter with 'em? Don't they want to be freed?" asked Pot Shot, taking a last look down over the labouring Urmen.

"They've been under the yoke too long," said Gutsy. "They just need someone to show 'em how, that's all. Guess we'll be doing that before the day's out."

Jeffries stood in Chandar's small chamber while he allowed his eyes to adjust to the gloom. He peered at the objects all around him, piles of Urman junk; pots, jars, jewellery, woven mats, crude shoes and animal skin clothing, wooden implements of every description. Some, given pride of place on earthen plinths or in niches around the wall, commanded the eye. Others, considered less important perhaps, sat in unsorted piles around the floor. He found himself reminded of the piles of their own trench equipment in the other chamber.

"Sirigar thinks this one is wasting its time, but this One's accident allowed it to see Urmen in a new way," said Chandar, standing proudly amid its collection.

"Accident?" said Jeffries, glancing around with indifference, now he could make out more detail in the lichen-light.

"This One's antennae were damaged," said Chandar, squatting and beginning to root though a pile. "This One can no longer sense odours. In Khungarrii terms this One is..." it seemed to struggle to find the right words.

"Ah. Scent blind. Unfortunate for you." Jeffries was becoming impatient with the small talk. After cornering Chandar into revealing what it knew about Croatoan, he didn't appreciate this new delay.

"No, GarSuleth wills it. To Khungarrii this one is pitied, unable to perform its duties, so I have undertaken new studies. Liya-Dhuyumirrii Sirigar allows this one to pursue its interest in Urmen, now this One only sees the world in the way they do. This One believes it gives it some insight into their old way of life."

"Where did you get these artefacts of yours?"

"Scentirrii would occasionally come across such things and bring them back. Once they were deemed to be of no harm or interest they were disposed of on the midden heaps, but this one retrieved them. This one can only speculate as to some of their uses. This One thought you might be able to enlighten it."

The old fool had been hoarding these things, not knowing what they were and no doubt extrapolating ludicrous theories about indigenous Urman culture on that basis. Jeffries wandered over to a niche in which was a pile of small metallic objects. Chandar followed, watching his reaction eagerly.

Jeffries stood before the niche, for once nonplussed, all thoughts of Croatoan suddenly expunged from his mind. Fingers trembling, mouth dry, Jeffries picked up the least of the trifles; a small round metal disc, and turned it over in his fingers.

"What do you think it is? A charm, a ward perhaps?"

It spoke volumes to Jeffries that the Chatt didn't recognise a coin when it saw one. He studied the copper disc between his thumb and forefinger. He heard the blood rush in his ears and his fingers trembled fractionally with every pulse beat. This... this was a Roman coin, a denarius, if he wasn't mistaken and, judging by the pug ugly, bull-necked profile on the obverse, from the reign of the emperor Titus. He struggled to keep his outward composure calm. Somehow, this all made sense. Somehow.

"In a manner of speaking," he croaked, having to cough and clear his throat as he shuffled through the pile of similar coins. "Do you have anything more?"

"Yes," Chandar's stunted middle limbs seemed gripped by spasms as if exhibiting childish delight. It led Jeffries to another pile of items and began sifting thorough them, looking for a choice find. With each new presentation Chandar made, it became harder for Jeffries to conceal his disbelief at what he saw. There were more coins, bone pins, a crushed and dried out leather sandal, a scattering of medieval brooches and pottery, a small carven Celtic cross, Elizabethan silverware, crockery and scraps of cloth, and what seemed to be medical tools; an incision knife, a spatula; the items came one after the other. With a lurching sense of vertigo, it became clear to Jeffries that they were not the first humans to visit this world from Earth. Even as he thought this however, another, more damning, hypothesis began to form in his mind.

The more Jeffries saw, the more he became convinced that there had been incidents of human displacement in history before. What had happened to those people? Well, that was a stupid question. If their own experiences were anything to go by, then most of them would have been killed, struggling to survive their first few days. But the survivors? Could these troglodytic Urmen be the descendants of others who had arrived here from Earth in the past? There were many legends of mass disappearances throughout history. For all the soldiers' hopes, for all their desires and dreams of Blighty, it appeared that there may not actually be a way back to Earth. But what did that have to do with his Great Working? With Croatoan? That he couldn't yet see, until his gaze fell upon what should have been an impossible object, or at least, until a few minutes ago, an impossible object. The sight of it caused him barely to suppress a gasp.

"Where... where did you find this...?" he rasped, picking up a weathered, hand-carved wooden sign that proclaimed boldly the legend, '*New Roanoke*'.

With that one name, the matter of Croatoan burst once more into the forefront of his mind. Croatoan, the fallen angel who communicated with the renowned Elizabethan Magus, Doctor John Dee. Several of his disciples were reputed to have been among the first English settlers in Virginia in 1582 when they attempted to found the colony of Roanoke, financed by the secretive School of Night. When the supply ship returned later, the colony had disappeared. The only clue they found was the word 'Croatoan' carved into a gatepost. That the opening of the New World was conceived of as an occult operation was an idea Jeffries had been aware of for a long time, he just didn't think they meant *this* new world, although he could certainly see how it fitted the bill as *prima materia*.

It was becoming clear to him now, beyond all doubt, that Croatoan was linked to the disappearances. Was the colony really an audacious early attempt at the very magickal operation he had performed, well away from prying Protestant eyes, where the necessary bloodletting could be practiced on the native population without being hampered by the moral imperatives of society?

Whatever the truth, it would seem the same fate had befallen the settlers of the lost Roanoke colony as befell the Pennines. From the weathered sign he held in his hands, it was clear that they too had been transported to this world in response to their Working. Here, they had sought to found a new colony, a new Roanoke, who worshipped Croatoan. If the Battalion's own experiences were anything to go by, then not many would have survived their first few weeks without help. He rounded on Chandar. "Tell me about Croatoan. That's the bargain. Tell me about Croatoan."

Chandar hissed at the mention of the name, but resigned itself to its side of the bargain.

"According to the notes of the Perfumed Chronicles it happened many, many queens ago. In the spinnings of the dhagastri-har queen -the forty third queen of Khungarr- a herd of Urmen passed into the lands of the Khungarrii and, seeking refuge in Khungarr, which they received willingly, they brought with them into our midst their own god... Croatoan. They began trying to convert the Urmen of Khungarr to their god and, as a sign, pointed out a bright spot in the sky that they claimed was their god come to smite down GarSuleth." Here Chandar made a brief gesture of reverence as if to protect itself and its god from its own heretical words. "The light grew brighter, brighter than all the other dew drops that shine in GarSuleth's Web and Urmen turned against the Khungarr. The liya-dhuyumirrii declared that GarSuleth would cast the false god from the Sky World. So it came to pass that the false god was hurled down in fire and the entire world felt his fall. Croatoan was consumed in flames and consigned to the underworld by Skarra. With their god destroyed the majority of Urmen turned rightfully to GarSuleth. Those that would not were, likewise, cast out and his worship declared heretical by Chemical Decree from the queen."

That Croatoan was woven into the fate of the Khungarrii was more than Jeffries had dared hope for. As all these thoughts circled round his mind, his eyes fell on a piece of parchment sat in a niche, pinned to a board of bark. Chandar looked on proudly as he studied it. It looked like a map. He must have made a noise because Chandar picked up on it.

"Does it mean something to you?"

"Hmm?"

"The dhuyumirrii studied it but it has no scent of meaning to them. The glyphs we cannot decipher."

"Did you not think to ask one of your Urmen?" said Jeffries, irritated at having to deal with these interruptions as he struggled to get to grips with all that he was seeing.

"Khungarrii Urmen can neither script nor scent. After the Croatoan Heresy their own ways were declared sacrilege. All that they were is lost. Urman culture was eradicated. All Urman writings and knowledge wiped out. They are Khungarrii now. No one can read the language, if language it is."

Jeffries stared at the map. It seemed to be a map of this world. He couldn't understand how Chandar couldn't see it for what it was, but then it was entirely probable that their cartography was scent-based and not visually oriented. He ran his eyes hungrily over every symbol, over every mark on the map. Everything he knew from his studies; the style of calligraphy, the type of parchment, told him this was Elizabethan. It was fine, if hurried draughtsmanship. The map was incomplete although it did indicate what seemed to be mountains, forest, rivers and presumably, other edifices. He saw blocks of closely written Enochian and Voynich text that he would have to decipher laboriously. And there, and there, despite the bad penmanship and the foxing, emblazoned on the map in several locations, Jeffries recognised the unmistakable sigil of Croatoan.

CHAPTER SEVENTEEN
"Louse Hunting"

Everson halted the party in a side tunnel to get their bearings. It was apparent to him that these rough tunnels were reserved for worker castes, designed as passing places or servant's passages, so that the ruling Chatts wouldn't have to come face to face with them. His father's house in Broughtonthwaite had similar features.

He got Poilus to ask passing Urmen if they knew where the prisoners were being kept, but he might as well have been asking them the way to the Alhambra Picture House. There was no way they would find the captured soldiers by blundering blindly about these tunnels, the place was a maze with numerous cul-de-sacs and dead ends, so it was just as well he'd got a plan.

"Atkins," he called.

The private turned from watching the mouth of the tunnel and Everson, crooking a finger, beckoned him back.

"Sir?"

"You still have that confounded creature?"

"Yes sir, it's getting a bit restless, though," he said, nodding down at his gas helmet knapsack, which was moving about in an agitated fashion. "I reckon he must be getting pretty hungry."

"Good, time to take it for a walk then. Let it out, will you."

He saw Atkins look at Hopkiss, who just shrugged.

"Don't look at Hopkiss, Atkins, just do it," said Everson.

He could see the looks in their eyes; *it's a bloody officer, who knows what he's thinking, just do as you're told.* But he'd learnt to let that wash over him a long time ago.

Atkins complied and pulled a large rat-like creature from his knapsack, its long nose already questing at the air with small, wet snuffles.

"Got a name has it, Atkins?"

"Ginger, er, Mottram, called it Gordon, sir."

"Very well. Get a leash on him. If Gordon is as hungry as I hope he is I think he might just lead us to our men."

Atkins put a loop of string over its head.

"What," said Sergeant Hobson at the sight of the creature, "is that?"

"I believe the men call it a Chatter, Sergeant," said Everson. "It loves lice. Apparently, it thinks them quite a delicacy. And thanks to this little blighter and Evans' entrepreneurial spirit none of us here is hitchy-koo anymore, so I'm hoping it'll sniff out any lice in this place, and the only place I know we can find 'em is on our own great unwashed."

Hobson gave a sceptical grunt before turning to Hopkiss and hissing, "You trying to tell me that's what I paid me thruppence for, Hopkiss, to have that thing rooting through my smalls and shirts?"

"Aye, Sarn't. Money well spent, I'd say," said Porgy with a grin. "Ain't scratched since 'ave yer?"

Hobson muttered unhappily until Poilus, who had been keeping watch, motioned them to keep quiet.

Gordon began scurrying about amongst their feet looking for his new favourite food and Atkins had to yank him back before they all got tangled up in his string leash.

Heads down, they stepped from the worker's passage into the main tunnel as an eager little Gordon took the lead, tugging at the string in Atkins' hand. Hobson rolled his eyes at the sight but took up point with him as he'd been ordered to.

The tunnels became lighter and airier. They must have been in an outer spiral because apertures high in the walls filtered bright beams of sunlight into the passageways. They passed several groups of Urmen repairing tunnels, perhaps after the recent tremors, without further incident but there was still no sign of the captives.

Everson watched expectantly as Gordon stopped below a vent shaft up in the wall and raised itself up on its hind legs, its forepaws scrabbling at the earthen wall, the nostrils of its thin wet whiskery snout flaring as it scented something. "Good boy!" praised Atkins, petting Gordon as if he were a prize ratter. The private peered at the opening above his head. "It runs upwards sir," he reported. He listened intently for a moment then added, "I think I can hear voices."

But were they Urman or Human? Everson ordered Hobson and Blood to move one of the weapon sleds across the curving passage to form a barricade behind which they knelt, pointing their Enfields into the tunnel behind them. Pot Shot and Porgy used the second sled as a mount for the Lewis Gun. Everson could see sweat beading on their foreheads. Wandering these tunnels wearing full kit and lugging an extra twenty or thirty pounds each was taking its toll.

He made his way through his men to the vent hole two or three feet above him. He removed his cap and gingerly tilted his head towards the vent, but could hear nothing above the curious pops and clicks that issued from it. "Hopkiss, give me a leg up will you?"

Hopkiss handed his rifle to Evans and linked the fingers of his hands together, palms up. Everson stepped onto the offered cradle and Atkins boosted him up so that he could get his head into the vent above.

He could feel a down draught cooling his face and, riding on the breeze, he heard the faint murmur of voices, human voices. If he could just... He put his hands up inside the vent, braced them on the walls and hauled himself into the mouth of the hole, until he was resting on his stomach, leaving his now flailing legs searching for purchase, which wasn't so much found as offered. Hopkiss' shoulders, he presumed. He used them to drive himself up into the shaft. With a cautionary *shhh* to his men below, he started to listen to the faint sounds filtering down from above.

In the warm, cramped confines of the shaft, he became aware of his own body odour. It smelt as if he hadn't had a bath in weeks, which wasn't that far from the truth. He began to wonder how long the scent from the dead Chatt would mask it. If, in fact, it still did. He lay still, held his breath and listened. There was a mutter of voices above, but he still couldn't tell what they were saying. He had to know whether they were Urman or Human before he committed his men. He cupped his hand round his mouth and hollered up the vent. "This is Second Lieutenant Everson of 'C' Company. Hello? Are you all right?"

The seconds ticked by as he waited, then he heard a distant, but definite, "Yes, sir!"

"We're on our way" he called back up. "Get ready to make a break for it!"

He was about to call down when Hobson's urgent whisper reached him. "Stay where you are, sir!" Then he heard the unnerving chitter of Chatt mandibles below and the familiar sound of magazine cut-offs being flicked open and loading bolts being cycled back in readiness. Slowly he swivelled round in the narrow vent until he was on his back, looking down the length of his body to the end of the shaft and the top of Hopkiss' steel helmet. He readjusted his pistol grip and waited.

"What do you here? Answer!" came the breathless glottal sound of a Chatt. "You block way."

"Us?" he heard Hobson's voice respond. "We're just taking food to the prisoners."

"Prihz nuhz."

Everson braced himself. Judging by their use of language, these Chatts knew just enough to deal with Urmen on a basic level.

"You not Khungarrii."

"We most certainly are."

"Scent no."

Well, that answered *that* question.

"You no Khungarrii." There was an inhuman scream and a muttered interjection of "Oh, hell," followed by the sound of a club smashed into something brittle and wet. Hard on its heels came a hissing and a pained yelp mixed with an electric crackle. A bluish white light flared briefly, illuminating the shaft.

"Damn!" said Everson, relaxing his body and allowing himself to slip from the vent.

He landed heavily on his feet, revolver ready, but the immediate problem had been dealt with. Two broad-headed Chatts, one with an electric lance, lay on the floor. One had its head staved in. The other had been stabbed through the chest. Private Blood was wiping his bayonet blade and Sergeant Hobson was hefting 'Little Bertha'. Corporal Ketch was clutching his arm.

"Damn thing spat acid at me," he coughed. "It's gone right through me bleedin' stripes!"

"Reckon someone's trying to tell you something, Ketch," sniped Evans. Ketch glared back at him.

Everson didn't need this right now. He needed them to be operating as a unit. He stepped in between the two soldiers.

"You all right, Corporal?" he said.

"I'll live," replied Ketch from between gritted teeth.

"Right. I don't need anyone blinded by this acid spray. So let's not take any chances. Gas helmets on."

"Looks like our smell-o-flage has worn off, then sir," said Hopkiss in a chirpy assessment of the situation, rummaging in his canvas bag for the gas hood.

"So it would seem, Hopkiss."

"We must move," urged Poilus. "They will have sent out an alarm scent warning the rest of the colony. More scentirrii will be here soon."

"We've lost the element of surprise, then," said Everson.

It was bound to happen. Their luck wouldn't hold forever. Mind you, they'd got further than he'd thought. Knowing they didn't have long before more Chatts turned up he wanted to push on as quickly as possible.

"This is it," he said. "Everybody ready?" There were grunts of assent from under the gas hoods as the men moved off. Everson rolled his gas hood down over his face, tucked it into his shirt collar, replaced his cap and took a place at the front with Poilus, behind Hobson and Atkins as Gordon sniffed out the way. Blood and Ketch followed pulling the weapons sleds while Evans, Nicholls, and their Flammenwerfer brought up the rear with Otterthwaite, Jellicoe and Hopkiss.

They pushed on up the gently spiralling passage. They'd only just managed to build up a head of steam when the first soldier Chatts appeared from a side passage to the left. Evans nodded and Half Pint opened the valve. A brief spurt of fire sprayed out of the Flammerwerfer's nozzle, like Satan's own piss. The Chatts began to squeal and thrash about, fire leaping high and blackening the tunnel walls. There was a sickening heavy smell like burnt hair.

"Passage," shouted Sergeant Hobson, indicating with his right arm as they advanced past the dark open maw of a side tunnel.

Blood, pulling a sled, pulled the pin on a Mills bomb, counted to three and tossed it into the shadows. There was a brief rattle of metal on clay then the tunnel shook and bloomed with a fiery light as the explosion spat hot shrapnel through the enclosed space, eliciting startled inhuman shrieks.

Everson heard the stutter of rapid fire as Hopkiss fired back down the tunnel. He glanced back to see a squad of Chatt soldiers retreating round the curve of the passageway. Jellicoe pulled the pin from a grenade and rolled it, clattering, down the passage. It exploded round the corner bringing baked earth crashing down.

The Chatts' weapons – spears, some form of swords, their acid sprays and electric lances – were all close range. If they could keep the damned things at bay, they may just have a chance. With all their firepower though, Everson briefly wondered if they'd gone over the top.

Jeffries gazed at the sigils on the parchment as one might at the photograph of a far away sweetheart.

"You recognise something?" asked Chandar.

"Hmm?" said Jeffries. He had to remember that this was a creature that had spent a good deal of time around Urmen. More so than its companions. It had learnt to mimic behaviour and gestures to gain confidences. He had done such things himself. It was trying to ingratiate itself. "What? No," he added almost absent-mindedly. This was important, but he didn't want Chandar to know how important.

The room shook. Dust showered gently from the domed ceiling.

"What was that?" asked Jeffries.

"A tremor. Continue."

But Jeffries was distracted now. He made out the faint faraway report of rifle fire.

Damn. Not now, bloody idiots. They'll ruin everything. That damn boy-scout, Everson!

The door shrivelled back and Rhengar and two of its scentirrii entered the chamber, pointing their electric lances at Jeffries and herding him against the wall, from where he could now only eye the map covetously.

Their commander hissed and chattered frantically at Chandar, its mouthparts and mandibles moving rapidly. Chandar took whatever comments the soldier was spewing at him, and then turned to Jeffries.

"Your herd has invaded the colony," said Chandar. "Rhengar thinks you have broken your agreement."

"No!" said Jeffries emphatically, shaking his head, arms wide. "This is not my doing."

Chandar turned back to Rhengar, slipping into its own language of hisses and clicks as a heated exchange developed. Eventually, Rhengar rounded on Chandar, emitting a long hiss with open mandibles and rose up on its powerful legs even as Chandar assumed a position of submission. Whatever argument Chandar was trying to put forward, it had just lost. Jeffries cursed silently.

"You must go with them," said Chandar.

"If you attempt to escape we will hurt you," Rhengar made sure to say in English.

Jeffries got the message. Rhengar strode off, its scentirrii, shepherding him along, their lances never wavering from his body.

As he was led away, Jeffries turned and called back to Chandar who stood in the entrance to the artefact chamber.

"It's a mistake. Let me talk to my men, Chandar. I can get them to stop the attack. It's all an awful mistake. Believe me!"

But Chandar didn't move and Jeffries lost sight of the creature as the guards urged him relentlessly on.

His mind raced. If Everson's damn fool rescue failed then there was no doubt that Sirigar creature would have them all culled. If the rescue did succeed, then he lost access to the map and those artefacts. He felt the stolen pistol in his waistband, but with electrical lances against his back, he doubted he could reach it in time. He needed that map. He felt sure it was the answer to all, well, *many* of his questions.

If they were stuck here on this world with no way home then he didn't need to be hampered with several hundred stranded soldiers. He could abandon them to their fate. They had served their purpose and delivered him this far. It was clear now that his destiny lay in a different direction, and that pointed to Croatoan once more.

"This wasn't my idea, you know," he said to Rhengar's back as the scentirrii frogmarched him back the way he had come; past the trench equipment, through the alchemical and library chambers towards the temple. Dhuyumirrii and their acolytes scurried about as he was escorted across the main temple chamber and out of the ornate entrance on the large thoroughfare tunnel. Masses of Chatts moved along it in well-ordered ranks, the only allowance to chaos was the haste with which they were moving. He assumed that it was not the weight of written law that made them obey but rather instructional semiochemicals lacing the atmosphere, filtered through the natural air conditioning of the nest, impelling them to comply.

The few Urmen that were allowed access to this level were directed down side passages or cloister tunnels by scentirrii that took up positions to direct traffic flow. A defence plan was being put into operation.

A squad of scentirrii ran down past them, their powerful legs barely containing their springing step in the confines of the tunnel. Then he heard the faint but recognisable judder of a Lewis gun and the dull, muffled thud of an explosion reverberated through his feet.

Great. What the hell else could possibly go wrong?

Edith Bell looked blearily around the chamber. The slumped Tommies around her were beginning to stir. The feeling of rapture was wearing off. Edith, in her naivety, could only compare it to that brief, special moment upon waking in the warmth of one's bed, when one is dozily blissful, before the cares of the day encroach and sully the transitory moment of peace. Some soldiers were already sitting with their heads in their hands, wondering what the hell had happened. For some, coming down from the drug-induced euphoria left them feeling depressed and melancholic. Others still wore blissfully stupid smiles. Captain Grantham sat staring into space. He was lost in his own thoughts and they didn't seem to be happy ones.

Napoo, who seemed to have recovered faster than they had, was already moving from one soldier to another, slapping them to bring them round.

"Yes, thank you, Napoo. That will be enough of that," said Sister Fenton, who was already standing, if a little shakily, but determined to show that she would let no insect muddle her mind.

"But the Khungarrii dhuyumirrii's blessing is strong," he said, unused to having his behaviour challenged.

"Yes, some sort of natural opiate, no doubt," said Sister Fenton. She smoothed out her blue nurse's uniform in an attempt to recover her authority and decorum, although her apron now hung out of the garderobe as a makeshift signal.

"I beg your pardon, Sister?" said Edith.

"The insect sprayed us with some sort of opiate, hoping to keep us docile and subservient. Nurse Bell, Abbott, start checking the men, if you would. Some may have had an adverse reaction."

Edith got unsteadily to her feet and had to brace herself against the wall as a brief wave of nausea washed over her, spots dancing before her eyes.

"Give a gel a hand," groaned Abbott. Edith clasped her arm and pulled. There was a groan as Nellie raised herself up, smoothed out her ankle-length khaki dress and turned to her with an irritatingly chirpy smile. "Don't mind me, Edi. I've had worse hangovers down the Estaminet in Sans German. Mind you some of these boys don't look as if they've handled it very well."

The chamber was filling with groans and sighs as the men came down from their non-consensual high.

Edith spotted the Padre sat by the door, his shoulders slumped. She hadn't noticed him being returned to the chamber, but something terrible must have happened to reduce him to this state.

"Padre, what's the matter. Where's Lieutenant Jeffries?"

The army chaplain lifted his head, his eyes rheumy and red-rimmed, his pupils dilated.

"What have they done to you?"

"Crushed my faith," he said, shaking his head despondently. "Wherever we are, we are far from God's sight."

Edith shook her head, as if that would somehow flush out the residual effects of the insect's spray. There was something she had been trying to remember, but it was a hollow in her mind. What the deuce was it?

Suddenly Napoo, stood below the air ventilation hole with his head cocked, urged them all into silence, his keen native senses straining to hear something. Then others heard it, too.

"This is Second Lieutenant Everson. C Company. Hello?" said a voice drifting from the vent.

"Give me a leg up," said one of the soldiers. A couple of his companions boosted him up towards the vent. "Sounds like someone said he's Lieutenant Everson," he said.

"Bloody hell, man, well shout back! It could be a rescue party."

"What?"

"Get down. Let me," The other man was dropped unceremoniously while a Corporal was boosted up. He grasped the lip of the vent and called down.

"Are you all right?" the voice called from below.

"Yes, sir!"

"We're on our way. Get ready to make a break for it!"

Napoo went to the door and tensed, waiting expectantly. Several men joined him.

"Captain," said Sister Fenton sharply, addressing Grantham. "Captain, it appears your men are here to rescue us."

"Hmm, what?" said Grantham.

"Captain," said Sister Fenton sharply. "You do not want to let your men down. They are looking to you to lead them. Whether you feel you can or not, it is your duty."

Grantham looked up at her as if something she said had reached him.

Some of the men, too, had got their dander up. Having heard the voice of rescue, they were up for taking a pop at the blasted Chatts. It was amazing how they rallied, Edith thought. They endured so much misery and suffering but their spirit, though dampened, was never truly extinguished and it took the merest spark to renew it. So it was she found herself swept up in their cheery confidence and for a brief, exhilarating moment she couldn't help but believe that everything was going to be all right.

Turning down another passage Rhengar and the scentirrii brought Jeffries to the gaol chamber. The two scentirrii on guard outside exchanged a few clicking sounds with Rhengar. One then hissed briefly at the barbed door, which opened just enough to allow Jeffries to be shoved through with a prod from his escort's electric lance. He staggered, almost losing his footing, and narrowly avoided stumbling against Napoo who had been by the door. He shot the Urman a glance, warning him off. It was hardly the triumphant entrance he'd intended. He noticed the men were up on their feet as he entered.

"Glad to have you back, sir," said one private.

"Don't worry you fellows. Help is on the way, apparently," said Jeffries. He looked down at the Padre with disdain. The Chaplain glanced up but quickly averted his gaze. Next, he spotted Captain Grantham. Hell's teeth, but he wouldn't be sorry to see the back of this sorry-looking shower.

"We heard them," said a Lance Corporal with a bandaged head. "It's Lieutenant Everson, sir. He'll see us right."

Everson. Bloody boy scout. Still, a plan was forming. He could use the escape as a diversion to return to Chandar's artefact chamber and collect the map.

That voice. Now Edith remembered. The recollection washed over her like a wave. The blood drained from her face and the room began to spin. She clutched at Abbott's shoulder.

"What's up, Edi? What is it? Are you all right?"

"That voice," she said weakly. "I know where I've heard it before. It's him!"

"Who, Lieutenant Jeffries?"

"No, not Jeffries. That's not his name at all."

"Edi, come on love. Of course it is. It's the effects of the insect drug. You're imagining things. We've been though a right old time. I'm sure you're mistaken."

"No," said Edith curtly. "It's him."

"Who?"

She found herself shaking, not with fear, but with anger. It was a fuse lit by the invitation to a private party, fuelled by the murder of her friends and her survivor's guilt, burning through the years of torment and horror on the Front. Unable to contain it any longer she felt it detonate deep within her. Edith broke away from Nellie's grip and strode belligerently towards Jeffries, with no thought for consequences. No thought but for this one remaining moment of reckoning.

"You!"

Jeffries turned towards her, nonplussed. "Me, Nurse?"

"I know who you are!" her voice quavered, barely able to keep the fury under control.

Jeffries smiled wanly at the men near him, who looked confused.

"Yes, dear and so do all these men here. Sister Fenton, if you wouldn't mind, I think one of your charges is becoming a trifle hysterical. It must be the shock, poor thing, hmm?"

Sister Fenton steamed in to cut across Edith's bows. "Nurse Bell, that will be enough!"

Edith balled her hands into fists, her knuckles whitening.

"Enough!" bawled the Sister, grabbing her wrists. "Do you hear? Desist from this foolishness."

But it wasn't enough for her. Not by a long chalk. Edith windmilled her arms trying to break Sister Fenton's grip, but she held her fast. Edith fell into Fenton and glared over her shoulder at Jeffries, whose mouth slid into an insincere smile as he stared not at her, but through her as if she wasn't there. As if she was inconsequential. Well she may well be, but her words weren't.

"I know who you are!" she cried. "His name isn't Jeffries."

"Bell, be quiet!" said Fenton. "Abbott. Help me!"

However, nothing could still her now.

"His name's not Jeffries at all," she cried. "It's Dwyer. Dwyer the Debutante Killer, Fredrick Dwyer, the Diabolist who calls himself The Great Snake. And snake he is," she spat. "*Murderer!*"

CHAPTER EIGHTEEN
"The Verminous Brood"

Restrained by her companions, Edith began to yell hysterically. The men glanced at each other, uncertain of how to react. However, Edith was oblivious to it all. She was focused on one man, the man who was the ruin of her life, the man whose very existence and proximity filled her with such a righteous indignation that, against all social decorum, she could no longer contain it. That he, of all people, should be here, hale and hearty, having perversely survived all the indignities that the war could heap upon him, when her dear friends had been cruelly dispatched for his heretical sport.

"You filthy murderer," she cried, spitting a gob of saliva in his direction. It fell short but the gesture shocked those watching.

Jeffries smiled and casually picked lint off his lapel.

"Bell. Stop this," said Sister Fenton. "You're making a spectacle of yourself."

Edith struggled to face the men gathered round, confused and unsure. "Please, you must believe me. That man there is Fredrick Dwyer. He's wanted for murder."

She heard the muttering of dissent ripple through the soldiers. She knew from the tales she'd heard that he was considered a snob and a martinet. Many men hated his guts, and more than one had a bone to pick with him.

Several men hesitantly pushed their way forward and, exchanging looks, seized Jeffries by the arms.

"Is this true, sir?" asked a Lance Corporal.

"No, of course it isn't, you bloody cretin, she's a hysterical woman," snapped Jeffries. "You're making a big mistake, hmm? Technically, you could both be up on a charge for assaulting an officer. You don't want to add disobeying a direct order to the charge sheet, do you? Apart from which you're messing up my uniform. Unhand me. *Now.*"

Napoo looked from Edith to Jeffries as if trying to weigh their claims.

Captain Grantham glanced at Edith Bell, shaking his head.

Edith tore herself away from Sister Fenton and collapsed into Nellie Abbott's arms, sobbing into her shoulder at the unfairness of it all.

"Let him go," Grantham said to the soldiers restraining Jeffries. The men shuffled uneasily. "I shan't ask again."

The two soldiers glanced at each other uncertainly and then, almost apologetically, at Edith herself.

"No!" she cried as they reluctantly let go and stepped away, shamefaced. "No." Barely more than a whisper now, defeated.

Jeffries smoothed out the sleeves of his tunic, gave his cuffs a cursory tug and nodded his head in acknowledgment to Grantham, who turned to Edith.

"Young lady, this is very serious accusation. The inquest jury found Fredrick Dwyer guilty of the 'wilful murder' of those two girls in his absence. The vermin is still on the run, an absolute coward. Are you seriously suggesting that Lieutenant Jeffries here – who I have personally seen exhibit such bravery as defies description; a man who has been mentioned in dispatches – is nothing more than a common murderer?"

There was a derisive snort from somewhere among the soldiers. Grantham stared hard at them, his glare sweeping like a searchlight, seeking out the dissenting voice but finding none. He bridled and pulled himself up, pushing his chest out.

"Fall in!" The crowd of soldiers jostled and resolved itself into well-drilled ranks.

"I will not have any insolence or insubordination. You are professional soldiers. To that end, you will follow all orders that are given to you. Is that understood?"

"Sir!"

Any help Edith might have expected from the men had now been snatched from her. Napoo was left hovering, still uncertain, his eyes flitting between Edith and Jeffries. The Padre was still slumped on the floor, muttering to himself. Sister Fenton had distanced herself from her charge and looked on frostily, as if she no longer knew her. Only Nellie stood by her, but Edith began to think it was more to stop her making even more of a fool of herself than for actually believing her. Edith sniffed, wiped her eyes, shrugged herself from Nellie's embrace and turned round to glare defiantly at Jeffries. He smiled back at her. The arrogance of the man! Well, there was nothing he could do to her here. There were too many witnesses. At least there was that.

Explosions and rifle fire sounded from outside the chamber.

"Sir, they're coming!"

"Oh, Edith, we're going to be saved!" said Nellie, clasping her hands. "Come on, love. Let it go. You were mistaken, that's all."

"No," said Edith, pulling her hands from Nellie's, adjusting her posture and straightening her back, trying to recover at least some dignity as Jeffries walked over to her.

"I remember you," he whispered. "You missed a frightfully good party, as I recall, hmm? I've just decided to invite you to another."

"Go to hell," she muttered from between clenched teeth.

Quicker than Edith was prepared for, Jeffries swung around behind her, locked his forearm round her neck and drew the pistol from under his tunic. "Oh, I am, but you're coming along, too, I'm afraid. Everson, its seems, has forced my hand."

He covered the startled men with his pistol.

"Jeffries! Damn it, man," said Grantham. "What's got into you?"

"It would be so easy to believe I've funked it like you, wouldn't it, old man? You pathetic oaf. You have no idea who I am, what

I've accomplished. It's every man for himself. You have served your purpose. I have no further need of you. Of any of you. Except you of course, Bell," he added, the intimacy of his warm breath against her ear making her shiver with revulsion.

"Edi!" cried Nellie. She took a step towards Edith.

Edith blinked away tears, shook her head, and watched, relieved, as Sister Fenton put a firm hand on Nellie's shoulder, holding her back.

Several men advanced slowly towards them. Jeffries stilled them with a wave of the pistol in their direction. Napoo, having made his decision, took advantage of the brief distraction and lunged for Jeffries. Jeffries was too quick and pulled the trigger. Edith squealed and Napoo dropped to the floor with a grunt of pain.

"Ah-ah. The rest of you stay back," said Jeffries. "You wouldn't want your little Rose of No Man's Land to wilt prematurely, would you? Don't try and follow me if you know what's good for you, hmm." As Edith struggled to find purchase with her toes in order to relive the pressure against her throat, she felt the last dying embers of her anger fade, leaving only the cold ashes of fear.

"Is it true then? Are you? Are you Dwyer?" asked Grantham with a look of hurt betrayal, like a whipped dog.

"Oh, I've been many people," said Jeffries as he continued to edge toward the door. "I was Dwyer once and I have been many others since. And now, it seems I am done with Jeffries too. The Great Snake sheds its skin once more. Adieu."

"Then where is the real Jeffries?"

"Dead in a ditch outside 'Bertie the last time I saw him," said Jeffries. He stepped back towards the barbed door and called out to the guards. "I want to see Rhengar. GarSuleth wills it!"

There was a brief pause and the doorway began to shrivel open. As soon as he got a clear shot, Jeffries fired through the gap, blowing away the head of the scentirrii outside. He then forced his way through the narrow opening and shot the second scentirrii as he dragged Edith through, her dress catching on the barbs and ripping as he yanked her into the passage. "Don't struggle. You're only alive for as long as I need you. You start struggling, you're a liability."

Some part of Edith, some small part of her, the part that had dried up and withered away that night long ago, accepted this and was at peace with it, perhaps even longed for it. It was as if she had been guided to this moment all along, and that now, at last, she would rejoin her friends. It was almost a relief.

"Ediiiiiii!" she heard Nellie scream before the plant door dilated shut.

Now that the Chatt scent had worn off, the week old stink of sour sweat, smelly feet and musty uniforms was telegraphing their position to every insect in the edifice. Everson and his party had to fight every step of the way.

The Chatts proved no match for the Tommies' weapons; a few had got off discharges from their lances, but otherwise they only had rudimentary spears and swords. However, their sheer numbers were another matter and the Chatts were reacting to their intrusion in a more organised manner now.

Hobson and Atkins continued their advance on point, sticking to the outer wall of the spiralling passage, maximising their field of fire as they fought their way up the edifice; a task made all the more awkward by the restrictive vision of their gas hoods. Everson followed with Poilus. Atkins had that dashed Chatter of his, nosing its way forward on its string lead. Everson felt he was taking a chance trusting the rodent, but it was the only lead they had in finding their friends and comrades.

"Keep a look out, Sergeant. We must be almost there," Everson yelled over the staccato chunter of the Lewis gun behind him. He was vaguely aware of a thick *whoosh*, a smell of fuel oil and a light blooming and fading as Evans and Nicholls sent a spurt of cleansing flame down an adjoining passage.

* * *

Atkins heard a roar from Sergeant Hobson ahead of him as he fired at another mob of advancing Chatts. They seemed to exhibit no sign of fear, despite their brethren being mown down in front of them. Atkins ran forward, emptying his clip into the Chatts as he did so, but they were upon him before he could reload. One lunged with its short sword, cutting Gordon's leash. Atkins parried with his rifle before driving his bayonet through the creature's thorax and twisting the blade. His weapon caught fast on the chitinous armour. Atkins lifted his leg and stomped forwards, driving his foot against the creature's chest, freeing the blade as a second Chatt lunged at him with a spear.

Hobson fired and the Chatt fell back. Atkins brought his hobnailed boot down squarely on the creature's head, smashing its facial plate and grinding his heel into the soft pulpy tissue beneath. He fired again and took out a further two, a single bullet driving straight through both of them.

There was a loud report to his right as Lieutenant Everson finished off another Chatt with his service revolver.

As a fifth lunged with a short spear, Atkins stepped aside and swung his rifle round, catching it in the faceplate with the shoulder butt, sending it reeling against the wall. He fell against it, the length of the rifle barrel against its throat, trying to choke it. He pushed harder on the barrel and felt something crack, but the Chatt continued to struggle. Something stabbed at his abdomen. He felt the claws of the middle limbs pressing into his skin though his tunic and shirt, holding him in a vice-like grip, as the creature's mandibles scythed lethally together again and again in front of his gas-hooded face.

Then the Chatt pushed forward with its powerful limbs, slamming Atkins into the opposite wall. He collapsed heavily to the floor, gasping for breath, lights bursting in front of his eyes. His gas hood had been knocked askew in the impact and he could only see out of one eyepiece. The Chatt's mouthparts filled his small circle of vision. Atkins struggled to keep the scissoring mandibles as far away as possible, saliva dripping thickly onto his mask. He felt his strength fading. In seconds, the weight of the Chatt would bear its mandibles down towards him. He thought of the face of the German soldier he had killed in the shell hole and began to sob with desperation. He didn't want to die, he couldn't die. He had to survive; he had to get back to Flora.

Oh, God, Flora. Poor Flora.

He roared in frustration as the muscles in his arms began to burn with the effort of keeping the thrashing louse at bay, then he heard a crunch and felt the weight lifted from him. He felt a hand find his.

"Up you get, son," said Sergeant Hobson, pulling him into a sitting position. Atkins ripped the suffocating gas hood from his head and sucked in a lungful of air, his face dripping with sweat. The Chatt lay by his side, its head caved in by 'Little Bertha.'

"You were bloody lucky. By rights, that thing should have spat acid at you," said Hobson.

"It tried," he said. "But I think I broke something in its throat."

"If you get in that close again – and I don't recommend you do – go for their antennae, lad. It doesn't always stop them but it does seem to confuse 'em for a while."

"Thanks, Sarn't," Atkins rasped. Coughing, he picked up his rifle and struggled to his feet, shoving his gas hood back into its bag. It was proving more a hindrance than a help. He noticed the string hanging limply on his belt. "Blood and sand! Gordon, where are you? Gordon!"

"I have it," called Poilus, rounding the corner, holding the thing up, its belly cupped in the palm of his hand, its legs hanging limply as its nose twitched eagerly. Poilus handed him over. Relieved, Atkins held it up to his face and cooed at it. Gordon's long tongue flicked out and licked him briefly, before the creature sniffed mournfully at his chattless khaki jacket. Atkins crouched down, intending to tie Gordon's broken string leash, but the little devil struggled out of his grip.

The Sergeant, back against the outside wall of the tunnel, edged forward, craning his neck in order to look as far forward as possible. "I can't see anything. They've pulled back."

"Gordon!" hissed Atkins. The Sergeant looked back to see the furry rodent dash past him. He attempted to grab it, but missed. It stopped just ahead, and sat up on its hind feet, sniffing. Atkins raced towards it but Hobson stuck out an arm to stop him.

"Shh."

Atkins froze. They felt a soft draught. A faint rumble from up ahead grew louder. Atkins looked at the Sergeant who raised his eyebrows, shook his head and shrugged. He obviously had no idea what it was either, but whatever it was, the noise was getting louder.

Gordon squeaked and darted back between Atkins' legs and down the slope toward the others.

"Good enough for me!" Atkins said. "Run!"

They ran back down the passage towards the rest of the party. Atkins told himself not to look back, but he couldn't help himself. He glanced over his shoulder and instantly wished he hadn't.

A large sphere of stone filled the tunnel, rolling down the incline towards them and picking up speed.

There was a sound like cellophane being scrunched up as the boulder crushed the bodies of the dead Chatts behind them.

"Shit! Come on!" grunted Gutsy as he tried to haul his sled of equipment.

"Leave it!" cried Atkins as he pounded past.

But Gutsy wouldn't. He leaned forward in his harness and cried out as he dug one foot in front of the other. The boulder was almost upon them now. Half Pint dashed forwards and gave the sled a shove from the back. The sled shot forward but Half Pint lost his footing. There was a sickening thud and the rumbling stopped.

The boulder had ground to a halt, jamming itself against the tunnel walls by the sled. Half Pint lay in front of it, screaming, his right foot under the giant stone.

Atkins reached him first and hurriedly knelt down to examine his leg. Not that he could have done anything. He had no medical training and the only medical supplies he carried were the regulation Field Bandages.

"Tell me the worst, I can take it." Half Pint said through a grimace of pain as he grabbed Atkins' forearm.

"Well, put it this way," said Atkins, "it'll really give you something to grouse about now."

Everson and Hobson trotted forward and examined the boulder.

"We're not going to be moving this any time soon," Hobson said. "Looks like this is their way to block access to the upper levels.

"The Chatts know they've got us cornered. They'll be here with reinforcements soon. We've got to clear this blockage and we can't do it with Nicholls there," said Everson. He paused briefly. "Get Blood up here."

Everson squatted beside Atkins to talk to Half Pint. "We've got to get through this boulder, Nicholls. We've got to blow it. We can't do that with you here." Nicholls looked up at him uncomprehendingly, eyes clouded with pain.

Out of the corner of his eye, Atkins could see Hobson talking quietly to Gutsy, flicking discreet glances at the trapped soldier. Gutsy sagged visibly then walked leadenly towards them.

Half Pint caught sight of him as he shucked off his pack and pulled out his cleaver, its broad blade reflecting the dull blue light of the luminescent lichen. He gripped Atkins' hand in fear, tears welling up in his eyes. "Oh God, no. Please. No. Only. No, don't let them cut my leg off. Please, Only, I'm begging you. Please!" Sobbing, Half Pint began clawing at the ground, desperately trying to drag himself free of the boulder. "Please Gutsy, don't do this."

"I'm sorry Half Pint, there's no other way," he said, avoiding his eyes.

He knelt by his comrade and tore strips from his trouser leg, making a tourniquet that he began to tighten around Half Pint's thigh.

"No, wait. Wait!" begged Half Pint.

"Sorry, mate," said Gutsy, before punching Half Pint solidly in the head. He went out like a light. "Right. Are we doing this?"

Everson nodded.

"Only, you're going to have to hold his leg steady."

Gutsy placed Atkins' hand on Half Pint's thigh. Atkins closed his eyes and heard a brief, faint whistle as the cleaver cleft the air before striking through flesh and bone and hitting the compacted earth floor beneath.

When Atkins opened them again the Lieutenant was trying to apply the field bandages to the bleeding stump below the knee as blood pulsed out, soaking them as fast as he applied them.

"Ketch, Hopkiss," he called, "get up here and take Nicholls back to cover."

They jogged up, looked at Half Pint and then at Gutsy, who was cleaning his cleaver with another field bandage. He glared at them, daring them to say something. Atkins shook his head. Silently, the two men carried the unconscious Half Pint back out of sight, round the gentle curve of the tunnel.

Atkins held out a Mills bomb. "Grenades, sir?"

"Yes, I think so, Atkins," said a visibly shaken Everson, before marching smartly back around the curve himself.

Atkins approached the boulder and chose spots to wedge the grenades while trying to avoid the crushed and bloody leg that protruded from under the great ball.

Gordon had found his nerve again and was snuffling hopefully about the base of the sphere, sucking hungrily for a faint air current. Atkins scooped him up and tucked him under his arm. He licked his dry lips, pinched his lower lip between his teeth nervously and put a finger though the ring of the grenade's safety pin. He braced himself, took a deep breath, pulled the pin out and ran.

"Take cover!"

The detonation filled the corridor with clouds of dust, smoke and debris. The force of the explosion blew Atkins over one of the sleds.

Once the dust had settled Atkins followed the others as they began to make their way over the litter of rubble that was strewn across the floor of the tunnel. Gutsy shouldered his sled harnesses again and moved out, an unconscious Half

Pint lying on the soft bed of fungus that covered the weapons supply. Ketch followed with his own sled. Atkins clipped a full magazine into his Enfield, fell in with Hobson on point and pushed on, Gordon nosing on ahead snuffling and sniffing, occasionally giving out little high-pitched sneezes. Then Atkins heard the familiar clatter of Chatt carapaces rubbing against each other.

"Ready, lad?" asked Hobson. "Look sharp, here come more of the verminous brood."

As the Chatts skittered toward them they opened fire, five rounds rapid, and the insects fell beneath their fusillade. Atkins and Hobson moved on, leaving any wounded to Gazette and the Lieutenant.

That was when they heard the scream. A human scream.

"Sir!" yelled Hobson, running up the incline to a junction where the floor levelled out. Gordon pattered excitedly past him, his tongue flickering out of his furry proboscis as he scampered off to the left.

Atkins followed and they came to a barbed plant door. Gordon was snuffling excitedly at the bottom of it. The bodies of two Chatts lay twisted and dead against the passage wall.

Everson came up and quickly appraised the situation "Evans, Hopkiss!" The pair came up with Evan's Flammenwerfer. "Get that door open!"

"Stand back!" cried Evans and, a few seconds later, with Hopkiss operating the valve, a spurt of flaming oil blasted the door. It shrivelled under the jet of liquid fire, spitting and popping, a sound like a human scream coming from it as it burnt. There was a crack and barbs exploded from the door, some embedding themselves in the wall opposite.

"Gordon!" cried Atkins, pushing men aside.

The little rodent lay bleeding and whimpering, impaled by one the barbs. His nose twitched as he sought comfort in the musty smell of fresh lice he would now no longer taste. He looked up at Atkins, pitifully, and was then still. Atkins sighed briefly and stood up.

Once the smoke and flame had dissipated, the chamber beyond stood revealed amid a circle of glowing cinders. The faces of about twenty men looked back at them.

There were brief cheers and backslapping as the parties were reunited.

"Where's Jeffries?" Everson said.

"He escaped, kidnapping the Nurse. It turns out his real name isn't Jeffries."

Porgy pushed his way though the huddle, Lewis gun slung from his shoulder. "Edith!" he called "Edith?" He found a tearful Nellie Abbott trying to staunch the bleeding from Napoo, who was lying wounded beside her. "Where is she? What the hell's happened here?"

"He's taken her! He's going to do her in, I know he is. You have to save her!"

Atkins exchanged a glance with Everson. He'd known there was something fishy about Jeffries. Their findings in his dugout had aroused his suspicions, now the latest events had confirmed them.

"Edith said he was that murderer, Dwyers," one of the Tommies said.

"Dwyers the Diabolist?" said Everson.

"The same, sir," replied the Lance Corporal.

"We've got to save her, sir!" said Porgy.

"Damn!" muttered Everson. "Hobson, start moving these men out. Hopkiss go with him."

"But sir!"

"That's an order. Atkins, with me."

Hobson and Ketch began handing out weapons from the sleds and a chain quickly formed as the men passed them on. Gutsy carefully lifted a semi-conscious Half Pint so they could get to the rest. Poilus helped lift Napoo onto the empty sled.

Everson found Grantham slumped against the wall, muttering to himself.

"Sir!" he said, shaking the officer.

Grantham looked up at him blankly. "Jeffries."

"I know," said Everson. "We need to leave. Now, sir."

Grantham shook his head. "I've served my men badly, Everson. Funked it. If I go back, it's a court martial for me. At least here, I can do something useful. Give me a gun. I can buy you some time, watch your back."

Everson studied the man carefully. He didn't have the time or the inclination to talk him out of it. He was a bad officer, but if he wanted to buy himself some dignity, so be it.

"Sergeant, get the Captain a Lewis gun and magazines. Leave him some grenades and an Enfield, too."

"Thank you," Grantham whispered.

Everson caught sight of the Corporal. "Ketch, follow me!"

Ketch fell in behind him and glanced at Atkins, barely managing to suppress a sneer.

"Hobson," called the Lieutenant, "we'll meet you in that fungus farming chamber where we got the sleds. Maybe you can rally some of those captive Urmen to rise up, give Jellicoe a chance to exorcise his Labour urges. I think we could use a General Strike after all."

Porgy grabbed Atkins' forearm as he left with the Lieutenant. "Save her," he said. "And make that bastard pay!"

CHAPTER NINETEEN
"While You've a Lucifer..."

"D'you think it's true then, sir, Jeffries is that bastard Dwyer?" asked Atkins as he jogged to keep up with Everson. He'd promised Porgy he'd save Edith. But what could he do up against someone of the likes of Frederick Dwyer? He was infamous, the Most Evil Man in England according to the *Daily Sketch*. As a hate figure, he was second only to Kaiser Bill. Half the stories that were in the press you didn't know whether to believe or not, they were so far-fetched. And even though they had been thinking that maybe the Chatts had brought them here to this god-forsaken place, what if it had been Jeffries... Dwyer... whatever, all along? Could he do that? The papers had been full of sensational stories of his past, the adventure magazines doubly so. Had he really made a pact with the devil?

"Well he's as good as admitted it, by all accounts," said Everson. "Even if he isn't, he's still in a hell of a lot of trouble. If those papers are anything to go by that's fraudulent enlistment, impersonating an officer, at the very least. Not that any of that matters a jot against a death sentence. Chap was going to swing before we ever came across him."

"I can't believe it," said Ketch. "He seemed like such an upstanding bloke."

"Well, he would to you," said Atkins. "Man after your own heart by the sound of it."

"Watch your mouth, Atkins, I'm still your NCO and don't you forget it."

"How could I?" muttered Atkins. "You never bloody let me."

Behind him, Atkins heard the rattle of the Lewis gun and the confused squealing of Chatts as Captain Grantham covered their escape.

Everson halted at a junction. Ahead, the passage branched. There was an opening to their left, decorated with some kind of hieroglyphs. After the unadorned, functional nature of the rest of the edifice, this struck him as something important, at least to the Chatts.

"Damn! I think Jeffries has given us the slip."

The excited clicking of alien jaws and joints alerted them to another approaching troop of insect soldiers ahead.

"Heads up, chaps," Everson warned as he backed against the wall, pistol arm extended. Ketch stopped beside him, dropped down on one knee and raised his rifle. Atkins fell in behind him, rifle at the ready. The troops of Chatts skittered round the corner, some carrying lances, others carrying short swords and spears.

"Wait for it," said Everson. "Fire!"

Atkins and Ketch fired and cycled, fired and cycled. The Chatts went down in a hail of bullets.

"Well Jeffries obviously didn't go that way," said Everson, and looked again into the dark opening to his left.

The distant sound of the Grantham's machine gun had stopped. It was replaced by several rifle shots, followed by several high-pitched squeals. There was a brief silence then a defiant shout. "Come on you bastards. I'll show you what backbone is. For the Pennines!" The tunnel echoed to the sound of a roar of rage and, following closely on its heels, a drawn out wail of anguish, pain and terror, punctuated by the explosions of Mills bombs.

"Sir?" said Corporal Ketch, looking at Everson expectantly.

"We can't help him."

A muffled pistol shot rang out from somewhere beyond the ornate doorway.

"This way!" said Everson, reloading his revolver before advancing cautiously. Behind him, the two soldiers slotted fresh magazine cartridges into their rifles.

Jeffries strode confidently through the dark high space of the temple, his hand tightly around Edith's wrist, dragging her along like a recalcitrant child. A large scentirrii in a silk scarlet tabard approached him with a spear. Jeffries shot it in the head. In the shadows, he saw dhuyumirrii and acolytes withdraw, melting into the shadows, clicking in agitation. He only had a few rounds left in his pistol but he only had to make it to the chamber where the Khungarrii had deposited their trench equipment. But his main priority was Chandar's little heretical collection.

"Please, stop," said Edith. "Whatever you thinking of doing, please don't!"

"What?" he said distracted. He stormed into the library chamber of niches where he saw again the scriptural jars filled with their holophrastic scents. "Chandar!" he called, waving his pistol and swinging Edith brusquely round in front of him for a shield, like a clumsy dance partner.

The acolyte Chatts backed away. He shot a jar, taking delight in the Chatts' alarmed reaction as it shattered, leaving a sticky sour smelling unguent to drip thickly from its niche. "Chandar!" he bellowed at a cowering insect. "Chan-dar, you arthropodal cretin! Where. Is. He?"

The old, maimed Chatt appeared. "What is this? We had an agreement."

"We did," said Jefferies. "Change of plan. I'm afraid it's off. However, if you want my men they're yours. Keep them, cull them, it's all the same to me."

"This trait of disloyalty is one we know runs through Urman culture, but you took the Rite of GarSuleth. How can you do this?"

"It's called individuality. You should try it sometime," said Jeffries.

He pushed the pistol into the holster of his Sam Brown and flung Bell to the floor before picking up a jar of sacred unguent. He swirled it around and watched particles of aromatic compound dance in a thick suspension of what he surmised was some sort of oil. He pulled the stopper from it and sniffed cautiously.

"It contains a distillation of ancient proverbs," explained Chandar.

"And this?" Jeffries asked, indicating another jar.

"The commentaries of Thradagar."

"And this?"

"The Osmissals of Skarra."

"And this?"

"The Aromathia Colonia."

All Jeffries could smell was rotting plums, pine sap and a hint of motor oil. It was intensely frustrating. All this knowledge and no way to access it. He pulled out a monogrammed handkerchief from his trouser pocket and poured some of the oil onto it, soaking the cloth before stuffing the handkerchief into the neck of the bottle. From his pocket, he withdrew a battered packet of gaspers, put one in his mouth, took out a packet of Lucifer matches and struck one against the box. It flared brightly.

Chandar staggered back, awed by the sight, and watched nervously, its eyes locked on the jar.

"What are you doing?" The pungent smell of phosphor drifted around the room, which seemed to alarm and frighten the other Chatts, who backed up against the wall, all except Chandar.

Jeffries casually lit his cigarette, took a deep draw, and smiled before holding the lit Lucifer to the corner of the oil-soaked cloth. He hurled the improvised petrol bomb down a gallery where it smashed with a splash of flame, catching other containers which quickly combusted. Jeffries watched in satisfaction before making another makeshift bomb, this time ripping a strip of cloth from Bell's already torn dress to use as a wick.

"What have you done?" cried Chandar, his mouth parts slack with horror.

"I've done you a favour," said Jeffries, pulling his pistol from his belt once more. Thick heady smoke coiled against the roof of the Receptory chamber and began to sink down. He grabbed a coughing Bell and a shocked Chandar, bereft at the sudden brutal loss of its precious scent texts. He urged them at gunpoint down the interconnecting passage that led to the Chatt's alchemical work chambers, closely followed by tendrils of smoke.

The smell of the smoke had already alerted the Chatts in the Olfactory, where they worked their strange mixture of theology and alchemy. They were running hither and thither in great agitation as Jeffries shoved Bell and Chandar into the room. Jeffries casually surveyed the space and chose his target.

"No! You can not," wheezed Chandar.

"Dwyer, you're mad!" said Bell. It earned her a vicious slap across the face and she staggered back, stunned.

Taking the lit cigarette from his mouth and touching it to the oil-soaked wick, he watched the flame lick up the cloth before casting the bomb into a workshop beyond. It smashed in a spray of fire amongst the volatile distilling jars, prompting soft *whooffs* of combustion whose gentle sound belied their ferocity.

Waiting only long enough to watch the fire catch, Jeffries took a last drag and flicked the glowing Woodbine into the strengthening blaze, before pushing his hostages on.

In the chamber beyond, where the Chatts had stored the trench equipment, Jeffries reloaded his pistol and picked up a webbing belt of Mills bombs. Keeping a wary eye on Bell and Chandar he hastily emptied boxes of small arms ammunition into haversacks along with tins of Machonochies, Plum and Apple and bully beef. Using webbing, he tied them together with several rifles and, as gently but hastily as he could, lowered them out of a window opening on a length of rope. He could hear the rifles clatter against the face of the edifice below. Then the rope ran short and he had to drop his load to tumble down onto a midden heap far below. He could only hope it wasn't all damaged beyond use once he retrieved the items.

He noted the trench mortar 'Plum Puddings' and smiled to himself. They should go up nicely. There would be little danger of pursuit after that. And after his sacrilegious arson a state of such enmity should exist between the Khungarrii and the Pennines that there would be no chance of a ceasefire. They would be locked in a cycle of mutual attack and counter attack. Everson and his men would have stepped from one war only to find themselves in another, leaving him free to follow his own path unchallenged. All he needed was that map.

"Take me to your Urman artefacts," he ordered Chandar. Gripping an increasingly dishevelled Bell by the unravelling bun at the nape of her neck he dragged her along impatiently as Chandar led the way, leaving the sounds of explosions and dying Chatts in his wake.

Outside the artefact chamber he beckoned Chandar to open the plant door. Inside, Jeffries swung Bell around and flung her against the wall. She dropped to the floor, dazed by the impact. He jerked his chin and ushered Chandar over against the wall beside her. Bell felt the back of her head and examined her hand, blinking incomprehensibly at the blood she found there.

"You know, until I met you I'd begun to lose all hope," said Jeffries, addressing Chandar, as he glanced around at the priceless archaeological treasures.

He strode straight to the niche containing the map, lifting it from its bark backing where it had been pinned like some entomological specimen. He folded it along well-worn creases and thrust it into his tunic.

Jeffries wheeled about, his eyes sweeping across the niches and exhibits of Chandar's collection. He walked to the wall and swept several items into the open maw of his haversack.

"So you were aware of these things? They do have meaning?" said Chandar.

Jeffries had the feeling the Chatt was learning more about 'Urmen' now than it had done in all its studies and it didn't like what it was seeing.

"Oh yes," said Jeffries. "More than you can ever know. I will be eternally grateful to you. I'm sure you'll be eager to know that you've served your part as an instrument of Croatoan."

"You dare accuse me of heresy! This one serves only GarSuleth."

"Only at the behest of Croatoan," countered Jeffries, grabbing the wrists of the dazed nurse and ushering her out of the chamber. "And as an instrument of Croatoan, I shall spare your life, as it was you who showed me the next step on the road toward communion with Croatoan himself. But that is the only grace you have earned from me."

Once outside the chamber Jeffries pulled the pin from a Mills bomb, before tossing the grenade into the room and ushering Chandar and Edith swiftly away. No one else would have access to the secrets he now possessed. The explosion brought the earthen walls crashing down behind them. Weakened, several chambers above collapsed, leaving a gaping breach in the side of the edifice through which they could just make out the jungle beyond.

A venomous hiss was the only warning Jeffries received before Chandar launched itself at them. Jeffries swung Bell into the creature's path. She screamed as she collided with the Chatt, sending them both careening into the wall. He put the pistol against the bony chitin of Chandar's head.

"Try that again, old thing, and I'll break more than your antennae. I'll blow your bally head off, hmm?"

Chandar hissed again, but this time in impotence, its mouthparts waving in frustration.

Dazed, Edith caught sight of the folded parchment peeking out from inside Jeffries' jacket as he bent over the insect. She was sure he would kill her but she wouldn't die quietly like Elspeth and Cissy. She had finally faced her demon – and he was just a man. And what did men want? Power. That parchment had to mean a great deal to him if he'd gone to these lengths to obtain it. So if he wanted it, she wanted it. Maybe it would give her something with which to bargain. Before she even knew what she was doing she slipped her hand into his tunic and snatched the parchment. He lashed out with a howl of fury, grabbing the hem of her torn uniform. She kicked out, ripping it away from him. He stumbled. Edith darted back into the chamber where the trench equipment was held. Perhaps there she could find something with which to defend herself.

"Come back here, you bitch!"

Edith threw herself behind one of the piles of trench equipment, her heart pounding. What was it that was so important about this parchment? Fingers trembling, she unfolded it, desperately hoping its contents might give her more leverage. It was some sort of map but she could make nothing of the symbols and writing. Shaking her head she refolded the map and continued to search for a weapon.

She heard Jeffries enter the chamber. There was a crash as he lashed out at a pile of equipment. "Give me the map, girl. Give me the bloody map."

There was a hiss and chatter. Peering out, Edith watched as Chandar attacked Jeffries again. Jeffries pistol-whipped the old Chatt and send it sprawling against the chamber wall, the last of its strength and anger dissipated. She let out an involuntary gasp. Hearing the sound, Jeffries turned. She ducked back out of sight, but too late. Jeffries strode round the pile, hauled her up by the hair, tore the map from her grasp and shoved it back into his tunic.

"I warned you," he said.

As Everson followed the trail of death and destruction through the temple, a screaming, flaming apparition ran towards them. A Chatt ablaze, sheets of fire wrapping themselves about it as it stumbled. Startled, Atkins let off a shot. The screaming stopped and the shape tumbled to the floor.

Next they came upon the burning library and alchemical chambers. Scrolls were crisping, shrivelling and burning while jars cracked and exploded in adjoining galleries, Chatts flinging themselves on the flames in a vain attempt to extinguish them. They were so intent on saving whatever was stored there that they paid no heed to the three Tommies that hurried through their midst.

Racing down a short tunnel, the soldiers heard a scream and burst into a chamber containing large piles of trench equipment to see Edith struggling with Jeffries.

"Halt!" yelled Everson, his pistol aimed squarely at the man's head. "Give yourself up, Jeffries."

"Everson, what a surprise. I might have known it would be you. Ever the boy scout, hmm. However, I'm your commanding officer. You're only a second Lieutenant. I think you'll find *I* give the orders around here."

"We both know that's not true, don't we?" said Everson. "You signed up as a private under a false name. You're no officer."

Atkins and Ketch covered Jeffries nervously as he held Nurse Bell to his chest, one arm around her throat. The injured Chatt lay crumpled against the wall, one arm seemingly broken, its antennae stumps twitching feebly.

"Let Nurse Bell go," Everson said, calmly.

"No."

"Let her go, Jeffries – or should I say, Dwyer?"

"Ah, so it's come to that has it?"

"Look, we can talk about this."

"Can we? I don't think so. Let's ask Nurse Bell, shall we?" Jeffries tightened his arm around her throat and her face began to turn purple as he applied more pressure.

"You've got nowhere to go, Jeffries."

"That's where you're wrong, though I must admit for a while there, when we first arrived here, I was worried."

Atkins, who had begun to edge along the wall, trying to flank Jeffries, found himself in Jeffries' sights as the man pointed the pistol at him.

"I think you'd better stop right there, Atkins, yes?"

"Sir?"

"Don't move, Atkins," said Everson, taking a step forward. "Jeffries, for God's sake man, give yourself up. It's a court martial. I swear you'll be dealt with fairly."

"If you know who I am then you'll know I'm facing the drop. Call that a fair trial? Besides, if you kill me you'll never get home. You're here because of me. Did you know that? I brought you here. Without me, you'll never get back. Never. It's taken the deaths of thousands of men to achieve this. I worked for years to this end; do you think I'm going to let you stop me now?"

Atkins was shaken. A way home? *Flora, oh dear God, please let it be true.* But having to deal with a rogue like Jeffries to get back? Atkins began to lower his rifle.

"Don't believe him, Atkins," snapped Everson. "The man's a congenital liar, a fantasist." He appealed to Jeffries again. "Can't we talk about this like rational men?" he asked.

"Talk about what, Everson? Your ignorance, your fear of responsibility? Do you even realise what it is I've accomplished here? Do you realise that you've been party to the greatest occult undertaking of the age?"

"You can't be serious, Jeffries. Listen to yourself. That's utter humbug!"

"Is it? Look around you, Everson. Can your small provincial mind even conceive the scope of what has happened? No, don't bother. Only a handful of people would truly understand my achievement. Magi for centuries have failed where I have succeeded. Only death on a truly industrial scale could have been sufficient to invoke Croatoan. I saw to it that those pointless deaths on the Front weren't wasted. I harnessed them. Used them to charge a pentagram set into the very landscape itself."

"You're mad!"

"That's what that hedonistic mooncalf, Crowley, said and where is he now? Skulking in America, plying his lies to Colonial toadies and lickspittles."

"It's shell-shock. Jeffries, you're not well."

"You want to go home? You want to see Blighty again?" roared Jeffries. "Well I know the way. Kill me and you're stranded forever."

Everson faltered and his pistol arm slowly lowered.

"He's bluffing, sir," said Atkins. "Isn't he?"

"He's got some sort of map," said Nurse Bell. "He's gone to a lot of trouble to get it."

A grin slid onto Jeffries' face as he arched an eyebrow. "Tick, tock, Everson. The Captain's funked it, and you're Commanding Officer now. It's your call. Your responsibility. Do daddy proud. These men that survived? Nothing more than the dregs that Croatoan rejected. I have no more use for them. I commend them into your care. It may be that their deaths can return you the way they brought me!"

"The devil take you, Jeffries!"

"The name, Everson, is Dwyer!" he spat, and with that Jeffries opened his arm, threw Nurse Bell aside and fired.

Everson grunted as the impact of the bullet into his shoulder drove him back and spun him around.

Ketch fired back. Jeffries ducked behind a pile of trench supplies and returned fire.

Behind Jeffries, Bell hoisted up her ripped skirt and swung her foot between Jeffries' legs. It connected with a satisfying thud and he doubled over.

Tears filling his eyes and distorting his vision, Jeffries fired again. Atkins ducked only to hear tiny clangs as metal struck metal. He looked around for the source and saw hissing green gas escaping from two chlorine cylinders, almost buried under a pile of trench supplies.

"Gas! Gas! Gas!" he shouted.

Jeffries grabbed hold of Bell again. "That," he said, pulling her head back with a sharp jerk, "wasn't nice. Just for that you don't get to die quickly." He released her and punched her in the solar plexus, winding her, before flinging her across the floor towards the punctured gas cylinders.

CHAPTER TWENTY
"The Caterpillar Crawl..."

Jeffries fled the way he had come, diving out past Chandar under a fusillade of bullets from Atkins. Seconds later, there was an explosion as he set a off a grenade bringing the entrance down and cutting off any pursuit. Clouds of dust and debris billowed into the room, mixing with the rising gas and blocking the doorway. The fires they passed had spread and the entrance they came in by was now ablaze and impassable. Everson and the others were trapped.

To Atkins it smelt just like the trenches again and he almost gagged. Shouldering his rifle, he dashed over to Edith who was on all fours, gasping for breath, a deadly green tide lapping about her hands and feet. Atkins pulled her to her feet before rifling through the pile of equipment. The Chatts must have taken a gas hood or two, but try as he might he couldn't find one. He turned around in a panic to see her giving him a pleading look as the gas, still pouring from the cylinders, began to rise around them. There was nothing else for it. He undid the bag around his neck, took out his own gas hood and pushed the stiffened flannel into her hands.

"Mouthpiece between your teeth. Tuck it into your collar and remember, in through the nose, out through the mouth," Atkins explained as he guided her to the wall where Lieutenant Everson lay slumped. His eyes scanned the room. The only way out was a vent hole in the wall.

The stench of chlorine began to sting his nostrils and he coughed thickly as he levered the Lieutenant to his feet.

"It's all right, Atkins. He just got me in the shoulder," said Everson through a grimace, a dark stain spreading over the arm of his tunic.

"Gas, sir. You need to get your hood on," he said, unbuckling the officer's canvas bag and pulling out the contraption. Everson pulled it over his head with his good arm.

"The air shaft looks to be our only way out," said Atkins. Linking his fingers, he boosted Everson up to the hole. Once he was in, Atkins was about to do the same for Edith, when he noticed the state of her now torn and ripped uniform. Embarrassed at the sight of her stockings he averted his eyes and caught sight of a pair of part-worn khaki trousers that he had scattered from one of the piles. He picked them up and offered them to her. She took them and he turned away as she stepped into them and tore a strip from the remains of her dress to use as a belt. "I'm ready," she enunciated from inside her gas hood, tapping him on the shoulder.

He boosted her up on his hands and she disappeared into the vent.

The gas was thickening rapidly now, swirling in the rising currents of heated air from the blazing chamber next door. Atkins began to cough. Christ. This was no way to die. Something sprang into his mind from his early days in training. He pulled out his handkerchief, unbuttoned his fly and fished about inside. Thank God he was scared enough. After a brief moment when he thought he couldn't, he managed to pee on the cloth, rung it out and, blanching slightly, tied it over his nose and mouth as he went back to look for Ketch in the rapidly thickening lethal mist.

"Ketch!" he cried.

He began wafting an arm about in front of him, disturbing the gas, creating eddies that swirled sullenly apart. He spied Ketch slumped awkwardly on the floor by the chlorine cylinders, a broadening stain on his tunic, one hand clutching weakly at his throat, Atkins knelt beside him. Ketch attempted to smile when he saw him, but produced nothing more than an ugly snarl, as if it were sheer vitriol that was keeping him alive.

"Bastard's done for me," he gasped. "You could let me die here with our secret. Nobody else would know. But you can't, can you? That would mean you were really *were* a bad person. And you're desperate to prove yourself otherwise, aren't you?"

"Let me help you."

Ketch coughed again and grinned through the blood and the green foam that began to froth at the corners of his mouth. "You can't help me now, Atkins."

"I can! We can get out of here." He put his arms under Ketch's armpits and began to lift him but the corporal retched and coughed, his face beginning to blacken from exposure to the gas. "Ketch!"

The corporal clawed at his throat as the chlorine reacted with the moisture inside his lungs. His eyes widened with terror. He began to kick and thrash, reeling around the floor, gasping for a life-saving breath that would never come. It was all Atkins could do to hold him.

"Atkins..." he gurgled, "one... thing..."

"What?"

"...She's... *pregnant*..."

"Who?' he asked, before he realised. *Flora.*

"S'you in hlll..." gurgled Ketch, his back arching as he patted his tunic pocket and his last breath bubbled up out of him, leaving a satisfied sneer etched on his face.

"Ketch! Ketch!"

Coughing and spluttering now, his own eyes watering, Atkins shook the corporal's body. Unbidden he felt Flora's lips on his; insistent, soft, yielding. He could taste the salt of her tears as they lost themselves in a rising urgency that, for a moment, washed away the grief; fingers fumbling at buttons and petticoats by the light of the parlour fire. Even as he recalled the moment, he tore open Ketch's tunic and rummaged through the pockets. Inside Ketch's pay book, he found a letter, addressed to himself in Flora's own hand. It had been opened. The bastard! How long had he had it? He quickly shoved it inside his own tunic. Please God, let him not have told anyone else.

He took Ketch's gas hood from its bag and rolled it down over his head in place of the urine-sodden cloth. As he headed back to the vent, he passed the Chatt wheezing for breath in the rising chlorine. He was going to leave the disgusting thing to its fate, but overcome with grief and remorse he took pity on it, if only to prove to himself that he *was* a good person. He squatted down to lift it up. The creature attempted to scuttle back against the wall, hissing, its mouth palps fluttering briefly with the force of the exhalation. As he put it over his shoulder it protested weakly, like a drowsy wasp in the first chill of autumn.

The blaze from the adjacent room was beginning to spread now. The encroaching flames cast surreal shadows on the rising chlorine fog. Atkins hoisted the Chatt up and fed it into the vent above his head, then took several steps back and ran at the wall, leaping up towards the hole and catching its lip. He pulled himself up into the shaft and found himself looking at the Chatt.

"Why?" it asked.

"Because it's the right thing to do. Because I am a good man. We're not all like Jeffries. And because no one deserves a death like that. We have to move."

The shaft angled down steeply and Atkins could feel a strong, cold draught blowing over him as they slid down for what seemed a long way. The Chatt in front of him suddenly dropped and Atkins found himself sliding out of the vent and falling to land heavily below.

"Steady, Atkins," said Everson, helping him as he climbed to his feet. Atkins pulled off his gas hood to see Edith looking nervously at the Chatt, who cowered against the wall of the passage.

"Shouldn't you shoot it?"

"No, Bell, I don't think so," said Everson, wincing with pain from his shoulder wound.

One of her eyes was starting to puff up and bruises were blooming on her cheeks. Her hair was in complete disarray. She looked like some kind of wild woman. Atkins felt a surge of anger at what Jeffries had done to her, immediately followed by self-recrimination. Was he really any better? Oh Flora, what had he done? His whole world had been turned upside down. Again. If she was pregnant, then it wasn't going to be hard for anyone to work out it couldn't be William's child. She would have to bear the barrage of gossip, the barbed comments, the withering fire of disapproving glances and the machine gun stuttering of tutting. And she would have to bear it alone.

He was aware of Lieutenant Everson shaking his shoulder.

"Atkins, where's Corporal Ketch?"

"Gone west, sir. Gas."

There was a series of explosions high above. Rubble erupted out of the vent followed by faint wisps of chlorine gas and, from somewhere behind them, the noise of gunfire grew louder.

"Damn." Everson crouched down in front of the Chatt. "Which way to the fungus farming chamber?" he said. The Chatt looked up at him. "Do you understand me? Can you speak?"

"Yes, this one can speak Urmanii."

"Do you have a name?"

"Chandar."

"Well, Chandar, we need a way out and you're going to have to show us. On your feet."

The Chatt rose as Everson ushered it to the fore. Atkins took up the rear, making sure that Bell was in front of him as he cycled his rifle bolt. They hadn't gone a dozen yards when Atkins heard shouts and shots behind him.

"Sir," he said turning round at the sound of running feet. Sergeant Hobson, Gazette and Pot Shot came hurtling round the bend.

"Sir?" gasped Hobson. "How the hell did you get here?"

Everson nodded towards the smoking vent. "Snakes and ladders."

The burly Sergeant took it in his stride. "Right you are then, sir."

There were several bursts of rapid fire from behind them as the rest of the Black Hand Gang, freed Tommies and nurses crowded along the passage, pulling the sleds with the injured Napoo and Half Pint on them, Poilus among those at the back fighting a rear-guard action.

"They're hard behind us, sir," called Hobson.

"Only!" called Porgy pushing through the throng. "Only! Where's Edith? Did you find them?" Atkins smiled as he turned aside to reveal Edith Bell stood behind him.

"Edi!" squealed Nellie Abbott, pushing past Porgy and flinging herself into Edith's arms, then stood back and looked her up and down, taking in the khaki trousers. "Edi Bell! I never took you for a suffragette."

"Times change," said Edith.

"You did good," said Porgy, clapping Atkins on the back.

Atkins didn't feel as if he had. He could hardly bring himself to look his mate in the eye. "Where is the bastard? Did you get him?" Porgy pressed.

"Jeffries? Got away," said Atkins. "But he won't get far out there, even if he makes it. He'll be something's meal by night-time, I'll bet on it. Ketch bought it, though. Gut shot and gassed."

"Hell's Bells," said Porgy. "Can't say I'm sorry, but I wouldn't wish that on a bloody Hun." Nellie and Edith broke their hug and he caught sight of Edith's face. "What's the bugger done to her?" Porgy cried, starting forward.

Atkins grabbed his shoulders. "Not now, mate. She's fine. She's a tough old girl."

Reunited, the Black Hand Gang pressed on, fighting a rear-guard action against the pursuing Chatts, the tunnel taking them inexorably downward. It soon became clear they'd missed the fungus farm chamber that marked the way to their excavated exit point. They were lost.

"Where the hell are we?" Everson asked Chandar, but the Chatt refused to answer.

"Sir," said Gazette, addressing Everson. "There are more Chatts coming the other way. We're caught between 'em."

"Not again," sighed Everson. "Atkins, I don't want to get

caught between a rock and a hard place. This isn't a good place for a last stand. See if you can't blow us an exit."

Atkins placed a couple of grenades against the wall of the passage and pulled the pins. "Grenade!" he hollered, dashing back round the curve. He was beginning to hate these damned tunnels. There were several dull explosions and Atkins felt his ears crackle and pop like a dropped needle on a scratched gramophone record as the concussion wave overtook him.

A cool breeze blew through the resulting hole. Everson braced his hands on the sides and stuck his head through tentatively.

"What's through there?" he asked Chandar. "Can we get out that way?"

Chandar peered into the darkness beyond and said nothing.

"We mean no harm," said Everson. "We just want to leave with our people." Still Chandar remained obstinately silent. Everson shook his head in despair, and then addressed his men. "Right, 1 Section, secure the other side. Make it snappy. This whole thing's turning into a shambles."

The weary warriors made their way cautiously through the hole in the passage. As their eyes adjusted to the darkness beyond, they heard the scuttling and frantic clicks of hundreds of Chatt voices. Atkins' flesh crawled with revulsion at the sound. The only light came from the familiar luminescent lichens, their faint glow barely illuminating the chamber's details. Long sinuous dry channels covered the floor, converging on an entrance in the far wall. Atkins noticed the frantic activity in them about halfway across the chamber.

"This'll brighten the place up," said Mercy, brandishing his Flammenwerfer. Gutsy opened the valve for him. A fiery orange geyser of flame erupted from the nozzle, casting an infernal glow across the chamber, illuminating pale Chatt and Urmen workers dragging clusters of pearlescent white globes away from the intruders, down the channels toward tunnels in the far walls.

"Poilus, any idea what this place is?" asked Everson.

"It's their nursery," replied the Urman with mounting horror. "We are under the edifice now, underground. We shouldn't have come here."

Around them, the walls of the chamber were full of recesses. They reminded Atkins of a church crypt, only the bodies that lay in these weren't dead. Chatts and Urmen moved back and forth among them, dragging out helpless pupae. At the soldiers' end, however, the cavities had seemed empty until Pot Shot gave a startled yelp. Idly poking about in one with his bayonet, he had come across the desiccated remains of some sort of partially formed nymph Chatt.

"Scared seven shades of shit out of me, that did," said Pot Shot.

"It's dead. Mummified," said Gazette. "Been here a while, has that."

"Ugly bugger, ain't it?" said Porgy.

"You'd know," retorted Mercy.

Its head was enlarged and bulbous, three of its limbs withered and deformed, its metamorphosis gone horribly wrong. And the more they looked, the more deformed, dead Chatts they found.

They advanced slowly across the chamber. A round of rapid fire scattered the Chatts seeking to reach a dry channel filled with large fat, white wriggling larvae. Standing over the limbless grubs, Gutsy thrust his bayonet into one with a vicious satisfaction. Thick viscous fluid oozed out.

By now, the rest of the men had scrambled through into the chamber behind them.

"Light!" called Everson.

A Very flare arced up and hit the chamber roof. It fell into a channel filled with grubs, spitting out its harsh white light. The larvae began twisting and writhing in the intense heat, throwing macabre shadows on the walls as more Chatt workers, undeterred, crept forward again in an attempt to save them.

Gutsy let loose another burst of rapid fire.

"Stop!" Chandar cried.

"It's grubs, sir," said Gutsy with disgust.

"It's their young!" said Atkins in protest. "What are we now, Bosche baby-killers?"

Chandar, hissed, clicking his mandibles together in agitation. "This is the Queen's egg chamber. You have threatened Khungarrii young, there is no way out for you now. Rhengar and the scentirrii will crush you. A pity. You are like no Urmen this One has known. Jeffries promised you to us. This One would have liked to have learned more. This One senses there is much he will never know about you, but GarSuleth wills it."

"Let us go and we will leave them unharmed," said Everson.

"I have not that power."

"They're coming through!" said a private keeping watch by the bomb-blasted aperture through which they had entered the chamber.

With no choice, they moved further into the nursery. Everson and 1 Section led the way along the runways between the dry channels. "Which way out?" Everson asked Chandar.

The Chatt gave a kind of shrug, as if any answer was useless now.

Atkins noticed a glint in the shadow beyond one of the apertures, the dull sheen of lichen light on carapaces. From an opening across the chamber came the martial sound of marching.

"Stand To!" said Everson. "We'll make a stand against this wall, use the channel in front as a fire trench. Sergeant Dawson, set up the Lewis gun on our flank. Hold until they spread out and we can take down the maximum number."

The group of thirty-odd soldiers, barely even a platoon, fell into a practiced routine, seeking what cover they could in the shallow channels and setting their rifles on the banks.

"Otterthwaite, see if you can't persuade them to stay back in the tunnels a little longer," ordered Everson.

"Right you are, sir." The sharpshooter looked down the barrel of his rifle towards the tunnels. He picked his target and squeezed the trigger. A squeal followed the rifle's echoing report. Otterthwaite fired repeatedly, but the march of feet and the dull clatter of armoured insectile shells grew into a din as the first of the Chatt soldiers emerged from the gloom of the tunnels.

The nurses, Padre Rand, still under the influence of his otherworldly ennui, Half Pint, Napoo and others too wounded to help were set to the rear against the chamber wall. Nurse Bell took up a rifle from one of wounded men. "They're not going to take me," she said through gritted teeth when she met Nellie Abbott's questioning look. The driver acquiesced mutely. A private with an arm in a sling offered her his bayonet. Nellie took it.

Sister Fenton stepped forward and Bell thought she was about to scold them but she, too, nodded sternly at another wounded soldier. "Give that to me," she said, indicating his bayonet. He handed it up without protest and she gripped its handle self-consciously. The other two nurses looked at her nonplussed. "Belgium," was all she said. All of England had heard of the Bosche atrocities there in the early years of the war.

In the fire channel Atkins nervously awaited the order to shoot. Seeing the massed ranks of insects before them was unnerving, but seeing them along the rifle barrel, it became business, and a business he knew how to do. He picked his targets and waited for the order.

To his left and right Gutsy, Porgy, Gazette, Pot Shot and Mercy were doing the same. He met their eyes one by one, an unspoken conversation of wordless encouragement and silent goodbyes. If this was it, they would give as good as they got and take as many of the damn things with them as possible when they went. The anger he'd felt at himself, Atkins now turned outwards towards the Chatts.

The first wave of Chatt soldiers swarmed onto the floor of the nursery chamber.

Brandishing his revolver, Everson stepped forward, bringing Chandar with him. "We just want to leave," he called out across the chamber.

A Chatt stepped forward from the ranks.

"Rhengar," said Chandar. "Njurru scentirrii of the Khungarrii Shura."

"Let us go," called Everson. "Allow us safe passage out of here with our people or we will destroy your young, your nursery!"

He deplored the tactic, but he felt he had no choice if he wanted to save his men. They were cornered.

Rhengar hissed. In turn, the Chatt soldiers began to hiss, some beating the flats of their short swords against their chests.

"Well, that's not good," muttered Everson, and then nodded to his Platoon Sergeant.

"This is it, lads," called Hobson. "Pick your targets. Fire!"

The Lewis gun opened fire, raking across the lines of Chatts who fell, toppling into the partly vacated channels only to be trodden on by ranks of their fellows as their advance continued.

Covered by insects wielding electric lances, spitting Chatts charged forward spraying jets of acid from their mouths, leaving several men screaming and clutching their faces.

Any moment now, they would be upon them. Atkins readied himself for fighting at close quarters.

"We're going to need something bigger than bullets," yelled Gutsy to Gazette, hefting a grenade from his pack, from the bottom of which projected a stick. "Rifle grenade."

"Not from my rifle you don't," said Gazette. "Bugger up your own bore."

"Well there's nothing to lose now, is there?" said Gutsy inserting the shaft of the stick into the barrel of his rifle. He put the stock of the rifle butt against the ground and aimed the barrel towards an opening on the far side of the chamber, through which Chatts were swarming. He pulled the safety pin from the grenade and then pulled the trigger. The bomb arced across the chamber and exploded within the ranks of Chatts, shredding body limbs in a hail of shrapnel. Showers of dust and debris rained down from the chamber ceiling.

"Bloody hell, Gutsy, you'll bring the whole place down on top of us," said Pot Shot.

The tremors grew stronger and a deep rumble filled the chamber.

"That wasn't me," he protested.

The Chatts wavered uncertainly, their leader – Rhengar – holding them in line as the rumbling continued. To the Tommies' left, the wall began to crack and crumble before exploding out into the chamber with a tremendous roar as the great bulk of an armoured beast crashed through it.

It was the Ironclad, *Ivanhoe*, covered in the dust and dirt of shattered earthen walls as it rolled implacably forward. It came to a halt, its engines growling and filling the chamber with acrid exhaust fumes, its great six-pounder guns trained on the ranks of Chatt soldiers. Light from the breached wall behind it filtered through the settling dust, bathing the tank in an ethereal glow.

A cheer went up the from the Tommies, while the Khungarrii hissed and backed away from the terrible vision before them, sinking down on their long-limbed legs, cowering as if in obeisance to the enormous beast.

"Skarra," hissed Chandar, also sinking down.

"Skarra?" said Everson.

"God of the Underearth. Dung Beetle Brother to GarSuleth himself, who takes the dead and guides them through their last metamorphosis so that they can rise and dwell in the sky web of GarSuleth forever."

Another rumble filled the air. Everson looked up at the roof and, in that moment, Chandar saw its chance and scuttled back along the wall behind the line of Tommies to the hole through which they'd entered, now covered by another cohort of Chatts.

"Sir!" said Hobson, swinging his rifle round to follow the limping arthropod.

"No, let him go, Hobson," said Everson. "Best save your bullets. We might need 'em."

Safe, Chandar turned, and its eyes met Atkins', who stared back wonderingly before the scentirrii parted and the old Chatt was lost in the swarm.

"Follow the bloomin' light," yelled a face peering out from a loophole in the side of the ironclad. A hand pointed needlessly to the gaping hole behind the landship.

Everson ordered the men towards the breach, the nurses and injured going first while a burst of fire from the landship's forward machine gun kept the Chatts at bay. Everson and 1 Section kept the retreat covered, before abandoning their position and falling back to the tank. The confused Chatts, hampered by their superstition, held back.

Everson banged on the small door in the rear of the left gun sponson. It opened a crack. "You're not coming in. There ain't room!" the leather and chain-mail masked crew member retorted.

"How the hell did you find us?" Everson bellowed above the growl of the engine.

"We didn't," yelled the cockney gunner. "When the explosions went off in the tower, Lieutenant Mathers ordered us forward, we hadn't got twenty yards across the clearing when the bleedin' ground collapsed beneath us. How were we to know it were riddled with tunnels and the *Ivanhoe* here a bleedin' twenty eight ton behemoth? Wah-la, as the Frogs say. We found ourselves down here."

"Well thank God you did," shouted Everson. "They think the tank is the god of their underworld, but I don't know how much time that will buy us."

"Well that's handy to know. You follow the others back to the surface. We'll keep the buggers busy." The door clanged shut again.

Everson waved 1 Section back as the tank's forward machine gun spat another hail of bullets across the chamber, keeping the Chatts at bay. They scrambled back along the tank's rubble-strewn path of destruction and into the bottom of a wide sinkhole. Ahead men were scrambling up the sides, hauling the injured up with them. Atkins and the others scrambled up the slope after them as the tank reversed back out of the nursery chamber towards them.

One of the gearsmen was looking out of a loophole at the rear of the tank, attempting to guide it. The landship lurched as it begin to climb up the side of the sinkhole; the engine labouring to propel its twenty-eight ton bulk up the steep sides, the tracks squealing in protest as they struggled to maintain purchase. At one point it looked as if wasn't going to make it but then it reared over the lip and, with a heavy crash, it slammed down onto level ground.

They emerged from the ground not thirty yards from the great earthen edifice that now towered above them, black smoke roiling up from a break in the wall high above. Further down the edifice, a familiar sickly green gas vented lazily from holes and sank down along the walls. Atkins was astounded at how much damage they had caused. And they hadn't stopped yet.

As Chatt soldiers poured out of the edifice, the air filled with the chatter of machine guns as interlocking fields of fire from the flanks mowed them down. The *Ivanhoe* fired shells at the entrances to the edifice, bringing rubble crashing down to block them, slowing any further pursuit. The hollow *plomps* of trench mortars sent shells arcing over the clearing to drop down among the remaining Chatts now trapped outside the edifice, while rifle fire and the odd grenade mopped up the rest. Plumes of smoke drifted slowly across the increasingly pock-marked clearing. It was all beginning to take on a familiar feel to the men of the Pennines. As Atkins took in the commotion, he caught a movement on the side of one of the midden piles buttressing the edifice. It was a soldier. Had they left someone behind? Atkins squinted and recognised him at once. Jeffries. The man stopped on the crest of the heap and turned to watch the carnage briefly.

"Atkins!" Do you want to get yourself killed?"

Atkins looked towards the cry. Hobson was ushering the last stragglers into the undergrowth where Hepton was cranking the handle on his kine camera, filming the battle of a lifetime. Atkins dashed for the cover of the encircling woodland and the rest of the support sections. When he looked back in Jeffries' direction, he had gone.

INTERLUDE 5

Letter from Flora Mullins to
Private Thomas Atkins

22nd October 1916

My Dearest Tom,

I write, praying this finds you safe for I do not know what else to do. You are the only friend I have left in this world who will understand. I could not bear to lose you as well.

Although we vowed that we would never speak of the passion that overcame our prudence that night, I fear we must. I have got myself into such a mess. Oh Tom, I am with child and the child is yours. Of that, there can be no doubt.

At first I denied the possibility even to myself, but my condition has begun to show and can be hidden no longer. I cannot continue to work at the Munitions Factory for the shame of it. There was a frightful row and my father is in a terrible rage for they know the child cannot be William's. He demands to know who the father is, but I have not told them. William was always a hero in their eyes but since he has been missing, he has become a saint and they will have nothing gainsay it. They told me that to do such a deed behind my fiancé's back I must be a wicked girl and he was all for throwing me out on the street there and then, but my mother, God bless her soul, calmed him down. They are to send me to board with my Aunt Peggy in Ulverston. Tom, I am afraid they mean to take the baby from me once it is born and give it up to an orphanage. I do not know what is to become of me. Alive or dead, I fear William will never forgive us and that is anguish enough, but to lose my child, Tom, that would be more than I could bear.

Oh, Tom, I know you are a good man. You have to come home to me and make this right. I do not know what I would do if I lost you, too. I need you, Tom – we need you. I pray ardently for your safe return. Write by return of post if you are able. Each day I do not hear from you weighs heavily on me.

Your loving
Flora

CHAPTER TWENTY-ONE
"Glorious, Victorious..."

Atkins read Flora's letter several times on the long journey back to the entrenchments. The tear-stained paper in his hands left him reeling with a vertiginous sense of guilt. He was so self-absorbed he barely noticed as Gazette fell in beside him.

"Want to talk about it, mate?"

"No. Not really."

"Fair enough. Fag?" he said, offering a crushed Woodbine. Atkins shook his head.

"So, Dwyer the devil worshipper, eh?" said Gazette. "Bloody hell, that was a turn up for the books and no mistake. The most notorious man in England. Think of the reward money we'd get if we could turn him in, eh? Pity he scarpered. If there's any justice in this world he'll be a bag o' bones by now."

"I said I don't want to talk about it."

Porgy trotted up and was about to speak when Gazette shook his head, so Porgy just matched his stride with theirs and they walked along in uneasy silence.

"Wait, something's wrong," said Pot Shot behind them, holding up a hand. "Half Pint's stopped grousing."

Eyes turned to look at the curmudgeonly private being carried along on a makeshift stretcher. Behind him, Napoo was being carried on another, Poilus now constantly at his clansman's side. Around them walking wounded limped along in ones and twos or helping those blinded by Chatt acid, all of them constantly herded along by the nurses, like sheep.

"Half Pint, what's the matter?" called Gutsy, over the ever-present rumble of the tank up ahead.

"Shhh!" warned Sister Fenton. "Poilus has given him crushed berries of some sort. It seems to have numbed his pain."

"And his ability to complain, too, by the sound of it," said Pot Shot.

"No it hasn't," said Half Pint drowsily, "I just don't know where to bloody start."

"Off on the wrong foot, knowing you, probably!"

"No thanks to you, you bugger," said Half Pint, sticking up a pair of fingers in Gutsy's direction. Gutsy puffed out his cheeks with relief.

Everson drove the men on. They had made longer marches than this in France and in worse conditions and he knew they wouldn't be safe until they reached their entrenchment. But would it still be there? That was the question that went through the mind of every man in the column, the thought that made every one of them sick at heart.

Weary, footsore and hungry the bedraggled column marched on, although the two day trek back was not without incident. Along the way, a small group of Chatt soldiers harried them, although they mostly kept their distance, still awed by the sight of the ironclad.

When they reached the open veldt the trail they had followed days ago was still there, cutting across the vast expanse of tube grass, but to what would it lead them?

The answer to their prayers came on the wind in the form of a faint insect drone. A dot in the sky resolved itself into the flimsy shape of Tulliver's Sopwith as it circled them. Seeing the biplane raised their spirits and sent their hearts soaring. A rousing cheer went up as it passed low overhead. They waved their rifles and hats jubilantly above their heads and were delighted to receive a waggle of the wings in return. Knowing that that the muddy field they called home had not disappeared in their absence, their mood became more ebullient. The aeroplane wheeled above them once more, then flew on ahead, leading them home.

Jeffries staggered up the hill, away from the crashing sounds in the forest below. Whatever it was, it had been following him for some time now.

Escaping from the edifice in the confusion, he'd managed to pick up his dropped weapons and equipment, although the barrel of one Enfield was broken beyond use and he'd had to discard it.

Panting, he reached the crown of the hill and dropped his equipment. Paled into grey by the distance he could make out the Khungarrii edifice behind him, still smoking. He took the map out of his pocket, unfolded it and smoothed it out on a rock. His eyes flicked from the parchment to the landscape and back again as he orientated himself, matching landmarks to symbols. He turned the map. Satisfied, he studied it more closely. He tapped a Croatoan sigil thoughtfully and looked out over the forest towards a line of hills some twenty miles away before folding the parchment away again. He checked his rifle, picked up his load and set off down the far side of the hill.

He was on the final road to meet his god and when he did, The Great Snake would rise again.

Everson hardly recognised the trench system when they saw it. In four days, Company Quartermaster Sergeant Slacke had begun to turn the field of Somme Mud into something resembling a defensible stronghold, a corner of a foreign field that was to them, for now, all that was England. A fire trench now ran all the way around the perimeter with saps and OPs projecting out into the scorched earth cordon.

Everson went to the hospital tents, where Napoo and Half Pint were made comfortable. They were gravely ill, but stable. All they could hope for was that infection didn't set in. Padre Rand, who had been melancholic all the way back from the edifice, insisted on discharging himself from the MO's care. Everson was keen to hear about his experience.

"I don't know what to say, Lieutenant," he told Everson. "What I experienced there severely tested my faith to the point where I rejected my God, but then," he said with a self-effacing smile, "even St. Peter failed that particular test as I recall. Jeffries had me fooled. He had everyone fooled. I'm sure he had some machinations of his own. What they were I don't know, but I do know he was willing to sell us all into slavery to get what he wanted. And these Khungarrii, although they look hideous to our eyes and their culture is like none I have encountered before, would we have reacted any differently in their shoes? Even so, I have a horrible feeling that we may have started a war where none was looked for."

Everson rubbed his eyes with the heels of his palms, briefly wishing the entire world away, before dragging his hands down his face to confront it again with a sigh of resignation. "Could we have avoided it? Did we do the right thing?"

"'When I was a child I spake as a child, I understood as a child, I thought as a child,'" quoted the Padre. "We're warriors, Lieutenant. We understand as warriors, we think as warriors. Was it the right thing to do? Only God can judge, although in mitigation, I must say, we *are* British."

"Well, you're back on form, then," said Everson.

The Padre patted his Bible "I shall pray for us."

That evening the elation of the men, while temporary, was a pleasant and much needed diversion. The nurses danced gamely with as many men as they could until, exhausted by the constant demand for their attention, they retired for the night.

The noises of revelry and the slurred sound of a battered, hand-cranked gramophone warbling at varying speeds drifted down the steps into Everson's dugout. *"-Take me back to dear old Blighty; Put me on a train for London Town. Take me over there, drop me anywhere; Liverpool, Leeds or Birmingham, well I don't care..."*

Everson sat looking dolefully at the light of the hurricane lamp through a glass of whisky. He was now the highest-ranking officer left in the 13th. Like it or not, these men were now his responsibility and it was a heavy load to bear. It was everything he never wanted.

On the table before him, the Battalion's salvaged war diary lay open on blank pages. He didn't know how the hell he was going to write this one up. Beside it, under a now empty bottle of whisky from his father's own cellar, lay several maps and orders from Jeffries' chest. On the edge of the table sat the man's journal with its incomprehensible ciphers and sigils. Everson had spent the last hour or so examining them, looking for any clues that there might be a hint of truth in what Jeffries had said, looking for a shred of hope.

"I don't know what to think. Is he pulling the wool over our eyes, are we chasing him up a blind alley, Hobson?"

"Not my place to say sir," said Hobson.

"This is the last of it," he said, swilling the malt around the dirty glass. "I was fully expecting to get another case when we went back into the reserves. Doesn't look like that's going to happen any time soon."

"S'not true sir. It could happen tomorrow."

"And if it doesn't, Sergeant, what then?"

"With the help of Napoo and his people we can always find more food."

"And ammunition? The only reason we survived that attack on the Khungarrii edifice was firepower. They hadn't seen anything like it. And that's another thing. I didn't see anything there that would remotely suggest they had the ability to bring us here in the first place. No great scientific or technological advances. They were little more than savages. Mind you, once our ammunition runs out, we'll be reduced to fighting on their level. And they have the superiority of numbers. They know where we are. They've come for us once. They'll do it again. That's a certainty. If nothing else, we've proved we're a threat to them now and I'm not sure that's a good thing. Slacke has done sterling work the past few days. We've got the beginning of a stronghold we can defend until we can go home, but how long will that take?"

"Can we get home, sir?"

"Jeffries – Dwyer said he had a way, a map, information."

"He could have been lying. Slippery bastard like that, you can't trust a word that comes out of that man's mouth."

"He could have been lying to save his own skin, yes, but what if he wasn't? I have to believe he's telling the truth. Who knows what information he garnered from the Khungarrii? He was willing to sell us all into bondage over it, so it must have been important. No, we have to find him, Hobson."

Atkins found himself summoned to Everson's dugout. His stomach turned. You never knew what to expect when sent for by an officer.

"Atkins!" said Everson as the private entered and snapped to attention in front of the desk. "At ease, Atkins. At ease."

Atkins relaxed his stance. "Thank you, sir."

"Your section's lost two NCOs in almost as many weeks. Sergeant Jessop was a good man. He had family, I believe."

"Yes, sir. A wife and three children. Last were born a month ago. He hadn't even seen him."

"I'd write to his wife, but –" Everson gave a dismissive wave towards the curtained doorway at the world outside and shrugged. "Even if I could I wouldn't know what to say."

"No, sir."

"Which brings me to you and your recent behaviour, Atkins. Ketch didn't have a good word to say about you, apparently."

"Sir?" said Atkins. He was not sure where this was heading, but an awful suspicion formed in his mind.

"It's all right, Atkins. Relax. I knew Ketch of old. A cantankerous old sod and one hell of a toady. Was when he was working at my father's brewery, was in France by all accounts."

"Sir."

"On the other hand, I've been impressed by your courage and actions. You've certainly proved your worth on all our recent Black Hand Gang stuff. I've spoken to Hobson, here. He tells me you're popular and a good man to have in a tight spot. Your section needs a new NCO. I can't promote you, but I need NCOs, so I'm giving you a field appointment to Lance Corporal."

"Sir, I can't. You don't want me." Atkins forgot himself and started forwards. A warning cough from Sergeant Hobson made him catch himself and stand fast.

"Nonsense, Atkins. You've earned it. If there's one thing I need, it's people I can trust. You've proved yourself worthy." Everson stood up, stepped round his makeshift desk and grasped Atkins' hand in a firm handshake he barely had the enthusiasm to return. If only Everson knew. If only his dugout mates knew his true colours.

"Is that all, sir?"

"Not yet, Lance Corporal. You and I are the only ones who have any idea what Jeffries – Dwyer – was talking about back at the edifice. I've just been looking through the papers you found in his dugout. From the bits I can make out it's quite a sordid tale."

"Sir, did he bring us here with some diabolic pact?"

"I'm sure he thinks so, but look –" Everson lifted the empty whisky bottle out of the way and turned the uppermost map around. It was an artillery map, showing British gun positions and barrage targets across the Harcourt Sector. Marked in red were five locations, two beyond the German lines, two behind the British, one in No Man's Land, all joined by pencil lines to form a perfect pentacle.

"He must have been planning this for weeks, typing up his own orders on blank order sheets, impersonating artillery officers – Tulliver thought he recognised him.

"Is that what he was saying about a geographic whatsit?" said Atkins, looking at the five-pointed star.

"I'd say so, yes. Don't believe in the mumbo jumbo lark myself. It looks like a magic circle or something, but see here." Everson took a pencil and a piece of string. Holding one end of the string on a mark in the centre of the pentacle, he drew a circle. Atkins watched with mounting apprehension and dismay at the pencil intersected each point of the five-pointed star on the map.

"So it's true, then. He did conjure some spell and transport us here?"

"He certainly thinks so," said Everson, now planting the fingertips of his hand on the map and moving it aside, only to pull another map out from underneath. It was a similar map, only this one had a much cruder circle drawn over it encompassing the Harcourt sector, enclosing the British trenches currently held by the 13th Pennine Fusiliers. "This one was taken from observations made by Lieutenant Tulliver after we arrived here and surveyed by CQS Slacke in our absence."

"So?"

"Whatever happened, whatever brought us here, I don't think it was the result of Jeffries' occult practices. Look." He took the one map, laid it on top of the other, and held both up in front of the hurricane lamp for Atkins to see. He adjusted them slightly with his thumbs so the trench positions matched up. The two circles however, did not. Oh, there was an overlap, but they didn't cover the same ground.

"What do you think of that?" Everson said.

"They're not the same, sir,"

"No. Jeffries' circle doesn't correspond to the one we're stood in right now. It's just coincidence, d'y'see?"

"So it's got nothing to do with Jeffries. And when he said that he knew the way home?"

"That, I can't be sure about. It seems he may have learnt some things from the Khungarrii. He mentioned the name Croatoan. Poilus has mentioned it too. There's something else going on here and this Croatoan thing seems to be key, it keeps cropping up. That can't be coincidence, it means something but I don't know what. All I have are Jeffries' indecipherable notes. That damn man has caused irreparable damage. But he's left us with one thing – the *possibility* of a way home and I suppose for that we should be grateful."

Lance Corporal Thomas 'Only' Atkins stepped out of the dugout an NCO, but it was a hollow moment. He didn't deserve this. He felt he was deceiving his friends and the Lieutenant. He had left chaos and calamity in his wake, as Jeffries had. He took out the letter he'd taken from Ketch, Flora's letter to him, the last post. He held it tightly in his hand as he refused to let the tears fall.

Above, the unfamiliar stars were coming out one by one; the constellation they called 'Charlie Chaplin' hung low in the heavens against the gaseous red ribbon that trailed across the alien sky. This new world, like Atkins' fortunes, continued to turn, but for good or ill, he couldn't say.

A bright point of light rose above the horizon. It was the brightest star in the sky, the star they had christened 'Blighty'. Atkins looked towards it, held the thought of Flora in his mind and made the most fervent wish he could.

THE END

The Pennine Fusiliers will return...

GLOSSARY

Ack Emma: From the *Signalese* phonetic alphabet; AM. Morning.

A.M: Air Mechanic; ground crew in the RFC.

Battle Police: Military police assigned to the Front Line during an attack, armed with revolvers and charged with preventing unwounded men from leaving the danger area.

Battalion: Infantry Battalions at full strength might be around a thousand men. Generally consisted of four *companies*.

BEF: British Expeditionary Force. Usually used to refer to the regular standing army who were the first to be sent to Belgium in 1914. Kaiser Wilhelm called them a 'contemptible little army' so thereafter they called themselves 'The Old Contemptibles'.

Black Hand Gang: slang for party put together for a dangerous and hazardous mission, like a raiding party. Such was the nature of the tasks it was chosen from volunteers, where possible.

Blighty: England, home. From the Hindustani *Bilaiti* meaning foreign land.

Blighty One: A wound bad enough to have you sent back to England.

Brassard: Armband.

British Army Warm: An army issue knee-length overcoat worn by officers.

Boojums: Nickname for tanks, also a Wibble Wobble, a Land Creeper, a Willie.

Bosche: Slang for German, generally used by officers.

Chatt: Parasitic lice that infested the clothing and were almost impossible to avoid while living in the trenches. Living in the warm moist clothing and laying eggs along the seams, they induced itching and skin complaints.

Chatting: De-lousing, either by running a fingernail along the seams and cracking the lice and eggs or else running a lighted candle along them to much the same effect.

Comm Trench: Short for communications trench.

Communications Trench: Trench that ran perpendicularly to the *fire trench*, enabling movement of troops, supplies and messages to and from the Front Line, from the parallel support and reserve lines to the rear.

Company: One quarter of an infantry battalion, 227 men at full strength divided into four platoons.

CQS: Company Quartermaster Sergeant.

CSM: Company Sergeant Major.

Enfilade: Flanking fire along the length of a trench as opposed to across it.

Estaminet: a French place of entertainment in villages and small towns frequented by soldiers; part bar, part cafe, part restaurant, generally run by women.

FANY: First Aid Nursing Yeomanry. The only service in which women could enlist and wear khaki, they drove ambulances, ran soup kitchens, mobile baths, etc. in forward areas.

Field Punishment No 1: Corporal punishment where men were tied or chained to stationary objects for several hours a day for up to 21 days. At other times during their punishment they were made to do hard labour.

Fire Bay: Part of a manned fire trench facing the enemy. Bays were usually separated by *traverses*.

Firestep: The floor of the trench was usually deep enough for soldiers to move about without being seen by the enemy. A firestep was a raised step that ran along the forward face of the fire trench from which soldiers could fire or keep watch.

Fire Trench: Forward trench facing the enemy that formed part of the Front Line.

Five Nines: A type of German high-explosive shell.

Flammenwerfer: German liquid fire thrower.

Fritz: Slang term for a German.

Funk: State of nerves or depression, more harshly a slang word for cowardice.

Hard Tack: British Army Biscuit ration, infamously inedible.

Hate, the: Usually a regular bombardment by the enemy made at dawn or dusk to forestall any attacks; the Morning Hate and the Evening Hate.

Hitchy Coo: Itchiness caused by lice infestation and their bites.

Hom Forty: French railway freight wagons used to transport troops at excruciatingly slow speed, so-called after the signage on the side; *Hommes 40, Chevaux 8.*

Iddy Umpty: slang for Morse Code and, by extension, the Signallers who used it.

Jack Johnsons: Shell burst of a 5.9 or bigger, know for its plume of black smoke and nicknamed after famed black boxer, Jack Johnson.

Jildi: From the Hindi – get a move on, quick, hurry.

Kite Balloon: An observation balloon, carrying a basket for an observer but attached to the ground by a winch.

Landship: a tank.

Lewis Machine gun: air cooled, using a circular magazine cartridge holding 48 rounds each. Lighter and more portable than the Vickers.

Linseed Lancer: Slang for a stretcher bearer of the *RAMC*.

Maconachie: Brand of tinned vegetable stew. Made a change from endless Bully Beef, though not by much.

Mills Bomb: Pineapple-shaped British hand grenade, armed by pulling a pin and releasing the trigger lever.

Minnie Crater: Crater formed from the explosion of a Minniwerfer shell.

Minniewerfer: German trench mortar shell.

MO: Medical Officer.

Napoo: All gone, finished, nothing left. Mangled by the British from the French phrase; 'il n'y en a plus' – there is no more.

NCO: Non Commissioned Officer; Sergeant Majors, Sergeants or Corporals.

No Man's Land: Area of land between the two opposing Front Lines.

OP: Observation Post.

QM: Quartermaster.

Parados: Raised defensive wall of earth or sandbags along the rear of the trench to help disperse explosions behind the line.

Parapet: Raised defence of earth or sandbags at the front of a trench to provide cover for those on the *firestep*.

PH Helmet: Phenate-Hexamine Helmet. Early type of full-gas mask. Not so much a helmet as a flannel hood soaked in neutralising chemicals, and a mouth tube and distinctive red rubber valve for exhalation.

Pip Emma: From the Signalese phonetic alphabet; PM, after noon, evening.

Platoon: A quarter of an infantry company, commanded by a Subaltern. Consisting of 48 men divided into four sections.

Plum & Apple: Much derided flavour of jam because of the cheap and plentiful ingredients used by jam manufacturers on government contract.

Plum Pudding: Nickname for a type of British trench mortar round.

Poilus: Nickname for a French soldier, like the English Tommy. From the French poilu meaning 'hairy', as French soldiers were often unshaven, unlike the British Tommy who was required to shave every day.

Pozzy: Slang for jam.

Puttee: Khaki cloth band wound around the calf from the knee to the ankle.

RAMC: Royal Army Medical Corp, often summoned with the well worn yell, "stretcher bearer!" Uncharitably also said to stand for Rob All My Comrades.

Reading Your Shirt: The act of Chatting.

Red Tabs: Slang for Staff Officers, after the red tabs worn on the collars of their tunics.

Revetment: Any material used to strengthen a trench wall against collapse; wooden planking, brushwood wattling, corrugated iron, etc.

RFC: Royal Flying Corps of the British Army.